Disgraceful Conduct

by

Colin Rowland

One Good Sonnet Publishing
Publishers of Fine Romance and Fantasy Fiction

By Colin Rowland
Published by One Good Sonnet Publishing:

PRIDE AND PREJUDICE ADAPTATIONS

By Colin Rowland

Disgraceful Conduct
Hidden Desires
The Parson's Rescue

By Jann Rowland

With Love's Light Wings
Another Proposal
A Matchmaking Mother
The Challenge of Entail
The Impulse of the Moment
Mr. Bennet Takes Charge
A Gift for Elizabeth
Whispers of the Heart

By Jann Rowland, Lelia Eye, and Colin Rowland

Mistletoe and Mischief, A Pride and Prejudice Christmas Anthology

This is a work of fiction based on the works of Jane Austen. All the characters and events portrayed in this novel are products of Jane Austen's original novel or the authors' imaginations.

DISGRACEFUL CONDUCT

Cover Design by Colin Rowland

Published by One Good Sonnet Publishing

ISBN: 1-989212-58-1
ISBN-13: 978-1-989212-58-5

To my family who have, as always, shown
their unconditional love and encouragement.

To my editor, who encouraged me
to publish this novel when I doubted my ability.

To Elly Mae. Although she does not realize it, her
unquestioning loyalty and companionship are
a godsend.

CHAPTER I

It has often been said that love arrives on its own schedule, often at the most inopportune time. On the first point, Miss Elizabeth Bennet could agree.

She was, as on most mornings, walking the paths of Longbourn, her home since birth and, she supposed, likely to remain so forever if recent history was a sign.

Spring this year was late in arriving, winter's snow fighting for all its worth to remain as long as possible. Its advent, though delayed, brought warm days and cloudless skies, which were sorely needed, in Elizabeth's opinion.

The weather this morning was magnificent, with nary a cloud to spoil the view, or a breeze to divert the aromas wafting from the delicate flowers sprouting in abundance alongside her path. Bees flitted from flower to flower collecting nectar to take back to their nest where it would shortly become honey. Their movements took them from one blossom to the next, and to the hive to deposit their sweet treasure, after which they set off again to repeat the process over and over until sunset.

She envied the insects their single-minded focus, unbothered by anything unconnected to life's overriding purpose of supplying their queen with the fruits of their labors. And Elizabeth missed her sister Jane, who, with their Aunt Gardiner, had gone to London without her because of an inconvenient illness which had confined Elizabeth to her bed.

To add insult to injury, her recovery coincided with the arrival of Mr. Collins, her father's sickeningly obsequious cousin. The purpose of his visit was purportedly the resolution of a long-standing disagreement between their fathers. It was soon plain, however, that he wanted a wife and had resolved to choose a Bennet daughter, with the full support of Mrs. Bennet.

Elizabeth, confident she would soon have the honor of a marriage proposal from another, rebuffed his repeated advances, despite her mother's insistence. Mr. Collins, to his credit, was not the buffoon he appeared to be and soon transferred his attentions to Elizabeth's closest friend and neighbor, Charlotte Lucas.

News of their betrothal sent Mrs. Bennet into paroxysms of panic, interspersed with despair over her certain destiny of homeless scrabbling on the streets of Meryton for scraps of food.

"We are ruined," cried she to her husband. "Upon your death, the entail on the estate comes due, and Mr. Collins will not hesitate to throw us into the street immediately!"

Mr. Bennet's amusement at his wife's rantings only worsened her mood, sending her upstairs many nights to settle her nerves.

Elizabeth, who endured her mother's censure without complaint, tried her utmost to reason with the woman, to no avail. Even though Mr. Edwin Sadler was, with Mr. Bennet's blessing, courting her, Mrs. Bennet refused to listen, preferring instead to nurse her injured feelings, justified or not.

Late yesterday had seen the delivery of a post from Mr. Sadler. Elizabeth, although surprised, tore open the envelope and perched herself in a chair to devour this missive from her love.

Her joy, however, soon became anguish. The purpose of the letter was not to profess undying love, but to bid farewell, as he had taken passage on a ship bound for sea. His plans to make a fortune as a privateer, an occupation where death was a common occurrence, did not include the promise of an eventual return to resume his spurious pursuit of her hand.

Elizabeth's world lay in ruins, her plans all for nought. Carefully she read it again, her tears staining the page until the ink ran. When at last she put the paper aside it was all but illegible, the words having merged into a blot of ink covering the page.

Her sleep was fitful, inhabited by dreams of wedded bliss which became nightmares as each ended in betrayal, awakening her to the reality of her dismal future.

She rose early, unable to endure another disturbing episode. After dressing quietly so as not to wake the household, she left the manor and set out along her favorite path, determined to forget about her former beau.

The day's beauty was the temporary remedy she needed. Within an hour, the majesty of surrounding flowers, from the yellow and purple of the pansies to the bright orange marigolds which appeared to bloom just for her, captured her heart.

Her walk took her into the small forest bordering Longbourn, its trees standing as sentinels and appearing to prohibit entrance to all but a select few. She loved this path and its ability, proven countless times, to soothe her troubled spirit.

The further she went, the greater the calm that descended upon her, until the heartache of the previous day was only a distant memory, banished temporarily to a corner of her mind. As the journey progressed, her steps grew lighter and her appreciation for the world around her rose until, with astonishment, she caught herself singing a carol to the birds cavorting gaily in the sky overhead.

Turning to watch them, she saw the lengthening shadows and realized with a start she had tarried all day.

Before hurrying home she stopped and looked heavenward in gratitude: *Thank you, Lord, I needed solace and you, in your wisdom, gave me just that.*

Mr. Bennet was waiting as she came from the cloakroom, having doffed her cloak and hat: "Please come to the library, Lizzy."

"You wanted to see me?" said she, entering the room and closing the heavy door behind her.

"Take a seat." He gestured to a comfortable chair by the fireplace, its burning logs enough to remove the spring chill from the air.

Joining Elizabeth by the fire, a goblet of brandy in his hand, he favored her with a smile: "I guess you enjoyed your walk. I was beginning to fear you decided to keep going."

"It never entered my mind. If I were to leave, who would provide you with stimulating conversation, or arguments to challenge your mistaken opinions?"

"Indeed," he chuckled. "You, more than any of your sisters, can defend yourself in debate, and I value that. Our discussions are the best part of my day."

Elizabeth laughed: "So why did you invite me to your sanctum sanctorum? Was it to question another of my beliefs, or is there more to your summons?"

"You know me too well," said Mr. Bennet, smiling at his favorite daughter. "I received a letter from Jane. She needs to stay in London a while longer."

"I know this is not what you hoped," said he as Elizabeth's face fell, the disappointment clear to see.

An involuntary sigh escaped before her smile returned: "I will be fine. Did she give a reason?"

"Your aunt has fallen ill and asked Jane to extend her visit while she recovers. "You know your sister; she cannot say no to anyone in need, more so if it is someone she knows and loves, such as your Aunt Gardiner, who has always been her favorite relative."

Elizabeth smiled, nodding her head in agreement. "That is my sister, always an angel of mercy. I would be disappointed had she said no."

"This news of your aunt's illness has me wondering," offered Mr. Bennet, his lips spreading into a playful grin. "Did you infect her? As I remember, you were deathly ill while she was here."

"I hope not. She would never forgive me, and rightly so."

"I was only teasing you," said Mr. Bennet with a laugh. "No one else was stricken, and if you passed your illness to your aunt, one or more of us would also have caught whatever you had."

Elizabeth shook her head, unable to take offense at her father's ill-conceived joke. "That was not nice. I will repay the favor someday, I promise."

"I have no doubt," was his response.

"Dinner must be ready," said Mr. Bennet, rising in response to a knock at the library door. "Come along, we do not want to make them wait."

Elizabeth followed her father to the dining-room, seating herself and bowing her head as Mr. Bennet gave the blessing on the food.

Dinner at Longbourn was always a boisterous affair, and tonight was no different. At the prayer's conclusion, hands were thrust forward and serving dishes grabbed, with no consideration for decorum or manners. As on most nights, Elizabeth was grateful there were no guests sharing the meal, as the embarrassment would have been too much for her.

"I heard from Jane," said Mr. Bennet when the meal was well under way. "Mrs. Gardiner requested she stay a few weeks longer, and she has agreed."

"But she was to be back in time for Midsummer Day," whined Mrs. Bennet petulantly. "What am I to do without her?"

"I think you will survive," said he with a wink at Elizabeth. "The day will not differ from what it was last year. If I recall, you did not do anything to mark the day, unless retiring early to bed is your idea of a celebration, and you do not need Jane for that. Should you need someone to replace her, you can always ask Lizzy."

"She would turn me down, like she does every time I ask her to place this family before her own selfish needs," was Mrs. Bennet's reply.

Elizabeth sighed and shook her head, knowing her mother had been waiting for an opening to air her grievances, as she had every evening meal for the past few weeks.

"You know that is not true," said Mr. Bennet, again stating the facts of the matter. "She had a suitor, one, I might add, that you approved of."

"If she loved me, she would have accepted Mr. Collins' offer of marriage. Because of her selfishness, I will be homeless."

"Need I remind you, again, that I have not passed on, and do not expect to anytime soon? As to Lizzy's refusal of marriage to Mr. Collins, I gave her my full support then, and have seen nothing since that would induce me to change my opinion."

"What about my future?" cried Mrs. Bennet, her voice shrill enough to cause the estate's hounds to wail at the moon.

"That is enough," said Mr. Bennet, his patience obviously wearing thin. "The decision is made, and no amount of complaining will change it."

Mrs. Bennet sat back in the chair with her arms crossed in disgust, a pose Elizabeth knew well.

"I almost forgot," remarked Mr. Bennet, rising from the table to go back to his library for the evening. "Jane included a letter for you as well. It is waiting on my desk whenever you want it."

Elizabeth called to her father as he left the room: "I will get it now. Hopefully she has some good news for me."

"I did not look at it," answered Mr. Bennet when she caught up to him. "What you and your sister write each other is none of my business."

"Thank you," said Elizabeth, taking the letter from her father's outstretched hand. "I have missed talking with Jane, so this comes as a welcome surprise."

"I thought it would," he chuckled as Elizabeth left the library and made her way to her bedroom. She clutched the note securely in her hand, unopened until she was alone to enjoy its contents.

Safely in her room, Elizabeth readied herself for bed, her desire to read something, anything, from her sister adding urgency to her preparations. At last she pulled the chair away from her writing desk and sitting, unfolded the letter and read:

Gracechurch Street, March 12

"Dear Lizzy,

"I hope this letter finds you in better health than you were when we left last month for London. I could not help worrying about your condition, as you looked so wretched at the time.

"Our journey was uneventful, although long and tiring; I cannot imagine where those children find such energy! They fidgeted and fussed the entire time, and nothing we tried seemed to calm them enough to be still for even an hour.

"By the time we arrived at Cheapside, Aunt's patience had ended, and she informed me that nothing short of putting them to bed would suffice for the rest of the evening. Accordingly, we fed and tucked them in, after which we repaired to the sitting-room for a review of the day's events before turning in ourselves.

"I must confess that London, while always enjoyable, is not as much fun without your company, and I miss you terribly. Aunt took me to explore the shops, and I dreamt of the dresses you and I might create to impress our friends at the Meryton balls and assemblies, but it was not so much fun without your company. Your humorous observations and opinions are the most enjoyable part of visiting the London merchants.

"Aunt Gardiner took me to a ball which I enjoyed, but the experience left much to be desired. I found those in attendance to be cold and most uncivil, both in their greetings and their conversations. Never have I heard such denigration of others, and from so many people.

Everyone had an opinion regarding everyone else, and none were complimentary. "By the time the evening came to its end, I was missing our local assemblies and balls thoroughly. At least in Hertfordshire everyone puts on a friendly face, no matter whether they care for each other or not. It is rare to hear derogatory opinions about anyone, and that is how it should be. I do not need to be told of someone's dislike for their neighbor, or the reasons they hold that opinion.

"I guess Papa has told you I will not be back to Longbourn for a few weeks. Please forgive me, but our aunt is ill, much as you were, and is in bed for the foreseeable future.

She practically begged me to stay and tend to our young cousins, and I could not refuse her request. I know that, were our situations reversed, she would not hesitate to do the same.

"I promise to leave as soon as Aunt can resume caring for her children. In the meantime, I will write to you as often as I can. I know it is not the same as being there in person, but it will have to do for now.

"Please pass along my love for everyone; I would have asked Father to do this, but he would be unlikely to remember, so it is up to you, Lizzy.

"All my love and best wishes,

"Jane Bennet."

Elizabeth placed the letter on the desk and waited for the melancholy brought back by Jane's news to pass.

Her thoughts again turned to Mr. Sadler and the last ball they attended together, only a week before his letter of dismissal. He had been, in looking back on the evening, distracted the entire night, treating her with indifference as he focused his attention everywhere but on her.

She had felt so ignored that she accepted dance invitations from everyone who asked, and his apathy only made matters worse.

The man's request for her company, offered before the final dance of the ball, angered her. She flatly rejected his request, suggesting his time would be better used in learning expected manners and etiquette for an event such as this.

Mr. Sadler did not bother to defend himself, which angered her even more. His response was to nod in acceptance of her rejection and make his way to the opposite side of the ballroom, where he remained until the event finished, whereupon he donned his cloak and departed without so much as a farewell.

Elizabeth was incensed, and everyone in the Bennet carriage became the object of her scorn; from her poor father to Kitty and Lydia, no one escaped.

When they reached Longbourn, the carriage emptied at once, the passengers eager to escape her vitriol. Mr. Bennet took her aside and talked with her, encouraging her to give vent to her feelings until at last she quieted, her emotions spent. He then encased her in a fatherly hug and sent her to bed, where she tossed and turned before finally escaping into dreamless sleep.

Elizabeth shook her head, the memory of that evening still an unhealed wound, each recollection more painful than the last.

I cannot continue to let his actions control me. It is time to put him from my mind altogether.

Her decision made, she got herself into bed, determined the memory of Mr. Sadler would never again darken her thoughts.

She reached over to extinguish the lamp, then laid back down. For an hour or more she thought about Jane's letter before closing her eyes to let slumber remove the cares of the day.

CHAPTER II

Elizabeth rose to the sound of birds greeting the new morning, and found herself eager to join them in welcoming the sun. Dressing quickly, she all but burst from the manor in her eagerness to commune again with nature.

Her mood, initially elevated by the serenity of the paths, gave way to a somber and pensive consideration as her thoughts turned to the sister she missed more than she wanted to acknowledge. Jane's absence robbed her of the chance to discuss her failed romance. Her sister's delayed return added to her sorrow, until she turned back toward Longbourn, the beauty of the day lost to despondency.

She turned into the drive, her head hung low, and struggled to find a smile for Mr. Bennet, who watched her approach the house.

"To what do we owe the honor of your sunny disposition?" asked he when she halted on the stoop in front of him. "It is unusual to see you this happy."

Elizabeth smiled in spite of herself, unable, as always, to defy her father's attempts to lift her spirits.

"That is better," said he. "What troubles you this morning? Let me help."

"I miss Jane," confessed Elizabeth. "The prospect of facing summer without her depresses me. This will be a lonely season, and a boring one as well."

"And without Miss Lucas, too," said he, to Elizabeth's nod, "it could be worse, but you will manage. You always do."

"I suppose so, although it will be difficult."

Mr. Bennet opened the door for his daughter, who ascended the stairs and shut herself in her room, unwilling to endure her mother's reviewing of the same complaints she repeated whenever Elizabeth came near.

She stayed there the rest of the day, not stirring until the summons came for supper, which she answered, albeit hesitantly.

Mrs. Bennet fixed her with a disapproving frown before turning her attention to Lydia and Kitty. Elizabeth, experienced in her mother's displays of ire, hoped this signalled the woman's intention to ignore her this evening, a prospect she welcomed, given her present state of mind.

Said Mrs. Bennet, to no one in particular: "Charlotte Lucas is to be married next month. The banns are to be read beginning this Sunday. Her mother is waiting for the day I am evicted so she can lord it over me while she celebrates my poverty."

Mr. Bennet stopped any reactions Mrs. Bennet hoped to evoke. The shake of his head and stern visage he wore quelled any response Lydia or Kitty might have thought to make.

Mrs. Bennet, though, was not to be denied her moment of pique. When her statement provoked no reply, her acrimony increased, her voice rising to drown out all other conversations.

"That woman has always envied our ownership of Longbourn and has lusted over it since the first time she called upon me. Now, because of a selfish daughter who I have decided to no longer acknowledge, she will be mistress of this estate while I am reduced to living by my wits, a beggar by someone else's choice, not my own."

"Lady Lucas will never be mistress of Longbourn," was Mr. Bennet's reply, offered with a smile for Elizabeth. "That honor will go to Mrs. Collins, unless you are privy to information kept from me and Sir William."

"You know very well what I meant," snapped Mrs. Bennet to her husband, whose mirth was unmistakable. "The woman cannot wait to move Charlotte and that nasty man she is marrying into my home, and to see me evicted. Why are you not alarmed? Have you no concern for our future?"

Mr. Bennet watched his wife until her rant subsided. He was quiet, but Elizabeth could tell he was considering his next words, weighing his desire for amusement against the string of complaints any remarks would raise.

"I think, Mrs. Bennet, that this matter is better left alone. As I told you repeatedly, and will reiterate one last time, my death is not imminent, so Longbourn is in no danger of slipping from your hands. Lady Lucas has no claim to the estate, nor would she, even if I should suddenly pass away.

"These irrational fears result from your overactive imagination, and are no more substantial than puffs of smoke on a windy day. Your claims are unfounded and I will thank you not to repeat them at this table. For the last time, woman, let them go."

Mrs. Bennet did not reply, choosing wisely this time not to defy her husband. Elizabeth fled to her bedroom, where she tried, unsuccessfully, to compose a suitable response to her sister's letter. An hour later, without a single word recorded upon the page, she extinguished the light and retired for the night, hoping for a better tomorrow, while doubting the possibility.

The following day was much the same as the one before. The weather was again exceptional, calling her out of doors to bask in the sun's warmth. Her appreciation for the beauty of the day was, however, again diminished by the recurrence of her memories, which, in defying all efforts to push them away, dimmed her enjoyment of the path she trod.

In a fit of obduracy, Elizabeth ignored the urge to return to Longbourn, resolving to walk until her spirits lifted and she could welcome the peace that normally accompanied her, like a trusted friend. Resolutely she carried on, forcing herself to observe such things as birds tending their nests of newly hatched offspring, each chick calling out for nourishment. She studied the forest, with its trees reaching ever higher toward the heavens, and young saplings destined to grow into mighty oaks. The grassy meadows she encountered were coming alive with flowers of every color imaginable, growing amid the grassy carpet which covered the ground.

Elizabeth walked farther than intended, retracing her steps only when she reached Oakham Mount. Her love of the neighborhood had drawn her onward, hoping to rediscover her awe for the majesty of God's creations. Try as she might, though, her heart remained closed, rebuffing all attempts to revive her spirit.

Her return to Longbourn was a solemn procession of one, her loneliness threatening to unleash a torrent of tears. As on the previous evening, she went to her room, refusing this night to join the family for supper, deciding instead to go to bed and, hopefully, to sleep.

When Elizabeth opened her eyes, the sun sat high in the heavens, its rays piercing the upper pane of windows and shining in her face. She grumbled at the annoying shaft of light and flung herself to the side, but the heat of the sunbeam, focused as it was on her coverings, drove her from the bed.

With a sigh, her mood already darkened by the necessity to rise, Elizabeth dressed and left her room for the sitting-room, her desire to eat still absent. She had almost reached the last step when the library portal opened and Mr. Bennet stepped into the hall.

"Come see me after you eat, please," said he before backing into the library to close the door.

"I am not hungry," said she, following him into the room before the portal swung shut.

Her father waved her to a chair, choosing its companion as she made herself comfortable. Mr. Bennet studied his daughter while she settled into the seat, waiting until she sat before speaking.

"I am worried," said he when she looked up at him. "I am watching my lovely, vivacious daughter wander the estate and its surrounding paths despondently, as if nothing interests her any longer. You rarely eat, and when you do, the meal is hardly enough to feed a mouse."

"I am sorry, Papa, but I am upset, and nothing I try has lifted my spirits."

"What is troubling you, Lizzy? I know you miss your sister, but that does not account for this change I am seeing. Jane has been away before and you coped. Please let me help you, as much as I can. It bothers me to see you in such a state."

Tears formed in Elizabeth's eyes, and she tried to force them back. She dreaded telling her father, for Mr. Sadler was an estimable match in his eyes. In vain she shook her head while Mr. Bennet looked on, his concern plain.

"What has happened? Have Mrs. Bennet's rants and complaints brought you to this state? I will speak to her again and put a stop to her tirades."

"That is not it." Elizabeth's tears were now running unhindered down her cheeks.

"Then please, tell me what it is so I can help you."

"I cannot," sobbed Elizabeth. "I do not want to disappoint you."

"Lizzy," said he, leaning forward to capture her hands in a loving grip. "You could never do that. I love you, and want to comfort you, but I cannot unless you tell me what has upset you."

"It is Edwin Sadler," she wailed as salty tears spilled from her eyes to fall on the front of her dress.

"What of Mr. Sadler?" asked Mr. Bennet, his voice calm, as if preparing himself for the worst. "Has he harmed you? If so, he will answer to me."

"No, Papa. He gave me a letter, the contents of which I could not forget," came out between heartbroken sobs, which gave way to hiccups. "He did not even have the decency to tell me in person!"

"And what were the contents of this letter?"

"He has left off courting me and gone to sea." Elizabeth was now gasping for breath as her hiccups made speech difficult. "He offered no reason, other than he wants to make his fortune as a privateer. Someone filled his head with dreams of untold wealth and acts of derring-do."

"The man is a fool," said Mr. Bennet with disgust. "What he will find instead is a watery grave. But tell me, what made you so sure I would blame you?"

"You held him in such high regard," said Elizabeth, her tears now spent. "I was afraid you would suspect I had driven him away. I could not bear to face your disgust."

"You should know me better than that. Tell me one time, if you can, that I ever displayed such an emotion because of something you might have done. In all your years, Lizzy, I have never been disappointed in anything you did."

"But you were so looking forward to the conclusion of his courting, and our eventual wedding. It will never happen, and the responsibility is mine."

"Nonsense. If he could not see your worth, and prize you accordingly, he does not deserve you."

"Do you think so?"

"I know so. There is no doubt in my mind."

An immense weight seemed to lift from Elizabeth's shoulders: "Thank you, Papa."

Mr. Bennet stared into the fire, as if pondering some of the greatest questions in the universe. Elizabeth waited patiently, knowing he would speak when he was ready. Pressing him would not induce him to hurry, a fact she had learned as a child.

"Your mood worries me," said he at last. "I think you should spend the summer away from Hertfordshire. Time away from home might help you mend."

"Thank you for your concern," replied Elizabeth, "but I have nowhere to go, and with Jane gone, nobody to go with."

"My sister lives in Derbyshire with her husband and four children. Bannerman is the family name, and she would welcome a visit from you."

"I had not heard of any relations there."

"You and Jane visited once, but you were only a year old, so I would not expect you to remember. And your aunt Gardiner lived there in her youth, in a town called Lambton, which is a larger version of Meryton."

"It does not sound like you and your sister are close," said Elizabeth. "You never mentioned her, as I recall. I do not want to visit a stranger who may regret her invitation after I arrive."

"We have exchanged monthly letters since before you were born, Lizzy. I never shared our correspondence because I assumed there was only a slight chance you would ever meet them again.

"We keep each other informed with news of our family's progression, what has happened to our children, and so on. My sister, Rebecca is her name, has commented on you and your sisters' triumphs and achievements, such as your constant need to improve your mind, and Jane's charitable nature, to name just a few.

"I have responded with compliments and best wishes for her husband and children over the years. Rebecca says she knows all of you, almost intimately, so detailed have our letters been to each other. She has told me, many times, that she has a certain affinity for you, Lizzy. You remind her of herself when she was young, with your inquisitive nature and need to set things right when they go astray."

"But what gave you the idea for a visit now? It seems a bit sudden to me."

"It was Rebecca's idea. She asked in a letter last year if you and Jane might like to visit this summer. I was going to propose it, but Jane left for London before I had the chance. With her delayed return and your troubles, a visit might be just what you need. She is not aware that Jane cannot join you, but that will not matter, I am sure."

Elizabeth pondered the proposal. Had her distress been so obvious that her father thought it vital to step in and save her? She was closer to him than any of her sisters, so his concern was no surprise, but she was certain there was a detail he had not mentioned.

"As we grew, we were the closest of siblings," said Mr. Bennet, interrupting her contemplation. "My failure to call on them bothers me; it was a decision I made shortly after their marriage. I know, from Rebecca's letters, they are blessed with sons and daughters, two of each. You would like them, and certainly Louisa, their oldest girl."

"Why did you decide not to visit? Was it something Aunt Rebecca did? Surely you could forgive her, Papa. I have seen you act as peacemaker and admired the ease with which you can mend hurt feelings and repair broken relationships. What happened, that you would turn your back on her?"

Mr. Bennet sighed and leaned back in his chair, his eyes unfocused. Elizabeth waited for him to gather his thoughts, content to bide her time until he was ready.

"Her husband, George, and I never warmed to each other. It seems he felt her acceptance of his marriage proposal disappointed me."

"Was there something about him that made him unsuitable as a husband?"

"Not at all. George's problem arose from the difference in our estates. Kingsdown was his father's and was not one of the larger, or more successful, properties in that area. Longbourn was better situated than his own, and it bothered him. To prove himself my equal, or my better, he took steps to increase his capital, and thus his status. I had never, to my knowledge, given him cause to assume I considered myself above him, but he wanted to prove me wrong.

"He made ill-advised changes to Kingsdown. I tried to offer my advice, but he would accept no part of it, convinced his judgement concerning what the estate needed was better than mine.

"His schemes failed, and as a result, he almost lost Kingsdown. I wanted to help, but his pride would not allow him to accept my offers. Rebecca came to me to talk about the situation. In the end, I agreed to distance myself. That was over eighteen years ago, and we have not been back since."

"Then what makes you so sure Uncle George will welcome my visit now? If he pushed you away then, would he not still hold the same opinion?"

Mr. Bennet rose and paced the room, shaking his head as he did. "Rebecca tells me his feelings are softened," said he, "and he voiced no opposition to her idea. If you decide to go, I will take you. With your help, I might establish a friendship with the man. I will try, for Rebecca's sake. Our estrangement has bothered her, and the time has come to put some of our past differences aside."

"And?"

Mr. Bennet stopped his pacing and turned to look at his daughter. There was a look akin to regret on his face, as though he had said more than he wanted.

"What is it, father?" she asked, not willing to let this question pass unanswered. "Tell me, so I can make an informed choice. I do not want my decision tainted by incomplete information."

"My brother-in-law has never been supportive of Rebecca's efforts to improve her children. Rebecca is much like you; she has an inquisitive mind, one that chafes at being told to ignore the unknown. She encouraged her children to learn while they were young, and before they lost the chance to the necessities of life.

"George holds a different view on the matter. He feels that other than the need to read the simplest of sentences and perform basic mathematical functions, education is unnecessarily frivolous. If you decide to accept her offer and pay a visit to Kingsdown, this will be plain to see, and I know it will bother you."

"You worry too much, Papa," laughed Elizabeth. "I can control any revulsion to my cousins' personal shortcomings, especially those thrust on them by an inflexible parent."

"Are you decided, then? If so, I will notify Rebecca so she can prepare."

Elizabeth raised her hands to dampen Mr. Bennet's eagerness: "Not so fast. I need time to think about this; I am not comfortable being asked to reach a decision so fast."

"I understand your hesitation," said he, "and I sympathize, but a journey to Derbyshire would be good for you. The chance to go away somewhere new will help you forget."

"Give me a day or so to consider the idea. The prospect of meeting previously unknown relatives is exciting, but it is also disconcerting. What if they dislike me? What if I dislike them? Let me think about it so I can be sure whatever decision I arrive at is best for me."

"I will respect your wishes, Lizzy, though I urge you make your choice without delay, before fate steps in to make it for you."

"Yes, Papa, and thank you for listening to me blubber and carry on as if I were a little girl. Our talk has already improved my mood."

"You are welcome. Now off with you so I can return to my brandy and my books."

Elizabeth pulled the library door shut behind her and made her way down the hall, intent on going to her room to ponder her father's idea.

The sight of blue skies and light, airy clouds pulled her outside and onto one of the well-trodden paths around the house. It was some minutes before the call of a bird awakened her to the realization that her plans had changed. The next few hours were a joy as she drank in nature's beauty, displayed in abundance on every side. When she returned to the manor, her mind was clear of the clutter that had dragged her down for so long.

Elizabeth answered the call for supper, ravenous for the first time in a week. Her face wore a smile and nothing, not even her mother's complaints about Mr. Collins and Charlotte Lucas, could remove it.

Her happiness lasted through the evening and was still there when she woke the next morning.

CHAPTER III

Elizabeth rose early, eager for her usual pre-breakfast walk. She dressed and made her way to the cloakroom, where she chose a wrap warm enough to ward off spring's chill but light enough to wear comfortably.

The gentle clearing of a throat startled her, and she turned to find Kitty, the second youngest of her sisters, standing nervously in the doorway.

"May I come with you?" asked the girl timidly, as if expecting an emphatic no to her question.

"Of course you may." Elizabeth stepped aside to let Kitty into the room. "Choose a wrap for yourself. It will be cool this early in the morning."

Elizabeth inspected her sister, impressed with the preparations the girl had made even before entering the cloakroom to pose her question.

"You were expecting this," said she, looking at Kitty's face. "And you are for the most part dressed appropriately, although you might want to change your shoes for a sturdier pair. What you are wearing will be uncomfortable, and you will be limping well before we finish our walk. I have no desire, or strength, to carry you back to Longbourn."

Kitty responded with a laugh and followed Elizabeth's advice with alacrity. "Is this a good choice?" asked she, showing off her feet encased in the new boots.

"That will do nicely," was Elizabeth's verdict as she led the way, setting off for a path she rarely walked, leaving Kitty hurrying to catch up.

This morning was quiet, as if the animals had slept late. They heard few birds chirping, which was an unusual experience for Elizabeth, who loved the daily aerial symphony. She looked to the sky, hoping the silence did not portend a coming storm but, other than an occasional cottony white cloud, it was clear, a stunning shade of azure.

"This is nice," said Kitty, breaking the spell and bringing Elizabeth back to the present. "I can understand why you do this so often."

Elizabeth laughed, its spontaneous occurrence a surprising relief: "I love being so close to nature." She spun in a circle, her arms gesturing to include the path and everything about them. "There is something about the beauty of a bright yellow daffodil or a meadow of bluebells, their blossoms hanging as if waiting to be rung.

"I love the trees as well. The oak is my favorite; it is so strong and majestic. To see the robin's nests among the branches, their babies crying for food, touches my heart. There is so much I have yet to discover in these woods that I will never grow tired of my morning ritual."

"I see what you mean," replied Kitty. "I might have to join you again. If you will let me, that is."

"You can anytime you like, but why did you choose to come today? You normally rise much later; I am often back and finished my breakfast before you are awake."

"Lydia made me angry," said Kitty, after a moment of silence. "She claimed the only reason you spend so much time walking, or reading, or any of the things you do most every day is because you cannot attract a suitor. According to her, with nobody willing to pay their regards you must find other interests. She thinks you will be an old maid, alone forever, while she will be fending off her many suitors, who will be heartbroken when she finally gives her hand to only one."

"Lydia is a foolish girl, and one you should pay less attention to. There is more to courting than simply flirting with every man or boy who crosses your path. She is going to learn, probably the hard way, that carrying on in that manner can be a dangerous game, with terrible consequences."

"I have tried to tell her," said Kitty, "but she will not listen. She knows better than me, or you, or Papa, for that matter. She says her comely looks and delightful figure are enough to enthrall any man, married or not.

"She is always sneaking off to Meryton, where she looks for anyone in uniform so she can give them a thrill by talking to them. I am uncomfortable watching her carry on like that and have tried to warn her, but she ignores me.

"In her opinion, I am too unsophisticated to understand men like she does, but she is in no danger, as they are too rivetted by her beauty to do anything but hang on her every word. To her men are nothing more than lapdogs, eager to accept any attention she pays them. It is disgusting to watch her throw herself at them like she does."

"Then why do you follow her? Every time Papa catches Lydia misbehaving, you are with her," sighed Elizabeth. "You have a mind of your own, Kitty. Lydia is not your chaperone, nor is she a good example of obedience or propriety."

"But life at Longbourn is so boring!" Kitty exclaimed. "There is little to do and nobody to do it with. Mary's only interest is studying her bible or other religious publications, like Reverend Fordyce's sermons. I hesitate to speak to her because I know she will lecture me on the sins she thinks I am committing. According to her, I am bound for hell."

"Mary can be a little self-righteous," agreed Elizabeth, "but she means well."

"I prefer to avoid her, if possible, but there is no one else to spend time with, other than you or Jane. But you are always busy with one thing or another, and Jane never seems to stir from the sitting-room, when she is not away visiting."

"Jane's absence was not unplanned," said Elizabeth. "She and I were both supposed to return to London with Aunt Gardiner, but I was too sick. As luck would have it, Jane had to extend her stay because our aunt came down with something and is now too ill to leave her bed. You know Jane, there is no way she could refuse to stay and help; that would be against her nature."

"I know, and I cannot fault her for that, but what else is there for me to do? I know Lydia welcomes my company; she invites me to go to Meryton with her. She is always up to no good, and I know Papa will also punish me, but I keep hoping that she will finally listen to me and decide to change her ways. Of course she never does, so Papa thinks I am as bad as Lydia."

Elizabeth shook her head in disagreement: "He does not. What baffles him is how she can talk you into participating in her schemes.

"Despite Lydia's belief in her own sophistry and superior intelligence, it is easy to predict where she is likely to be found, because her plans are always the same. She has been like this since shortly after her twelfth birthday, a change that has bedevilled both our parents, Papa more than our mother, who will not acknowledge there is a problem."

"I know, and I am sorry," said Kitty, her head hung low in apparent shame.

This openness had taken Elizabeth unawares, although on further consideration she should not have been surprised. Kitty often seemed reserved and hesitant to voice an opinion, as if the mere mention of her own views might cause her elder sister displeasure, although once she started speaking, she did not hold back. She displayed no such reticence with Lydia, however, boldly espousing contradictory ideas, which her sister would most times ignore or belittle.

Kitty was not a stupid girl, notwithstanding her tendency to join Lydia in her foolhardy defiance of their father's rules. On every occasion the girls escaped to Meryton unnoticed, Kitty had been the one to devise a workable plan.

Their inevitable discovery upon returning home was because of Lydia's inability to keep their adventures secret. Where Kitty would say nothing about a forbidden or clandestine jaunt, Lydia seemed to have an ungovernable need to boast about her latest exploit. She looked on the resulting censure and punishment as a personal affront, as if she were being unjustly accused and persecuted.

Elizabeth feared for her youngest sister's future if she continued to pursue her present course. The girl was headstrong to the point of obstinacy, unwilling to entertain any suggestion that her troubles were self-inflicted. Kitty, on the other hand, while easily led, would accept her guilt and the discipline that followed.

Walking beside her gave Elizabeth a chance to study Kitty's reaction to the subjects they were discussing. She knew, from the responses to her observations, that Kitty agreed with her. What she did not know was Kitty's reason for coming along on this morning's walk. Did she want something, or was it nothing more than the desire to draw closer to her elder sister and disprove Lydia's declarations?

What if there was something Elizabeth could do to reduce Lydia's influence? Would Kitty be amenable to such a suggestion, or would she resist any offers of help? The nub of a solution nibbled at the edges of Elizabeth's consciousness, prodding her to consider its possibility. Like the buzzing of a persistent fly, it continued to bother her, stubbornly refuting all the reasons she could conjure up for dismissing it as an unrealistic gamble.

A surreptitious glance at Kitty revealed a young woman who, while paying close attention to their discussion, was also enjoying their surroundings. Her eyes danced from woodland to wildlife, watching everything from the birds overhead to the squirrels and rabbits, darting through the branches or along the forest floor between the trees.

"I never expected to find such beauty along a simple path," said Kitty. "Why have you kept it to yourself? If Lydia could experience this, the peace and solitude might convince her to spend some time in more constructive activities!"

"I love your enthusiasm," laughed Elizabeth, "but doubt she would take the time to appreciate anything this simple, or beautiful. To be honest, I am surprised to see you enjoying yourself this much.

"If you remember, I have suggested, frequently, that you come with me and spend a morning exploring our neighborhood. I have tried to tell you of the wonder I find in God's creations, and the magnificence of the first birdcall of the day.

"You have, along with Lydia, rejected every invitation, and in fact ridiculed me for making the suggestion. And you are astonished that I would decide to stop talking to you about it?"

Kitty did not respond, and Elizabeth was content to let her absorb the mild censure. For some minutes the sisters trod the path, Elizabeth willing to let Kitty break the silence, but ready to let her finish the walk wrapped up in her thoughts if she chose not to speak.

"Forgive me." Kitty's voice was subdued, her manner regretful: "I was indifferent toward your feelings. It was foolish of me, all the more so now that I can feel the peace and solitude of this path. I cannot think of a better way to begin the day than out here, basking in the sun's warmth."

"I do this every morning," agreed Elizabeth, "even when it is raining or snowing. The weather must be severe to convince me to cancel my walk. This is my favorite part of the day, something I look forward to."

"Have you ever spotted deer or other large animals?"

"I have seen deer a few times, and glimpsed a fox following me from within the trees, but none of them approached. The sight of a human scares them off."

"Why not take one of Longbourn's dogs with you for protection?" asked Kitty, looking nervously about her as they emerged from the trees and approached the manor. "I would worry about something like a badger deciding I was its enemy. Their temper is formidable, and the damage their claws can do to a person is worrisome."

"I did once, and that experience convinced me I was better off alone," was Elizabeth's response, accompanied by a laugh. "The dog was more interested in chasing every animal he saw than he was in walking with me. I should have realized that before I asked Papa's permission, which he gave after he tried to tell me it was a foolish idea."

"What do you mean?"

"Longbourn's dogs are for hunting. They are used for chasing game through the woods, or retrieving fowl that Papa or other hunters have shot. They are not pets and are uncomfortable around humans when we use them for something other than what they are trained for. By the time I finally got the dog back to the stable, I was tired and frustrated, and to make matters worse, the stable hands laughed at me when I complained.

"Papa was amused to hear of my misadventure, and teased me mercilessly for a week. Eventually I found the humor in my experience, but it taught me to listen more to advice when it is offered."

"I can almost picture you returning to the stable with that dog," laughed Kitty merrily. "It must have been a memorable sight."

"I am sure it was," replied Elizabeth, "but if you want more details, ask old Richard. He remembers it clearly and is not above reminding me of the incident whenever he decides I am too full of myself and need to be humbled. He is always right, and I try not to take offense. Richard is older, and has more experience, so I try to heed his counsel."

"I will ask him someday," said Kitty with a chuckle as Hill opened the door, admitting them to the house. "It might be rewarding to hear his version of events."

"I am sure it would. Just try not to trust everything he tells you. He is known to exaggerate, while I told you nothing but the truth of the matter."

Kitty stopped and looked at her sister as if trying to decide whether to believe her. Elizabeth tried to maintain her composure, but the expression on Kitty's face was too much and the mirth burst from her in an explosion which soon had Kitty holding her sides as she convulsed in gales of laughter.

When they were able to calm themselves, Kitty declared: "I am going to ask him for sure, now. I have to hear his version of the story."

"You should wait until after breakfast," said Elizabeth, "or it will be time for dinner before he finishes. Richard can be long-winded when you get him started on a story, and this is one of his favorites, so you might be there for hours."

With another laugh Kitty followed Elizabeth to the dining-room, where a hearty breakfast waited for them. Quickly they sat down and ate, consuming the cook's offerings with abandon.

Elizabeth spent the afternoon in her bedroom, considering the proposed journey to Derbyshire. The idea was intriguing; the possibility of meeting cousins she had until yesterday been unaware of particularly attractive. She had never been a timid girl, and in fact was usually the first in her family to extend a welcome to strangers. Failing to convince Elizabeth of the need for caution had exceedingly vexed her father when she was young.

The unknown held a special attraction for the girl, possessed as she was with an inquisitive nature. It was to her a conundrum whose mysteries, once exposed, demanded resolution usually at the expense of caution.

This outlook was an integral part of her, and had been all her life. Many were the times that her habit of rushing headlong into a new and exciting situation had caused misunderstandings and embarrassment, most often for Elizabeth.

Mr. Bennet, as proud as he was of his second daughter, was always ready with an amusing anecdote or story concerning the predicaments this obsession had raised in the past. Supper guests rarely escaped without hearing one of these tales, and its solution, which was never complimentary to her.

To relive her escapades, with their inevitable embellishments, no longer bothered her. Mr. Bennet's skill as a spinner of tales was a legend in the county, something friends and neighbors alike enjoyed.

Though embarrassed as a teen, she now encouraged her father, knowing how much he enjoyed his role as a storyteller. Visitors, informed by neighbors, often raised the subject, hoping to be regaled with new stories they could repeat throughout Hertfordshire.

It was this same perspective that tempted her to accept the invitation without knowing any of the details concerning her relatives, or the situation she might encounter upon arrival. Elizabeth found the possibilities, either good or bad, impossible to dismiss. The longer she thought about the prospect of meeting her cousins, the more enticing the idea became.

She could not help but wonder, though, at Mr. Bennet's insistence that she consider her aunt's offer. Try as she might to dismiss the notion, she remembered the tone of his voice when he introduced the possibility, which suggested another reason behind the offer, one her father did not wish to reveal.

Could he have another purpose for raising the subject, one which necessitated her absence for the summer months? Searching her memory brought no forgotten events to the surface, other than the late arrival of spring.

Elizabeth held a special love for the season. The snow's retreat, accompanied as it was by the fresh growth of new grass and the budding of leaves on the branches, excited her. The promise of warm days and gentle breezes after the harsh season just passed, wrought a change in her demeanor year in and year out.

Gone were the depressing sights of fresh snow and icy paths, replaced by new life and babbling brooks. Each tiny hatchling and kit sent her spirits soaring in celebration of spring's renewal. The first weeks of the season would find her walking further and returning later as she gloried in nature's rebirth.

Surely this season, and her heartache, could have nothing to do with the invitation could it? Try as she might, Elizabeth could establish no connection between the two seemingly unrelated issues. Resolutely she put the matter away until she could pursue it with her father.

Her decision brought the memory of her walk with Kitty back, accompanied by the idea she had wrestled with as they followed the path. What were the chances her father, or her aunt and uncle, would accept the plan? Would they entertain her suggestion, or might they take offense at her presumptuousness in proposing such an idea?

Elizabeth worried about Kitty's fate should she leave Longbourn for an extended period. Kitty wanted her father's approbation, but Lydia's influence always seemed to overrule her good intentions. She was the type of girl who would not, of her own volition, take chances. Lydia seemed to believe it was better to beg forgiveness than ask permission, knowing that her plans were, without fail, contrary to her father's rules.

Without Elizabeth's guiding hand and loving instruction, she was certain chaos would reign supreme in Longbourn and Meryton. With Elizabeth gone, the fear of discovery would not hamper Lydia on her unallowed visits to town. She would have no reason for concern over the chances of being caught, as Mr. Bennet, though a loving father, was a lax disciplinarian. And Mrs. Bennet was apt to object, vehemently, any punishment imposed on her youngest daughter, deserved or not.

Elizabeth wanted to protect Kitty from Lydia's machinations but no other options came to mind. Jane's presence might work to divert Lydia's attention, but with her absence expected to last for a minimum of another month, Elizabeth could find no other workable approach. Reluctantly she reached the decision to request permission, hoping it would be given.

The call to supper ended her deliberations,, and she answered it at once, her mouth watering in response to the aromas issuing from the kitchen.

"Was your afternoon productive?" asked Mr. Bennet of Elizabeth when the blessing on the food finished and the meal's typical disarray was underway. "I noticed you did not leave your room."

"The entire day was enlightening," said she, "but I now have almost as many questions as answers. Prepare yourself; I need them resolved to my satisfaction before I decide."

Mrs. Bennet paused, her fork almost at her mouth, before placing the utensil back on her plate and saying: "What is this about being enlightened?"

"Has Elizabeth come to her senses and accepted Mr. Collins' charitable offer of marriage? I can just imagine Lady Lucas's discomfort, having lorded it over me for so long. I shall call on her tomorrow, just so I can watch her squirm."

"There is no longer any offer for Elizabeth to accept," reminded Mr. Bennet, his exasperation showing in the firm set of his mouth and the anger in his eyes.

"Mr. Collins will marry Miss Lucas, and no amount of wishing or hoping on your part will alter that fact. For the last time, accept the reality that is staring you in the face."

"I hoped she might respect my wishes," muttered the woman, resuming her meal. "It is only fair that I should be protected in my old age."

"What questions do you have?" said Mr. Bennet to Elizabeth, ignoring his wife for the sake of peace and a modicum of tranquility, temporary though it might prove to be.

Elizabeth waited a moment before replying, relishing a somewhat perverse joy in her father's obvious curiosity: "The usual kind. The type that would occur to anyone when presented with a choice as important as this. And one or two more."

Mr. Bennet studied his daughter, as if hopeful the intensity of his gaze might coax her to bare her soul. "Are you ready to ask them, or do you mean to make me wait, with bated breath, until you decide to share them with me? You are a deceitful girl, Lizzy, an attitude most unbecoming in a young woman."

"Is that so?" Elizabeth laughed. "What is it I am accused of hiding? My comment pertained to answers I need to make an informed choice. Forgive me, but I see nothing misleading in what I said.

"I will review the matter with you tomorrow morning, then you can write to inform Aunt Rebecca of my choice."

"That will suffice, I suppose," said Mr. Bennet, his smile informing Elizabeth that his stern look had been in jest.

"What is this of your sister?" asked Mrs. Bennet, her previous outburst forgotten. "Have you heard from Rebecca? It has been such a long time, and I have missed her. When can we visit, or have they made plans to come to Longbourn?"

"This is about another matter entirely," replied Mr. Bennet. "It does not concern you right now. Should things change tomorrow, I will tell you everything. Now, if supper is concluded, I am going back to my library for the evening."

Mr. Bennet stood to signal the meal's conclusion and left the room. Elizabeth, wanting to review her ideas a final time, returned to her bedroom to pass the rest of the night in solitary contemplation.

CHAPTER IV

Elizabeth's walk the next day was shorter than usual. Her appreciation for the day's wonders was undiminished, as was her joy in the experience. Rather, her thoughts on this morning centered on the conversation she would have with Mr. Bennet upon her return.

Much of the previous day, and all the evening, she spent in contemplation of her idea, and the negative reaction she might expect from her father or her aunt. Try as she might, Elizabeth found no valid reason they might deny her request.

Well before reaching the halfway point of the path, she reversed her course, determined to present the notion to her father without delay. His answer would be the impetus for her final decision to remain at Longbourn through the summer, or experience the delights of the season in Derbyshire.

Upon her return she went directly to the library. Approaching her father, she pulled a chair up to the desk and seated herself.

"Lizzy," said he with a smile as she settled into the chair, "might I inquire as to your lack of manners this morning?"

"My apologies, Papa, but were you not waiting for my decision?"

"I was, although I would rather you not come barging into my library uninvited."

"In the future I will," was her laughing reply, "and will, from now on, remember to show the requisite amount of piety upon entering this holiest of shrines to the printed word."

"Thank you," said Mr. Bennet. "What was so important that you did not enter on bended knee to begin with?"

"I promise to genuflect doubly the next time. May we be serious now, or should I return tomorrow?"

Mr. Bennet watched her for a minute before nodding his head to continue, his grin never wavering as he matched her insouciance with good humor. The tension which had bothered Elizabeth left her and she spoke without fear, confident her father would accept the choice without rancor.

"I have determined what I would like to do, but first there are questions, as I told you at supper last night."

Mr. Bennet nodded, so Elizabeth continued: "You talked about four cousins in Derbyshire, and that Aunt Rebecca has written regularly with news about her family. What can you tell me about them? Will they welcome me, a stranger, or will they be resistant to my presence?"

"Rebecca's children are, as far as she has told me, delightful human beings. Of course you will want to make your own determination once you meet them.

"The first is Robert. He is nineteen and, as their firstborn male, the heir to Kingsdown. Rebecca claims he is a studious young man where it pertains to the care and upkeep of the estate. He is not much for reading, probably because he has had only the most basic of instruction. His father subscribes to the belief that anything more than that is throwing time and money away.

"Louisa is the oldest girl. She is almost eighteen and, according to her mother, the prettiest girl in Derbyshire. Rebecca says she is painfully shy in company but is sure that will change with some instruction on etiquette and manners.

"Next is Amelia, who is fifteen and reminds Rebecca of you. She has an inquisitive and outgoing nature, like Lydia, and a healthy interest in members of the opposite sex, although she is not in the habit of throwing herself at every man in uniform."

"How then is she like me?" interrupted Elizabeth. "I am not interested in chasing men, or flirting with them. Unlike Lydia, the regiment in Meryton does not interest me, and I never sneak off to town to attract their attention."

"My I finish?" said he with a smile when Elizabeth's protests died down. "Rebecca says Amelia is a lot like you, because she is not satisfied to let the unknown go unchallenged, like a certain daughter of mine. She is obedient but apt to challenge injustice or maltreatment of friends or strangers. Does this sound familiar?"

Mr. Bennet paused for Elizabeth to reply, continuing as she chose instead to remain silent.

"The youngest is Christopher. He is just turned seven and was a surprise, as Rebecca thought her days of child-bearing were over. I can imagine George's shock when his wife told him they were expecting another. Rebecca says he is a quiet boy, possessing a quick intellect and an inquisitive mind. She says that of all her children, he might be the most intelligent."

"Tell me more about Louisa. Why would she need instruction? Did she not receive that prior to her coming out?"

"I do not have all the details in front of me," said Mr. Bennet, casting his eyes about the room. "That is a subject you can raise with your aunt when you get to Kingsdown."

"What are you keeping from me? You say Aunt Rebecca has told you everything about her family. Why then would she keep you in the dark about problems her eldest daughter is facing? I know you, Papa, and can tell when you are hiding something. Tell me, or I will remain at Longbourn."

Mr. Bennet regarded Elizabeth, who returned his gaze resolutely, determined he would give her the information he did not want to share. Father and daughter locked eyes, Elizabeth's stare competing with Mr. Bennet's vacillation, until finally, to her satisfaction, Mr. Bennet sighed in defeat.

"Louisa is not out," said he. "Her father has not given his permission, so she has received no instruction for what is acceptable and what is not. She has never attended an assembly or a ball, despite being included in the invitations."

"How is she to attract the attention of eligible suitors when she does not attend the public events in her area?" asked Elizabeth in surprise. "Her father cannot expect them to magically appear to ask for her hand. Unless he plans to support her forever, because if he does not fulfill his duties as a father, that will be the outcome."

"George Bannerman thinks the lack of a dowry for either of the girls excludes them from marriage to any but the poorest of men. His reasoning, according to Rebecca, is that none of the Derbyshire gentlemen will pay attention to a young woman from a family with no standing and less money to offer as a dowry. He cannot, in his mind, justify the expense of gowns and accoutrements that will go to waste. If that is to be the destiny of his daughters, why spend money he cannot afford on such foolishness?"

To say Elizabeth was astonished would not do justice to the confusion and bewilderment that ran through her thoughts. How could any man, a gentleman no less, come to such a nonsensical conclusion? The lack of preparation would hinder his daughter's marriage chances more than the absence of any monetary inducements.

"Just because Louisa and Amelia do not possess respectable dowries does not mean they will marry commoners," said she, trying but unable to hide the despair she felt for her cousins. "With no dowry, any gentleman who wants to court them will do so for love, rather than the expectation of financial gain. That, to me, should be the basis for a marriage anyway, not a happy accident that occurs after the wedding is over and their life together has begun. I would much prefer knowing my husband loves me, not the funds he will gain should I consent to his offer."

"That is my Lizzy," laughed Mr. Bennet. "Always the dreamer."

"Is it not better to marry for love than for convenience?" asked Elizabeth, not afraid to challenge her father on this point.

She had observed her parents' loveless partnership through the years, and it served to convince her that a marriage without love and respect was not worth having. If she found no attraction to a suitor, she would not permit his courtship. It was a decision reached before her first ball and, in the years since, she had found no reason to change her mind.

Mr. Bennet sighed before answering with what Elizabeth knew was an uncomfortable admission: "I wish I had an answer to give you. What I hoped was love turned out to be nothing more than infatuation. Not a day goes by, but what I am reminded of that fact. I agree with you and would never advise that you take the hand of any man you did not genuinely love with all your heart.

"Your aunt hopes that if you visit, you might also agree to assist with Louisa's instruction. Rebecca worries she does not have the knowledge or skills to take on such an important task herself. She is confident you will prove to be a competent and caring teacher, and Louisa's insecurity will fade.

"It surprised her to learn Mrs. Bennet saw to preparations for all our daughter's introduction to society before they turned sixteen, because George will not entertain such an idea."

"I will not be drawn into a family dispute, Papa, nor will I be the one to plead her case to my uncle; that is the responsibility of Louisa's mother."

"I would not involve you in a situation you were not prepared for, Lizzy, and I said so to Rebecca. She simply wants you to undertake to instruct your cousin, and adequately prepare her to enter society. Rebecca has promised, and I trust her, that she will be the one to discuss the matter with George. She seems to feel that he is ready to give in to her request.

"The choice is yours; I cannot make it for you. If you decide not to visit Derbyshire, I will respect your decision."

Elizabeth wondered about the problems she might encounter at Kingsdown. She did not fear for her safety, and her father had voiced no concerns. She trusted his judgement and, if she were to be honest with herself, was interested in the opportunity her cousin's inexperience presented.

A chance to help was an exciting challenge, and had been since she was a child. Many morning walks had seen her return to the estate, cradling an injured creature she felt compelled to mend. Mr. Bennet, after fruitlessly counselling her against such actions, had allowed her space in one of the unused stable pens, and she had gone about equipping it for the recovery of her next injured discovery.

Her rescues were as often unsuccessful as they were rewarding, but that did not diminish the girl's need to try.It was this integral part of her personality that ultimately decided for her.

"I will go." Her answer was apparently no surprise, for Mr. Bennet smiled and nodded.

"I will tell Rebecca. Be prepared to leave in four weeks, on the last Tuesday in April. You will arrive on the Thursday or Friday of the week, which will give you time to prepare for church with the family on Sunday."

"I want to take Kitty with me," declared Elizabeth before her father dismissed her. "She might gain from the experience."

"Are you sure? I would suggest taking Mary instead. She will be less trouble."

"Kitty wanted to join me on my walk yesterday morning, and I told her yes. We had an interesting discussion about Lydia, me, and a lot of other topics. Some of what she told me was surprising, as I would never expect to hear such things from a girl so willing to take part in Lydia's escapades.

"Kitty and Lydia would both benefit if she were to accompany me to Derbyshire. Kitty would see that there is more to life than unquestioning obedience to every foolish scheme her sister dreams up, and Lydia would need to find some other companion to spend time with."

"The only person left is Mary," was his thoughtful reply, "and I doubt Lydia would subject herself to the unavoidable lectures, or to her pious attitude."

"Can it hurt to try? She might surprise you."

"We will see," said Mr. Bennet. "In the meantime, I will write to your aunt and tell her Kitty will be with you, instead of Jane."

"We should ask Kitty first," stated Elizabeth, rising and crossing to the library door. "I wanted your approval before inviting her."

Opening it, she stepped into the hall, returning a few minutes later with her sister. Pointing to an empty seat she had drawn up to the desk, she said: "Sit there." Kitty obeyed, but her expression was pensive, as though she feared she was in trouble but could not remember what she had done wrong.

"Do you recall the conversation we shared yesterday on our walk?" asked Elizabeth, to which Kitty nodded. "We talked about Lydia, and your penchant for following wherever she leads."

"I did not go with her today." Kitty's fear was now manifesting itself as she looked from her sister to her father: "She was going to sneak off to Meryton again, but I wanted to stay on Papa's good side, for once."

"A wise decision," agreed Mr. Bennet. "It is good to see you finally paying attention, to me and your sister."

"You do not need to worry," said Elizabeth, placing her hand on Kitty's arm to calm the girl's fears. "I did not bring you in here because Papa wanted to punish you. Yesterday's discussion gave me an idea. May I share it with you?"

Kitty nodded hesitantly so Elizabeth continued, hoping her plan would capture the girl's interest.

"Jane and I are invited to spend the summer in Derbyshire. Papa says we have relatives there, and they want us to visit. Of course, Jane's being in London means she cannot go, so I thought you might like to come along instead."

"Mama told us nothing about other relatives," laughed Kitty nervously. "I mean, other than the Philips and the Gardiners, who I know well."

"They are relatives of mine," said Mr. Bennet. "My sister Rebecca sent the invitation, and Elizabeth accepted her offer."

"Are you sure you want my company?" asked Kitty. "Should you not rather ask Mary? She would be less apt to embarrass you, a talent I possess, or so I am told."

"Forget what others say," replied Elizabeth. "I am not worried about it, and you should not be either. If anything you might worry about the chance I might embarrass you; Papa has cautioned me more than once about holding my tongue until my thoughts can catch up to my mouth."

Kitty's quick giggle was cheerful: "You are injudicious at times, and your comments often mortify Mama. Lydia and I find it funny to watch."

"I will try to control myself," laughed Elizabeth before continuing. "Does my idea intrigue you at all? Would you like to spend the summer somewhere other than Longbourn, with cousins to boast about meeting before Lydia? She always insists on being the first to try something new; the bragging rights would bother her to no end."

"I had not considered that," said Kitty with an enigmatic smile that to Elizabeth looked cunningly devious. "I will come with you. A summer away from home sounds like a wonderful idea. But there is so much to do, I will never be ready in time!"

Kitty jumped from her chair and hurried from the room, all the while muttering to herself about the many preparations she needed to complete.

"Now you may inform Aunt Rebecca and Uncle George," said Elizabeth to her father, who had pulled a sheet of paper from his desk and was dipping his quill into the ink. "I hope they are ready for us. Kitty can be a handful when she is excited, and her mood will probably not change once we get to their estate."

"I suppose you are right." Mr. Bennet raised his hand as Elizabeth rose to follow her sister from the room. "Please stay a minute more so I can make one more request."

"Kitty might benefit from the instruction you give Louisa," was his remark after Elizabeth seated herself again. "As I recall, her training prior to coming out was little more than superficial. Mrs. Bennet was more interested in Lydia's instruction so Kitty suffered.

"She is uncomfortable at the assemblies; that explains, to me, why she stays with Lydia instead of participating in the dances or mingling with others. If you were to include her, unobtrusively of course, in Louisa's training, she might attract the attention of Hertfordshire's single gentlemen and that might lessen Lydia's influence."

"I will do my best," said Elizabeth, pondering how to include the girl. "It might work to ask her to help me teach her cousin. She cannot help but learn while she is assisting me."

Elizabeth barely heard her father's reply: "Thank you, Lizzy; I can always count on you." The words were muffled, as he was already bent over the desk in the act of composing his letter.

They began preparations for their departure the next day. Kitty, at first hesitant in asking for Elizabeth's advice, was soon so caught up in the excitement that she could not remain quiet. Everything raised questions, from the length of the journey to the route they would follow, and so on.

Inquiries about Derbyshire were unrelenting and, for the most part, unanswerable. Elizabeth tried to explain that she did not remember their relatives, but that did nothing to satisfy Kitty. Surely she knew something about the Kingsdown estate, or Lambton, or the county of Derbyshire itself.

In desperation, Elizabeth wrote to Mrs. Gardiner, posing the questions she could not answer. She hoped that her aunt, having lived in the area, would provide some knowledge before they departed. She thought that London, being closer than Lambton, would allow for a quicker response than sending a letter to her Aunt or Uncle Bannerman.

Accordingly, she wrote and posted the letter, but Kitty's interrogations, or that is what they seemed like to Elizabeth, persisted without stopping.

"Will the weather be different there than at Longbourn?" asked Kitty one day, standing at the door to Elizabeth's room with a coat in each hand. "I am unsure which to bring, my spring or my summer one. If it is colder I shall want the heavier spring coat, but if it is the same, or warmer, the summer one would be better."

"Why not take them both?" said Elizabeth, absent-mindedly folding fabric to place in the trunk she was packing. "That way you will have the proper one, no matter the weather."

"That is a clever idea. Thank you, Lizzy." Kitty happily watched Elizabeth putting the cloth bolts away in the trunk.

"Are you planning some additions to your wardrobe when we are at Kingsdown?" asked she with a giggle. "Or will you need something to keep monotony in check?"

"I expect we will attend a ball or an assembly while we are there," said Elizabeth. "If that is the case, I want to make us some new gowns to wear."

"Can we not take some with us? The gowns we wore to the last ball should be good enough, should they not?"

"That is possible, but I want the option of making new ones."

Elizabeth saw that her answer confused Kitty but, to Elizabeth's relief, she did not pursue the subject, electing instead to return to her room to continue her packing.

She had not intentionally misled her sister regarding the muslin and other cloth she was taking to Kingsdown. Kitty's inquisitive nature guaranteed a round of questions Elizabeth had neither the time nor the patience to answer so, to protect the girl's tender feelings, she deflected the initial question.

After the discussion with her father regarding her uncle's opposition to presenting Louisa in society, Elizabeth was certain he would not approve the purchase of a new gown for her debut. She therefore decided that Louisa would wear something new to her first ball, should they get the opportunity to attend one during their visit. Accordingly, she had purchased supplies to fashion something Louisa would be proud to wear.

Her only worry was that her uncle would also oppose any plan to equip his eldest daughter for her appearance as an available young lady in Derbyshire society. Elizabeth, though, was a determined young woman and knew that, if called to defend her viewpoint and her cousin's future, the challenge was not an impossible one.

"Rebecca responded to my letter," was Mr. Bennet's news three weeks after his missive had been posted. "She says our acceptance excites the entire family."

"I confess," said Elizabeth, "I am looking forward to this journey, although not nearly as much as Kitty."

"I can tell," was his chuckled reply before disappearing back into his library.

The response to Elizabeth's letter arrived ten days after she had written it. Quickly she perused its contents before going to Kitty's room and knocking on her door.

"Lydia?" she heard from the other side of the portal. "Please leave me alone. I am busy packing, and have no desire to sneak off to Meryton today."

"It is Elizabeth, not Lydia, and I have a letter from Aunt Gardiner about Lambton and the surrounding county. Do you want to read it?"

The door was flung open before she finished speaking, revealing an excited Kitty, who reached for the letter while hopping excitedly from one foot to the other. She snatched it from Elizabeth and hastily unfolded the page before sitting at her dressing table to devour its contents.

"Aunt Gardiner says she cannot tell us much about Lambton, or Derbyshire," said Kitty in a dejected tone. "It has been years since she was there, and not since she married our uncle. According to her letter, it was a smallish town filled with friendly people. She cannot say if they use the assembly hall much during the spring and summer months, but assumes they do, based on her recollections."

"She does not mention the Bannermans," said Elizabeth. "I presume that is because she does not remember them from her time in Lambton. As I recall, Aunt Gardiner moved from the area before Aunt Rebecca married, so she might not know them."

"I hoped she might be able to tell me something, even if she had to repeat rumors," sighed Kitty. "We will form our own opinions, I guess."

Elizabeth laughed: "That is always best. Opinions based on rumor or insinuation do nothing but taint the first meeting between strangers. A viewpoint, once decided, can be impossible to adjust. Why not delay judgement until we get to Kingsdown?"

"I suppose," answered Kitty. "I thought I might get to know them a bit before they met us, but I guess that was foolish."

Elizabeth replied quickly to bolster her sister's confidence: "Not foolish, but unwise. Are you finished packing? We are leaving tomorrow morning, so complete everything tonight. Father will not want to wait."

"There are only a few more minor items. I am waiting for Mrs. Hill to bring them so I can put them with my luggage. I will be ready tonight; Papa will not need to wait for me."

True to her word, Kitty was waiting by the cloakroom when Elizabeth descended the stairs the next morning. Her trunk sat by the door, ready to be set in place on the carriage.

"What kept you, Lizzy?" smiled Kitty, her excitement clear. "I have been ready for hours. You picked a fine morning to oversleep."

"I am well rested," responded Elizabeth. "Unlike a certain sister, I will not be falling asleep before we are out of the county."

"Would you care to place a wager on that?" asked Mr. Bennet, coming from the dining-room, where he had consumed a hearty breakfast. "If this journey is anything like our last, and the one before that, your eyes will be closed before hers."

Elizabeth laughed: "There is not much else to do so I try to make myself comfortable."

"That you do," said he with a nod to the servants to begin loading the luggage onto the carriage. "If the two of you are ready, we can get started."

"Kitty, you can sit beside Lizzy while I enjoy the solitude of the other bench," were the instructions as he handed his daughters into the conveyance.

With his daughters settled, Mr. Bennet gave the order and the driver, with a shake of the reins and a snap of his whip, started the horses moving.

"I can hardly wait!" exclaimed Kitty as they pulled out of the Longbourn drive. "This will be so exciting."

"For the first hour, at least," said Mr. Bennet sardonically, shielding his eyes against the swirling dust as the carriage entered the lane and picked up speed.

CHAPTER V

"Are you finally ready, or should I lie down and nap for an hour or two?" asked Fitzwilliam as Darcy came into the entrance hall.

"Would you deny me a proper breakfast before following you on this fool's errand, Colonel?" answered Darcy, stopping in front of the man who waited impatiently, tapping a foot on the tiles.

"Fool's errand? As I recall, you raised the matter. I wanted to ignore you but, thanks to the goodness of my heart, I graciously offered my opinion. I would advise you to appreciate gifts freely given, *Mr.* Darcy. And, as I told you more than once, I am no longer a colonel, having retired, if you recall."

"My appreciation for your so-called gifts knows no bounds," laughed Darcy, leading the way from the house and nodding to the servant, who closed the door behind them. "I am well aware of their value and acknowledge their worth accordingly. And I will continue to call you Colonel. It amuses me to see the discomfort it causes you, although I suppose I could call you by your first name, Richard, if that is more annoying."

"Never mind." Fitzwilliam's reply was no surprise, as Darcy knew he had never enjoyed being called by his given name.

The banter between the two, who were as amiable as two cousins could be, continued as Darcy led the way to his orchard.

More than mere relations, they were close friends, and had been since childhood. Darcy, despite his complaints and reticence to acknowledge the gesture, was grateful for the man's help.

Darcy stopped at the orchard and gestured to his trees' branches, which bore few blossoms, unusual for this far into spring. Instead, the tree appeared to be moving, its branches covered with worms, wriggling among the few remaining leaves and dropping on gossamer threads to the ground, which was also covered with them.

"That is quite the infestation," observed Fitzwilliam. "What has your gardener done about it?"

"I no longer employ a gardener," answered Darcy, to a surprised look from Fitzwilliam.

"What happened to him? Did you run him off like you did Georgiana's chaperone?"

"I would be careful about referring to Mrs. Younge. Her employment ended because of her association with Mr. Wickham. If not for the questions Georgiana was asking about Mrs. Younge's actions, he might have talked her into marriage and gained control of her dowry. "Georgiana has not taken the disappointment well. Since then, she has adopted a rebellious streak. She seems compelled to defy me, although not openly, yet. I suspect my trouble in retaining a chaperone is her way of lashing out at me for thwarting Wickham's plans for their future.

"To answer your question, my gardener retired and moved to Luton, as per his son's request. Thomas was getting on in years and his arthritis made it increasingly difficult to tend the estate's grounds properly. I wished him well and sent him off with a gift of one thousand pounds for his years of service."

"So you are not the skinflint everyone assumes," came from Fitzwilliam with a laugh, prompting a look of reproach from his cousin. "Relax, Darcy, they regard you as a kind and generous employer, besides the widespread belief that you are too full of yourself.

"I apologize if my reference to Mrs. Younge upset you. I agree, Wickham came too close to eloping with Georgiana. As I said then, and repeat now, should fate put him in my path again, he will not escape my justice as easily as he did yours."

Darcy shook his head and chuckled at the retort before turning back to his suffering trees. "Mr. Wickham is aware of the love you hold for him. As to the matter of the orchard, I do not know how to deal with this. You, as I recall, mentioned a problem like this at Thorndell."

"That happened while I was on the continent battling Napoleon for England's future," said Fitzwilliam, "and it was my gardener who dealt with it, not me. I would ask one of your esteemed neighbors for their advice. It is possible I may be mistaken but, while it is certainly the most imposing and pretentious estate in all of England, yours is not the only one with this problem."

"Pemberley is not pretentious, but you are probably correct," sighed Darcy. "I will not see much of a harvest this season."

"I will be surprised if you see any," was Fitzwilliam's opinion as they left the orchard and returned to the house. At his side, Darcy contemplated the difference five years had made.

He was the product of his upbringing, nurtured at his father, George's, knee. To say he was the apple of his daddy's eye would be an understatement, as Mr. Darcy saw to it the boy had everything imaginable.

He was coddled as a child and indulged, although not spoiled, as a young man. An only child until he was twelve, his father raised him to believe in the superiority of the family's name and lineage.

George Darcy's death five years ago forced many unplanned changes, the most important of which was the appointment of Darcy and his cousin as guardians of Georgiana, who was almost twelve.

Darcy took to his role with a dedication nobody, including Darcy himself, had foreseen. Together, the two men undertook to honor the elder Darcy's wishes in caring for the young girl.

He provided for and protected Georgiana much like his father had done with him. Her every wish was granted, first by Darcy or his cousin, and then by a string of matrons. These were replaced with regularity whenever Georgiana voiced a complaint. He did not investigate their validity, although he knew he should, which gave rise to rumors concerning the youngster.

He justified his actions by telling himself he owed it to his sister, whom fate had deprived of maternal companionship and instruction in her formative years.

In time, competent matrons became scarce, which led to the hiring of Mrs. Younge, and the incident with Mr. Wickham that followed.

"Fitzwilliam, I was afraid I had missed you!" called Darcy's sister from the entrance as the two approached the house. "Will you be staying more than a single day this time?"

The colonel opened his arms to sweep her into an embrace, a part of their welcome that had become a ritual in the years since the passing of her father.

"It is always good to see you," said he, hugging the young woman closely as Darcy watched, making faces to mock his cousin's obvious affection for the girl.

Fitzwilliam taunted his cousin: "Your brother finds this amusing," while sticking out his tongue in an imitation of a child.

"What he finds humorous should worry you," responded she, twisting to catch Darcy contorting his visage, to his cousin's amusement. "Please never descend to his level, it is most unbecoming."

"I promise," he laughed, while Darcy smiled at their antics.

"Why are you here?" asked she, disengaging from the embrace and stepping back. "I mean, other than to spend time with your favorite relative. Thank you for the sacrifice, it has not gone unnoticed."

"Sacrifice?" asked he. "What sacrifice?"

"Why, your willingness to endure William so we can spend a day or two catching up, of course."

"The things I will put up with for your company are amazing, are they not?" said he with a chuckle as Darcy scowled at them. "But we should try to include him before he throws a tantrum. You know how childish he can be at times."

"Are you two finished having fun at my expense, or would you rather I come back in an hour? I can occupy myself elsewhere, and you can continue to deride me."

"Stay, William, please," begged Georgiana. "It is not as much fun when you are not here."

With a shake of his head, Darcy made his way to the kitchen to speak with the cook, while behind him Fitzwilliam roared with laughter.

"I was just leaving when I saw you," Georgiana was saying as he entered the sitting-room. "Sarah is waiting and I am already late, but if you are spending the night, I will see you at supper."

"Darcy wants me to leave so he can escape further teasing," chuckled Fitzwilliam. "So I am going to remain until tomorrow."

"Then we will talk later," offered Georgiana, leaning over to kiss the man's cheek. With a wave to them, she left.

"Your sister is growing into a beautiful woman," observed Fitzwilliam as the sound of horse's hooves signified Georgiana's departure, "but I still see a little girl with braids and skinned knees."

"Those days are long past," sighed Darcy wistfully. "She has gained friends now from a lot of the neighborhood families, although she spends most of her time with Miss Sarah Haversham."

"I hope Miss Haversham is a friend who will not lead Georgiana astray. Poor choices might have unanticipated consequences."

"She is the daughter of Roger Haversham, one of Derbyshire's most respected gentlemen," replied Darcy. "If they were to misbehave, Roger would punish his daughter and send Georgiana back to Pemberley with a note explaining their sins. Miss Haversham is one of the few people I am not worried about her spending time with."

"Have you found a chaperone for Georgiana? She needs one, with you away in London so often on business."

"Mrs. Annesley has been with us for a month. She came highly regarded, and even better, Georgiana has taken a liking to her."

"I did not see her when I arrived this morning. Is she ill?"

"She requested a week off to deal with a pressing family matter. I had no plans to be away, so I agreed, so long as she returns before I leave next week."

"I hope you give her the time to become the chaperone Georgiana needs," said Fitzwilliam. "That young lady is nearing the age where you will need to plan for her coming-out. Mrs. Annesley should teach her proper manners and how to participate in the dances that go on at these types of things."

"Mrs. Annesley is qualified in those areas, or I would not have hired her. Kindly quit worrying: you are worse than a mother hen."

"Forgive me for wanting to ensure my cousin is properly prepared for one of the biggest days of her young life. It is one of my few failings."

"You are sadly mistaken if you think your failings are few," chuckled Darcy, to which his cousin did not reply.

"I am not raising Georgiana properly," he confessed after a minute of silence. "There is so much I will never know that our mother would have taken care of if she had not passed away."

Fitzwilliam sat still, saying nothing to counter the statement. Darcy knew his cousin was studying him and felt he was coming up short in the assessment. He waited for the appraisal to finish, feeling less confident with each passing minute.

"Find someone to assist you," said Fitzwilliam at last. "A woman who can take Georgiana under her wing and teach her the finer points of membership in the first circle."

"That is what I hired Mrs. Annesley for, but I fear people will still judge her because of my failure as her guardian."

"You will not bear the entire condemnation should something like that happen. Remember, the responsibility is upon both of us, so they would call me out as well."

"But I am her brother and should be able to protect her from that kind of shortcoming. The problem is I am ill-equipped to deal with this."

"Then take it upon yourself to find someone," repeated Fitzwilliam. "It should not be difficult. You are a Darcy, after all."

"That is why I hired Mrs. Annesley, or were you not listening?"

"Are you being deliberately obtuse today? Find yourself a wife, Darcy, someone who will take on the challenge you say you are so poorly equipped to handle."

The insult did not upset Darcy, as he had chosen to misunderstand his cousin's implication. The problem was that he was not going to accept a loveless marriage, like the ones so many of his friends and acquaintances had blindly entered.

The marriage Darcy wanted for himself was the same type of union he had grown up with as a child. His father loved the woman he married with his entire being, a feeling the man displayed every day they were together. She was his first thought in the morning, and his final one each night. When Lady Anne passed away, George was beside himself with grief. Her death took the life out of the man, leaving a mere husk in place of the former kind, generous individual he was while she lived.

In response, he had taken to visiting the pubs in Lambton in a futile attempt to drown his sorrows. The result of his injudicious habit of crying in his cups had given rise to rumors, most of which, Darcy was sure, were not kind or flattering.

While Darcy did not fear the possibility of a woman he cared that much for predeceasing him, his difficulty was the idea of a marriage where passion and love did not co-exist as equal partners.

"Forgive me for being blunt, but that is not an attractive proposal," said he, to Fitzwilliam's amusement.

"What about it is unattractive? All you require is a partner, someone who will undertake the responsibility you are unwilling to assume. If you had married your cousin Anne, as Lady Catherine wanted, Georgiana's instruction would not be the problem it is now."

"Anne has been dead for some time, cousin, so it would still be a problem, anyway."

"But with Lady Catherine as your mother-in-law, she could bring her favorite niece up in the de Bourgh tradition, unyielding and resistant to the airing of unwanted opinions."

Darcy shook his head at the remark, knowing that Fitzwilliam's aim was to provoke a reaction, but the very idea of his aunt involved in the training of Georgiana caused him to shudder in revulsion.

The quality of instruction would dictate Georgiana's success, or failure to prepare for her presentation. Lady Catherine's involvement only complicated things, he was sure.

The woman's indomitable nature and self-assured manner would allow no opposing viewpoint to contradict her insufferable opinions. The result, he knew, would be a woman unable to function at any public event, an outcome he found reprehensible.

Darcy caught Fitzwilliam eyeing him in amusement. The man was, he knew, enjoying this conversation and the discomfort it caused.

"Enough about my lack of a wife. What about your future now that you are a former member of His Majesty's military? Have you given any consideration to marriage, other than arranging mine?"

"I am in no hurry to enter that blessed state," replied Fitzwilliam sarcastically. "Let me enjoy a month or two of freedom before I am tied down by the responsibilities of matrimony."

"But you are quick to see me ensnared," said Darcy, "to the first available woman, and it matters not a bit to you if we suit."

"I am more interested in Georgiana's future happiness and security than I am in yours, Darcy. You can marry the meanest harridan in England for all I care, so long as she does well by Georgiana."

"Your attempts to avoid my questions are truly pathetic," laughed Darcy. "There are many handsome women in Derbyshire, of flawless character and morals. Some of them possess dowries of sufficient size to keep your own Thorndell in good repair far into the future. Why not stay long enough to meet them? Are there other commitments so urgent you cannot stay a week?"

"There are. I have an engagement next week I must not miss, an event that might adversely affect my future if I miss attending."

"What kind of commitment, if I may be so bold, is more important than spending a few days with Georgiana and me?"

"I am meeting someone. It is nothing important, but I promised to attend and I do not want to disappoint them."

"While you are there, take the time to find a proper woman to court," said Darcy. "If you wed, it will spare me the necessity."

"I will be much too busy to spend my time casting about for unattached women," responded Fitzwilliam, rising from his chair. "Now please excuse me, I would like a nap before supper."

Darcy watched his cousin walk from the room, the ambiguity of the discussion playing upon his imagination. Although the man's response to his question had been anything but clear, Darcy knew someone had captured his interest, but who it might be, he could not say.

Georgiana spurred the horse on, wanting to make it to the Haversham estate quickly. She sat astride the mount, having no desire to ride side-saddle, like a proper gentlewoman was taught.

She held little regard for the restrictions of society, preferring instead to choose her own path. That people had not observed her sitting a mount in this fashion was attributable as much to good fortune as to astute planning.

Dismounting outside the view of the Pemberley staff, who might report her disregard of these rules, had kept her safe from her brother's censure, as had threats of retaliation against any who accidentally observed her unladylike behavior.

When she arrived at her destination, she rode the animal directly into the stable before jumping to the ground and handing the reins to the stable boy, who was no stranger to her unorthodox manners. After a word with him, she went to the house, reviewing her plans for the rest of the day as she walked.

Georgiana lifted the knocker and let it fall against the door, producing a sound which echoed through the house. Seconds later Hawkins, the manor's butler, opened the door.

"Welcome, Miss Darcy. Miss Haversham is in the music room. You know the way, I presume."

"Yes, I do. Thank you, Hawkins," laughed Georgiana as she hurried down the hall to the room in question.

"Georgiana," said Sarah. "You are late, again. What delayed you this time?"

"My cousin made a surprise visit and I stayed to greet him."

"He is a fine specimen of a man," sighed Sarah. "Bring him with you next time."

"I wish you would control your animal desires," laughed Georgiana. "It is in poor taste and, frankly, embarrassing."

"Says the girl who cannot keep her eyes off many of the finer examples of single men in Lambton," responded Sarah. "You would do well to keep your own counsel."

"Are you still upset that I won our little wager?" laughed Georgiana. "I told you he would kiss me first."

"But you failed to tell me how you were going to entrap the poor boy. You cheated!"

"No, I used my feminine wiles to press my advantage. It is not my fault you did not come up with anything similar."

"You told him you were going to call for help, and threatened to say he accosted you. That is not using your feminine wiles, it is coercion," said Sarah. "He had no choice but to obey; the threat of an accusation of improper advances toward a Darcy is probably still causing him sleepless nights!"

"Harold was not in any danger," said Georgiana with a mischievous grin. "This was not the first time we had kissed, and will probably not be the last, either."

Sarah's venomous glare did not go unnoticed by her friend as she boasted of the ease with which her subterfuge had enabled her to triumph.

"I should remember you would never stoop so low as to allow honest effort to decide the winner. I cannot understand why I let you goad me into these foolish bets; you never follow the rules, even when you are the one to set them!"

"Pouting is very unbecoming," laughed Georgiana. "It certainly does not present you in a favorable light. If you suspect I will bend the rules a little, why do you continue to accept my challenges?"

"Bend the rules? A little?" exclaimed Sarah. "I would like to see that happen. Just once would satisfy me because it would give me the chance to win. You do not bend the rules, Georgiana. What you do is shatter them, leaving me no chance to come out the winner."

"If you are so sure I will go to that extreme, and the contest is so uneven, why do you take part?"

"Because one day I will be the victor, and I want to see the look on your face. To realize you are bested, despite all your underhanded schemes, will be worth the humiliation you inflict upon me."

"It is good to know one's foe," laughed Georgiana. "What do you think, is there time to go to Kympton for the afternoon? It has been a while since we browsed the shops, and a visit might relieve the boredom for a few hours."

"Are you sure you want to go there instead of Lambton? You are not so well known in Lambton, and it is much larger. Kympton has only the one shop, and it is not stocked with the latest merchandise."

"Lambton is twice the distance, and I am expected back at Pemberley early today. Fitzwilliam likes to visit when he comes from London, and I snuck away the last time he was here. I do not want to make him suspicious."

"I should be the one asking you if there is time," said Sarah. "I am under no restrictions to be home at a certain time; my father has gone to Bath and is not expected back before Friday.

"Why not just enjoy an hour or two on horseback? We can take the opportunity to appreciate the leaves budding on the branches or the early blossoms this spring. Winter stayed so long I thought the season would never change. You would not have to worry about getting back to Pemberley late, so Mr. Fitzwilliam would not suspect you of anything."

"Or we can simply stay indoors and sample the Haversham port, as we did the last time your father left on business," snickered Georgiana, with a look of avarice.

"I suppose," said Sarah, although Georgiana knew she was not very much in favor of the idea.

"We need to be careful; I think my father wonders if Hawkins is imbibing when he leaves. I overheard him questioning the poor man upon his return from his last journey to London. It did not sound to me like he accepted Hawkins's denials."

"We could always refill the decanter from the bottles in the cabinet. You claim to know where he hides the key, or were you just bragging to impress me?"

"I was not bragging," whispered Sarah, as if fearful the servants might be listening. "It is at the back of his desk drawer, hidden unless the drawer is pulled out to its stops."

"Then lead on, Miss Haversham. All this talk of your father's finest alcohol is making me thirsty."

Sarah led the way from the music room, down the hall to the manor's library. Georgiana smiled inwardly, knowing her friend did so hesitantly, fearful of being discovered.

The allure of the escapade was not the liquor; Georgiana had no love for the strong, bitter taste of the liquid. Rather, it was the possibility of being caught which fired her imagination and prodded her to take such risky chances. The ease with which she continually coerced Sarah was also an enticing lure.

Sarah approached the door on tiptoe, as if the slightest sound might announce their intention. Grasping the handle, she pushed the door open and rushed into the room, reaching behind her to pull Georgiana in with her.

"Close the door before someone notices us," said Sarah in hushed tones as she walked behind the desk and pulled on the drawer. She reached into it and felt around blindly for the key to the liquor cabinet, stopping after a brief time to fix Georgiana with a worried look.

"It is not here. I cannot find it. I wonder if my father moved it, or forgot to put it back the last time he opened the cabinet."

"That is because I moved it." Both girls looked up to see Hawkins, standing in the doorway with the key in his hand. "I decided, after Mr. Haversham's accusations, that I would move the key and watch who might try to use it to help themselves to the liquor. I must confess, Miss Haversham, I did not suspect it was you."

"Forgive me, Hawkins, I did not intend to cause you any trouble," said Sarah, tears misting her eyes. "Please don't tell my father."

"I would not dream of it."

"Thank you," said Sarah, her head downcast.

"It might be best if Miss Darcy were to return to Pemberley," remarked Hawkins, with a nod toward Georgiana. "We look forward to seeing you again soon, but Miss Haversham needs to practice her pianoforte. Mrs. Sims has been looking for her."

"I will take my leave," said Georgiana before turning toward the main door of the manor. Crossing the grounds to the stable, she took her horse's reins from the stable hand, who stood there holding the bridle to Sarah's horse, which he had saddled in response to Georgiana's request. With a smile and a rueful shrug of her shoulders, Georgiana climbed into the saddle, shook the reins, and dug her heels lightly into the horse's sides, heading for home at a gallop.

CHAPTER VI

As Mr. Bennet feared, Kitty filled the start of their journey with questions and conjectures. Her queries covered everything, from the route their carriage might take and the likelihood of inclement weather along the way, to the reception they should expect from their cousins, etc. How the girl went on! Each answer raised another question, often unrelated to the one preceding. Elizabeth seemed content to observe the discussion while showing her amusement with Kitty's indefatigable curiosity, which was not surprising. From the look on her face, she was enjoying Kitty's success in keeping him from his reading, which he preferred over conversation.

"Is Derbyshire similar to Hertfordshire?" asked the girl, breaking into his reveries yet again. "Does Kingsdown look like Longbourn, or is it much more prosperous?"

"The counties are similar," replied Mr. Bennet, "but also different in many ways. As to comparisons between the two estates I could not tell you, as I have not been there in years."

"The country in that part of England is more rugged," responded he to Kitty's look of bafflement. "But so is much of the county."

"Papa is trying to say that, although there are estates within Derbyshire much like Longbourn and its neighbors, the country farther north runs to hills and untamed forests," explained Elizabeth. "The change begins as you approach and continues all the way to Scotland, with some exceptions, of course."

"You said you did not remember visiting your aunt and uncle Bannerman," said he. "Yet here you are, describing the neighborhood as if you lived in the area."

"I was much too young to remember," laughed Elizabeth, "as you well know. You do, however, possess an assortment of maps, and an Encyclopedia Britannica collection that contains a lot of information."

"Of course you would do what you could to satisfy your curiosity. You were, I hope, careful with those books; they are among my most valuable."

"Have no fear," was Elizabeth's somber reply, although Mr. Bennet could detect a hint of amusement in the tone of her voice. "I placed them in perfect alignment with the corners of your desk, and they remained unopened until the noon sun passed its zenith. I allowed no dust to fall upon the pages, and Hill was present to ensure I bowed twice and touched my hands to my waist three times before touching each page. When I finished, I fell prostrate upon the floor and cried aloud, asking forgiveness from the publisher's gods of the printed page, whomever they may be."

"But did you circle the desk three times opposite to the direction of the prevailing wind, while chanting a Gaelic rite; in reverse order, mind you?"

"I did not, Papa. Please forgive my insensate attitude, but I substituted the Vulgate chant instead. If such an egregious error should occur again, I will throw myself from the spire of the Longbourn chapel in remorse."

"See that you do. I will not sanction such disrespect a second time. And what about Kitty? Was she a willing participant in your desecration of my library?"

"No, she is innocent of the crimes and misdemeanors I committed while in that revered alcove."

"Then I will spare her on this occasion," said Mr. Bennet. Upon observing his daughter's expression of concern, he asked: "Is something bothering you, Kitty?"

"Why did Lizzy need to take such precautions?" asked she, a tremor in her voice. "She only wanted information about our destination. What did she do that was so wrong?"

"Well," stated Mr. Bennet, his stern countenance and voice appearing to cause further unease in the girl, "let me see if I can explain." At this point he paused to gain control of himself, as the urge to break into laughter became almost overpowering.

"He is teasing you." Elizabeth threw a look of reproach toward her father, which did nothing to detract from his mirth. "He knows my habit of searching through his precious books when I want answers to my questions. In fact, he gave me permission to read any of them, with the understanding that I treat each book with respect."

Kitty gave an unsure nod and, turning to the carriage window, focused her gaze on the passing scenery. Peace reigned for twenty minutes, to Mr. Bennet's relief.

"Have you read many of them?" asked Kitty.

"Many of the books?" responded Elizabeth. "Yes, and there are more that I want to read."

"Why did Papa give only you permission to go into his library and pick out a book?"

"Because Lizzy is the only person, other than me," said Mr. Bennet, "who has shown an interest in learning any more than what she was taught as a young girl. She came to me, on her own I might add, to ask permission to explore my collection. I was more than happy to oblige her."

"Will you give me permission, the same as Lizzy? I might like to learn too."

Mr. Bennet looked at his daughter in a new light. Who was this girl sitting across from him in the carriage? In appearance it was Catherine Bennet, but she had until now never displayed a propensity for self improvement, preferring instead to follow Lydia from one misadventure to the next, often without a break between catastrophes.

Was it possible that a separation this brief had affected the girl, and she might now be inclined to reconsider life's priorities? She was barely eighteen years old, but that was an age when many young women were already married and bearing children, something which Lydia had until now eschewed and, of course, her sister echoed.

Kitty, to his annoyance had, from the time Lydia took her first steps, been in thrall to her sister's every whim. Where Lydia went, Kitty followed, in defiance of Mr. Bennet's efforts to control them.

In his estimation, she had no personality of her own, reliant instead on Lydia to supply her with the opinion she should adopt. If Lydia took a stance, no matter the issue, Kitty would support her, despite the probability of future censure for acting on Lydia's misguided ideas.

If she wanted the use of Longbourn's library, he would not interfere. She would be under the same rules as Elizabeth, but they were not onerous. All he insisted was that she respect and care for any book she wanted to read, and that she return it as soon as she finished. Elizabeth had agreed without reservation and faithfully adhered to those rules since the day she chose her first book. Mr. Bennet would expect the same from Kitty.

"I will give you the same access as Lizzy," said he at last, "but not at first. To begin, you will be confined to the library itself. When I am satisfied you can be trusted to follow my rules and respect the books, I will allow you to take them to the sitting-room, and eventually to your bedroom if that is more convenient."

"Thank you, Papa," clapped Kitty gleefully until another thought intruded. "Will Uncle Bannerman let me read some of his books?"

"That is a question you will need to ask him," said Mr. Bennet. It would surprise him, though, to learn that George owned anything as pedestrian as a mere book. Was there any value in something like that to a man who held such a low opinion regarding the importance of an education? Any books to be found in the Kingsdown manor would have been accumulated by George's father who, while relatively uneducated himself, recognized the advantages to be found in the pursuit of improving one's mind.

Mr. Bennet's choice to stop for the night was more for the relief it gave him from the necessity of answering further inquiries, than for a need to rest the horses. After renting rooms, they shared a supper of mutton stew, whereupon he retired for the evening, leaving Elizabeth to deal with her sister.

Their journey resumed the next morning, as did Kitty's interrogations. This time Elizabeth sat back with a smile when the onslaught began with the carriage's first movement.

"I told Kitty you would answer her questions," said she. "It was not until I promised her that she would go to sleep."

"Lydia was so jealous when she learned Lizzy had asked me to come with her," boasted Kitty. "She threatened to make a scene before we left."

"Lydia was upset because she thought there might be a regiment in Lambton," agreed Mr. Bennet. "Her jealousy was that you might meet some of them without her."

"That is not what she told me," replied Kitty. "According to her you chose me to go because I was not trusted to behave in your absence. She insisted you would not let me stay with Lizzy, but would bring me back when you returned."

"If trust were the problem," laughed Mr. Bennet, "Lydia would be in the carriage instead of you. I have no idea what mischief she is up to now, but it is certain she will do something, or cause some sort of problem for me to fix when I get back to Longbourn. I will probably need to visit our neighbors to apologize or talk to Colonel Forster about the inappropriate attention certain members of his regiment pay to her, or something else entirely. I will not find out until I get home, but I am familiar with Lydia's habit of laughing over the consequences of her actions."

"Why did you choose not to bring her?" offered Kitty. "She might have enjoyed a visit to cousins she has never met."

"Well, Lizzy, was it wrong to leave her at Longbourn?"

"If we had not," said Elizabeth, "our aunt and uncle might have disowned us and demanded we leave at once."

"I agree," said Mr. Bennet. "Lydia does her best to ignore my attempts at shaping her into a young gentlewoman. Her inclination to obey Rebecca or George would be less than it is for me. I shudder to think what might happen should Louisa or Amelia fall prey to her manipulations."

Kitty seemed astounded: "All of Derbyshire might curse the Bennet name?"

"You grasp the enormity of the problem, I see," winked Mr. Bennet toward Elizabeth, at which point Kitty laughed.

"I can just see them tarring and feathering Papa, like they did to that thief in Luton last year," said Kitty when her laughter subsided.

"Please, Kitty," smiled Mr. Bennet, "keep your imagination to yourself. I do not wish to entertain that kind of mental image, thank you."

"Sorry, Papa." Kitty's grin was impish: "I will behave."

"See that you do," said he, still smiling at the thought. "Now if you do not object, I would like to read this book I brought to pass the time."

The remainder of the day was quiet, with Mr. Bennet immersed in his book, and Elizabeth and Kitty content to watch the passing scenery until the carriage stopped at another inn for their second night.

Elizabeth watched the world go by as the carriage neared its destination on the third day of their journey. Where Hertfordshire was mostly farms interspersed with smaller forests and sedate, gently rolling hills, the road the carriage followed comprised a series of hills which grew ever steeper. The forests bordering the lane were denser than those at home, the trees more closely bunched, with thick trunks and sturdy branches.

This county's inhabitants were friendly if the reception they were receiving so far was any inkling. Passengers in the carriages they passed smiled and waved without exception, as did the drivers, and the servants perched atop. The greetings reminded her of home, where everyone was your friend, and all were ready with a companionable wave or a nod of the head.

She noted with interest that, as the Encyclopedia had stated, the land was more rugged in this part of England, although if asked she would not have called it untamed.

"We will arrive in about an hour," said Mr. Bennet, "early enough for proper introductions before you unpack your trunks.

"Rebecca claims they are beside themselves with excitement at the prospect of meeting you, and I believe her, knowing my sister and her welcoming ways. She says that George will try to be there when we arrive, but he might be too busy in his orchard. Insects infested the trees, and George is battling to save them."

"How much of a problem is it?" asked Elizabeth. "Will they have a harvest this year?"

"The gardener gave me an idea that might help if he will consider using it. Longbourn suffered the same problem two years ago, and he created something to lure them away from the fruit. He supplied me with a copy of the recipe to give to George."

"Is that Kingsdown?" interrupted Kitty, pointing excitedly at a house off to the side of the road.

"It must be," said he as the driver turned the carriage into the lane and pulled up in front of the building.

The house before them was smaller than their own, but that did not make it any less imposing a structure. It sat facing the rising sun, and though it was past the noon hour, most of the front windows remained curtained.

Wings flanked the entrance on either side, extending in a manner similar to home, although shorter. Each end was rounded, as if the original design called for turrets, which were never constructed. The windows Elizabeth saw appeared smaller than she would have expected in a house such as this.

The portions of the house and property visible from the carriage were neat and tidy, the flower beds on each side of the drive well maintained. Kingsdown bore a look of shabby gentility, and Elizabeth wondered if the family was the same.

Before the carriage came to a stop, the manor's door opened and four people came hurrying out to greet them.

A soft laugh pulled Elizabeth's attention to Kitty, whose face wore an amused expression. "What do you find so funny?" she asked as her sister's humor increased.

"They came out so fast it almost looked as if the house expelled them," she laughed, before becoming serious. "I hope they like us."

"We should find out," said Mr. Bennet, opening the door and exiting the carriage. Turning back, he extended his hand to assist them from the conveyance before facing the house once again.

"Rebecca," said he to a woman who was approaching almost at a run, "it is good to see you again. It has been too long since I was last here.

Further words stopped as his sister launched herself at him with a cry of delight, while throwing her arms about him, enclosing him in a loving embrace.

"Henry," she sighed, her hug continuing until he gently disengaged himself and stepped back. "I am sorry, but it has been so long since you visited that my emotions got the better of me. Please forgive my exuberance, but I could not help myself."

"You are forgiven," said he with a chuckle. "Truth be told, I had the same temptation when you came out of the house, so one way or another an embrace was inevitable."

"How was your journey? I hope you were comfortable; to travel any great distance can be a trying experience. Were you able to find clean accommodations along the way? It would be unbearable if there were no rooms to rent and you had to sleep in the carriage."

Elizabeth fought back a laugh as her aunt prattled on without stopping for breath. The woman reminded her of Mrs. Bennet, whose tendency, like Aunt Rebecca, was to carry on until she ran out of breath. Maybe this trait was what had attracted her father to her mother!

"Rebecca, you have met my second eldest daughter Elizabeth, and this is my next to youngest daughter Catherine, or Kitty as we have called her almost since the day she was born."

Elizabeth curtseyed at the introduction and Kitty followed suit. Her aunt smiled and shook her head in amusement.

"It has been so long since I saw you last, Miss Bennet, or Elizabeth if that is acceptable."

"That is fine, Aunt, although everyone at home calls me Lizzy."

"No, Elizabeth suits you better," said Mrs. Bannerman after a moment. "Lizzy is too informal and suggests a young child, which you are not anymore. Elizabeth it will be while you are here."

Elizabeth smiled in agreement as her aunt turned her attention on Kitty.

"Now Kitty suits you perfectly," laughed she. "Your youth and demeanor remind me of a willful child, one who occasionally rebels against what she thinks are unfair demands, although I would wager that you are an absolutely delightful young woman."

"She can be, when the mood strikes her," laughed Mr. Bennet, "which it does not do nearly enough, unfortunately."

"Never mind, Henry. If first impressions are any sign, both of your daughters will be perfect gentlewomen while they are here.

"Now it is my turn to make introductions. Louisa is my eldest girl, and beside her you will find Amelia. Next to Amelia is my youngest, Christopher. Robert is off assisting his father."

"We are pleased to make your acquaintance," said Kitty. "I hope we become the best of friends while we are here."

Elizabeth watched each cousin as her aunt made the introductions. Louisa was, as her father said, a pretty girl with an air of innocence about her as if unexperienced in many of the ways of the world. She was the same height as Elizabeth but slimmer, with honey brown hair and bright hazel colored eyes. Louisa seemed nervous, as she fixed her eyes upon the ground at her feet. Her occasional glances up were quick, as if she feared Elizabeth or Kitty might notice and pay attention to her. Her smile, when it appeared, was fleeting and hesitant, giving the impression that she wanted to be accepted but was unsure of how best to achieve the goal.

Amelia wore her self-confidence like a badge of honor. She was, in Elizabeth's estimation, an outgoing girl, one who made friends easily. The welcoming smile dancing upon her lips gave Elizabeth the impression of someone who was probably playful in the most serious of situations, an uncommon trait in her experience.

Christopher was an active boy, as evidenced by his impatient fidgeting and squirming as his mother made the introductions. His green eyes were alive, moving first from Elizabeth to Kitty, and then to Mr. Bennet before coming back to Elizabeth. He wanted to be moving rather than standing still, and Elizabeth wondered when his restless spirit would come to the fore.

"Let us go inside," suggested Mrs. Bannerman, releasing her hold on Christopher who, upon being set free, scurried off around the side of the house toward what looked to be the estate's stables. As he ran, she could hear him calling out the news of their arrival to his father and brother, a fact that brought a smile to Mrs. Bannerman's face.

"If anyone can get George and Robert to come inside for a moment, it will be Christopher," said she as they made their way into the house.

The main entrance to the manor was simple but clean, a fact which confirmed Elizabeth's first impressions of the Bannerman family's attention to detail. The front hall was a decent size but not huge, a staircase in its center leading to the second-floor rooms.

"Louisa, Amelia, show Elizabeth and Kitty where they will sleep," directed Mrs. Bannerman. "Henry and I have some catching up to do."

"Come," invited Amelia, "Your rooms are between Louisa's and mine."

As if by prearranged plan, Amelia showed Kitty to her assigned bedroom, leaving Louisa to take Elizabeth to hers.

"It is probably not as large as your own but it is sufficient for us," said Louisa as the servant placed Elizabeth's luggage on the floor and left. "May I help you put your things away?"

Elizabeth smiled at her cousin's attempts to ingratiate herself: "Thank you. That would be appreciated."

Elizabeth opened the trunk and began removing her clothes. Guessing that her cousin was still nervous, she kept up a steady stream of questions and comments, hoping to lessen the girl's uneasiness. In a brief time the job was complete and the two sat together on the bed.

"That was quick," said Elizabeth, "and I appreciate your help. I find that a chore, no matter what it might be, is much more enjoyable with company."

"I agree," Louisa replied, "although Amelia and Christopher would not."

"Louisa, Amelia," came a summons, "come to the sitting-room, please."

"That is Robert." Louisa sprang from the bed to answer the call: "He probably wants to meet you and Kitty."

The two left the room and followed Kitty and Amelia, who were already halfway down the stairs, to the sitting-room, which was occupied by Mr. Bennet, Mrs. Bannerman, and two additional people.

"Elizabeth, Kitty," said Mrs. Bannerman, "I would like you to meet your uncle, Mr. Bannerman, and our eldest son Robert. George, Robert, these two young women are your cousins, who have come to visit for the summer."

Elizabeth curtseyed to the introduction, as did Kitty, at Elizabeth's prompt. "We are pleased to meet you. Thank you for the invitation to stay with you this summer."

"Your aunt is the one you should thank," observed Mr. Bannerman. "It was her idea, after all."

"How are you, George?" offered Mr. Bennet. "You look good, and not that much older than when I was here last."

"Hard work will do that for a man, and tending to the needs of the property. My tenants can only plant so much, so Robert and I do the rest. I suppose with so large an estate, you are not required to do any physical labor yourself."

"I am no stranger to the work of a farm," responded Mr. Bennet mildly, the tone of his voice unwavering despite the implied insult.

Elizabeth, looking at her father, saw his smile tighten in response to her uncle's words as the tension in the room increased. He was a pleasant man by nature, not given to confrontation and possessing an excess of patience. It was unlikely, she knew, he would take offense to a gibe like this. Robert seemed unconcerned, although whether he agreed with his father she did not know.

"Supper is ready." Mrs. Bannerman rose from her seat to lead the way into the dining-room. With her movement, the budding hostility evaporated, seemingly replaced by the anticipation of a family meal.

"We can ignore custom for the night," said she. "Henry, please sit here beside me. I want you to tell me everything about Longbourn and your wonderful wife. Elizabeth, sit beside Louisa and Kitty beside Amelia. This should be an effective way for you to get to know each other.

Elizabeth took her aunt's advice and struck up a conversation with her cousin as the meal progressed. Louisa was slow at first to reply to Elizabeth's remarks but, by the end of the meal, she seemed to overcome her shyness, and become wholly involved in the discussion.

Amelia and Kitty started talking before they sat, and engaged in the liveliest of conversations throughout the meal. To anyone watching, they would have appeared to be lifelong friends, so animated and joyous was their discussion. When supper ended, they went to Amelia's room without pausing their conversation.

Elizabeth smiled to herself, pleased that she and Kitty had both found kindred spirits in their cousins. The additional sight of her father and her uncle disappearing for some after supper port and conversation of their own was also gratifying. Maybe, between them, they might mend their rift before her father returned to Longbourn.

CHAPTER VII

The week that followed was for Elizabeth, one of getting acquainted with the Bannermans. Her aunt seemed, to Elizabeth's delight, a happy, intelligent woman who informed her, every day, how delighted she was that Elizabeth and Kitty were spending the summer.

Louisa was once again a timid girl the next morning, to Elizabeth's consternation. With the determination that had always set her apart from her sisters, Elizabeth decided she would find the happy, fun-loving young woman who had briefly appeared during their first supper at Kingsdown.

She made a special point to find Louisa each morning and involve her in the day's activities. Her persistence worked as Louisa responded to Elizabeth's attention. Over the course of the week, they formed a bond, which resulted in a friendship destined to last their entire life.

When Mr. Bennet departed at the end of his stay, Louisa was the first to wish him a pleasant journey and her hope to see him again soon, after which she took Elizabeth by the hand and led her away on another activity.

Kitty and Amelia hit it off from their first introduction. They were together constantly, either laughing and playing or engrossed in deep conversations, the subjects of which they were not prone to share. Elizabeth's aunt expressed her pleasure with their growing friendship, as Amelia had none with any of the girls from neighboring estates.

The relationship between Mr. Bennet and Mr. Bannerman started as a concern for Elizabeth, however. Her uncle displayed his animosity from the initial greeting, and she held little hope it might lessen. Her father, though, proved her wrong.

At the completion of supper on the evening of their arrival, Elizabeth had seen her father and uncle disappear down the hall together. "That is a good sign," said her aunt, who was also watching the development.

"What do you mean?" asked Elizabeth, who had some worry over the conversation which might be going on out of the sight of everyone. Had they gone off to air past grievances, thus raising the spectre of hatred along with the disinclination to find common ground? Would their mutual dislike descend to fisticuffs and bloody noses, or worse?

"If George has invited Henry to his study, it means he might be ready to leave their former animosity in the past.

"Your uncle is a private person who does not like to share his thoughts or feelings with others, not even me, and our marriage was twenty years ago.

"For him to take Henry to a room he rarely lets any of this family enter suggests he might have re-examined the issue that caused their disagreement."

"Can they find common ground?"

"We can hope," said Mrs. Bannerman, "but it will take time."

When the men joined everyone in the sitting-room an hour later, some of the tension between them had eased. Mr. Bannerman smiled as he joined the group, nodding in a friendly manner toward Elizabeth, which surprised and pleased her. He even took part in the conversation for a while before bidding his wife and guests a good night and going to his bedroom.

She saw the two men conversing frequently the following week, and by Thursday Elizabeth observed them together in the orchard. They moved from one tree to another, her uncle pointing while continuing their discussion.

By the time of Mr. Bennet's departure their conversations were more relaxed and amiable, and to Elizabeth they seemed almost friendly. Mr. Bannerman's farewell to her father was warm, although reserved, and Mr. Bennet's was the same.

"I will miss you at Longbourn," said Mr. Bennet to Elizabeth as he was leaving. "The thing I will notice most is the absence of your wit and charm when I am forced to punish Lydia, which is far too often. Your defense of her, misplaced though it seems, has on occasion persuaded me to reconsider my opinions regarding some of her activities."

"I only defend her when you accuse her unjustly," laughed Elizabeth. "The problem is that it happens so rarely it surprises us both."

"Whatever the case, I will miss your company. Enjoy yourself and please, keep Kitty from embarrassing us."

"I will, Papa, and I will also remember to write," said she as her father settled into his seat, "so please, do not feel too lonely without me."

As the carriage disappeared, Elizabeth was glad the animosity between her father and her uncle appeared to be thawing. They were not yet close but, given time and further amicable visits, mutual respect and friendship might someday result.

Robert was an enigma. He was a tall lad, towering over his father by a good two inches. To say he was handsome would have been an understatement, in Elizabeth's opinion.

His head perched upon the broadest shoulders she had ever seen, and the face it sported would have set her heart to fluttering had he not been her cousin. His hair was a tousled brown, the perfect compliment for his deep green eyes, which were the same color as his brother Christopher's. He possessed a strong nose, a wide mouth with full lips, and a prominent chin sporting, in its center, the cutest cleft. A powerful neck supported the whole, the cords of which stood out when he spoke.

He was a taciturn young man, having addressed her no more than once or twice since her arrival. His only shortcoming was that he had yet to laugh or display so much as the hint of a smile, a failing she resolved to correct. From her perspective, his greatest enjoyment was in working the land, whether in the fields or the orchard did not seem to matter.

"Thank you, Lizzy, for bringing along," said Kitty one evening as they were going to their rooms for the night. "I like my cousins; Amelia most of all. She is so much like Lydia!"

Elizabeth could not believe what she was hearing. Had her attempts to distance Kitty from Lydia's troublesome influence been all for naught? Was Amelia going to prove to be just as bad as Lydia in leading Kitty astray?

"They are nothing alike," declared Elizabeth. "Your cousin is obedient and considerate, which Lydia is not. She asks permission before trying something new, and listens to her mother if the answer is no, unlike your sister, who jumps into things with both feet, ignoring the consequences."

"What I meant is she is funny and a bit surprising," said Kitty. "I can never tell what she is going to say next, not that she is rebellious or disobedient. We get along well, and I have not missed Lydia much, if at all."

"That is good to hear," said Elizabeth, pausing at the door to her room. "Just remember, when we go home you do not need to go along with every one of Lydia's ridiculous ideas."

"I will, Lizzy, I promise."

"I am not the person you should make promises to. Promise yourself, and see that you honor the commitment. How proud will Papa be if you show him Lydia no longer controls your behavior? Good night, Kitty."

Kitty seemed to be pondering their conversation as she went to her room. Her face was screwed up in thought, which Elizabeth took as a good sign.

She rose early the next day, eager to recommence her habitual morning walks, which had fallen by the wayside. This morning's air was crisp but not cold, and redolent with the scent of fresh blossoms, bursting forth in profusion around the trees which formed a wall bordering her path on either side. It was a scene that transported her back to Longbourn's woods, where a similar sight was displayed to any who took the time to look.

The path she followed was barely a trail, not well used or easy to find. She picked her way carefully, mindful of hidden branches that might trip her or unseen holes waiting to capture an unprepared foot.

She wondered about her uncle who, while civil, displayed little enthusiasm for her visit. They exchanged no words beyond those of his initial tepid greeting and, it appeared he intended to keep it like that until she departed. Elizabeth did not know if his reticence was a cultivated affectation, or if he opposed his wife's invitation.

Preparations were yet to start for Louisa's instructions, and the delay bothered her. The promises her aunt made to secure permission were unfulfilled, tempting Elizabeth to begin with the lessons before her uncle gave his approval. She was not, however, willing to undertake anything likely to sow discord between them, so she ignored the urge. If this foretold how the summer would pass, she might just as well return home as waste her time at Kingsdown.

A faint rustling pushed her thoughts aside, replacing them with a wary vigilance and an increased pace. Her eyes searched the seemingly impenetrable forest walls surrounding her, but no break large enough to admit her presented itself.

The noise increased, now accompanied by the sound of breathless exertion, suggesting her pursuer was battling the same tangled timbers and vines that her trail led through.

Catching sight of a sturdy branch lying on the ground, Elizabeth picked it up and turned to face the threat, her limbs shaking as she readied herself for a confrontation she did not want, but was not about to run from. The thrashing grew louder as her stalker neared, and Elizabeth raised her arms, determined to incapacitate whatever denizen of the animal kingdom it was that wished her harm.

When the branches parted she swung with all her might, using the branch she clutched as a weapon with which to defend herself.

"Wait, Elizabeth!" cried Louisa, jumping to the side to avoid the makeshift club which whistled past her ear, missing her by the width of a hair, if that.

"Louisa, what are you doing?" asked Elizabeth, dropping the branch like it was a hot coal. "I might have hurt you; why did you not call out to me?"

"I did not realize you were this close. I expected you to be almost to the end of the path by now."

"And I feared you might be a wild animal, like a weasel or badger, upset with me intruding on their territory."

Elizabeth stepped back from her cousin, the shock of this encounter causing her to shake. She might have hurt or killed the girl! How was it possible to mistake the sounds of Louisa passing through the forest for something as small as a badger? Though they were formidable, and ferocious when riled, they were also small, and unlikely to announce their proximity in so obvious a manner.

"I like to take time to admire my surroundings. It is not my habit to hurry just so I can reach the end of a path. Remember, I am not familiar with Kingsdown, like you or your siblings," said she when she calmed.

Louisa smiled, shaking her head in denial of Elizabeth's comments: "I am as unfamiliar with these woods as you. This is the first time I have been this far into them since I got lost here as a little girl. Since then, I have been unwilling to venture further than the first tree or so."

"Then come with me today. I walk every morning, although I have been lazy since arriving. It is a habit I decided to start again, and plan to continue every day, weather permitting. You are welcome to join me; we can discover the countryside together."

"I am not a complete stranger to the estate," laughed Louisa. "I have explored the grounds, as much as I can, although Father discourages Amelia and me from spending much of our time anywhere but in the house. He says there is little need for us to get too familiar with the outside world. Our duties are within the manor, where we should learn to cook the meals and clean the house."

Was this part of the reason her uncle had not given her permission to teach Louisa? Did he cling to the notion that women were to be kept indoors, chained to the kitchen stove or the washboard?

If this were the case, should she raise the issue with her aunt, or wait until an opportunity presented itself to ask her uncle? Elizabeth was not a bashful girl and had no compunction about approaching Mr. Bannerman. Her hesitation lay in the possibility that such an action might cause problems between her aunt and uncle, and damage whatever good relations existed between her and them.

"What a lovely path," said Louisa. "I was not aware we had anything like this on the estate. How did you find it?"

Elizabeth laughed and waved her arms, encompassing the trail and woods they were walking through: "I stumbled on it by accident. When I left the house this morning I had no idea which way to walk, so I went straight when I came out the door. I found where the shadow of a trail came out of the woods, so I followed it. But I had not planned to use this path today, so how did you find me?"

"Amelia saw you enter the forest, and pointed me in the correct direction. I confess, though, I almost quit before catching up with you. The path is so faint I was not sure you were still ahead of me. If you had not been singing, I would have given up and gone back home."

"Was I singing? If so, I was unaware."

"Your voice was easy to hear; I just had to follow it to find you."

"That is another habit of mine," chuckled Elizabeth. "I hum while I walk, without realizing it. Often I will break out into song without realizing. I have startled myself in the process."

Louisa's responding laugh was bright and cheerful, and a welcome accompaniment to their discussion. To Elizabeth, she seemed a happy and intelligent girl, and one who found joy in the simplest of circumstances, unlike many of the girls Elizabeth knew in Hertfordshire. An outlook like this, if she maintained it, would serve the girl well in the difficulties that were sure to beset her as life continued.

"I love my morning constitutional, as much for the exercise I get as for the beauty of the world around me," said Elizabeth. "There is nothing better than walking into the middle of a woodland, familiar or not, and being enveloped in the peace and solitude of the area. No matter what is bothering me, when I set out on my walk and step into a forest or a meadow, I can forget my troubles, for a time, anyway."

"I wish I could do that," sighed Louisa. "Unfortunately for me, once a problem comes up, I cannot forget about or ignore it until I see it resolved."

"Like Kitty and her begging to visit Lambton?" chuckled Elizabeth. "She wants to go to town, and will not take no for an answer."

"She keeps asking me, too," laughed Louisa. "She wanted to walk, until I told her it was five miles. Since then she has been suggesting we take the carriage."

"She can be persistent when she sets her sights on something. I feel guilty; she has not come to ask me more than four or five times."

"I told her we do not go there much. My father needs the horses to work the land; he cannot afford to lose them for an entire day. I could tell she was disappointed."

"She will get over it," was Elizabeth's opinion, "but we should return to the manor. I am starving."

Elizabeth saw Louisa looking at the thick woods on either side, the brambles growing amongst them dense enough to form a wall. The trail ahead seemed to disappear into a thorny bush, leaving them with no easy exit. Worriedly she turned to Elizabeth, the apprehension in her eyes hard to mistake for anything else.

"How do we get back? There is no way forward, and I paid little attention to the path I followed to find you."

"Not to worry," said she, turning and pushing a sickly bush to the side. "I have been looking for a way out, and this will do nicely."

Elizabeth held the bush to the side as Louisa slipped through it onto the lane which ran past the estate. In the near distance was the house, the sight of which set her to skipping happily.

"How did you know?" asked she when Elizabeth joined her. "I assumed we were miles from home, but the estate is right beside us."

"The trail I followed runs alongside this road, and I was fairly sure we were close. I have a lot of experience walking unfamiliar paths, so I am careful to pay attention as I go along. I kept track of where Kingsdown was approximately, although I thought it was further from here."

Louisa gaily ran ahead, while Elizabeth followed at her own leisurely pace. Soon they were sitting down to a delicious breakfast, livened by Louisa's excited comments about their morning's adventure.

Elizabeth had Louisa's company on her walk the following three mornings, and they spent each day exploring the neighborhood in Kingsdown's immediate vicinity. She was, as Elizabeth expected, a curious and intelligent girl. Louisa varied and usually raised the subjects they talked about, to Elizabeth's delight. She learned quickly, rarely asking Elizabeth to explain more than once.

Mr. Bannerman was waiting for her Saturday morning when she emerged from the path, which was now easier to follow because of the increased traffic. She stopped when he approached, looking like there was something he wanted to talk about.

"How was your walk?" said he, but in a tone of voice which showed his lack of interest in the answer. "I see you every morning, usually with Louisa."

"Kitty told her I like to walk, and she came with me on Monday, and every morning since, until today. We have the most interesting discussions about almost anything under the sun. We have explored so much of the estate; I feel it is almost as familiar as Longbourn."

"Louisa does not need to explore the estate, and I would rather you not fill her head with strange notions. She needs to be in the house with Mrs. Bannerman and Amelia, not out traipsing around the woods."

"But Uncle, Louisa and Amelia will benefit from learning whatever they can before their marriage. I walk every day and find something new each time I go out. Intelligent women attract discerning men, because they have someone to carry on a conversation with besides what's for dinner or if the clothes came out of the wash clean."

"My daughters will be lucky to attract the attention of one of the tenant farmers in the neighborhood. They have little dowry to garner the attention of a man such as you describe."

"The size of their dowry is not the only thing that will secure them a husband, Uncle. Let me prove it to you. I will take Louisa under my wing and prepare her for coming out. You will see how much she improves and what kind of attention she receives. The change should impress you."

Elizabeth expected her uncle to deny her request, and was pleasantly surprised to hear him say: "I am not convinced, but you may try. You need to be aware, though, that I will not purchase gowns or anything of that nature. Do what you can, but do not ask for money."

"Thank you, uncle, you will not be sorry," said Elizabeth, excited to tell Louisa the news.

"I hope not," she heard him say from behind her, which elicited a smile, and a confidence in her ability to teach her cousin and surprise her uncle with the results.

"Good morning," greeted Louisa when Elizabeth entered the house. "I am sorry I missed our walk today, but Father asked me to stay behind."

"We had an interesting discussion when I got back, about you and Amelia. He gave me permission to prepare you to come out, although we did not discuss when that might happen."

"I had not given it much consideration," said Louisa. "The one time I asked, he told me it was not something I needed to worry about so I have not pursued the subject, with him or Mother."

"I had to convince him, but he agreed to let me teach you, which I am more than willing to do."

"What about me?" asked Amelia from the other side of the table. "I would like to be instructed. I will be old enough in another few years."

"Your father might not let me," laughed Elizabeth, before turning back to Louisa: "We can start as soon as breakfast is over. The day is nice, so we will begin outside in the garden."

"I am ready now, if you are," declared Louisa, rising from the table to follow Elizabeth.

To Kitty, she said: "You should come with us. Maybe you can help me with Louisa's instruction."

Kitty nodded happily and fell into line with Louisa as they filed through the house and out the back to the garden.

"You will need to know how to act at events, such as assemblies, balls, and public gatherings," stated Elizabeth once they were comfortable on the garden benches. "You must follow certain rules closely, so you do not become the victim of gossip, or worse, censure. Ladies, especially ones who are attending their first ball, must be on their guard against letting the excitement of the evening overcome their manners."

"That would never happen to me," Amelia's confidence was emphatic. "I am far too cultured a person to let frivolity or childish behavior interfere with my good taste."

"Do not repeat that to your father," said Elizabeth. "He did not give me permission to teach you, so I cannot share any instruction your sister receives."

"This is so unfair!" pouted Amelia,

Kitty laughed: "You remind me of Lydia. That is something she tells Papa every time he punishes her."

"Never mind, Kitty. Amelia does not need to hear tales about your sister and her ideas concerning proper behavior."

"Amelia has never given our parents any trouble, have you?" asked Louisa, but the girl did not answer the question, as the sound of voices in the orchard captured her attention.

Elizabeth watched as her expression went from curiosity to bliss in less than a second.

"He is here," said she breathlessly, "and I almost missed him."

"Who is here?" asked Elizabeth of Louisa, who was laughing at her sister.

"Mr. Darcy, our neighbor. He is the master of Pemberley, the estate on our northern side, and the largest in Derbyshire."

"Is he a frequent visitor?"

"Not so much. He calls when he needs to talk with our father, but he has never, to my knowledge, made a personal call to the estate.

"He is friendly enough, for a man of his standing. Anytime Amelia or I come upon him, he takes the time to nod and tip his hat to us. He has never ignored me or given the impression he considers himself better than me. He seems personable, but no one here has spoken to him, other than Father."

"He is so handsome," sighed Amelia. "Marriage to a man like that would be heaven on earth."

"You might as well forget that dream," said Louisa. "He would never marry someone like you or me. Our family is not wealthy or influential enough to be noticed by someone like Mr. Darcy."

"Anything is possible," suggested Elizabeth. "Just because he is rich and owns a sizable estate does not mean he cannot fall in love with you, or your sister. Let her have her dreams. They do no harm and can be the difference between a boring, unfulfilled life and one with a bit of excitement. That is as important as anything else."

"Do not let Father hear you saying such things. He discourages daydreaming because it wastes valuable time. If he catches you, he will not be happy."

"Well, everyone should have at least one dream, something to hold onto when life gets discouraging. I do not recommend letting your dreams rule your every action and decision, but they are important just the same."

Elizabeth let the subject lapse, but the memory of the conversation would not leave her. After supper she wrote to Jane, a task she had meant to complete within the first night or two of arriving.

"Kingsdown, May 5.

"Dear Jane,"

"How I miss your company! Each night before turning in, I think of the fun we might have had together, visiting our forgotten relations. As I mentioned in my previous letter, I chose Kitty as your replacement and she has been a surprisingly delightful companion since we arrived. She is cheerful and personable, always eager to please. She and Amelia have become close, which is a relief. I hope Amelia's influence rubs off on Kitty, and she develops enough willpower to refuse Lydia's attempts to cause trouble.

"Kingsdown is a wonderful estate, although not as large or well maintained as Longbourn. Our cousins Louisa and Amelia are dears, and so easy to get along with. I do not know Robert or Christopher well enough to venture an opinion, although they are personable to Kitty and me.

"Uncle George is a nice enough man, but his ideas are a little strange. He says women are good enough to cook and clean, but not worth educating, if you can believe that. He did not trust me when I told him I love to read, and when Kitty asked if she could look through his library he seemed unsure what he should say!

"To answer your obvious question, Kitty has decided it is time she improved herself. She even asked Papa if he would let her read some of his books. He gave his permission, provided she obeys his rules, which she vowed fervently to do. Our little sister is changing, and for the better, I might add. Getting her away from Lydia was a clever idea, despite Papa's fears she would be an embarrassment to the Bennet name.

"I have attended church every Sunday since my arrival and must tell you it is nothing like a Longbourn service. The people here are friendly, just like at home, but the pastor is meek and almost timid, unlike Pastor Ramsbury, whose fire and brimstone sermons are enough to scare you into repentance!

"I hope you are getting along well in London. Please give our aunt my wishes for a speedy recovery. I am counting on you to write and tell me when you are planning to return home. In the meantime, I will rely on you for all the latest gossip, both good and bad.
Please take care and be safe. You know I love you,

"Your sister, Elizabeth."

CHAPTER VIII

Elizabeth's walk the next morning took her past Kingsdown's garden, which was comparable in size to Longbourn's. The well established plants drew her attention, and she paused to view them. There was something about straight lines and manicured plants that never failed to draw her interest. Although this was still late spring, early plantings of carrots, radishes and peas looked almost ready to harvest.

As she looked along the rows, she noticed some invading plants that were thriving among the vegetables and competing, successfully it seemed, for the moisture in the soil. Without a second thought she went into the field and, kneeling among the offending plants, was soon as work pulling them from the ground and piling them, to be disposed of when she finished.

So absorbed was she in her work that Robert's voice startled her: "Why are you on your knees? Are looking for something? If so, I can ask a servant to help you locate it."

Elizabeth quit tugging at the weed she grasped and sat back on her heels to see her eldest cousin looking down at her. His expression was one of disapproval, the corners of his mouth turned down and his eyes flinty and narrowed.

"The garden needs tending," said she, "or the plants will suffer. I am pulling weeds so your beans, peas, and other plants do not die."

"You should not be doing things like this. Are you not the daughter of a gentleman? Or has your father never taken the time to teach you what is proper for someone of your status?"

At first Elizabeth thought her cousin was teasing her, and took his statement lightly. The way he regarded her, however, convinced her there was no intended humor in his statement.

"I do the same in Longbourn's gardens, and enjoy the opportunity, both to be of use to our servants, and to ensure a healthy and sizable harvest for future consumption."

"Kingsdown has servants assigned to the task, unlike Longbourn, apparently."

"Longbourn's servants appreciate the help, and I enjoy the feeling of soil in my hands. I am not the only one in Hertfordshire; many of my friends also work their gardens. My closest friend finds the exercise relaxing."

Robert's head was shaking in disagreement as she explained her position. When she finished, he said: "My worry is that you will teach Louisa and Amelia that such behavior is acceptable, when it is not. Gentlewomen, as you supposedly are and my sisters will eventually become, do not stoop to common labor such as this. Kindly refrain from teaching them differently."

Elizabeth waited to respond, wanting to make her views clear without causing offense. Various replies presented themselves, each more confrontational than the previous. Robert watched her for a moment before turning away, apparently satisfied that he had carried his point.

"Am I mistaken? It was my understanding that women, which includes me and Kitty as well as your sisters, are good for nothing more than the work of running a household. We should confine ourselves to the cleaning of our homes and the preparing of meals for the family.

"Would that not include tending to the garden, with its plants that are grown for nothing more than the consumption of our husband and children? Correct me if I am wrong, but that is your father's position on the matter."

"What father meant is that women are to tend to the daily needs of the household, which does not extend to the grounds. Kingsdown has servants whose responsibilities include the cultivation and maintenance of the garden. I am sure Longbourn has as well.

"Lowering yourself to perform that kind of manual labor does nothing to elevate you in the eyes of a potential suitor, and might have the opposite effect. Please do not encourage my sisters to follow your example."

"I promise to do nothing your father would find objectionable. My intent this morning was to satisfy my desire to tidy your garden, something I missed doing since leaving home."

"Thank you, Elizabeth," said Robert as he turned toward the gate. "That is all I ask."

Elizabeth watched him leave, noting to herself how much like his father the young man was.

I will need to be careful not to anger him again, she decided as she watched him walk away.

The conversation was still on her mind as she resumed her instruction later that day. Louisa was, to her delight, an apt pupil who grasped the lessons quickly and once taught, kept the knowledge. Manners and etiquette were a natural for the girl, whose questions regarding points of confusion were short and direct.

It surprised Elizabeth when Louisa offered no argument concerning the more difficult rules she would need to follow. Lydia had refused to accept them and still occasionally voiced her opinion with no concern over who might overhear her complaints.

When the time came to introduce Louisa to the dances she needed to learn and become proficient in, Elizabeth could not help but worry. As someone who found pleasure attending balls and assemblies, she was an accomplished participant, at ease on the arm of her dance partner and admired by friends and prospective suitors alike. She did not, though, consider herself talented enough to instruct her cousin, who was sure to be judged on the ability she displayed in her first dance, no matter who it was with.

Louisa needed to comport herself well if she were to have any hope of being noticed by the area's eligible suitors. If she should stumble or appear unsure of herself, the gossips would notice and rumors would spread quicker than the plague.

To her amazement, Louisa proved herself up to the task. Elizabeth, humming a tune to help keep the time and associate the music with the proper sequence of steps, took on the man's role, leading her cousin through a set. When they finished, they started again, but Louisa proved her aptitude by recalling each step, in proper order and with the correct tempo.

"I think I am wasting my time," pronounced Elizabeth at the end of the second practice. "You know these steps better than Kitty or me, and I have been attending balls for a few years now. Have you been practising in secret?"

"No, I have not." Louisa was smiling, and blushing at the same time. "I could never persuade father to allow it, and did not want to pursue the matter too vigorously. You are a wonderful teacher, Elizabeth, and one who makes learning fun."

"We will be admired so much at the balls, everyone will want to partner with us," said Amelia. "I cannot wait for my first; I shall be the most popular person there."

Elizabeth, knowing her uncle's thoughts on the matter, was quick to say: "That will have to wait until your father says you are old enough. You are only fifteen, so there is no need to hurry. Enjoy your childhood while you can."

"I suppose," grumbled Amelia, "but it is so hard to be patient!"

"You had better resign yourself to the fact, or the years will drag," Elizabeth smiled. "I am finished for today, and you are learning faster than I had imagined. Practice with Kitty for another hour, and we will go over them again tomorrow."

"I felt like you before my first ball," commented Kitty from the side of the room, where she had watched Elizabeth's instructions. "I feared it would never arrive, but it did, and I am glad I had to wait. The anticipation was as much fun as the dance."

"Kitty, come here and take my place," said Elizabeth. "Louisa needs more practice and I have other things to do."

Elizabeth left the music room once Kitty replaced her, having decided that the day was so nice she would take a rare afternoon walk. Gathering a light wrap, she walked out into the garden and from there to the stables, wanting to walk through the orchards on the far side.

When she approached the trees, she could see the apples, still green and unripe, hanging down from the branches. The blossoms from which the apples derived were gone and so, unfortunately, was the scent the flowers carried.

She was part of the way to the other side when her uncle stepped into the row in front of her.

"Good morning, uncle." She stopped to greet him instead of walking around, as she wanted to do. "The orchard is lovely today, is it not? I see apples are growing, although not in the numbers I would expect."

"They are delayed this year. A late spring, followed by an infestation meant it was touch and go but everything is at last under control."

"The fruit looked a little stunted," said Elizabeth, "but I was not going to say anything. I did not want you to think I was being critical for no good reason."

"I appreciate your thoughtfulness. I also want to commend you on the improvements I have seen in Louisa's manners since you started teaching her. She seems happier and more thoughtful, thanks to you."

"Louisa is an intelligent girl. I am surprised by her aptitude and her willingness to learn. She is a joy to teach."

"I am sure she is. Again, I want to thank you for the difference you have made in my eldest daughter. I suppose the same goes for Amelia."

"I did not intentionally go against your wishes, but she takes part when she can, and I have not the heart to send her away."

"Do not worry," he chuckled. "Amelia is an inquisitive girl, and I did not expect you to deny her an opportunity I gave to her sister. While I am still not convinced the lessons will help either of them, I will acknowledge the fact that they are both happier and more content. My only request is that you not fill their heads with unrealistic promises or expectations. I am not a wealthy man, and their lot in life is already determined. Nothing you or I can do will change that."

"I will abide by your wishes, Uncle," said Elizabeth, although she did not know how it was possible to keep either of her cousins from setting their sights higher than their father assumed they would ever achieve.

"May we take a different path today?" asked Louisa a day later. "The land on the north side of the estate is a bit more rugged, but beautiful. I thought you might enjoy something different, after spending so many days walking the same trail."

"Lead the way," Elizabeth replied. "I will follow you."

The two set off, Louisa happily skipping along a trail that was wider and easier to follow than the one Elizabeth had taken since resuming her walks. The trail led past fields planted with grain, the plants set in orderly rows and sprouted evenly, with few gaps between them. A gentle breeze blew across the fields, moving them in undulating waves from side to side, each followed closely by another.

Elizabeth saw that the healthy green of the crop was almost to the stage where it would begin to ripen, changing into the golden hue she loved before the cutting and threshing of the harvest.

The path they trod led past the field the tenants worked and into hills that started as a gradual incline but steepened as they progressed. Soon they were entering another growth of trees, this one less wild than the one Elizabeth was used to closer to the house.

"Where are you taking me," asked she playfully as the trees closed in around them and the quiet sounds of the woods overcame the cheerful ones of birds chirping. The deeper they went, the quieter things became, the only sound that of their footsteps scraping the forest floor and the snap of an occasional twig, broken by a foot landing on it.

"Why do you ask?" said Louisa with a secretive grin. "Do you not trust me? I promise there are no plans to mislead you, or at least I had none when we left the house."

"Is there a reason for the secrecy, then?" asked Elizabeth, as Louisa kept walking. "Are you taking me to a hidden treasure that is known only to you?"

"What if I was? Would you refuse to come along? Or would curiosity override your common sense and compel you to follow until it was too late to do anything else?"

"I am not sure. It would depend, I guess, on the time it took to get there, and how ominous your manner became."

The trees were thinning as they pressed on, and Elizabeth could see the edge of the forest, presenting as a solid line past which was only meadow.

They emerged into a field of daisies, the white petals and yellow disk of the flowers sitting upon green stems that, like those in the farm fields, waved in the breezes playing across the expanse. Hollyhocks grew in what seemed a haphazard profusion amidst the flowers, their deep pink and vivid red blossoms a bold emphasis to the daisies.

Elizabeth stopped, spellbound by the beauty revealed in front of her. She turned from side to side, imprinting the scene to memory for her to recall later.

"This is what I wanted to show you," said Louisa, jarring Elizabeth from her trance and pointing to the valley below. "I used to come here just to sit and observe the house, and dream about living in something like it one day."

Elizabeth followed the pointing finger to a sight which took her breath away. Below them was the most immense house Elizabeth had ever seen, dwarfing any of the largest ones in Hertfordshire. It was three floors high, and possessed enormous wings, one at each end of the main house. The manor sat back from the lane, at the end of a drive lined with stately pine trees, each taller than the roof of the mansion.

Windows broke the walls up on every side, enough of them that she wondered if any of the exposed rooms required lamps or candles to light them during the day.

The drive passed in front of the house and turned to exit back onto the road. A roof extended from the entrance, providing shelter in case of inclement weather.

"That is the biggest house I have ever seen," whispered Elizabeth, her breath catching in her throat. "Some of the houses in Hertfordshire are large, but this is massive. I can imagine the size of the family that lives there. It must be large to require a manor that size."

"That is Pemberley," said Louisa, "and its owner is Mr. Darcy, the man that was talking to my father yesterday."

"Have you ever visited, maybe with Uncle when he goes?"

"My father does not go to Mr. Darcy's house, not because he is too proud, but for the simple reason Mr. Darcy never needs to ask him for help. Mr. Darcy is an astute landowner and has multiple servants to tend his grounds and house. I do not recall a problem arising that he needed Bannerman help to solve."

"Have you never met his family?"

Louisa shook her head and gave a chuckle that Elizabeth did not understand.

"Mr. Darcy lives there with his sister, and only his servants for company. Now and then another man, a relation I assume, visits for a day or two, but he receives no other visitors that I have noticed."

"Are you acquainted with his sister?"

"I have met her once or twice, but we are not friendly. She is a bit of a hellion, if the rumors are accurate, and not the type of person I would want to spend what free time I have with." "What about their parents? Do they not live there as well?"

"No," said Louisa, "they passed away a few years ago. Mr. Darcy looks after her alone, although there are rumors he has hired more than a few matrons, who never seem to last long."

Elizabeth thought about the challenges he must face raising a sister without benefit of instruction from his mother or father. If the girl were like Kitty, it would be a straightforward task, but should she possess Lydia's unbending attitudes and disregard for rules, the poor man might feel lost and alone.

Her heart ached for him, with no one except one sister and a household of servants, most of who would care little for the welfare of an orphaned girl. With no other relatives in the vicinity, they might both be dying of loneliness while showing the world a brave face.

"How old is Miss Darcy? Is she out yet?"

"I think she is a year or two younger than me, but that is just a guess. Mother says she is out, although I do not know if that is the case or when she was presented. Either way, mother is of the opinion she is too young, but Mr. Darcy would be the one to decide."

"We should return before Father comes looking for us," said Louisa. "The morning is almost over and he will not be happy if we stay away too much longer."

Elizabeth took one more look at the estate spread out below them: "That is a house worth remembering."

As Elizabeth followed Louisa back to Kingsdown, thoughts of the Pemberley mansion filled her mind. What would it be like to live in a house that enormous? Would there be so many servants they would not know one another all that well?

And what of the servants tasked with maintaining such a residence? Would they be familiar with the house, or would they get turned around and require direction to find their destination? Were the upstairs and downstairs servants strangers to each other, or did they tend to work wherever they were needed in the house, like the Longbourn servants?

Elizabeth put her thoughts to the side as she and Louisa neared Kingsdown, where her uncle waited, seemingly concerned, for their arrival.

"Where have you been?" he asked Louisa as the distance narrowed. "Mrs. Bannerman and I expected you back an hour or more ago. I was preparing to start a search, although I can ill afford the time."

"I showed Elizabeth the woods and meadow at Kingsdown's northern boundary," answered Louisa. "While we were in the vicinity I also took the time to show her the Pemberley mansion."

Mr. Bannerman did not, to Elizabeth, look pleased upon hearing the news of their morning's escapade. He crossed his arms and planted his feet in an aggressive stance, to where she feared they had broken a rule or committed a sin she had been unaware of.

"You should not be spying on Mr. Darcy. I made myself clear on this when you were still a young girl. The man deserves his privacy; your habit of going to stare at the property is something Mr. Darcy would find objectionable."

"We did not go to spy on him," protested Louisa. "Pemberley is a massive property, and I thought Elizabeth would appreciate the beauty and stately presence of Derbyshire's largest and least known estate."

"It is less well known because Mr. Darcy does not advertise its presence or his wealth. The man deserves his privacy, and I do not wish to see him disturbed unnecessarily."

Elizabeth wondered about the man at the center of their dispute. Was he so prejudiced that he avoided those of lesser station? The idea such a person existed aroused a feeling of dislike that she fought to suppress. She did not know the man, and was not about to judge him.

There might be a valid reason for him to avoid the notoriety his wealth and status afforded, wanted or not. Maybe he was by nature a solitary man, one who shunned company because he was uncomfortable with unknown people, but until she knew the reasons, she would withhold her opinion.

"George, what is going on?" asked Mrs. Bannerman as she crossed the garden toward the group. "I heard you from the house. Can this not wait until Elizabeth and Louisa are inside?"

"Louisa took her over to our boundary with Mr. Darcy to spy on our neighbor. I have been telling her since she was young that such attention is inconsiderate and unbecoming for a young woman, but she chose to disobey me today. She must realize my distaste for such behavior."

Mrs. Bannerman studied both girls while her husband spoke. "Did you bother Mr. Darcy or his sister?"

"No, we did not. I took Elizabeth to view Pemberley from the hill on our side of the property. It is such a beautiful house, and I hoped she would appreciate it like I do."

"Did anyone notice you? Did they know you were in the area and paying an unusual amount of attention to Mr. Darcy's home?"

"I do not see how," said Louisa with a shake of her head. "We did not call attention to ourselves and spoke to nobody while we were there or on our way to or from the area. We viewed the estate from the meadow above, the one with so many daisies and hollyhocks. We were far enough away that Mr. Darcy would not have seen us without the use of a spyglass. I suppose he might have used one, but why would he want to?"

Mrs. Bannerman came quickly to her daughter's defense: "George, you are overreacting. Louisa did nothing wrong. Mr. Darcy was unaware of their presence, and they did not, according to her, trespass on his property. If he saw them there and finds fault with their actions, we can apologize and promise it will not happen again. Should he not appear at our door demanding one they have no reason to feel guilty."

"Do not let it happen again," said he. "I have the privilege of counting Mr. Darcy as a friend and I will not let foolish actions by my eldest daughter or my niece jeopardize that friendship. It is too valuable to lose."

Having finished, Mr. Bannerman stalked off toward the stable, the rigidity of his back showing his anger.

"Thank you, Aunt," offered Elizabeth. "We had not intended to raise any issues with your neighbor. I am sorry it upset Uncle George. I will apologize to him before supper."

"George will calm down when he stops to think about it," Mrs. Bannerman sighed. "He has always been a little unsure regarding the state of his friendship with Mr. Darcy although, to my knowledge the man has voiced no displeasure or given George reason to suspect anything was amiss.

"In the interest of peace and stability, try not to call attention to the differences between the two estates. The sheer size of Pemberley makes us all a little uneasy when Mr. Darcy visits, so I can understand George's concern. Should you decide to visit that meadow again, try not to announce your intention. From my experience with Mr. Darcy, he would not mind even if he were aware you were up there, but it does not hurt to take precautions."

"Thank you, mother," said Louisa. "The next time, if there is one, we will be more careful."

"That is all I ask," was Mrs. Bannerman's admonition before returning to the house.

CHAPTER IX

"I love these morning walks," declared Louisa as they stepped onto the road in the early morning hours a few days later. "The temperature is perfect, and the world is just beginning to wake and rise."

"The world has been up and about for a few hours," laughed Elizabeth. "It is past eight, and most of the birds rise with the sun. That lets them catch the worms and grubs before they disappear underground for the day."

Louisa tramped through the grass along the roadside, the tassels waist high and threatening to stain her clothes the verdant hue of the stems. Emitting a spirited laugh, she reached to grasp one reed, pulling it from the soil with a quick tug.

"It will not please your mother if you come home green from your feet to your middle," said Elizabeth. "Maybe you should come back to the lane before your clothing gets too stained to clean."

"I was only admiring these plants beside us," pouted Louisa as she rejoined Elizabeth. "They're pretty, and I wanted bring some back with us.."

"Most of those plants you admire are weeds, which grow with no competition. They are usually first to sprout and last to die when the weather turns cold. The marks they leave on clothes are the hardest to remove, so your mother will probably thank you for avoiding them."

Elizabeth gave off talking as they followed the lane, content to admire the scenery they passed.

The road was narrow, so much so that when two carriages met, one would have to give way by reversing course until it widened. Pine trees grew close on either side, the uniformity of the resulting wall suggesting their appearance was neither random nor accidental. Unlike the oak and ash Elizabeth was familiar with, the boughs of the pines did not interlace over their heads, leaving a bright, sun dappled roadway on which to walk.

"This is so much fun I never want it to end. If we could only spend the rest of the day walking, I would be happy."

"That would be impractical," said Elizabeth. "What would you do when you got hungry? There are no inns along the way from which to purchase a meal, and if there were, I would not want to go inside, anyway.

"You would tire well before day's end and then where would you be? Would you simply curl up in the weeds and try to sleep, with the ants and spiders crawling all over you? There would be no blanket to cover yourself, or bed to stretch out in."

"You are such a killjoy," laughed Louisa. "The sun's warmth and the beauty of the day captivated me, but I was not serious."

"I cannot help myself. If an opportunity to tease you presents itself, I have to take it."

"Well then, I hope…" Louisa's reply stopped, cut off by the appearance of a man on foot, who had entered the lane from an intersecting road and was approaching them.

As they neared each other, Elizabeth was able to study him, an opportunity as enjoyable as it was unexpected.

He was a medium sized fellow, sporting dark wavy hair and eyes so deep a shade of brown they looked black. His nose was straight and prominent in a mildly attractive way, his nostrils flaring provocatively with each inhaled breath.

His lips were full and formed into a most attractive smile, which brightened his eyes until they seemed to have a light burning within them. The crowning glory of his face, though, was his chin, which looked to have been chiseled with loving care, setting him apart from anyone else Elizabeth had ever seen, or ever would, in her opinion. Her heart, already pounding against the restraints of her chest, increased in speed as the stranger neared, stopping before them and bowing with a flourish in Louisa's direction.

"Miss Bannerman," said he with a welcoming smile, "what a pleasant surprise. I did not expect to encounter anyone this morning, yet here you are."

"Good morning, Mr. Darcy," mumbled Louisa, "it is good to see you today."

Bowing once again to Louisa before turning to Elizabeth, he said: "If I may be so bold, I am Mr. Darcy, Mr. Bannerman's neighbor to the north. May I assume you are a relative of Miss Bannerman's?"

"You may," responded Elizabeth, amused almost beyond measure at her cousin's tongue-tied embarrassment. "I am Miss Bennet. Mr. and Mrs. Bannerman invited my sister Catherine and I to spend a few months at Kingsdown. Forgive me for asking, but how did you guess? I bare only a slight resemblance to Louisa or any of the Bannerman family, and neither I nor my sister have left the estate since we arrived last week."

Mr. Darcy began to laugh, but cut himself off with a sheepish grin. "I am sorry, but I can tell from your question that you are not a native of Derbyshire. Your arrival became common knowledge throughout the neighborhood, as you stepped out of the carriage you arrived in, would be my guess. The gossips described you and your sister precisely, I might add, down to the color of your bonnets and the dresses you were wearing.

"Let me warn you, there is no such thing as a secret around here; the Lambton busybodies make sure of it. If they can find a way to report on the contents of your breakfast, or the conversations you conduct with your cousins, they will. As it is, they must make do with conjecture, most of which is pure balderdash. That does not stop them, unfortunately."

"The more things change, the more they stay the same," chuckled Elizabeth, to a look of confusion from Mr. Darcy. "What I meant is gossips will be gossips, no matter where they live. If our situations were reversed and Louisa was to visit Longbourn, the Meryton gossips would praise her to the skies, or deride her words and actions, depending on their mood. In some ways, I am afraid this county is not so different from my own."

"And on that note I will excuse myself. Please accept my apologies for interrupting your walk, but I recognized Miss Bannerman and wanted to introduce myself properly. It is good to meet you both but be warned; my habit is to explore the country around my estate, when I am not away on business that is. My preference is to do it earlier in the morning but I was delayed today, so our meeting is fortuitous, or not, depending on your point of view."

"An early walk is the best way to start the day," said Elizabeth. "The quiet of the first few morning hours is welcome preparation for the day's problems."

"We are of like mind. Take care Miss Bannerman, Miss Bennet. May all our meetings be this cordial." With a nod and a bow, he departed, leaving Elizabeth and Louisa to talk about him as they returned to Kingsdown.

Louisa stood watching the man until he was lost to view before turning to Elizabeth: "What a charming man. I can understand why Amelia is so enamored of him."

"He was friendly," agreed Elizabeth, "but I prefer to wait until I know someone better before deciding whether or not I want them as a friend. Who knows, he may be hiding a dark secret."

"I find it hard to believe he is a cruel, unfeeling monster," laughed Louisa. "He is rich, and the most prominent citizen in Derbyshire. There is little chance he could conceal a liking for the cruel or perverse."

"Neither his status nor his wealth would guarantee he is of sound mind, but I will agree that he is easy to look at."

The conversation continued in this vein until the two regained the house. Entering the sitting-room, Amelia and Kitty, who looked like they were beside themselves with anticipation, set upon them.

"It came! It came!" cried Amelia, her excitement matched by Kitty's, with the two hopping from one foot to another in almost perfect unison. The sight of the girls dancing about the room amused Elizabeth almost to the point of laughter.

"What came?" asked Louisa, reaching for a crumpled envelope clenched in the hand Amelia was waving about, as if its contents were too hot to hold.

Amelia snatched her hand away from her sister's grasp, as if what she held was too precious to surrender. "A letter from Mr. Darcy, of course."

"What does it say?" asked Louisa, impatience coloring her voice. "Have you opened it, or are we to guess?"

Amelia's face took on a sly look, as if she were in possession of secret information: "I did not open it, but I know what it contained."

"And how is this possible? Are you suddenly prescient?"

"I opened it," said Mrs. Bannerman_from her position beside the fireplace, "and it is not from Mr. Darcy. It is from the Pemberley estate, of which Mr. Darcy is the master."

Mrs. Bannerman waited for the girls to sit, while Amelia threw herself onto the settee and crossed her arms, all the time glaring at her mother.

"Show a little patience, Amelia. According to our parson, it is a virtue, and one you should cultivate."

"I am as patient as I can be under the circumstances, but it is difficult when you draw the announcement out until I am driven mad."

"A fitting revenge for the treatment you inflict on me whenever you can," laughed the woman, unaffected by her daughter's demands. "I will share the news as soon as I am ready, and not before."

Elizabeth watched the discourse with interest, marvelling at the difference in tone and manners when compared to similar discussions she had witnessed between her mother and Lydia. Had she been at home, a discussion of this nature would long since have descended into harsh words, interspersed with mild vitriol from both sides of the argument.

Amelia was eager for her mother to share the news, while her mother seemed content to spend some time teasing her youngest daughter. The give-and-take was not strident in Amelia's case, or condescending in her mother's. It seemed, to Elizabeth, this was a game they had played more than once.

"If you do not read the notice," threatened Amelia, her smile calculating and confident, "I will tell_them all what it says without waiting for you."

"It is not important," said Mrs. Bannerman, sitting back in her chair. "In fact, it might be better to wait until tomorrow."

"They have invited us to Pemberley!" burst from Amelia, as her mother laughed. "He is inviting us to a supper he is having in a fortnight. I cannot wait to visit him at his estate, and to sup with him. It is a dream come true!"

Elizabeth looked from her aunt to her cousin, wondering if there was something she had misheard from either. Mr. Darcy had mentioned nothing about inviting the Bannerman family to supper, and according to Louisa, her father did not consider him anything more than a neighbor. That he would invite them to Pemberley to share a meal was not an impossibility, but it was unlikely.

"The Darcys have not invited us to dine with them," sighed Mrs. Bannerman. "Amelia, as usual, has leaped to the conclusion she wants, and she is once again wrong."

"But you said it was an invitation for the family," spluttered the girl. "And it is from Mr. Darcy, or Pemberley, which is the same thing, is it not?"

"In this case, it is not. We are invited to a ball being held in a fortnight, that much you had correct. As is customary, there will be light refreshments served. No one asked us to enjoy a meal with Mr. Darcy, and you are not invited. You will remain here with Christopher that evening."

"I guess Kitty and I will just have to find some way to occupy ourselves," huffed Amelia, "while the rest of the family is off having fun."

"Kitty will be at Pemberley," said Mrs. Bannerman, to Amelia's shock. "The invitation includes Elizabeth and Kitty. In fact, it makes special mention of our guests."

"How did Mr. Darcy know I was here?" asked Elizabeth. "I had not met the man until this morning, and he would have sent his invitation before that."

"Did you not hear him talking about the neighborhood gossips?" laughed Louisa. "Mr. Darcy knew we had company before you were in bed that first night. He included you in the invitation because he is a gentleman, and it would not be proper to exclude you."

"Louisa, you will have the chance to show how good a dancer you are," said Elizabeth. "Although I think we might devote a few more hours to honing your talent. It would not do to stumble or appear unsure of yourself, would it?"

To Elizabeth, Louisa now looked as unsure of herself as anybody she had ever seen. Her eyes went to her mother and back to Elizabeth, before flitting to Amelia and Kitty, resting on none of them for more than a second.

She seemed to arrive at a decision, saying abruptly: "I need to change my dress. I must have stained it on our walk this morning."

With that she rose in a hurry, and in fact almost ran from the room to Elizabeth's dismay. Curious about the reason for such a hasty departure, Elizabeth followed the girl to her room, where she knocked on the door.

"Louisa, it is Elizabeth. May I come in?"

Three times she knocked until at last the door opened and she was invited into Louisa's bedroom.

"Are you bothered by the prospect of attending this ball at Pemberley?" said she to Louisa, who shook her head in denial. "What is wrong then, if that is not the case?"

"My father will not allow me to attend." Louisa's gaze was locked on the floor at her feet. "He feels activities such as balls are nothing more than markets, where parents send their daughters with the goal to ensnare unsuspecting young men foolish enough to fall into the trap. To him, it is unseemly for a young woman to take part in such an immoral endeavor. I have not asked permission because he will not let me go."

"Does he not realize the disadvantage he causes by keeping you at home, instead of somewhere you can meet the local bachelors, one of which may be your future husband?"

"I have never discussed it with him. It has been more than a year since I asked and was told, in no uncertain terms, no."

Louisa's distress shook Elizabeth to her core, making her decision easy: "I will talk to your mother. Surely there is some influence she can exert, otherwise the time I spent teaching you is wasted."

Elizabeth let herself out of the room and went in search of her aunt, all the while rehearsing the situation in her mind. How could her uncle think to keep Louisa confined to Kingsdown, when most of the neighborhood's residents would be in attendance? Did he not realize the importance of having his daughter seen at an event like this?

And what about her aunt? Had she invited Elizabeth to visit hoping to force this issue? If so, Elizabeth would return to Longbourn at once. She would not be pulled into a family squabble; her father had promised her nothing of the sort would occur. Her decision reached, Elizabeth squared her shoulders and marched back into the sitting-room, which by this time was empty of everyone but Amelia.

"Where is Aunt?" asked she, which brought a smile to her cousin's lips.

"She is talking to father; did you not hear their discussion when you came back down the stairs? I thought everyone in the house was listening to them. It was loud enough."

Amelia chuckled, though to Elizabeth's ears the sound was without mirth.

"I heard nothing," said Elizabeth, "but my thoughts were elsewhere, so I would not have paid attention to voices, even if I did."

"That is probably best. She wanted to speak with Father, no doubt about his resistance to allowing Louisa and me to take part in balls or anything he considers immoral or degrading to a young woman. She might be awhile; my father can be stubborn, more so when it involves my sister. To him, I am too young, although I expect to face the same opposition in a year or two."

"Amelia, kindly refrain from airing family secrets," said Mrs. Bannerman, entering the room as her daughter finished speaking. "You will give Elizabeth the impression that there is no peace at Kingsdown, or worse, that I am a shrew, never satisfied and always harping on George."

With a nod to her mother and a smile toward Elizabeth, Amelia left the room, leaving Elizabeth to wonder if it might be wise for her to do the same.

"She tends to the dramatic," Mrs. Bannerman smiled as she settled herself again in her chair. "She means well but her words often get ahead of her thoughts, so she speaks before realizing what she is saying."

"I was not really listening to her. My interests were more in Louisa's distress. She wants to go to the ball at Pemberley but is afraid to ask Uncle for permission. Is there nothing we can do to help? This ball is exactly the event Kitty and I have been preparing her for."

"I agree. That is why I spoke with George, and he has given his consent. Louisa can accompany us to Pemberley for Mr. Darcy's ball.

Elizabeth jumped to her feet, eager to share the good news with Louisa: "I will tell her. She will be so happy; she has been dreaming of this since I began teaching her."

"Wait," said her aunt, waving her back to the chair. "George agreed to let her attend, but he refuses to purchase a gown for her, or anything else of that nature. We will have to do the best we can with what Louisa already has. I think I might have some lace or suitable pieces of fabric we can use to remake one of her dresses; that will have to suffice."

Elizabeth smiled, remembering the supplies she had packed for this exact circumstance. With Kitty and Louisa's help she could create something her cousin would love, without costing her uncle so much as a farthing.

To have the girl attend something as important as her first ball without proper clothing would, in Elizabeth's mind, be unforgivable. She recalled the assembly she had gone to when she was fifteen, and the inspections, both overt and concealed, conducted as she entered the hall, and throughout the evening.

Had she attended the event in anything less than her best, condescending attitudes and comments would have accosted her, from friends and enemies alike. To subject Louisa to such treatment was unthinkable.

"Elizabeth? Did you hear me?" asked her aunt, pulling Elizabeth from her reminiscences and back to the present.

"Forgive me, but I was thinking about the fabric in my trunk that I brought to modify one of my gowns for an occasion like this. I will remake one of Louisa's dresses instead. And Uncle told me before I started teaching Louisa that he would not be persuaded to purchase a new gown for her."

"I cannot ask you to do that. Any fabric you brought is for you and Kitty to use."

"There is more than enough for all of us," said Elizabeth, "and I would love to do this for her. She deserves the chance to put her best foot forward. Together we can make this ball the best of her life."

"Thank you, Elizabeth," said Mrs. Bannerman, tears appearing in the corners of her eyes. "Your father told me you are a compassionate person, second only to your sister Jane, and have a compulsion to do whatever you can to help. In my opinion he has understated your true worth."

"I am no better than anyone else," said Elizabeth, her cheeks coloring as the blood rose to become the warmth of a blush on her face. "Louisa will enjoy herself as much as Kitty or me; together we will make sure of that. So, if you will excuse me there is much to be done."

"Is it true?" whispered Kitty, stopping Elizabeth before she reached the stairs. "Does Louisa have permission to attend Mr. Darcy's ball?"

"She does, but there is no money to purchase a new gown for her to wear, so we will make her one, or update one of hers."

Kitty's smile at Elizabeth's statement lingered before expanding to transform her face. With a gleeful titter she joined her sister in climbing the stairs to the second floor, pausing in confusion as Elizabeth carried on past Louisa's door.

"Are you not going to give her the news?" asked she when Elizabeth stopped at the door to her own bedroom. "She thinks we are going without her; would it not be best to let her know she can attend?"

"I will tell her," said Elizabeth, opening the door and stepping inside, "but first I want to look at the fabric and other supplies I brought with me. I want to check for something specific before I talk to Louisa."

Elizabeth grasped her trunk and pulled it from the nook where it sat. Throwing back the lid, she dug into the contents, looking for a certain item. Though she searched carefully, the prize she needed remained hidden.

"We might have to go to town," was her comment upon closing the lid and rising to her feet. "I want a certain pattern of lace which I thought I packed, but cannot locate. I will ask Uncle for the use of the carriage in the next few days so I can purchase what I need unless I can find it before then."

Kitty, Elizabeth knew, was only too happy at the prospect of spending a day in Lambton. "We can all go. I have been asking Amelia about going to town but she insists it is too far to walk."

"It is almost five miles," said Elizabeth, leading the way back to Louisa's room. "That is a lot farther than Meryton is from Longbourn, so Amelia is correct in not wanting to walk. By the time you arrived it would be time to leave again."

"Louisa," shouted Kitty as the girl opened her door to Elizabeth's knock. "Uncle George says you can go to the ball! It will be so much fun you will never want to leave; I promise."

Louisa looked at Elizabeth, her brows raised in a silent question, which caused Elizabeth to laugh. "Your father gave his permission after Aunt pleaded your case. You will attend your first ball, and at Pemberley, no less!"

"But first we are going to Lambton tomorrow," added Kitty breathlessly, "to purchase a new gown for you. Is the town like Meryton? I hope so; a journey there is always an adventure."

"I did not say we were going tomorrow," said Elizabeth. "There are a few matters to take care of first."

With an amused shake of her head, she turned to Louisa. "She gets so excited when someone mentions a visit to town. I hope she can get control of herself, or I will leave her behind.

"May I look through your closet? Despite Kitty's enthusiasm, your father, in giving his permission, denied your mother's request for funds to purchase a proper gown for your first ball. I told her that Kitty and I can change one of yours. If you are not comfortable wearing anything you might have worn previously, I will make you a gown myself, with your help."

Louisa sat heavily on her bed, shaking her head in disbelief. "Are you sure this is something you want to do? I can stay behind, as I have in the past."

"Nonsense," declared Elizabeth. "We will all attend or we will all remain here. To begin, where are your clothes, I need to view them. I am looking for a certain cut of dress that I can remake."

Louisa's nervously shaking finger pointed to the closet, and Elizabeth attacked the clothing with, for her, an uncommon fervor. One after another she inspected the garments, holding them beside Louisa to look at their fit and form. The dresses were placed into one of two piles, the smaller of which she expected might lend themselves to change.

When she completed her scrutiny, she rechecked the items in the lesser pile, looking at each more closely than she had initially. Again she lifted each to view, but this time she had Louisa stand as she held each dress against the girl.

At the end of an hour, she had chosen the garment she thought would best lend itself to her talents as a seamstress. "This one will serve the purpose. With the ribbons and lace I brought, you will have the prettiest gown at the ball."

"But what about your own dresses?" asked Louisa. "Did you bring enough to tailor them as well?"

"That is why a journey to Lambton might be in the future," Elizabeth's smile was directed toward Kitty. "It will allow me the opportunity to purchase a few more necessary items while giving Kitty the chance to satisfy her burning curiosity."

"I see," said Louisa. "Do you have a certain day in mind? We will have to arrange it with Father. Kingsdown has only two teams of two horses each and we use them throughout the day."

"We can ask him tomorrow," said Elizabeth. "There is one thing I want you to know before we start with these preparations. I will change your gown for the ball and you can assist. While I can readily mend and patch, and have made some of my own clothing in the past, I am not proficient. We employ a seamstress, so we do not need to create our own garments. It will take me longer to complete the dress, but I do not mind."

"I cannot ask for anything more," said Louisa, throwing her arms around Elizabeth, and then Kitty, in warm embraces. "Thank you for everything."

Elizabeth ushered Kitty through the door and into the hall before turning back to address the happy girl: "We will start tomorrow, after we complete your lessons."

"Thank you again, Elizabeth," said Louisa as the door started to close. "Or maybe I will call you Lizzy. The name fits you."

"Whatever you like," laughed Elizabeth. "I will answer to either."

CHAPTER X

Sarah closed the stable door and, taking the reins from her friend, walked her horse to the rear of the building.

"Georgiana, please!" said she as her friend mounted her own horse, throwing a leg over the saddle to ride as a man. "We are too close to the house. What will happen if Hawkins, or any of the servants, see you riding like that? They will inform my father, who will tell Mr. Darcy. They will do so cheerfully, hoping your punishment is severe.

"They dislike you because of the way you treat them. If they see a way to cause inconvenience for you, they will jump at the chance, so please, pretend to be a gentlewoman, at least until we are away from the estate."

"Your servants should learn their places," Georgiana sniffed and, with an upturning of her nose, said: "It is not up to them to monitor my activities, nor is it their responsibility to tell your father of my indiscretions. If you had better control over them, this would not be a problem."

"If you would accept your status as a woman of breeding, and act like one, you would find that life is easier."

"Easy is riding astride my horse, not trying to balance on the side of the animal. One stumble and I am unseated, sitting on the ground in the dirt. That, to me, is not the definition of easy, or convenient."

"That is something I would pay to see," Sarah giggled gleefully. "Miss Georgiana Darcy, upended and forced to grovel like a peasant in the dirt. Your enemies would pay a princely sum for the chance to observe you in such a state."

"Enemies?" said Georgiana with a wicked smile. "I have no enemies. My opinions are considered wise, and my slightest wishes are granted. People look up to me, and pattern their lives after mine."

Georgiana was aware that there were people in the county who wished her no small amount of ill will, but they were not worth taking the time to worry about. Her manner toward them was looked upon as that of a condescending, spoilt child. This had gained her few acquaintances she considered true friends, but had attracted hangers-on, many of which hoped to witness the day she was brought low, for scandal or another reason, they cared not.

She professed no interest in the dregs of society, which included any who, whether by necessity or by choice, engaged in work. That her brother did so willingly was immaterial.

Georgiana's friendship with Sarah was forged in the fires of competition. For as long as she could remember, Sarah had bristled anytime Georgiana referred to her supposed superiority.

Since childhood, friendly antagonism had ruled their relationship, based, thought Georgiana, on Sarah's need to prove herself Georgiana's equal. Georgiana, never one to refuse a challenge, wholeheartedly accepted Sarah's proposed contests, no matter how outrageous, and sometimes suggested her own variations. The competitions, which she usually won, did not lessen their bonds of friendship.

Today the two planned to visit Lambton, something they did once or twice each week. Georgiana knew Sarah enjoyed the excursions, as they afforded her an excuse to browse the many shops and visit with the merchants, who treated her as a valued customer because of her friendly mien. Sarah usually confined her purchases in town to the confectioner, but her considerate attitude endeared her to all, to Georgiana's envy.

"Have we come far enough, or do you want me to submit to this unnatural position all the way into town?" sighed Georgiana, pulling her leg from the pommel and throwing it over the horse. There it dangled without benefit of a stirrup, which she no longer noticed, having sat the horse in this manner since her first time, years ago, riding the animal to the Haversham estate.

"There, that is better. You should try it, Sarah."

"Thank you, but I will ride as a lady should. I do not want my father to catch me, or hear reports of my untoward behavior. His punishment would be considerable."

"You worry too much about punishment for minor disobedience," laughed Georgiana. "Fear keeps you from enjoying life. Look at me, comfortable and unworried about William's censure."

"Is your brother still enjoying the company of his cousin? He is such a beautiful man," sighed Sarah. "You should invite him along one of these days so I can bask in the glow of his attentions."

Georgiana burst into laughter at the mental picture of the Colonel fighting for comfort on a sidesaddle, while his horse fought the unfamiliar sensations of its off balance rider. As the picture unfolded in her mind, she saw the horse finally rearing up to deposit its unsuspecting rider on the ground, before galloping back to the stables.

"What is so amusing about my idea? I think the man might enjoy spending a day with his favorite cousin and her best friend."

"Best friend?" said Georgiana, her laughter continuing. "That is a little presumptuous of you, I think. You are a friend, I confess, but my best friend? You are more than a little too sure of yourself."

"I am not only your best friend, I am your only friend, or the only one who is not ashamed to be seen with you in public."

Georgiana's laughter subsided as the reality of Sarah's declaration hit her. Sarah *was* her only friend, the one she spent most, if not all, of her free time with. The fact did not bother her; like her brother, she was not overly fond of large gatherings.

At balls she was normally found with Sarah and a few others she had, over the years, grown comfortable with. Unlike her companions, though, she did not flit from group to group like a gadfly, preferring instead to remain within the confines of one company.

Her reticence to mingle unabashedly with other than her peers had earned her a reputation of improper haughtiness. Because her mother was daughter to the Earl of Matlock, people assumed that Georgiana improperly considered herself Lady Georgiana Darcy, even though Lady Anne's title had been only a courtesy.

Georgiana did not try to silence her critics, believing that if her true personality was revealed, the knowledge would provide more ammunition for attacks on her character and family. To allow attacks on herself, baseless though they might be, was in her mind a way to protect her brother.

She was not a cruel person, although many in Lambton thought of her in that way. Her haughty mien had been cultivated since the death of her father, when rumors of his immoral, licentious escapades had arisen, concocted by those who harbored ill will toward the Darcy name. The county's gossips took and embellished them in the spreading until the mere mention of George Darcy was enough to set tongues wagging.

The residents of Lambton were fond of his son, and cautious about repeating any of the rumors where he might hear them. That did not stop the speculation regarding his probable predilection for the same type of depravity attributed to his father.

Though Darcy suspected there were rumors, he was not privy to the more debauched versions, for which Georgiana was grateful, knowing his anger would compel him to seek redress for the effrontery behind such accusations. To her, keeping the peace was more important than chasing unsubstantiated tales, which in too many cases leant an air of truth to them. In fact, she had not heard them repeated in the past twelvemonth, and hope they were forgotten.

"What of your cousin," asked Sarah. "You have not mentioned him for a few days now. Is it because the man has been asking after me and you have interfered with him romancing his future wife?"

"He is not even aware you exist, so there is no need for me to shatter your dream, or his nightmare, should he ever have the misfortune of noticing you."

"Need I remind you we have met? It was you, remember, who introduced us, and he was overcome by my beauty and manners. While I was present he was unable to take his eyes off me, if you remember. He would probably ask my father right now for permission to court me were it not for your meddling."

Georgiana made no attempt to hold back the laughter that burst forth at Sarah's claim, and her friend soon joined her. The peals, though loud, disappeared in the trees on either side of them, and they soon calmed, the statement forgotten.

"The colonel is not at Pemberley. He left last week when William did. "

"And you are all alone? Does it not get lonely there by yourself, with no one for company?"

"Mrs. Annesley is there, so I am not completely alone. William will be back Friday or Saturday, so I have only two or three days without his company."

"I cannot imagine being left by myself every day. I would be bored to tears within the first hour."

"Which is why I come to visit so often. Your father has tasked me with keeping you active, which is not a simple thing to do. You are a boring person, Sarah."

"I am not boring! It is just easier to let you find something to keep us busy, although most often we would both be in trouble if my father or your brother were to discover our activities."

"What we have been doing is getting tiresome. If only Lambton were more exciting, like London. I have heard there are so many new and exciting attractions in the city that one has no time for boredom."

"We are getting close," said Sarah as the town's buildings came into view. "Please seat yourself properly so we do not attract attention."

With a huff of displeasure, Georgiana pulled her leg up and positioned it around the pommel to mollify Sarah. When she settled again, she spurred the horse forward, leaving her companion to catch up.

"What Lambton needs are decent suitors," said Georgiana as her friend pulled up beside her. "The few that are available do not interest me; they are too timid. The town needs some men like William, who are sure of themselves and unafraid of other's opinions. Lambton has none of either persuasion."

"Lambton has a lot of potential suitors, but they will not approach you because they are afraid of what you will do to them. You have not been the most feminine example of womanhood, Georgiana."

"Can I help it if none of them were born with a backbone? When I approach they run to their mothers, as if I am going to hurt them, poor dears."

"That attitude will doom you to life as a spinster," laughed Sarah. "You will be the twisted old hag all the neighborhood children are afraid of. Parents will use your example to scare their children into obedience."

Although Georgiana laughed along with Sarah, the girl was correct. Her life to this point had been a contest to prove she was as good as or better than anyone else in Derbyshire. The result was, as Sarah said, the fear, held by any of the town's young men, that she was unapproachable or worse, vindictive toward any who might have the temerity to disappoint her.

Georgiana worried Sarah might be correct in predicting her future, and that she would never attract the attention of a man fearless enough to pursue the possibility of marriage to a member of the Darcy family.

"There are eligible bachelors in Lambton, although none are foolish enough to ask Mr. Darcy for permission to approach you. I would not worry though, you are not yet old enough for your first kiss, much less an offer of marriage. Your brother would most likely kill anyone brave enough, or stupid enough, to try."

"Need I remind you I have enjoyed my first kiss, and my second, and my third? Or have you forgotten the humiliating defeat you suffered when you bet me that Harold Trowbridge would kiss you before kissing me?"

"But you had to cheat or you would not have won._You had me believing that he kissed you out of fear you would accuse him of trying to have his way with you, when you had arranged everything with him before agreeing to the wager."

"Your anger is false, as is your outrage. You are more upset that I managed to win than you are that he kissed me and not you."

"You cheated! There was no way you could have triumphed by following the rules we agreed upon. Mark my words, Georgiana, eventually one of your wagers will cost you everything, and I will be there to rub salt in the wound."

Georgiana's composure was failing her under the onslaught of Sarah's counterfeit indignation. The wager the girl was harping on about was in the past, but she would not let it go. Yes, Georgiana had arranged with Harold to kiss her instead of Sarah, but Harold had confided in Georgiana, revealing her friend's attempt to make the same arrangement so she would be the victor instead.

Sarah was unaware of Harold's confession, and Georgiana had no intention of informing her. She would not throw the fact in Sarah's face to spite her, but knowing of her failed attempt to guarantee victory gave Georgiana an important advantage she would use in their next wager. As her friend carried on, an idea began to form, one that was almost too risky to suggest, which decided the matter.

"You are correct," said she, stopping Sarah's diatribe in the middle of a sentence and causing her friend to stare at her. Georgiana knew she was probably wondering what new subterfuge she had in mind.

"I cheated, and that was wrong. You deserve a chance to even the score."

Sarah gazed at Georgiana for what seemed an interminable length of time before raising her hands in front of her, giving the appearance that she was defending herself from Georgiana's assault.

"What new trickery is this? You are not sorry for cheating; you have yet to play fair. If you are offering an olive branch, there is a snake curled around it somewhere, waiting to bite me when I least suspect."

Georgiana knew that whatever Sarah might deny, she was interested. To Sarah, the possibility of the game was like the offer of laudanum to an addict. The poor sot wanted to refuse the drug but his willpower was weak, and easily swept aside for the promise of an hour or two of drug-induced stupor. The offer of a new match had, for Sarah, the same hold on her emotions.

"I am offering you the chance to turn the tables on me. The rules are simple, and it should be easier for you to win than for me. I suggest we choose one of Derbyshire's young men and compete for his attention. We can do anything within reason, as long as we observe the bounds of propriety."

"What you are proposing is the same as our last competition, where you convinced Harold Trowbridge to abet your underhanded actions. I will not fall for that again, Georgiana. No thank you."

"This is not the same wager, I promise. The contest will not end with a kiss, although they are always a wonderful reward for a hard days' work.

"No, the winner this time will be the one who gets him to either confess his love or ask our permission for him to pay his attention to us, with the intention to court."

"There is no way that one of the young bachelors in Lambton, or any in possession of the smallest amount of intelligence, would ask my father or your brother for permission to court either of us.

"And what will happen when they discover it was nothing more than a silly little competition? We might find ourselves forced to marry against our will, with a man we might never grow to love. Not that love is all that important in the grand scheme of things.

"If my father were to discover our despicable contest, I would be severely punished, as would you when he told Mr. Darcy."

Georgiana laughed as Sarah pointed out all the reasons she had for considering the idea too ridiculous to explore. The more she objected, the more Georgiana could see that the suggestion had taken hold of her imagination, to the point that she was probably weighing the various approaches she planned to ensure victory over her sometime foe.

"We will have to be careful; I agree. We cannot let him so much as entertain the idea of going to my father or Mr. Darcy to ask their permission. As you so aptly pointed out, the consequence of that would be terrible for ourselves and possibly the suitor as well.

"But that is part of the appeal. We must control him, to where he will do nothing without asking permission of us beforehand. If he does anyway, the game is over and we deny any interest in his attention."

"That is a cruel way to treat someone," said Sarah, "and one that would lower people's opinion of our worth. It might mean nothing to you, as the gossips in town already call you undesirable, but it might ruin my chances for a marriage to anyone of breeding or status."

"I will withdraw the offer if you are too afraid to try. It is regrettable; I thought you wanted the chance for revenge for my supposed ill treatment, but I guess that will have to wait for some time in the future, or never."

"Who would we choose? We are competing for the same person, correct? If so, he must be acceptable to both of us, and not someone you have already coerced into assisting you."

"Then you choose our victim. That way you cannot claim I bent the rules, although you probably will anyway."

Sarah guided her horse to the side of the road and stopped to think, mumbling names of the town's young men and rejecting each.

"What about Roger Hampstead? No, he is too short. Edwin Robertson? Too pudgy and he smells of rancid butter. Erasmus Blackmore? Heavens no, he has not bathed in years!"

"Do you need my assistance?" asked Georgiana as Sarah continued to suggest and then reject name after name. "I can offer a few names that might not have occurred to you. The choice is still yours, but you seem to be having some difficulty arriving at the best contestant for our game."

"Keep your suggestions to yourself and let me select someone," commanded Sarah before returning to her review of seemingly every person she had met in all her visits to Lambton.

"Yes!" said she, just when Georgiana was about to give up all hope. "I know who our victim will be."

"Please, tell me," prompted Georgiana when Sarah fell silent. "Unless you do, I cannot compete."

A sly look came over Sarah, causing Georgiana a moment of fear before a smile she would have ascribed to a fox, for all its cunning and evasiveness, replaced it.

"We will compete for the attention of Robert Bannerman," said she with a look of complacency, combined with ruthless determination.

"What made you choose someone as inappropriate as Robert Bannerman?" asked Georgiana, as the thought of trying to ingratiate herself with her neighbor's son caused a bit of indigestion to rise, which she fought to control. "The family is poor and unsophisticated. He rarely comes to town, and when he does, he stays just long enough to fill a list his father has given him.

"He associates with nobody when he is in Lambton, and the one time I tried to talk to him he walked past me as if I did not exist. I have seen him at town balls or gatherings once or twice, but no more. If he attends, he stays with his mother and father. Not once have I seen him on the dance floor or visiting with those of his own age.

"I cannot decide if he considers himself better than all of us or just has no desire to be friendly. Surely you can find someone better for our competition."

"Your objections are more reason for me to choose him. I suppose if you are afraid you might lose, we can forget about it and I will tell all our friends you were too scared to try. They should enjoy hearing that I bested you in a contest you refused to enter.

"There is nothing about Robert that makes him a poor choice. He is a fine young man, and good looking to boot. He is also the son of a supposed gentleman, so his attention and our response to it will get nobody in trouble."

"Fine," said Georgiana petulantly. "When should we begin? We can start today, if you like, or next week; the choice is yours."

"Why not the night of the Pemberley ball? You will be there, I assume, and my father will let me attend, so there really is nothing standing in our way."

"But will Mr. Bannerman be there? Remember, he is not frequently at these types of events. If he stays home that night the contest cannot begin, or we need to choose another from those who are there."

"We need *him* to be there, or we cancel the wager. I chose Robert Bannerman, and no one else is acceptable."

"Do not worry," said Georgiana, a plan already hatching in her mind. "I will make certain he attends. You will not face disappointment again, until I win our little wager, anyway."

"What do you mean? Nothing will affect my enjoyment in this competition, if it means I have the satisfaction of beating the great Georgiana Darcy at her own game."

"We shall see," mumbled Georgiana to herself. "I would not be counting myself triumphant yet, there is still a contest to endure."

"So we agree then?" asked she, wanting to get Sarah's commitment before she came to her senses and changed her mind. "The wager will start at my brother's ball?"

"Yes," came Sarah's hesitant agreement, before she drew herself up and stated emphatically: "Be prepared to lose, and to lose badly. I do not plan to let you win, my dear friend. The bragging rights will be mine, and mine alone."

"I hope you are successful, but remember, my intentions are also to win, and I have more experience at it than you. Shall we continue to Lambton, or are we going to argue about this for the rest of the day? If that is your intent, I will return home so I can map out my strategy for your next humiliating defeat at my hands."

Georgiana spent the remainder of the day browsing the town's shops, dreaming of victory while avoiding thoughts of the possibility of failure to triumph over her opponent.

By the time she made it back to Pemberley that night she had a plan worked out in her mind, one she was confident would work to her advantage, while interfering with anything Sarah might use to gain her own victory.

The plan would start with a visit to Kingsdown and an introduction to Mr. Robert Bannerman.

CHAPTER XI

Georgiana was uncomfortable, and the constant jostling was not helping the situation. This carriage was not her favorite mode of transport, but choosing it was a necessity if she wanted to make a good impression on this first visit.

If she should arrive mounted astride a horse, their perception of her as uncultured and rebellious would last forever. The consequences would be the opposite of what she hoped to accomplish, and her plans would be for naught. Sarah would be the victor, a humiliation she would spread far and wide.

She was using William's fortuitous meeting of Miss Bannerman and her cousin while on his walk as a reason to call at Kingsdown and introduce herself. If she should, accidentally of course, come upon Robert, she could easily arrange an introduction to him also, which would serve her well in the upcoming competition with Sarah.

Her brother, in describing his brief encounter with the two girls, had expressed some admiration for Miss Bennet, and Georgiana was curious about this new arrival. Was she as beautiful as he seemed to think, or had the unexpected occurrence so caught him so off guard that his recollection was suspect?

If Miss Bennet were half as enchanting as he described, Georgiana would have to be careful. She was not about to let William fall in love with someone who might, as a result, come to upset the life she enjoyed at Pemberley.

The carriage turning to the left startled her from her musings, and Georgiana looked up to 3.see the driver pulling the conveyance to a stop at her destination. Tying off the reins, he let himself down to open the door and extend a hand to help her from the cabin. She stepped onto the drive, surprised to see a welcoming committee of a woman and five others lined up to greet their surprise guest.

Georgiana faced them, uncertainty sitting like an unsettled lump in her stomach. She was unsure of the proper manner to approach these people as up to this time in her life, Georgiana had always been the person receiving an invitation. This was, for her, an unfamiliar experience, and she was not sure how to proceed.

"Miss Darcy." The woman, stepped forward to offer a small curtsey, "it is good of you to call. I am Mrs. Bannerman. Welcome to Kingsdown."

"How did you know who I was?" asked Georgiana in confusion. "I do not recall a prior introduction."

"It was not needed," smiled the woman in a friendly manner. "I have seen the carriage in Lambton, and the Darcy coat of arms on the doors is unmistakable. I assumed you were Miss Darcy, as there are no other female residents of Pemberley, to my knowledge, except the servants, who would have little reason to call upon us."

She is intelligent and intuitive, thought Georgiana, listening to the explanation that was, when she pondered it, perfectly logical. Everyone in Derbyshire was familiar to the Darcys, and all their carriages, from their curricles to their chaise and fours, sported the family's distinctive crest and heraldic flourish. Mrs. Bannerman knew, by process of elimination, who was gracing her door before the driver left his seat. What she did not know was Georgiana's reason for calling, and Georgiana was not about to tell the truth.

"How discerning of you," said she. "My brother speaks highly of you and your family; I can see his esteem is not misplaced."

The look Mrs. Bannerman fixed upon Georgiana took her aback, and an inner voice warned her that this flattery was having the opposite effect from what she intended. The woman recognized her praise as insincere. She was probably wondering what motive Georgiana had in calling, when she had not, since childhood, taken the time to befriend Louisa, or acknowledge the slightest acquaintance with any of the family members.

Her superior status would answer just a small part of Mrs. Bannerman's curiosity. To Georgiana's brother, neighborly relations were a point of pride. William liked to visit the estates around Pemberley, for no other reason than to inquire after each family's health or offer help when needed. His willingness to give of himself to aid those in need was the biggest reason most of the rumors which ran rampant after his father's passing had never attached themselves to him.

Georgiana did not consider herself above her neighbors. George Darcy had seen to that. It was her fear of the unknown that hampered her attempts to follow her brother's example. She was unsure how to make someone's acquaintance, and taking the first step frightened her almost to the point of immobility. The decision to visit Kingsdown was not taken lightly, and if her competition with Sarah had not made it vital, she would not be here now.

"When William informed me you had a guest, I decided I would like to meet her and renew my admittedly scant acquaintance with Miss Bannerman. I have been remiss in offering my friendship and want to apologize. It was never my intent to dismiss the possibility of gaining her friendship; I let the grief from my father's passing drive all thoughts of proper behavior from my mind.

"To make matters worse, I took no steps to acknowledge my lapse, thinking in my grief it was unimportant. I am ashamed, but am here to confess my thoughtlessness. I would like to earn your forgiveness for my inexcusable behavior."

Georgiana drifted into silence, hoping her supposedly abject confession would convince them of her honest intentions and keep Mrs. Bannerman from inspecting her words too closely.

A superficial acceptance would work to ingratiate her into Louisa Bannerman's circle of friends, few though they might be. A closer investigation, however, would raise the question of why it took her more than five years to realize the error in her treatment of those she once might have called friends. George Darcy was dead a long time, and his daughter had not tried to repair damaged relationships, some of which might have helped her come to terms with his loss.

A new person stepped forward with a curtsey: "Mr. Darcy was the perfect gentleman. Good day, Miss Darcy. I am Elizabeth Bennet, and this is my sister, Kitty. It was Louisa and I who met your brother on his walk. We enjoyed a conversation, but it was so brief that I did not think he would remember."

"William has a remarkable memory," laughed Georgiana. "He can recall occurrences from years ago, and with amazing detail. I am lucky if I can remember what day it is or what I ate for breakfast this morning. If I were to ask him, he would probably tell me the color of your eyes and what happened the minute before and after you talked."

"He was the friendliest gentleman I think I have ever met," said Miss Bannerman, her voice so quiet Georgiana had to strain to make out the words. "He even warned us he likes to walk early in the day, which Elizabeth does as well. We should walk together one day."

"Only if William waits until the sun is up," was Georgiana's response. "He has invited me, but I do not rise at such an ungodly hour, even for my brother, who I love with all my heart."

"That is unfortunate," said Miss Bennet. "The hour or two after sunrise is when the birds are waking and the blossoms are opening to greet the morning. The woods are serene, and you can observe wonders you will not see later in the day. I walk in those first hours for that reason. Besides that, there is the complete absence of people sharing the paths and trails I like to explore. If I close my eyes, I can pretend that I am alone in the world, with no cares or expectations. It is a wonderful, though fleeting, mood."

"I can call upon the identical mood from the comfort of my bed. All I need to do is close my eyes, the same as you, and make believe I am alone in the garden of Eden. Of course, one of our servants always interrupts my meditations before I have the chance to explore my imagined surroundings."

"With your permission, I would like to introduce my youngest daughter, Amelia and Christopher, our second son," interrupted Mrs. Bannerman, indicating to each that they should step forward to greet Georgiana. "Louisa you already know, so I will not waste your time introducing her again.

"My eldest son, Robert, is occupied elsewhere, as is Mr. Bannerman."

"Please extend my warmest regards," said Georgiana, "and my regrets for missing them, but I understand their absence. The work of the estate cannot wait, as William likes to say. He does not lie about the house when he is at home; he would rather spend his days worrying one problem or another to a solution."

"May I show you around Kingsdown?" asked Louisa, breaking into the conversation, to Georgiana's relief. She had almost run out of small talk and was unsure what she might do to prolong her visit enough to make Robert's acquaintance. He was, after all, the real reason she had undertaken to call upon the Bannerman family today.

"What a wonderful idea. Lead away, and I will follow."

"We can start inside, if you like." Miss Bannerman turned toward the manor and paused, looking back over her shoulder as if to be sure her guest was following.

"I would, but could you also show me your orchards and some fields where your crops grow? William praises the estate whenever he visits, and claims the quality of your land is second to none, including Pemberley's."

"I suppose," said Miss Bannerman, "although my knowledge of that part of Kingsdown is minimal. I am not familiar with sowing or harvesting, as Father says there is no need to teach me such things. Outdoor labor is his and my brother's responsibility. Robert may show you if you ask him."

"I would like that. I have an interest in the workings of a farm, of any size. William says I am too curious for my own good, but I prefer to think of it as a healthy interest in my surroundings."

Louisa led Miss Darcy through the house, showing her each of the rooms and making small talk as they went. Elizabeth was proud she had showed the courage to offer the tour, knowing how shy she was normally. Miss Darcy seemed to show the proper amount of interest, but Elizabeth could see her indifference and wondered why she had come to Kingsdown when Pemberley had more to offer. Maybe her stated reason pushed her to introduce herself, but Elizabeth felt there was another, one Miss Darcy chose not to share with them.

"Are you attending William's ball?" asked Miss Darcy when they stepped into the sitting-room. "He is sparing no expense to make it an event worth remembering."

"I cannot," said Amelia from behind her. "Mother and Father will not give their permission."

Louisa gave her sister a look that Georgiana suspected was one of exasperation: "She is only fifteen, which is too young. Father wants her to enjoy her childhood first, which in my opinion is wise counsel."

"And what about you, Miss Bennet? Are you planning to go?"

"I will be there with my aunt and uncle. Louisa is also going, along with Kitty. She loves the balls we have at Hertfordshire, so I doubt she will choose to stay behind."

"It should be an enjoyable evening for everyone," said Miss Darcy as Louisa led the way up the stairs to the second floor, Elizabeth and Kitty following. Amelia, having already expressed her disappointment, remained in the sitting-room.

From there Louisa took them out to the garden, where she stopped, as if unsure of where to go next.

She pointed toward the paddock, and the horses grazing on lush green grass: "The stables are over in that direction. I can show them to you if you like."

Elizabeth felt the need to rescue her cousin: "Allow me, Louisa." The girl seemed only too happy to accept the aid, if the expression crossing her face was any indication.

"The building is probably miniature compared to Pemberley's, but there are only four horses at Kingsdown, so a larger one is unnecessary."

Miss Darcy gazed at the animals peacefully moving about the enclosure: "Your horses are beautiful, but I see just three. Is the other somewhere else?"

"Duchess is being re-shod," said Elizabeth, to Miss Darcy's confused look.

"Re-shod? Do horses wear shoes?" As she spoke, she lifted her feet as if to inspect them. "They must be difficult to fasten while the horse is moving about."

"They are metal and nailed to the hooves," explained Robert, emerging from the stable leading a horse. He removed the bridle, gave the animal a light slap on the rump, and watched it move off to rejoin the rest in the paddock.

"Does that not injure the animal?" asked Miss Darcy, her eyes wide in apparent horror, although Elizabeth saw through her charade. That Georgiana was familiar with the subject was easy to tell, from the way she watched the animal gallop past her. Elizabeth, though, was unsure what the girl hoped to gain in keeping the knowledge from Louisa.

"The nails grip the hoof, and that is all," said Robert, who looked like he was warming to his subject.

"We mold the shoe to the hoof, so it is comfortable on the horse. Without it, they are unable to pull the wagons and carriages that we depend upon. Our roads would wear the hooves down or worse, cause them pain and injury, which might shorten their life. Fitting shoes to a horse is an act of compassion, for which I believe the animals would express their gratitude, if they could talk."

"I hope I never live to see that day." Miss Darcy batted her eyes and giggled at Robert who, it was apparent to Elizabeth, enjoyed the attention.

He thrust his chest out just enough to show off its breadth, and his stance was tall and confident, as opposed to his normal slumped and exhausted pose. She almost expected to see him reach out to the top rail of the paddock, where Miss Darcy had rested her hand, as if inviting his caress.

"I think that would be impossible," was the reply, his preening catching even Louisa's notice, as Elizabeth heard her titter. Quickly she nudged the girl to keep her quiet, as she wanted to see what Miss Darcy had in mind.

Robert gave a quick glance to his sister and frowned at the noise, prompting Elizabeth to move her out of earshot. When they were a few paces away, he leaned forward and whispered something, which seemed to amuse the girl before stepping back.

"I have another horse to work on," said he, turning back toward the stables, "so I must get back to my duties."

"Wait," called Georgiana, "nobody has introduced us. In my confusion about the treatment of your horses I did not hear your name."

"I am Robert Bannerman, Louisa's brother and Miss Bennet's cousin, and I am pleased to meet you, whoever you are."

"My name is Miss Darcy, your neighbor to the north. My brother is Fitzwilliam, master of Pemberley. I came to meet your lovely cousin and make sure she was coming to my brother's ball. She assures me she would not miss it for the world, and I am looking forward to seeing her there. Will you also be attending? You will not regret it."

"I had not given the matter much thought, although I suppose I will be there, to protect my sister, if nothing else."

"Then I hope to see you and your family enjoying yourselves," said she as he walked back to the stable, leading another horse.

"Miss Darcy seems like a nice girl," remarked Louisa, following Elizabeth to her room that evening after supper, where she took her semi-tailored gown from the closet. "I would like to believe her apology and excuse for shunning me, but I find it odd. She has not called on us before today, nor has she shown goodwill or friendship, although we attend the same church every Sunday.

"I remember her father and brother entering their pew while the rest of the congregation fought over the few empty ones. She passed by me frequently but until today we did not speak. I wonder what made her change, but almost fear the answer to the question will not be what she claimed."

"She has never paid you any attention? I find it strange that she would suddenly decide to notice you, even though you live on neighboring estates."

"She spends her free time with Miss Haversham, who seems to avoid the lesser residents of the county. Miss Darcy is of the same opinion, I suppose."

"My opinion does not matter, unless she gives me reason to mistrust her," stated Elizabeth. "I have made the mistake of judging prematurely before and will not do that again. You might want to adopt a similar attitude."

"I will try." Louisa watched as Elizabeth sat to thread a needle. "May I help? This is to be my dress, but you have done all the work and I feel guilty just watching. Surely there is something I can do."

"You should harness the horses and ready the carriage," declared Kitty, entering the room without knocking. "I am sure Lizzy needs something in Lambton and now would be the perfect time to go to town and make the purchase."

Elizabeth surveyed her sister, begging for the chance to visit the largest town in the neighborhood. She knew that Kitty, while no longer under Lydia's control, still longed for the excitement of exploring the merchants as she dreamed of possessing enough money to order the newest, most fashionable gown from the town's finest dressmaker.

For Kitty, heaven was in the browsing, stopping at merchants such as the milliner's to inspect the bonnets, touching them ever so lightly unless chastised by Elizabeth or Jane for the potential harm she might cause.

Elizabeth wanted to take the girl to Lambton, or Kympton, which was almost within walking distance. She would, she told herself, when Louisa's gown was complete and she could justify the time spent on such an endeavor. Until then she did not want to waste a minute, or she might disappoint her cousin, which she would not allow. Kitty would have to wait, or talk her aunt into going with her, which was unlikely.

"I have enough to complete this gown," said she, pulling the needle through another stitch as she worked to complete a final seam. "There is nothing I need in Lambton that I do not have here."

"But you said we needed supplies," wailed Kitty petulantly, a behavior that Elizabeth had not seen since their departure from Longbourn some weeks prior. "How can you finish, when you have to go for them?"

"It turns out I exaggerated the amount of ribbon I needed, and I packed some I had forgotten in my trunk. I was lucky to find enough material, without having to waste a day looking for it in town."

"So we will not go, despite your promise? You claim I can trust you, but you lied to me, and you are breaking your commitment. How can you live with yourself?"

"If you recall, I said we *might* have to go to Lambton, not that we *would* have to go. I am sorry you are disappointed, but I do not need, nor do I want, to waste a valuable day going back and forth to town. We will go another day, but it will probably be after the Pemberley ball, not before."

"It is not fair," pouted Kitty. "I was looking forward to spending a day there; Amelia says it is a large town and thinks it is much bigger than Meryton. I wanted to browse and purchase some sugar sticks, but now, because of your lucky find, I cannot."

"There will be other days, and other journeys to town, Kitty. All I ask is that you exercise some self-control. Is that such a hard request to honor?"

"But I wanted to go, and so did Amelia. We made plans to visit the milliner and the haberdasher. Amelia says the merchant has so many knickknacks for sale that it would take days to see them all. She says every visit is like going to a new shop, and he does not mind her spending hours looking through them all. I wanted to see his merchandise."

"And you will, I promise, but it will not happen until after the ball, so you might as well accept the fact. Moaning and complaining will change nothing except your mood, and that for the worse. You will probably survive a delay of a few days. Take some time to change your attitude from complaint to thankfulness for the blessings you have received. Maybe Amelia can help, she always seems happy, whatever happens."

"I suppose," was Kitty's response, though her expression did not change the tiniest bit.

"I think she has yet to see the rainbow at the end of her cloud," said Louisa as Kitty left the room, the sour look fastened to her face.

"She will eventually," laughed Elizabeth. "Kitty is not a person who wallows in self-pity. By tomorrow she will either forget about her disappointment or set it aside until the next time she decides it is time to go to town. If she waits until the ball is over, I will ask Uncle for the use of his carriage. That will soothe her injured feelings."

"I hope so," laughed Louisa, "or the consequences might be severe."

"Then I will do my best to keep her content, so we do not have to face those consequences."

The conversation continued another hour, until Elizabeth was satisfied with the progress she was making, whereupon she placed the garment in her trunk. It would be retrieved the following day in the hope of completing the changes she had been working on for more than a week.

CHAPTER XII

"The post is here," said Mr. Bannerman, giving a letter to Elizabeth and one to Kitty, whose excitement matched her surprise.

"Who could have written to me?" asked she of her sister. "Nobody knows I am here. I did not even tell Maria Lucas I was leaving for the summer."

" It might be from Longbourn. Mary misses you and has informed you of the depth of her loneliness."

"Does Mary even know I am gone? She spends so much time in the music room practising the pianoforte or in the sitting-room pouring over scriptures that I sometimes wonder how aware she is of the world around her. If Mama has not told her, she might not realize either of us is not there."

"That was not a kind thing to say," giggled Elizabeth, "true or not. She is our sister and we must respect her choices."

"What about your letter? Is it from Jane? I think you have written her every night since we arrived, so it is time she wrote back."

Elizabeth rose to her feet before saying: "It is, and I will read it tonight after supper. Until then I will be in my room, working on

Louisa's gown. The ball is in a few days, and there is still a lot to finish."

When she got to her room, Elizabeth inspected the letter, looking for a postmark. The familiar Hertfordshire mark was a welcome relief, as it told her that Jane was back from London and would have local news to share. Putting the envelope aside for later, she set to her sewing.

The morning passed quickly as she worked on the finishing stitches for the gown. By noon she was putting the needles and threads away, the completed dress hanging on the closet door, ready for Louisa to try it on.

Opening her bedroom door, she went in search of her cousin; if Louisa modeled the gown for her, she could make whatever few alterations remained and present her with the finished article of apparel. She would then have two days to admire the garment and dream about attending the ball adorned in her new dress.

Memories of her first ball reminded Elizabeth of past daydreams, in which the men lined up for the privilege of escorting her onto the floor for a set, and flocked to hear her every word. Of course, the night had been nothing like she imagined, limited as she was to dances with her father and Sir William. To her disappointment, the handsome young men she had been so sure were breathlessly waiting for her appearance scarcely noticed her!

Louisa was not in the music room, where Elizabeth had expected to find her practicing scales on the pianoforte, or reading from the bible, one of the few printed works her uncle owned.

"She is outside with Miss Darcy," said Christopher from the corner of the room, where he sat looking at the pictures in a child's book. "She came to call on Louisa this morning."

"Thank you, Christopher, I will look there."

She found the two girls, along with Kitty and Amelia, walking through the orchard and engaged in conversation.

"It will be so much fun that you will not want it to end," Miss Darcy was saying as Elizabeth drew near. "Would you not agree, Miss Bennet?"

Elizabeth paused to choose the best response to Miss Darcy's question: "It is exciting, terrifying, confusing, but not boring. Your memories will be jumbled and, at the same time, crystal clear. Some things you will never forget but others will be hard to recall; the first experience for every young woman is much the same."

"That is not an appealing description," laughed Miss Darcy. "If you are not careful, Miss Bannerman will be too afraid to set foot on the property.

"I will be fine," averred Louisa, although to Elizabeth she did not appear as confident as she claimed.

"We were discussing what to expect at the ball," said Miss Darcy as they passed through the orchard and paused beside the fence enclosing the paddock, where Elizabeth watched as her quick, furtive glance scanned the field.

On this morning, the paddock held three horses who looked up at their approach, as if hoping to see treats such as apples, which Elizabeth or Louisa might give them. When none appeared in the girl's hands their attention returned to their grazing.

Elizabeth watched Miss Darcy's gaze stop and linger upon Robert as he emerged from the building leading a horse he set free to join the others.

"She asked how many people William is expecting and whether most would be familiar to her," said Miss Darcy, pulling her eyes, almost reluctantly Elizabeth thought, from their study of the young man and back to her companions.

"That is something I would also like to know. Although I have met no one other than you and Mr. Darcy, Uncle Bannerman has. If he knows most of the guests, he might enjoy himself more than if he feels like a stranger, while I will do my best to fit in with a room full of strangers."

Miss Darcy paused as if to consider the question before smiling and shrugging her shoulders.

"William is well known in Derbyshire, as well as the surrounding counties, and London. There are a lot of friends to invite, but he limited the guest list to Lambton residents and others living close to the estate. He wants a smaller, more intimate type of gathering, one where everyone knows everyone else.

"According to his manservant, Snell, the guest list was kept to a maximum of two hundred so the guests would not overrun the house."

"Two hundred people?" Kitty's excitement was clear in her tone of voice. "Mr. Darcy considers two hundred people a small, intimate affair? Thank the Good Lord he kept it small!"

"For a Darcy fete, two hundred is a moderate number," said Miss Darcy, obviously amused at Kitty's outburst. "Are smaller gatherings common where you live?"

Before Kitty responded, Elizabeth jumped in: "Ours are attended by seventy-five to eighty people, at most. We consider anything over one hundred large.

"Hertfordshire is a small county. Our largest town is Meryton, and it boasts a population of only a few hundred. To see that many people at any kind of gathering is unheard of, to my knowledge. Two hundred people would tax the town's hall to its breaking point."

"Then this ball will be something new for all of you," observed Miss Darcy. "You will love it, I promise."

"She will, but it might her take a few days to realize it." Robert's comment caused Miss Darcy to jump and give a small squeal of surprise.

"Mr. Bannerman," said she, using her hand to stir the air in front of her face. "You frightened me! I did not realize you were here."

"I am sorry; it was rude of me to intrude like this. I will leave you to your conversation."

Miss Darcy reached out seemingly impulsively to grasp his sleeve as he moved away, dropping her hand when he stopped: "No, please stay. We were discussing the upcoming ball, and whether the number of guests was so large that Miss Bannerman might not enjoy herself.

"What do you think? I believe you have attended past gatherings at the estate. Will your sister have fun, or has my brother invited too many people?"

Robert seemed, to Elizabeth, to preen at Miss Darcy's touch. His eyes took on a lively glint and the hint of a smile graced the corners of his mouth. As she looked on, his spine straightened and his shoulders appeared to broaden as he squared them once again in reaction to her question.

If the situation had been less absurd, Elizabeth might have laughed. As it was, she felt sympathy for her cousin in seeing his usual stoicism wilt under the onslaught of the girl's charms.

Here was a young man who, if Elizabeth were any judge of human nature, was unprepared for the attention being lavished upon him. He seemed unsure of the answer she sought, and the reaction he might receive should she find fault in what he had to say.

Miss Darcy was no help, with the innocent look she fastened on the poor boy, whose neck and face were growing red with embarrassment, though from what Elizabeth could not determine.

"She will have the time of her life," said he at last before turning himself to face toward the stable.

"I need to get back to work, if I want to finish today," mumbled he, starting off at a pace just shy of a run.

"Goodbye, Mister Bannerman," called Miss Darcy as he entered the stable. "I look forward to seeing you at the ball."

With a half-hearted wave he disappeared into the building.

"I should also be on my way," said she, watching him walk away. "I promised Mrs. Annesley when I left that I would return in time to practice my lessons at the pianoforte, and I do not wish to disappoint her. Compared to my previous matron, she is a dear."

"I will see you next week at the ball," called Elizabeth as Miss Darcy went to her carriage, Louisa accompanying her. Miss Darcy did not acknowledge her farewell, so engaged was she in conversation with Louisa.

That young woman bears watching, thought Elizabeth as she went to her room to read Jane's letter. The attention the girl had paid to Robert troubled her. Why was she so interested in him, where she had not in the past so much as acknowledged any of the family's existence, according to Louisa?

Elizabeth would have assumed that his subdued personality and quiet, almost subservient manner made him all but invisible to Miss Darcy and her friends. If that were the case, what had caused her to take notice of him? As far as she could tell, Robert had done nothing out of the ordinary since she had arrived and this change had not happened before Mr. Darcy's decision to play host to a ball.

Robert seemed a sober young man, not given to boasting or showing off to attract the attention of the fairer sex. The man she saw at the paddock today, strutting and preening for Miss Darcy, was not the cousin who had reservedly greeted her upon her arrival. His actions this afternoon were not conspicuous, but Miss Darcy had noticed them. If she had not, Elizabeth had misinterpreted the self-satisfied look of avarice she had momentarily displayed.

A soft knock on the door interrupted her thoughts.

"Elizabeth?" said Louisa, opening it just enough to stick her head through the resulting crack, "I am here to look at my gown, if it is ready."

"Your timing is perfect. Come in and try it on, so I can see how it looks on you. I want to be sure there are no other alterations needed."

Louisa was happy to comply, and soon she stood in front of Elizabeth's mirror admiring the garment.

"It is beautiful. Thank you Elizabeth; this is more than I dared hope for."

"You needed something to wear, and I did my best to provide it for you. Please enjoy yourself; that will be thanks enough."

"That will be no problem, I think. May I put this in my closet, or do you want me to leave it here with you?"

"It is yours, so it belongs in your closet, does it not?" Elizabeth laughed. "Now take it and leave; I have a letter from my sister to answer."

Louisa's answer came as a surprise: "I will, after I tell you what Georgiana asked me."

"She has requested that the both of us call her Georgiana instead of Miss Darcy. She asked permission, and I gave mine, although I thought she would need to ask you herself. I considered it wrong of me to offer your permission. After all, you were not there."

"Thank you, Louisa. You are correct, and I would expect Miss Darcy knows that. No matter, I will wait until she raises the issue with me."

"Enjoy the letter, and thank you again, Elizabeth," said Louisa, stepping through the door, the newly tailored gown held like a precious gem in her hands.

Elizabeth sat at the small desk in her room and, unfolding the neatly creased pages, began to read:

"Longbourn, May 25.

"My Dearest Lizzy,"

"Please forgive my delay in writing to you, but so much has happened that I do not know quite where to begin. I suppose it best to start where I left off with my last letter, which was before I left London to come home.

"My journey was, as you might expect, boring and uncomfortable. Why there is not more padding on the coach seats, or tighter fitting curtains over the windows is something I will never understand. I suppose that is neither here nor there, and complaining will do nothing to rectify the situation, so I will move on to other, more interesting matters.

"I no sooner got back home than Papa came to request my help in controlling Lydia, who was, unsurprisingly, up to her old tricks. She was refusing to listen to his directives and going to Meryton anytime the mood struck her, which was every day, it seemed. He went to

Mary for help, but her approach was to lecture Lydia on the evils of licentious behavior. This only spurred the girl on to more scandalous instances of disobedience until finally Papa took the step of locking her in her room until she agreed to abide by his rules.

"I confess I was doubtful his approach would have any effect, but Lydia surprised us both by agreeing to his demands, so her confinement was not long. Since her release, she has been spending time with Mary, which has been beneficial to both. Lydia's manner is a little subdued, and Mary has expressed a desire to experience more of what the world offers. Who would have thought such a simple idea would yield such amazing results?

"I have the biggest news to tell you, Lizzy: Netherfield is let! The new tenant is a Mr. Bingley, and he leased the estate to help him decide if he would like to live in the country rather than London, where he has spent most of his life.

"He arrived with his sister, Miss Caroline Bingley, a nice enough person, although I could see she is not as attached to the idea as her brother. I called on her a few days after their arrival and we shared a delightful conversation.

"Miss Bingley does not wish to live so far from London, and wants to return as soon as she can. Apparently there is a potential suitor there, who had just started paying attention to her when Mr. Bingley announced his intention to lease Netherfield. She worries that if she waits too long, the gentleman will turn his attentions elsewhere. I expressed my hope that everything will work out for her, and she thanked me for my compassion.

"I like Miss Bingley, and think that if she were to remain in Hertfordshire, we might become the best of friends.

"Her brother is the most amicable gentleman I have ever met. His genial nature is a refreshing change from most of Meryton's young men. He is easy to like and even Papa speaks well of him.

"He has been to Longbourn three times to go after game with Papa and our neighbors, and their hunts have been successful, so much so that they have invited him to try his hand at fishing. When I mentioned the closeness of the friendship that has developed between the two, Papa gave me the strangest look and claimed he was doing it for me. I asked him what he was referring to but he would not give me an answer. His only response was that someday I would thank him.

"Honestly, Lizzy, how do you put up with him? I love my father, but his habit of avoiding an answer, no matter how simple the question, can be annoying.

"Mama sends her best and wants me to tell you she has forgiven you for refusing Mr. Collins's marriage offer. I want to believe her, but she still raises the subject at every meal, and continues to bewail the impending loss of the home she has known for over twenty years.

"Papa has promised to outlive her, but she refuses to listen. When he insisted he would not pass before her, she cried about Mr. Collins's plan to evict her daughters from their childhood home. Where she got this idea I do not know and do not want to ask her.

"The one time I tried to reassure her that he had no such plan, she began to cry, wondering how Mr. Collins calls himself a Christian while allowing the death of his cousins through neglect. At this point Papa left the room, but not before stating his hope that she will indeed survive him so she can experience what she seems to hope will come to pass.

"I miss you, Lizzy. Your presence at Longbourn is always the balm our father needs, and the foil that Mama plays off. Your capacity to endure her barbs and smile in response to her most pernicious insults is admirable; lately I want nothing more than to avoid her. If you had laid that sin at my feet six months ago, I would have denied it in no uncertain terms, but now I must own this shortcoming.

"I hope you are enjoying your visit with our aunt and uncle Bannerman in Derbyshire. I wanted to go with you but I could not abandon our aunt Gardiner in her time of need. The next time you visit I promise to accompany you.

"Aunt Bannerman has written to Papa, telling him how impressed she is with both you and Kitty. It seems the instruction you are providing is giving Louisa some much needed self-confidence and poise which, according to her mother, she was sorely lacking.

"I will close by wishing you the best summer and a wonderful visit with your cousins. I send you my regards, and the best wishes of our parents, as well as your sisters.

"All my love,
"Jane."

Elizabeth finished the letter and, returning to its beginning, read it again before hearing the call to supper. Folding it carefully, she placed it on the desk for perusing later, if the urge struck her.

When she entered the sitting-room after the meal finished, Kitty sat perched on the settee, the letter from Lydia on the table beside her.

"Would you like to read it before I put it away?" asked Kitty, "You are the first person she mentions."

"Did Lydia tell you she wanted me to read her letter?"

"No, but you might be interested in what she has to say, anyway. Most of it is unflattering, and some is rude and downright degrading."

"That does not surprise me. Lydia was angry when she learned you were going to spend the summer away from Longbourn and she was not included."

"It does not upset you?"

"No, Kitty, I have no time to waste worrying about Lydia's hurt feelings. Nothing I say or do while we are at Kingsdown will affect them anyway."

"I admire you, Lizzy. You can be serene, even in the face of criticism and unkind gossip. I should adopt such an attitude."

"All it takes is practice, and your personal decision to let issues you cannot change or control pass without striking out at them. Lydia has a quick temper, and has probably already forgotten what she wrote. She has been like that since she was born, and I doubt she will change anytime soon.

"Was there any news in her letter, apart from unintelligible ramblings and any unspecified vengeance she plans?"

Kitty laughed and shook her head. "You know her so well. She filled the first page with invectives and her opinions regarding how ill she is being treated.

"There is a regiment newly posted in Meryton and, according to her, filled with the most beautiful men she has ever laid eyes upon."

As her sister's past exploits sprang to mind, Elizabeth said: "To Lydia, any man in uniform is the most handsome she has ever beheld,"

"Do you remember the one who delivered the post from Aunt Gardiner last year? When she saw him, Lydia fell head over heels, and declared he was her future husband. The fact he was old enough to have grandchildren her age meant nothing, except that he could teach her things none of the lads in Meryton would know anything about."

"I remember," said Kitty with a laugh. "She was heartbroken when he departed without noticing her waving from the sitting-room window."

The memory of Lydia's tears when the fellow left brought a smile to Elizabeth. Lydia had been inconsolable for two hours, sure that her one chance for married bliss had deserted her.

"And now she has someone new to embarrass herself in front of while trying to attract attention. Jane says there is nothing to worry about, as Mary has taken the silly girl under her wing because Papa asked her."

"But she has been sneaking off to Meryton to flirt with them," insisted Kitty, "shamelessly, if her letter is telling the truth."

"According to Jane, Lydia appears to have changed her ways, and she attributes it to Mary's influence. She is not so apt to sneak off, and when she does go to town, Mary goes with her to act as chaperone. Jane thinks she is changing for the better."

"Lydia claims it is all a ruse. She pretends to pay attention to Mary so Papa will allow her to visit the regiment, where she can flirt and throw herself at the officers who, from what she says, are helplessly in love with her."

"Lydia loves to embellish." Elizabeth shrugged her shoulders and continued: "She has a talent for taking a mundane event and relating it as if it were a life altering experience. I would take her stories with a grain of salt if I were you."

"That is what I meant. I believe little of what she tells me, and even less of what she has written in this letter.

"The problem is she finished the page telling me how much fun we will have when you and I return to Longbourn. She assumes I will be ready to take up where we left off, chasing the members of the regiment."

"My advice is to ignore her," was Elizabeth's proposal, "and, above all, forget about what she wants to do when we get back. From the sound of her letter, she is still a wild and willful child. Please do not let her lead you astray again."

"I decided that I will not let Lydia influence me anymore. I am glad I came to Kingsdown and have not missed her in the slightest.

"That is good to hear," said a relieved Elizabeth. "Now, if you will excuse me, I am going to answer Jane's letter."

Back in her room, Elizabeth put pen to paper in response to her sister. To her missive she added the warning Kitty had related, in addition to the latest news about her relatives. When she completed it, she addressed the envelope and prepared the document for mailing, after which she went to bed.

Her dreams that night were about Georgiana and Robert. Elizabeth watched her chase the boy all night, in much the same way that Lydia was wont to chase after the members of the regiment. By the time she awoke the next morning, he had been caught and married multiple times.

CHAPTER XIII

The se'nnight before Mr. Darcy's ball was the longest in the history of the world, according to Kitty. Her excitement began on the Wednesday before the event and built through the weekend, including during the Sunday sermon, where she spent the service whispering and giggling to Louisa, until Elizabeth moved to sit between the two.

"You should be ashamed of yourself," were her words of censure when the sermon concluded and everyone milled about before heading back to Kingsdown for a light lunch.

"Your antics disturbed the concentration of everyone around you, including the vicar, who was not amused by your behavior."

Kitty hung her head, meekly accepting Elizabeth's chastening without protest. Louisa, standing nearby, did not completely escape her cousin's wrath.

"You are not my responsibility, Louisa, but your participation did not help. I will leave it to your father to decide if you deserve punishment, but to me, both yours and Kitty's actions reflect poorly on your names."

Mr. Bannerman, coming up beside Elizabeth and wearing an angry scowl, said: "I agree. If not for Elizabeth's efforts to mold you into a gentlewoman, I would confine you to your room the night of the ball. Instead, I will find another punishment."

"Yes, Father." Louisa's look was of one properly chastened and accepting her guilt. "Please forgive me; I behaved badly."

"Thank you for taking Kitty to task," mentioned he to Elizabeth as they boarded the carriage. "Louisa does not usually misbehave at Sunday service, and I thought you might not recognize that your sister is the one responsible. I believe I should punish both, and I will mete it to them equally."

"Thank you, Uncle. This is not the first time Kitty has done this during the Sunday sermon, but it is usually Lydia who causes the problem. My guess is that with her excitement over the approaching ball, she forgot this is the Sabbath, and that church is not the place to amuse herself. It will not happen again; I promise."

"I hope not," said he.

As a fitting punishment, it was decided they would clean the stable Monday and Tuesday, as directed by Robert. Kitty spent almost an hour at the end of the first day complaining to Elizabeth about their mistreatment at Robert's hand.

According to her, he seemed to take a perverse pleasure in making the chore as unpleasant as possible. He had her re-clean the stalls because she did not clean them thoroughly, and the straw was not evenly spread. He told Louisa the animals were not fed properly, either too little or too much, and she had done it at the wrong time.

When the girls led the horses out to the paddock, the lead ropes were too short and they did not make the animals yield their hind quarters. When the animals were returned to their stalls, they were not led properly.

In Kitty's opinion, their efforts that day accomplished nothing, as Robert found fault with everything they did, singling her out for additional tasks unrelated to the punishment Uncle Bannerman had decreed.

"We have tried to please him, Lizzy, but he refuses to accept our efforts and makes us redo the tasks repeatedly while he laughs at our efforts. Can you please talk to him? I tried, but he refused to listen."

Elizabeth smiled and shook her head. "Robert is making sure the stables are cleaned properly the horses are looked after correctly."

"But he is treating us unfairly! You were not there, Lizzy, to see him laugh when I asked whether Uncle Bannerman knew how many extra tasks he gave us. He told me I should get back to work, or it will be more difficult tomorrow. Is there nothing you can do to help?"

"No, Kitty, there is not. Remember, you brought this on yourself. If you had listened to the sermon instead of laughing and carrying on with Louisa, you would not be in this predicament. I do not feel sorry for either of you."

"I suppose you are correct," said Kitty, "but that does not mean I have to like it."

"No, it does not, but I hope you have learned your lesson. Think of it this way. You have made it through one day, so there is only one left. You know what Robert wants, so tomorrow should be easier.

"The ball is in a few more days and they will pass before you know it. Keep that in mind and you will be fine."

"I guess, but I am still not looking forward to working with Robert tomorrow. He takes a perverse pleasure in making us miserable."

The pout Kitty wore as she left brought a smile to Elizabeth's face. If Kitty learned her lesson, the punishment was worth it. Even if she did not, she deserved the penalty and might reconsider before engaging in that type of behavior in the future.

As Elizabeth promised, the days remaining until the evening of the ball passed quickly. Kitty was waiting for her when she returned from her morning constitutional on the day of the event, eager to prepare for the evening's festivities.

When Kitty asked for help with her gown, Elizabeth gave her the same advice she had received the day of her first ball: "You are putting the cart before the horse. The ball is hours away and there are other things you need to do first."

"There is nothing more important," said Kitty. "I have not worn this gown since you altered it, and I want to be sure it fits properly. I will be content to sit quietly until we leave for the Pemberley estate, but I wanted to satisfy myself that I am ready."

"The gown fits, we made sure of that weeks ago. You need to keep busy until it is time to leave; maybe go see how Louisa is getting along in the music room. She is afraid she might forget the dances we taught her and wants to review them. You can help her remember. If you walk through each of them with her, it will help her confidence."

Kitty left, albeit somewhat reluctantly, leaving Elizabeth to her thoughts.

She wondered about the attention Georgiana was suddenly paying to Robert, where previously she had scarcely acknowledged his existence. What changed her mind, and why had she seemed so worried he might not attend tonight?

Elizabeth suspected the girl wanted everyone to believe the coincidence of her sudden interest, occurring because of a chance encounter while visiting Louisa. She could see it was a ruse, but did not understand the reasons behind it. Not knowing the girl well did not alter her belief; Elizabeth had witnessed the same type of behavior in Hertfordshire. Each occasion ended in heartbreak and injured feelings.

Robert was an adult, and might not need Elizabeth's protection, but he had no experience regarding feminine wiles and was therefore unprepared. She considered asking Louisa, but her cousin was no more familiar with Georgiana than was Elizabeth, so inquiring of her would yield no useful answers.

The girl needs to be watched so she cannot cause problems, thought she as the time to get ready neared and Kitty appeared at her door, asking again for assistance in getting dressed.

Dressing herself, while doing the same with Kitty, proved an exasperating exercise. The girl seemed unable to do even the basic tasks, interrupting Elizabeth constantly with questions and suppositions about what the evening would bring.

Finally, Elizabeth reached the end of her patience and sent Kitty back to her room, telling her to ask for a servant's help in getting ready.

At the appointed time, the driver brought the carriage around and the six attendees boarded the vehicle, settling into their seats for the ride to Pemberley.

"You will have such fun," promised Kitty to Louisa, who did not look at all confident that Kitty might be correct.

"Remember your manners and everything will be fine," advised Elizabeth, to which Louisa presented a sickly smile. "Stay with me, and I will protect you. Remember, you are to dance with your father or brother only, unless your father gives you permission to dance a set with someone else."

"I will," declared Louisa, her confidence clearly increasing as she spoke, "and I will do my best not to embarrass you, Father."

"That should be the least of your worries," said he with the smallest of smiles. "Keep your wits about you and listen to your cousin. She appears to possess the presence of mind to keep you out of trouble. With Elizabeth beside you, nothing untoward will occur."

"We will have the best time together," Elizabeth assured the nervous girl, noting her uncle's less than enthusiastic vote of confidence.

"And if Elizabeth is busy, I will help," said Kitty. "You know, I have been to several balls and assemblies in Meryton. Other than the number of guests, this will be no different."

"Thank you." Louisa's spirits appeared to lift with Kitty's declaration.

"We are here," announced Mr. Bannerman, although to Elizabeth, he seemed to lack interest in the evening's activities.

I hope his mood improves as the evening passes, she thought as the driver handed them from the carriage to the drive.

"Miss Bennet, Miss Bennet," Elizabeth heard as the party approached the entrance. As she looked along the receiving line, it surprised her to see Miss Darcy waving from her place in the line greeting arriving guests. Beside her, Mr. Darcy bent over to whisper in her ear, whereupon Miss Darcy dropped her hand and refocused her attention on the line, to her brother's apparent satisfaction.

Georgiana looked toward the entrance for what seemed like the hundredth time since her brother placed her in the receiving line, but to her dismay, they had still not arrived. Turning back, she saw the line seemed to have doubled in length in the past five minutes. Would people never stop arriving?

"Quit fidgeting," whispered William beside her. "It is unbecoming, and people will assume you are bored."

"They will be correct," whispered she in return. "I do not know why I should be stuck here greeting *your* guests. I might know one out of every ten, and they do not know me, either."

"As master of Pemberley, it is my duty to thank everyone for coming. As my sister it falls upon you to do the same. And by the time you have thanked them all for attending, they will no longer be strangers, will they? Now welcome Lord and Lady Bancroft; they are here because I sent him a personal invitation."

Georgiana sighed and gave a quick curtsey to the couple, who returned her welcome before moving into the main hall.

How she despised these lines! If not for the fun she had planned with Sarah tonight, she would have tried to remain in her room, although William might not have allowed it.

"I should think it impossible to fall asleep in the receiving line," said a voice, interrupting her thoughts. With a start, she regarded the line, which had stopped because of her unintended lapse. Sarah stood in front of her, smirking at Georgiana's breach of etiquette and, without doubt, enjoying the discomfort her remark had caused.

Georgiana gave her friend a smile and a laugh while saying: "On the contrary. It was not inattention; I desperately wanted to avoid having to speak with you. Unfortunately, you did not have the manners to move along the line without calling attention to yourself."

"Has your special guest made his appearance yet? I should hope, for his sake, that he has. It would not do to keep the esteemed Miss Darcy waiting now, would it?"

"Who is Miss Haversham referring to?" asked Darcy. "Have you issued personal invitations? I wish you had consulted me first, so I could order extra supplies. It would not reflect well on Pemberley if we were to run out of food or drink tonight."

"No, I have not. She is referring to the Bannerman family. Miss Bannerman voiced concerns about attending. I urged her to accompany her cousin, and she agreed. Sarah's interest is mercenary, and not something to be concerned about."

Sarah's reply, which Georgiana knew would have been derogatory, was cut off by the necessity to move along. As a result, she would now be fuming, which would curtail her enjoyment of the evening until she created an opportunity to return the favor.

"I sometimes wonder about your friend," whispered Darcy before turning again to the line.

"Sometimes I wonder about her, too," mumbled Georgiana to herself, watching the Havershams enter the hall before turning her gaze once again to the drive and the carriages lining up to discharge their passengers.

Her attention sharpened at the sight of the conveyance she had been waiting for since the evening started. Anxiously she watched the footman open the door and extend his hand to the occupants who, one by one, emerged from the cabin.

"Miss Bennet, Miss Bennet," called she, waving her hand to catch the woman's attention while the guests in the line moved past her to accept their welcome from Darcy.

"Pay more attention to the line," commanded Darcy, "and less to everything else."

With a nod, she spoke to the next guest, offering a cursory welcome, which the gentleman thankfully took as a signal to move along. She made brief comments to the next few people and the line's progress quickened, to her relief.

"Welcome, Miss Bennet, Louisa," said Georgiana as they reached her position in the line. "I am so glad to see you tonight."

"And we are happy to be here, Miss Darcy," was Miss Bennet's response. "I know Louisa has been looking forward to this evening since her father gave her permission to attend. She is a little nervous, but that will pass. I assured her she is beautiful; she knows what to expect and how to act, so tonight will be memorable, and something to look back on fondly."

"Together we will make sure it happens. Trust Miss Bennet, Louisa. She will keep you out of trouble, and I will do what I can to help you enjoy yourself."

"Mr. Bannerman, welcome to Pemberley estate. How good of you to accompany your cousin and sister. I hope we have time to talk later, or maybe, with William's approval, you will escort me onto the floor for a set."

"That is Mr. Bannerman's decision, not yours," interjected Darcy. "Do not force the young man to do anything he is not comfortable with."

"I meant nothing by it, William. My intent was to let Mr. Bannerman know he is welcome tonight. Of course, the choice of who he wishes to associate with is his alone."

"Forgive me, Mr. Bannerman." She turned again to the lad: "I hope my remarks caused you no embarrassment."

"Your apology is unnecessary," said he, although Georgiana felt his discomfort. "I took no offense."

"Thank you and please, enjoy yourself tonight."

The family moved into the main hall, and Georgiana returned to greeting the last few guests, after which she followed Darcy into the ballroom.

"Were you reprimanded, or did I mishear?" taunted Sarah, joining her along the edge of the dance floor. "It seemed Mr. Darcy took exception to your manner of greeting."

"He did, but he will forget the issue within the hour. William does not dwell on minor annoyances."

"Your greeting might have been too forward, Georgiana. You almost threw yourself at the poor man.

"He was flustered by the time you finished with him," laughed Sarah. "I think Mr. Darcy got there just in time to rescue him."

"He did not need William's interference. Mr. Bannerman handles himself well whenever we speak."

"What do you mean whenever you speak? I thought you were not acquainted with him. Is this another lie, and in reality you know him well?"

"What I told you when you suggested him as the object for our game is the truth. As I told you at the time, I tried to speak with him once in Lambton, but he ignored me, so I took it upon myself to invite him and his sister to the ball to begin our competition."

"So you are confessing to cheating again," spat Sarah, her voice rising quickly. "I should have known you could not compete fairly. Miss Georgiana Darcy has no experience with honest effort."

"Sarah, keep your voice down, you are attracting unwanted attention."

"And I should care? You took advantage of my trust, and betrayed me again."

"No, I did not. I visited the Bannermans to encourage the young man to attend, which he might not have done if I had let things lie. Grow up, Sarah, and stop acting like a child."

"You are both acting like spoiled children, and I suggest you stop," said Fitzwilliam, coming up behind them with a frown on his face. "You are drawing attention to yourselves. Your brother expects you to show some manners, which you are not displaying now."

Sarah clearly enjoyed the sight of the colonel chastising her, Georgiana could tell. Her smirk had returned, and she tried unsuccessfully to hold her laughter in check. The colonel, though, turned on her when he finished with Georgiana.

"It would be advisable for you to listen as well, Miss Haversham, or I will take the matter up with your father."

Georgiana saw Sarah adopt a penitent demeanor, which almost caused her to laugh.

"I am sorry, Mr. Fitzwilliam. Please forgive me."

"See that you behave, or you will leave the floor, Georgiana, and you, Miss Haversham, I will take to your father."

"I did not cheat." hissed Georgiana as the colonel walked away to join Mr. Darcy.

Elizabeth witnessed the scene between the two girls, nodding with satisfaction as a gentleman stepped in to settle the matter.

"Miss Darcy seems to be having an argument," Kitty pointed and added, "I hope she does not cause a scene."

"Georgiana *is* creating a disturbance," said Louisa with a giggle. "And it appears someone has taken offense."

"As they should," stated Elizabeth. "That type of behavior is never acceptable. If you encounter a situation like that, remove yourself from the company of the person, if possible, or from the room. To respond reflects just as badly on you as on the instigator."

"Miss Bennet," said Mr. Darcy, who Elizabeth had seen approaching from the other side of the hall. "Might I have the pleasure of your company in the next set? I possess little talent, but I have been told that as I am the host, it is inhospitable to spend the evening on the sidelines."

"That is as roundabout an invitation as I have ever heard," laughed Elizabeth. "But I will be happy to join you." Grasping the extended arm, she accompanied him onto the floor as the music started.

The set progressed smoothly, and Elizabeth found herself surprised and impressed with Mr. Darcy's talent. His steps were sure and his transitions flawless, so much so it left her feeling that of the two, she was the weaker partner.

"You misled me, Mr. Darcy," remarked she to his querulous expression. "You possess much more talent than you would have me believe; in fact, your abilities are superior in every way to my own."

"Thank you for your kind words, Miss Bennet, but I am comfortable with my shortcomings. They are the reason you have not seen me taking part in many of the sets. I am mediocre and the fact discourages me from dancing."

"Modesty is an admirable trait, Mr. Darcy," responded Elizabeth with a laugh, "but false modesty is a sin comparable to vanity, according to Longbourn's parson. I think you are as talented as anyone in Hertfordshire, whether or not you agree."

"I have a friend somewhere in that general area," said Mr. Darcy, "but I cannot say where exactly. He is a new resident, and I have not yet visited him."

"I commend your friend on his choice," remarked she. "The countryside is beautiful and the people are the nicest in all of England."

"May I assume by your statement that you have traveled extensively through the country?"

His comment caused a giggle to rise unbidden: "No, but the people at home are so welcoming and personable that I stand by my claim without fear of contradiction."

"Your confidence is commendable," said he as the set completed, and he accompanied her back to where her cousin stood watching.

"May I have your company for this next set?" asked he of Louisa, who looked to Elizabeth for guidance.

"I spoke with Mr. Bannerman," explained Mr. Darcy, "and he gave his permission, because we are neighbors. If you would rather not, I understand."

"She is happy to be your partner," and with that Elizabeth pushed Louisa gently toward Mr. Darcy. "Do not mind her hesitation; she is a little nervous."

"I had not intended to make you uncomfortable," said he. "If you would rather not, I will take no offense."

"Yes," blurted Louisa before he turned away, "I would like the opportunity to dance with you."

Elizabeth watched as Mr. Darcy led the girl through the steps of the dance, his gentle way with the inexperienced girl gladdening her heart.

Louisa looked to be in heaven. Her steps, though tentative at first, gained confidence as her partner guided her patiently through the dance, and her smile bore witness to her rapturous delight.

"I think she is in love," laughed Kitty quietly. "Mr. Darcy might have to pry himself out of her grip when the dance is over."

"She is enjoying her set with him," agreed Elizabeth.

"He is such a wonderful man," raved Louisa when the dance concluded and she was once again at Elizabeth's side. "Mr. Darcy is so easy to dance with that I could do it all evening."

Elizabeth was grateful to the gentleman. His invitation to a girl who, understandably, felt overwhelmed was thoughtful and compassionate.

It allowed her to have the joy of an experienced partner, one sensitive to her insecurity and patient enough to guide her in something terrifying and transcendent, all at the same time.

Louisa spent the rest of the evening in a state of euphoria, to Elizabeth's amusement. To her, the evening was perfect, the music even more so, and Mr. Darcy the finest dancer in England.

"This has been better than I imagined," was her observation she as the evening drew to a close.

"I hate to be the bearer of bad tidings, but the ball is over and it is time to go home."

"Tonight was wonderful," said Louisa as the carriage left the estate. "Thank you for bringing me."

"The person you should thank is your father. He gave permission for you to attend and allowed me to prepare you for the evening."

"Thank you, Father, for making this night possible. You are the best in the world!"

"You are welcome," said Mr. Bannerman. "I am glad you enjoyed yourself; I guess you will want to attend all the balls in Derbyshire now."

Louisa answered with a smile and an opinion: "No, just those close to Lambton.

"We shall see," was the end of the discussion as the carriage stopped at the manor entrance. "But for now, it is time to retire."

"Thank you again, Father," sighed Louisa, before ascending the stairway to the second floor and her bedroom. "You really are the best ever."

"Go to bed," said he. "We can talk about it tomorrow, if you still want to."

As Elizabeth readied herself for bed, her thoughts were on the ball and the enjoyment everyone experienced through the course of the night.

Louisa and Kitty had both behaved themselves, something Lydia would not have done. Their demeanor had been exemplary, and Elizabeth took pride knowing her instruction had helped prepare them for the event.

She had not seen Robert much, as he spent the night with friends, only participating in a few of the dance sets. On one occasion, Miss Darcy appeared to be talking to him, but she could not be sure.

Not until the ride home did she ask him about his night, and received a mysterious smile in response. Try as she might, he would not elaborate on his activities, so she dropped the subject, although the curiosity stayed, like an irritating thorn, difficult to dislodge.

I will ask him again tomorrow or the day after, thought she as she sat at the desk to respond to Jane's letter.

The composition of her missive consumed three pages and took her an hour. When she finished, she placed it on the desk without addressing it to Longbourn. She would post it tomorrow after reviewing it once more, as was her habit. Retiring to her bed, Elizabeth fell asleep almost as soon as her head touched the pillow.

CHAPTER XIV

Breakfast the next morning was quiet, as Darcy waited for his sister to come to the table, while Fitzwilliam contented himself in sipping his tea.

"She is late this morning," Fitzwilliam observed after an hour had passed without Georgiana's appearance. "Either she has skipped the meal, or last night's ball was too much excitement, and she is still asleep."

"Or she wants to avoid me because of the spectacle she made of herself last night."

"The exuberance of youth," said Fitzwilliam with a laugh. "Try not to be too hard on her, she is still a child."

"She is sixteen, and should know what is acceptable at a ball, especially one held in her own home."

"Maybe she forgot herself in the night's excitement."

Darcy did not reply, as the subject of their discussion chose that time to appear in the doorway.

"Good morning, cousin," said she. "It is good to see you. When did you arrive? I hoped you would be here before the ball started, and when you were not, I assumed you were not going to be here at all."

"Your behavior made that clear," was his reply. "I did not expect to see you behaving like that. What happened, that you thought it acceptable to make a spectacle of yourself?"

"I am sorry; Sarah Haversham took exception to something I had done and would not stop, no matter what I did to calm her."

"From what I observed, you share as much of the blame as Miss Haversham. It seemed as though you wanted to continue the argument."

"I am sorry, Fitzwilliam."

"Your amusement while I spoke to Miss Haversham did not help, nor did your attempt to have the last word.

"Where is the girl Darcy spent so much of his time and effort raising to be a proper young woman? Did you forget everything we taught you?"

"No, cousin. I will do better next time, I promise."

"You had better, or your brother might confine you to your room until the end of time, correct, Darcy?"

Darcy let the conversation progress while he considered the steps he might take in response to her actions.

He was not her father but her guardian, like Fitzwilliam, a burden Darcy took seriously but loathed. She was his sister, a relationship neither had enjoyed since the passing of George Darcy some years ago.

Darcy, still reeling from the loss of his parent, was stunned when the reading of his father's will informed him of the responsibility he now bore.

Even five years later, he still thought himself unequipped for raising someone ten years his junior, and a girl at that. If not for Fitzwilliam's assistance, he would have given up within the first year, and sent the girl to a boarding school until she reached the age of consent.

Fitzwilliam did his best to see this formidable new task did not beat Darcy, giving him support, and allowing him the freedom to make the occasional journey to London on business.

It was Fitzwilliam who suggested hiring a governess to tend to Georgiana's needs as a growing young woman, and make sure her education progressed as it should. Unfortunately, the girl found amusement in disobedience, testing each until they resigned in frustration.

Darcy was no fool; he knew his sister was guilty of mistreating the poor women hired to teach her the finer points of being a gentlewoman. He struggled to find someone intelligent enough to instruct Georgiana properly, while possessing enough of a backbone to stand up to her attempts at intimidation. Through an almost disheartening process of trial and error he had found Mrs. Annesley, a woman even Georgiana respected.

"I said correct, William?"

Darcy started, pulled from his reverie by his cousin's question.

"Forgive me," he replied, "but will you kindly repeat your question? I had something else on my mind."

"I informed this young miscreant that another instance of that type of behavior would have dire consequences. Do you agree?"

"What happened last night? Did you not enjoy the ball?"

"Yes, William. I thought it was a grand affair."

"Then what came over you, that you would allow yourself to become involved in a public argument, such that the colonel needed to pull the two of you apart?"

"He did not need to interfere," complained Georgiana, a frown pulling the corners of her mouth down. "We simply had a discussion, that is all. I know our voices were louder than they should have been, but that was no reason to step in and threaten us. It was embarrassing."

"Fitzwilliam stepped in *because* of your loud voices, and you are lucky he did. I heard you from across the room. The only reason he interrupted you was because he was closer than I, so he arrived first."

"I did not even know he had returned until he interfered."

"He got back as the ball started," said Darcy, "and he did not interfere, he saved you, and me, I might add, from the embarrassment of a public row, in the middle of my ballroom."

Darcy gathered his thoughts. He disliked the necessity of having this conversation, and wondered whether Mrs. Annesley had been remiss in teaching Georgiana proper rules of behavior at an event such as the previous night's. In all other areas, the woman had been a godsend, keeping Georgiana in line and seeing to her training in every other area.

Was last night an aberration, never to reoccur, or a facet of her character that Darcy had not previously noticed?

With a sigh, he continued: "You were raised as a gentlewoman, the daughter of a Lady and granddaughter of an Earl. You know better, and I expect you to act in a manner more befitting a young woman of your status. If this sort of thing should reoccur, I will punish you. Do you understand?"

"Yes, William," mumbled she, her head lowered in seeming penitence. "Forgive me; it will not happen again."

"I expect it will not. Now go see Mrs. Annesley; she is waiting in the music room."

Georgiana curtsied and hastened to leave, as though she could not find the woman fast enough.

"She looks suitably chastened," said Fitzwilliam when she left the room, "but will she mend her ways?"

"Think back to yourself at that age," responded Darcy. "Did you repent and change when your father took you to task for something, or was your apology more likely to be mere lip service? I should talk to Mrs. Annesley; maybe she can steer the girl in a more genteel direction."

"If she listens, instead of telling the woman what she wants to hear."

"That is always a possibility. Only time will tell. I must confess, it surprised me to see you here last night. When you had not appeared by six, I assumed you had stayed in London to continue the pursuit of your young maiden."

A myriad of emotions flitted across the man's face, from surprise to consternation, but chief among them was bewilderment. Darcy laughed while watching his cousin, who was no doubt trying to remember when he had confided what he wished to keep hidden.

"Your secret is safe with me," said he. "And if you cannot recall telling me about your newest interest, it is because you kept me in the dark, or tried, I should say."

"So what made you think I was interested in a member of the fairer sex?"

"The last time you were here, you talked about a commitment in London you had to keep. You took great pains to convince me it was unimportant, yet you could not miss it, and then insisted you would be too busy to, in your own words, 'cast around for unattached women.' Your claim of disinterest tells me you were *already* interested in someone."

"That is a stretch even for you, Darcy, although I must compliment you on your active imagination. You should put it to use finding someone for yourself, like that beautiful young woman who so captured your attention last night."

"I paid attention to everyone last night. In case you have forgotten, I was the host."

"And a delightful, attentive host you were, especially to the woman you had your eyes fastened on the entire evening. One set with her captivated you the rest of the night."

"Are you sure we attended the same ball? I danced with more than one lady, and enjoyed each of them. I paid attention to every person in attendance, although I confess my attention was not on Georgiana, or that scene would not have gotten so far out of control."

"Finally, we agree on something. You ignored your sister to focus on someone else. You should court the woman; she would make a fine wife, and Georgiana seems to like her as well. You would not have to worry about conflict between your wife and sister, because they appear to know each other and are already friendly."

"If you are referring to Miss Bennet, we shared one dance, and I danced one set with her cousin, who was attending her first ball. We did not speak after that because my duties as the host occupied me. As you said, not too long ago, if memory serves, 'I compliment you on your active imagination'."

Fitzwilliam let loose a short bark of laughter when Darcy finished. "Prevarication will not avail you. I can see the truth is, for you, a malleable thing, good only as a tool to bend to your will.

"I know you did not speak with Miss Bennet after your dance, but that is the only part of your claim that comes close the truth. You spent the remainder of the night watching her closely. When she moved, you moved to keep her in view, and when she stopped, to carry on a conversation or to observe the guests, you also stopped.

"I would bet that you can recite the name of every man she danced with or spoke to the entire evening, along with those of the gentlemen whose approach to the young woman did not meet with your approval.

"Your attention was not as clandestine as you hoped, for the young lady with Miss Bennet caught you staring. She might or might not have mentioned the fact to her companion. I could not tell if she did from where I stood, but if she kept it to herself, be thankful."

"Miss Bennet is a personable young woman, and very polite," said Darcy, with more conviction than he had intended. "She was a welcome addition to those in attendance, and I have no regrets about including her in my invitation, but to suggest an ulterior motive is a flight of fancy, even for you."

Fitzwilliam leaned back in his chair and studied him. There was a gleam in the man's eye Darcy found unsettling, as if discerning any unrevealed meaning behind Darcy's ramblings came easy. As the subject of his cousin's scrutiny, Darcy was uncomfortable, but to mention that fact would give the man licence to poke and prod without pause, and that might last all day.

If he were to be honest with himself, Miss Bennet had caught his interest. She was a pretty woman, one of the comeliest he had met in some time. She carried herself with confidence, and seemed unafraid to speak her piece, regardless of the potential for criticism. Her affection for Miss Bannerman had been clear the day they met on the path, and elevated her in his eyes.

In speaking with Mr. Bannerman, Darcy learned that she was self-educated and well-read, qualities he considered essential in any person, male or female, and more so in a marriage partner.

Miss Bennet took her cousin under her wing and taught the girl what to expect at her first ball, and did so with a willingness that surprised Mr. Bannerman. To know that she possessed a caring personality raised her yet again in Darcy's estimation, and he wondered if establishing an acquaintance with the woman would be to his benefit.

"You are interested in her, that much is plain. At this moment, you are trying to ignore me while you decide what to do about it. You are debating whether the woman or her family would accept or deny your request to call on her, and have just about talked yourself into dismissing the idea.

"How accurate am I so far? Have you made your decision, or will you let this woman slip through your fingers, telling yourself you really have no interest in her?"

Fitzwilliam was having fun, no doubt. The trouble for Darcy was that, though he joked, his playful remarks hit close to home, too close for Darcy's comfort.

It was almost as if his cousin read his mind, and the thought left Darcy feeling exposed and vulnerable. To confess this to Fitzwilliam was out of the question; the man was too full of himself now. If Darcy agreed with him, the man's ego would take over, and it would be impossible to endure his company.

"I would not be making plans yet," said Darcy, "as I only met her once before last night, and at the time had only a few minutes to speak with her."

"You sly fox, trying to keep a prior acquaintance hidden," gloated Fitzwilliam, the scent of the chase clearly in his nose. "What else have you kept to yourself? Have you already offered for her?"

"I met her on one of my morning walks. The meeting was unexpected and resulted in introductions being exchanged, and that is all. Our conversation last night was a chance to become better acquainted while we enjoyed a set together."

"Well, cousin, from the look of you last night, I expect the sound of wedding bells in your future. I am leaving for home this morning to consult with the Earl, so you will have a month or more to set your wedding date."

"I will keep that in mind, cousin," laughed Darcy as Fitzwilliam left the room, before muttering aloud: "I will definitely keep *her* in mind."

Georgiana scrambled to conceal herself as Fitzwilliam rose from the table, the movement surprising her with its abruptness. In a panic, she slipped into the sitting-room and hid behind the door, her heart racing until her cousin passed by, seemingly without noticing her eavesdropping.

While she waited for her brother to exit the dining-room, she thought about the conversation she had overheard, the direction of which was disturbing.

She had noticed William's interest in Miss Bennet, but assumed it was nothing more than superficial, which was fine with her. To think he might hold the woman in some esteem was troubling, and something she could not allow.

Georgiana liked things as they were; she did not want them to change. She had grown comfortable with the life she led and did not welcome the possibility others might be allowed to intrude.

She did not remember her mother, Lady Anne Darcy, as the woman died in Georgiana's infancy. Her father's death, however, had left a gaping hole in her life, as the man had lavished his attentions on her as a replacement for losing his wife.

When he passed, Georgiana was inconsolable, and remained that way for months. It took the unconditional love of her brother and sustained encouragement from her cousin to regain the cheerful and ebullient personality she possessed from birth.

She had a good life at Pemberley, with servants tending to her every need and a brother who doted on her. She had only to voice a desire, and William would do his best to have it fulfilled. On those few occasions he had any objections, a few tears usually served to convince him of the error of his ways.

Her matrons were another matter. Georgiana had no objection to being taught. In fact, she thrilled at the opportunity to learn something new and was often in the Pemberley library, a book in her hand, as she chased down the answer to a vexing problem.

Conflict with her matrons inevitably arose when they attempted to impose their ideas of order in her life, demanding she accept certain hours for instruction and practice, as if those things could not happen later in the day, or be suspended a day or two.

Mrs. Annesley was different. She allowed Georgiana the freedom to abide by her own restrictions, so long as she paid attention during lessons, and respected Mrs. Annesley's authority over her for discipline and behavior.

The arrangement worked. Georgiana believed she had cowed the woman into submission, while Mrs. Annesley gained an attentive student, eager to be taught. Her knowledge grew, as did her ability to play the pianoforte and sing with a passably clear and tuneful voice.

This new intrusion by Miss Bennet was worrisome. If William developed an affection for her, his attention to Georgiana would suffer, replaced by swooning obedience to an outsider who would owe no fealty to the Darcy name. The words he muttered when his cousin rose troubled Georgiana greatly. She would have to pay close attention to William from now on. He would not develop an interest in Miss Bennet if Georgiana had anything to say about the matter.

She had nothing against the woman, who seemed in every way to be a pleasant person. Their conversations were friendly, and the woman left the impression she cared about Georgiana's health and wellbeing, which was a change, and something none of William's past love interests ever displayed.

From their first meeting, Miss Bennet had gone to the trouble to welcome Georgiana and to make sure she felt like a valued and trusted acquaintance. Her care and concern were not rushed, and Georgiana welcomed her open and carefree mien, something Miss Bennet's cousins, except for the eldest, Robert, seemed unwilling, or unable, to adopt.

Robert Bannerman. Just the recollection of his name sent a chill down her back as she remembered their conversation at the ball the previous evening. He had come upon her shortly after her set-to with Sarah, finding her perched in a corner, licking her wounds far removed from the evening's amusements.

"I did not expect to find you sitting by yourself." His welcoming smile was a relief from Fitzwilliam's dour countenance. "Were you banished to this corner because of the argument with Miss Haversham?"

Georgiana remembered her face coloring at the mention of her verbal altercation. She felt no chagrin over the incident; it was Sarah who lost her temper and spewed the accusations that angered Georgiana. If Mr. Bannerman had noted their spat and sought her out, all the better. With the judicious use of flattery, she thought, she might ingratiate herself with the young man.

"I came here on my own to ponder our disagreement," said she, her voice low and, she hoped, seductive, "and how best to make up with my friend. It is unfortunate that I angered Sarah; our friendship has lasted many years and I would not want to lose it over a silly disagreement, which is of no consequence, anyway.

"I hope our behavior did not bother you. Please do not think less of me because of a momentary lapse of manners."

Georgiana had lowered her head and looked up, gazing at Mr. Bannerman with half-closed eyes, a pose that men found irresistible, according to some of her acquaintances. The effect on him was almost comical, as he seemed to fumble for his response, hemming and hawing almost half a minute before finally squeaking out his reply.

"I, uh, that is, well, uh, I did not witness the disagreement," said he, his discomfort a quality she found charming. Georgiana watched him search for the words he needed, his embarrassment seeming to deepen while his nervousness increased.

"Todd Radcliff and his friends were talking about it," he finally blurted, "and having a merry laugh over the disturbance it caused. Some of them wagered on whether there would be a second part of the set-to, and if not, the chance they might arrange the possibility for one. I left them because I did not want to be a participant in anything like that."

"Why thank you, Mr. Bannerman," said Georgiana, batting her eyes at the boy, who had seemed to be, if not smitten, at the very least attracted by the attention. "That was genuinely nice of you. If only more of our so-called friends were as thoughtful, Derbyshire would be a much better place."

Mr. Bannerman had, to Georgiana's amusement, colored at her compliment and bid her a hasty farewell before hurrying off to another part of the ballroom.

Their discussion, she thought, had been a lone highlight to an otherwise dismal event. With his hasty departure, she tried to locate Sarah, but it seemed her friend had either left the dance or took steps to avoid her.

It was not until the last hour of the evening that she found the girl and pulled her aside to offer an apology, which was accepted begrudgingly.

She then looked for Mr. Bannerman, hoping against hope that she might maneuver him into asking William for permission to take her onto the dance floor for a set. Her brother would withhold his permission, as she was not yet out, but the act of requesting itself, if she could arrange such a thing, would place him further under her control.

Georgiana leaned against the wall, a daydream of being courted by Mr. Robert Bannerman playing out in her thoughts. Gentlemanly gestures and gallant actions she imagined him performing consumed her and caused her to swoon almost to the point of collapse.

When she came to her senses, she realized she had not moved from her hiding place behind the sitting-room door. With an inward laugh, she went to a chair facing the window to sit and ponder this young man who had taken up residence in her imagination.

What am I doing? thought she as the unfinished fantasy lurked at the edges of her consciousness, threatening to take control of her thoughts once again.

Is it possible that I have feelings for him? she wondered as a warm, peaceful feeling enveloped her. *No, I do not. He is the object of my competition with Sarah, nothing more.*

Another memory, that of his strutting and preening at compliments she directed toward him the previous week, flooded her mind. With a smile she recounted the way he had thrust out his chest and squared his shoulders to better present himself for her study, which she had been pleased to do, although surreptitiously.

She liked what she saw, and his return to his duties in the stable disappointed her, although she took care to disguise her regret from his sisters. It would be unfortunate if they discovered her subterfuge too early.

She could not let herself become enamored. The ridicule and torment from acquaintances, specifically Sarah, would never end. Any satisfaction she might achieve in her triumph would be lessened by their pity, and her exile from the group of acquaintances with whom she most frequently associated.

With William's constant absences, many of them long-term, her friendships were the family she did not have. To lose that would be too hard to bear.

It is time to press the advantage I gained last night, she concluded, rising from her chair with new determination.

CHAPTER XV

Elizabeth put her pen aside and, picking up her letter to Jane, read over her newest additions. When she finished this last review, she folded it, ready for posting. She smiled at memories arising from the ball, including the scene Miss Darcy and her friend had caused even before it had gotten well underway.

The conclusion of the argument, settled by a man stepping between them, had appeared to subdue Georgiana for only a short while after which Elizabeth observed her in Robert's company. Whether they shared a dance, or more than a brief conversation Elizabeth did not know, as her attention shifted momentarily; when she looked back, they had both moved from her sight.

The dance with Mr. Darcy, and his kind offer to share the next set with Louisa had been, for her, the best part of the ball. He was, in her opinion, a kind considerate man who had, with the simple act of extending his arm to a nervous young woman, made the evening one she would recall fondly the rest of her life.

Though Elizabeth had spoken with him but twice, including their conversation at the ball, the encounters had been pleasant. Mr. Darcy seemed a gentleman, showing respect for her and Louisa on both occasions.

While he seemed at ease with his duties as host of the ball, it was clear to her that, for the most part, he was not comfortable talking to people. She could see he avoided them as much as possible, giving the appearance he was involved in some important activity or another, thus saving him from having to stop and talk.

His efforts were endearing and amusing to Elizabeth, who was never at a loss for words. She looked forward to meeting new people, and was usually found at the center of a crowd.

Mr. Darcy seemed to prefer his own company above meaningless chatter with others. His comments, when offered, were concise, and rarely strayed from the subject at hand.

What would it be like to find herself the object of his affection? Would increased attention accompany his interest, such that visits to Kingsdown might become more frequent?

Elizabeth imagined a future as mistress of Pemberley, its servants at her beck and call. Mr. Darcy, madly in love with her, would see to her every desire and do his best to fulfill them. Their marriage, blessed with children, would endure through the ages, love never wavering and in complete agreement on every matter, important or trivial.

In her musings, the servants would love her immediately and do all within their power to keep her happy and satisfied.

It was a wonderful idea, and one she hoped to achieve, if not with Mr. Darcy, then with another some day.

A knock on the door interrupted her daydream. "Lizzy are you occupied?" asked Kitty. "May I come in?"

"You may," answered Elizabeth. Her sister entered and stood beside the doorway, as if wanting permission to speak, but nervous about opening her mouth before Elizabeth indicated she could. She waited for the girl to screw up her courage, knowing that if she spoke first, it would distract Kitty and she would forget all about the issue she came to discuss.

"May we go to Lambton?" asked Kitty, growing obviously uncomfortable with the prolonged silence. "It has been weeks since we came to Kingsdown, and we have not left the estate, other than to attend Mr. Darcy's ball. You promised days ago that we would go sometime. Please, may we go today?"

A hundred reasons to deny the request came to mind as Kitty waited for a response, the anticipation in her eyes impossible to mistake. The trouble, to Elizabeth's mind, was her impetuous tendencies, much like Lydia's, so the idea gave her pause.

Having taken Lydia and Kitty to Meryton many times, she was mindful of the problems that her youngest sister, with her impulsive streak, was never far from causing. Kitty, although rarely the instigator, succumbed easily to Lydia's harebrained schemes.

That Lydia was not with them did not entirely remove her concerns about going to town with Kitty. Elizabeth knew that if she agreed to the request, Amelia would want to come along, and she did not know how much she could trust the girl. The impression that Amelia did not appear to own a rebellious disposition did not give her much comfort. To watch Lydia at home or in the company of her elder sisters, a stranger might call her a well-bred, genteel young woman. Should that same stranger encounter the girl in Meryton, trying to attract the attention of members of the regiment, his impression would be the opposite.

The other impediment to Kitty's idea was in obtaining her uncle's permission to occupy two of his four horses for an entire day. Kingsdown was not an expansive property, and from what Elizabeth had observed, they needed the livestock most days for the operation of the estate. Mr. Bannerman might not care to lose half of his work animals so that four girls, two of which were not his own, might satisfy a whim by spending a day in Lambton, instead of remaining at home.

There was only one way to find out, she decided, and that was to pose the question.

"I will take you, but first we need to ask Uncle for permission to use his horses for the day. Wait here while I talk to him."

Elizabeth found her uncle behind the stable in conversation with his daughters, who seemed to have joined to present their case.

"Are you here to beg for the horses and carriage as well?" asked he. "I hope they understand me if I tell you what I told them. I cannot afford to lose two horses and a servant to drive them for an entire day. There is too much to be done, and not enough time to accomplish everything if I am reduced to a single team."

"But Father," said Amelia, her tremulous voice tugging even on Elizabeth's heart strings. "They have not been to Lambton yet. Have you confined them to the estate until they return home?"

"May I make a suggestion?" said Elizabeth, to which her uncle nodded his head. "Could you spare the horses long enough to take us to Lambton? The driver could return to the estate and you would have the use of the team for the day.

"When the work is complete, just send the carriage to pick us up and bring us back to Kingsdown."

"That would work, I suppose, as long as you send the carriage back immediately so Robert has the use of the team for the day."

"I will make sure we do, Uncle, and thank you. May Louisa come with us? I have not been to Lambton, so I hoped to use her as our guide for the day."

"She may. Remember who you are, Louisa, and why you are there. I trust you, but gossips will be gossips, so anything you do will reflect upon you and the rest of the family."

"I will be careful," promised Louisa. "Thank you."

"What about me?" demanded Amelia, somewhat indignantly, "I am as familiar with the town as Louisa, so I could be a guide as well."

"You are too young to go without me," said Mrs. Bannerman, who had approached unnoticed. "You will stay here and help mind Christopher."

"But Mama, that is not fair," cried Amelia. "Louisa and Kitty are both going; why must I stay home?"

"Louisa is eighteen, and so is Kitty. You were not old enough to attend the ball with them, and you are not old enough to go with them into town."

"Please let me go; I promise to be on my best behavior."

"I am sorry Amelia," said Mrs. Bannerman. Though her voice seemed calm and unaffected by the pleading, Elizabeth felt that she would not tolerate her daughter's arguments much longer. "I need you to mind Christopher, and that is final. Now, no more out of you or I will put you to work helping the housekeeper with the washing."

The protest forming on her cousin's lips died with the threat. Elizabeth knew, from experience, how difficult a chore it was, with your hands immersed, up to the elbow, in the harsh cleaning solution necessary to remove the sweat and stains from frequently worn garments.

Amelia wisely stopped arguing. Of course, this did not prevent her from fixing each with a glare as they went in search of the carriage and its driver.

"She was not happy," said Louisa while they waited for their ride to town. "I feel sorry for her. She really wanted to come with us."

"What if we visit the sweet shop," wondered Elizabeth, "so I can purchase some sugar sticks to give her when we get back. It is not the same as going with us, but it might make her feel a little better."

"Amelia is not one to hold a grudge. She will forget this before we are halfway to town. Despite her injured feelings, she loves Christopher and enjoys spending time with him."

"But a sugar stick is always a delightful treat, unless she does not like them."

"She will not refuse it, but I would not offer it as an apology; that would only remind her she was not with us today. If you simply give it to her, she will accept it with gratitude."

"I will remember," said Elizabeth with a laugh. "She differs from Lydia, that is for sure. If we were at Longbourn, Lydia would have already snuck out of the house and been on her way to Meryton, just to spite Papa's decision. At least Amelia listened. She may not have enjoyed being told to stay home, but she did not argue the point."

"She would never disobey our parents. As much as she might disagree with them, and that is often, she always does as she is told."

"What is taking them so long?" sighed Kitty, "will they never get the horses hitched?"

"Patience, Kitty," laughed Elizabeth as the carriage pulled up and waited for the girls to seat themselves. "Too much hurry will cause you to forget something important. A calm outlook and demeanor are much better than a hasty approach."

"Yes, Lizzy," sighed Kitty as the carriage entered the roadway and picked up speed.

"Is Lambton a large city?" asked Kitty as the journey progressed.

"No, Lambton is a town," laughed Louisa. "It is nowhere near the size of a city, with a population of about a thousand. They built it into the surrounding hills, so the streets can be steep, and occasionally crooked to accommodate the hillside they are on."

"Are the merchants friendly, or do they bar access to those who only want to browse?"

"I think they would much rather you make a purchase, but I have not met any who will not allow you to look at their merchandise. How else can they hope to make a sale if they forbid you from looking at their wares, and making a choice that satisfies you? After all, you are not buying it for the shopkeeper, you are making the purchase for yourself."

"I thought at first you intended to walk," said Kitty, "but I am glad Uncle let us use the carriage. It would have taken most of the day to walk this far, and I do not even see Lambton yet!"

"You asked if the town was close enough to get there on foot, and I told you then it was over five miles. Were you not listening, Lydia?"

"I am not Lydia," declared Kitty, to a smiling Elizabeth. "And I listened, I think. Maybe thoughts of the ball and what I would do there got in the way."

"They might have, Kitty and I apologize, but you reminded me of your sister. She pays no attention to anything that is not about her directly. I sometimes find it frustrating to carry on a conversation with her, because she is forever interrupting to ask questions that were already answered."

Kitty did not reply, as she was busy watching the passing scenery. The countryside was as wild as any Elizabeth had ever seen in Hertfordshire, including that around Oakham Mount. The road they were on was little more than a lane, the trees on either side growing almost close enough to scrape the sides of the carriage.

To Elizabeth, the beautiful landscape excited her instincts for exploring the unknown. The forest beyond the edges of the road was dense, with few laneways branching off in other directions. If she closed her eyes, she might imagine herself in an unknown country, at the mercy of brigands or highwaymen.

She *was* in an unknown country, she realized with an inner laugh. Just because it was still in England did not make it any less strange. She had been there before, she knew, but was too young at the time to appreciate the scenery, and even if she had, the memory would have long since faded.

After what Kitty complained was an interminable journey, the driver stopped the carriage at one end of a street that seemed, to Elizabeth, to stretch on for miles. Kitty, looking eager to begin her explorations, unlatched the door and threw it open before the driver dismounted to perform his duty. Jumping out, she beckoned enthusiastically for the others to follow.

"Patience, Kitty. Lambton will not disappear before you have the chance to poke your head into every nook and cranny of every merchant in the town. Be careful, or you will exhaust yourself before we are half begun."

"I know, Lizzy, but there is so much to see, and so many shops to explore. We could spend the entire day here and not get to a third of them!"

"She is right," said Louisa. "Lambton has what sometimes seems to be an excessive number of merchants for a town of this size."

"And I want to visit all of them." Kitty was by this time hopping up and down in anticipation. "Can we begin, please?"

"In good time," cautioned Elizabeth before turning back to Louisa. "Why are there so many, if the population is not large enough to support them?"

"The countryside in Derbyshire is much like it is here. It is not flat, and the further north you travel, the more rugged it becomes. Because the ground is so inhospitable, the estates are larger and more distanced from each other than what you probably find in Hertfordshire. To accommodate this, the merchants set up shop in which ever hamlet or town they can.

"While there are smaller hamlets like Kympton about, they like to restrict the number of merchants they will allow, according to Father, so the merchants go where they can set up shop. Lambton has not placed any such restrictions within the town's boundaries, and this is the result."

Kitty asked, in a plaintive voice: "May we *please* choose a shop to inspect?" Her voice, however, sounded distant, as though the girl was no longer close to them. When Elizabeth looked up she spied her sister pulling open a door and disappearing inside.

"I was afraid this would happen," said she to Louisa. "If I cannot get her to listen, we will spend the day chasing her, from one merchant to another, and that is something none of us will enjoy."

Elizabeth marched over to the shop Kitty had entered and, opening the door, peered inside. It was larger than she expected, stretching to the rear, rather than to either side. Rows of hats, bonnets, and sundry articles of lady's headwear were displayed, each mounted in such a way as to present them at their finest.

Hats made for Sundays occupied one complete row, while the row next to it contained nothing but sun bonnets. Other rows displayed hats so covered in lace that their basic shape was indistinguishable. The purchaser would have to trust the judgement of the merchant that the hat was perfect for them, she thought, because they could not tell, not even if they viewed themselves in the mirror.

Elizabeth trod each of the aisles, glancing at the many hats but not seeing them clearly as she searched for her sister. Not until she entered the last did she locate the girl, standing in front of the mirror wearing a most ostentatious hat and making faces at herself in the glass.

"Kitty!" Elizabeth's demand caused her sister to start and almost lose her grip on the hat. "Put that back where you found it and come with me."

Elizabeth led her sister outside, stopping at the front to compliment the shopkeeper on her merchandise and apologizing for her sister.

"If you do that again, this visit will be over," said she when they returned to the street. "I will not have you acting like Lydia, and I will certainly not chase you all over Lambton. You will spend the rest of the day sitting by the side of the road waiting for the carriage to return. Do you understand?"

"Yes, Lizzy. I am sorry," responded Kitty, her eyes focused on the ground at her feet. "I was excited and forgot myself."

Kitty's behavior improved as Louisa, at Elizabeth's request, led them from merchant to merchant, where they leisurely browsed through each, stopping whenever something attracted their attention.

Elizabeth could see that Louisa was well known in Lambton, and more important, well liked. Shopkeepers welcomed her into their establishments, and acquaintances, of her age and older, extended warm greetings along with best wishes for family members.

Elizabeth kept her attention on the passing time, eventually suggesting they make their way to the sweetshop to purchase some treats for everyone at Kingsdown.

"There are three, on this street alone," said Louisa when Elizabeth asked where she might make her purchase.

"Take me to your favorite, then."

"We are standing in front of it," chuckled Louisa to herself, as if she was enjoying a private joke. "I try to buy something from this shop every time I am in town. The owner is the kindest of gentlemen, and never complains about the time I take to decide, or the small amount I finally buy.

"Then he is the type of merchant I want to give my business to," decided Elizabeth, reaching for the door, which opened before she grasped the handle.

"Miss Bennet, how good to see you," Georgiana welcomed them, stepping back to allow the girls to enter. "What a welcome surprise to find you here, in a confectioner's of all places."

"Louisa is showing us around the town, and I promised to take some sugar sticks back with me," said Elizabeth, nodding a greeting toward Georgiana's companion, who did not look as thrilled as her friend.

"With your permission, I would like to introduce Miss Sarah Haversham," offered Georgiana, indicating the girl, who returned Elizabeth's nod with the barest one of her own. "She is one of my closest friends, and has been since childhood. Miss Haversham, this is Miss Elizabeth Bennet, Mr. and Mrs. Bannerman's niece. With Miss Bennet is her younger sister, Miss Catherine."

"Pleased to meet you," said Miss Haversham, although Elizabeth detected no enthusiasm in her greeting.

"Did you enjoy the ball, Louisa?" asked Georgiana. "I saw you dancing with William. Although he denies it, I believe he is the best dance partner in Derbyshire, would you not agree?"

"I would," laughed Louisa. "He was very patient with me, and not at all bothered by my missteps, which were unfortunately too frequent."

"Everybody is like that at first. You worry everyone will notice any mistakes, and you hope they are not bad enough to disrupt the dance for other participants."

"That is exactly how I felt, but Mr. Darcy told me to enjoy myself and not worry about such things. When I listened to his advice, my worries went away. Your brother is a wonderful dance partner."

As the conversation carried on, Elizabeth watched Miss Haversham, who seemed less than pleased at the interruption to her day. Twice she saw the girl roll her eyes as Louisa spoke, and the look she gave Elizabeth was like a challenge, daring her to mention it to Georgiana. She expected the girl to voice her displeasure, and was tempted to let her do so, but the afternoon waned, and it was time for them to meet the coach..

"Forgive my interruption, but we should be getting back to Kingsdown. It is getting late and our carriage should be waiting by now."

"Of course, I did not mean to delay you," said Georgiana, to which Miss Haversham rolled her eyes yet again and snickered, a mean sibilant hiss which, thankfully, Louisa did not hear.

"Sarah and I were going in that direction, so we will walk with you," said Georgiana, which caused a look of surprise from her friend, followed by a shrug of her shoulders as the group set off.

The discussion carried on without pause until they reached the carriage, where Robert stood waiting, his visage showing impatience, although Elizabeth did not think they were late.

"Mr. Bannerman," called Georgiana as they neared the conveyance. "It is good to see you again. Are you here for Louisa and Miss Bennet?"

"What a good brother you have." Turning back to Louisa, she went on without waiting for a response: "He seems as attentive to your needs as William is to mine. You are lucky to have such a devoted sibling. Not every brother would willingly bring a carriage to town to retrieve his sister."

Georgiana was not looking at Louisa as she heaped praises upon the boy. She instead batted her eyes shamelessly at Robert who, Elizabeth knew, drank in the compliments. His shoulders were up and his chest thrust forward, as it was at the Kingsdown paddock. If she had not witnessed the display, Elizabeth would have laughed upon hearing its description.

Miss Haversham, not to be outdone, stepped up beside her friend, in the process almost shoving Georgiana to the side.

"Mr. Bannerman, I have not seen you since the ball," said she, raising her voice enough to talk over what Georgiana was saying. "You look well. Did you enjoy yourself that evening? I know I did, although I was disappointed we did not share a dance. Promise me you will correct your oversight at the next ball."

Robert loved the attention, of that Elizabeth was sure. And who would not? To be singled out and greeted with such eagerness inflated any man's ego, and Robert was no exception.

Miss Darcy and Miss Haversham, however, were a different matter. The two looked as though they were competing for him, and Elizabeth did not understand why. He was a handsome boy, but his father was not wealthy, or even financially comfortable, and that would be common knowledge in a town the size of Lambton.

While Miss Darcy seemed to entertain some affection for him, Miss Haversham showed no such emotion, and her display worried Elizabeth. Did she intend to discourage Georgiana from paying too much attention to Robert, or was there another reason for her behavior?

"You are a good man, Mr. Bannerman," declared Miss Haversham in what Elizabeth realized was her attempt to give her voice a seductive quality. "It is not every brother who would take the time from important duties to come to Lambton for your sisters, when there are probably so many other things you need to do."

"I care for the Kingsdown livestock, and much of the estate's farmed land as well," Robert said, the timbre of his voice lowered, to

Elizabeth's amusement. Surely he was not so vain as to suppose his strutting and preening was impressing to his audience?

"And to sacrifice most of your afternoon to collect your sister and cousins, when you are no doubt needed in managing the business of the estate, is to be commended," said Miss Darcy, directing a beaming smile toward the nonplussed young man.

Deciding the show had gone on long enough, Elizabeth cleared her throat. "We should leave, or we will be late returning to the estate. It will take us more than an hour to get back to Kingsdown, and it is already past five."

"Let me know when you plan to return to town; Louisa and I will come with you," promised Georgiana while fixing Robert with a bright and enthusiastic smile. "I am sure Mr. Bannerman would not object to another passenger or two, would you?"

Robert did not respond, but the slight coloring of his face and neck told Elizabeth he heard the compliment. A quick look at Miss Haversham showed her displeasure at seeing her friend playing up to him in such an overt manner.

"My cousin is correct," said he, ushering the party into the carriage, and joining them in the cabin. "It is time we left."

With a shake of the reins, the driver put the vehicle into motion, but not before Miss Darcy gave a wave, directed, thought Elizabeth, primarily toward Robert, who was happy to return the gesture.

As the carriage left Lambton, she observed: "You have admirers, and they seemed happy to see you, Miss Darcy more than Miss Haversham."

"She was friendly, and nice enough to include me in her greeting."

"You appeared to be more than casual acquaintances, and she seemed happier to see you than I would have expected, given the fact you have exchanged only a dozen sentences at Kingsdown."

"We also spoke at the ball," said Robert, "although we did not say much."

"Did you dance with her? I do not recall seeing you taking part in any of the sets, but I might have been mistaken."

"No, you were not. After we spoke I joined my friends on the other side of the hall. I enjoyed a few dances, but I did not join every one of them."

"If I might offer some advice, be careful with her. I do not want to see you hurt or embarrassed. Remember, her brother is one of the wealthiest men in the area, and might not look kindly upon your attention to his sister."

"I have no designs on Miss Darcy. She has been friendly to us, that is all."

Silence took over for the rest of the ride, each passenger seemingly lost in their thoughts. Upon arriving at Kingsdown, Mr. Bannerman had Robert take care of the horses before joining the family at the supper table.

At the conclusion of the meal, Elizabeth repaired to her bedroom for the evening, where she sat at the desk and unfolded her letter to Jane. Dipping her pen into the ink, she added a few more sentences.

CHAPTER XVI

"That was the most shameless display I have ever seen," said Sarah when the Bannerman carriage departed. "Are you pleased with yourself?"

"To what are you referring?" asked Georgiana, though she knew her friend would never believe her protestations of innocence. "I did nothing wrong."

"Everything you did was wrong," spat Sarah. "If they had stayed five more minutes, I might have had to pry you off the poor boy.

"People watched you make a fool of yourself. What do you think would happen if I, or someone else, were to report your behavior to Mr. Darcy? I bet he would not be pleased."

"It would be in your best interest then," suggested Georgiana, "to make sure no one tells him, as your father would know about it as well. William would demand the details, and I would have to tell him about everything, including the wager we made. Your punishment might be worse than mine."

Sarah paused, and Georgiana could almost see the thoughts whirling about while she considered the consequences of carrying through on her veiled threats.

Georgiana loved the contests which put her and Sarah against each other, almost as much as she loved maneuvering her friend into proposing them. Sarah was no fool, and suggesting ideas in such a way so that she took them as her own was not always a simple thing to arrange.

While she often accepted Georgiana's ideas, her enthusiasm for them was moderate. For her full participation, she needed to believe the notion was hers and one she thought she might win, by whatever means necessary.

She was not above cheating, having convinced herself, Georgiana was sure, that it was her only path to victory. When it came to their wagers, Georgiana often won, a fact Sarah did not accept graciously.

It was common for her to accuse Georgiana of using the very tactics she herself employed in her failed attempts to claim victory. While Georgiana sometimes bent the rules slightly, she did not do so at the start of a wager, as Sarah invariably did, with sometimes comically embarrassing results.

Their friendship, based on competition and the resulting humiliation suffered by the loser, was not a healthy one, but that did not prevent Georgiana from using it to her advantage. Sarah, however, seemed to thrive on the rivalry and resisted any of Georgiana's suggestions that they find something else to occupy their time. To deprive Sarah of the chance to proclaim herself superior in any way was unthinkable, and a notion she would not entertain.

"To anyone unfortunate to observe you today, it would appear as though you and Miss Bannerman are the best of friends," teased Sarah, pulling Georgiana's thoughts back to the present. "The spectacle sickened me and served no purpose, unless you consider wasting the better part of an afternoon a wise use of our time."

"Did you forget our wager, Sarah, because I did not. I intend to win, and what better way is there of attracting Robert's attention than to let him see I am friendly with his sisters? Unlike the disgust and impatience you showed when I was talking to them, I pretended to have an interest in what they were saying.

"There is little chance Louisa sees you as a friend; you are barely an acquaintance, and judging by your manners, you regard her as even less than that. If her brother noticed your attitude, and I cannot see how he missed it, how likely is it he will pay any attention to you?"

"My attitude today is a part of my plan," said Sarah. "All I need is to convince him that his sister rejected my attempts at friendship and my behavior today, while regrettable, will be accepted as my reaction to her antipathy.

"But what about your behavior? I almost expected you to scrape the ground in your attempts to kiss the girl's feet, and to what purpose?

"The family are little better than commoners and, if not for this pointless wager, are not worth our notice. They are so uncouth they could be mere trades people, if not for Mr. Bannerman's ownership of Kingsdown. Their manners are poor and they know little about proper etiquette, judging by today's encounter. What do you hope to gain by debasing yourself like this? If you are not careful, they will pull you down to their level of filth and degradation."

The intensity of Sarah's rebuke surprised Georgiana. Did she really hold the Bannerman family in such contempt? If so, why did she feel that way?

Georgiana had not considered Louisa a friend, having entertained no urge to maintain more than a passing acquaintance with the girl until her wager with Sarah. This did not, however, mean that she harbored feelings of hatred or distaste for the family, such as those Sarah seemed to hold. Was there a reason for this enmity, or was it simple disgust because she thought them so far beneath her they deserved to be shunned? If so, Georgiana had not seen this side of her friend's character before.

Sarah took considerable pride in her level in society. Of this Georgiana was aware, but in all their years as friends, she had not witnessed such animosity, almost approaching hatred, as she had today. Sarah had, in the past, voiced uncomplimentary remarks that were in Georgiana's view uncalled for, but when taken to task she would retract her statement, although often unwillingly.

Maybe, Georgiana thought, in her need for friendship following the death of her father, she had begun a friendship with someone possessing none of the qualities her brother had raised her to value.

William would, she knew, disapprove of her choice of friends if he discovered Sarah held opinions like those she voiced today.

Was it Georgiana's responsibility, though, to encourage her friend to change her attitude toward others, especially with those Sarah dismissed as unimportant, because they had been less fortunate in life?

No, her duty was to treat others with kindness and respect, as William taught her. She could express disagreement with Sarah's views and try to correct her friend's behavior, but would not try and force the girl into changes she did not wish to make.

"Need I remind you that Mr. Bannerman is a gentleman, and as such holds a position equal to Mr. Haversham or William?" said Georgiana. "They are not disgusting or filthy, as you have so eloquently stated.

"Whenever I visit Kingsdown, I am welcomed without reservation. To be honest, every member of the family has been a pleasant surprise, but I suppose that is something I should expect because William is on friendly terms with Mr. Bannerman.

"Mrs. Bannerman is a neighborly woman who, as far as I can see, considers herself above nobody, including their servants, or the tenants who work their land. For you to defame her family and, by extension, Mrs. Bannerman, is beneath you, Sarah, and has no bearing on your *plan*, whatever that may be.

"It upsets you that I have been able to establish a friendship with Louisa, and the idea had not occurred to you. If I were you, I would find some other way of attracting her brother's attention, because heaping scorn and derision on them, done in private or not, will find its way back to the family, and Louisa's brother especially.

"While I agree we do not count them among the best of Derbyshire's residents, they are not, as you seem to think, the dregs of society. In fact, I quite like Louisa. You might feel the same if you got to know her."

Sarah laughed, a bitterly caustic sound which took Georgiana aback. "Your interest in Mr. Roger Bannerman is far more than you admit. You have feelings for the boy, don't you?

"I can hardly wait to tell everyone that the great Georgiana Darcy has fallen in love, and with someone like that, no less! You will be the laughingstock, of Lambton at least and eventually all the county. This is too good to keep hidden; everybody needs to hear the tale of how a simple farmer's son captured your heart."

"I will do whatever it takes to win, Sarah, and when I do, the entire town will know that *you* could not so much as gain his attention. Who will be the object of scorn then? I guarantee it will not be me."

Sarah's laughter died as the truth of the declaration hit home, as Georgiana felt it would. The potential for a loss of face was something she had not yet considered, if the fear manifesting itself was any sign.

"Remember, Sarah, the winner of our competition either has to get him to confess his love or his intent to ask for permission to court. I will do anything I must to win, and I mean it. Come up with a plan to compete; from what I have seen so far, your only plan is to deride the object of our contest, and his family.

"I am going to offer some advice, although I doubt you will listen. Take some time, the sooner the better, and decide what you need to do. When you finish, find an approach that will give you a chance to beat me or, if you prefer, prepare yourself for the humiliation that is fast approaching."

"What makes you think I have no plan, other than your own misplaced opinion of your supposed superiority? You are so sure you will win, and handily, to judge by your claims of better planning. Why, you have even wormed your way into a dubious friendship with a girl who, if I did not know better, I would assume is a scullery maid.

"Your opinion of yourself is inflated, Georgiana, and I am going to enjoy telling our acquaintances how I bested you, even with your underhanded attempts to cheat. The victory will be sweet, but your abasement will be even sweeter."

Georgiana laughed at her friend's vitriol, which brought Sarah up short. "Thank you, Sarah. It is always such a pleasure to goad you into losing your temper. Does it not occur to you when we argue like this that I am doing it for a reason?

"I should think that by now you would expect me to confuse or anger you, and you would prepare yourself. You do not learn from the past, because I have done the same thing every time we have agreed on a wager. That is part of why I enjoy these contests so much. Half of the fun is watching you beat yourself because you are so worried about what I might do or say next that you pay no attention to what *you* should do to beat me. If the spectacle did not amuse me so much, I would refuse to take part in these stupid affairs."

"And if you did not possess such a conceited view of yourself and your own self worth," stated Sarah, "I would not agree to the wagers you seem addicted to offering. It is the act of beating you at your own game that I love, and the look of abject misery you wear when it happens.

"There is no need for you to worry about my supposed lack of a plan because I have no intention of ceding victory, not when my triumph is at hand. I know exactly what I must do, more so after watching your shameful display of obeisance to Miss Bannerman and her brother. By the time I have finished with him, you will be nothing more than a distant and unfortunately painful memory."

"And on that note, I think it is time we were on our way home," said Georgiana, pointing to the Haversham carriage, which waited for Sarah's return.

"I will be home long before you, and will have a more comfortable ride as well. I cannot understand why you would confine yourself to a carriage, when the sun is shining, and the day is warm. They are an uncomfortable and dirty way to get anywhere."

Sarah's response was, in Georgiana's opinion, a declaration of agreement with her point of view: "A carriage is much more comfortable than a horse. I have no desire to subject myself to the torture device they call a woman's saddle, thank you."

"Then ride astride the animal, as I do. You have seen me do it, so the concept is not a foreign one. Why not give in and sample the freedom that riding like a man can give you?"

"Because a proper lady does not do such a thing. You would realize that if the idea were not so repulsive to you. I will arrive home at an appropriate time, with my clothing properly arranged and my dignity intact, while dust and who knows what else will cover you.

"Someone is going to catch you and reprimand you for your unladylike habits one of these days. I hope I am there to see it happen."

"If I am discovered, William will not reprimand me publicly, unlike your father. He does not air his grievances in front of everyone, and the sight of me astride a horse, while upsetting, would not be bad enough that he would feel it necessary to berate me in front of Lambton's gossips."

Sarah shook her head in response and, signalling to the driver, sat back as the coach moved. Georgiana watched until it turned the corner before proceeding to where her mount waited. Retrieving the animal, which she walked it out of town. Upon reaching an area empty of witnesses, she mounted the animal and, riding astride the beast, set the horse toward Pemberley, five miles distant.

The ride relaxed her, and her thoughts returned to her conversation with Sarah. Was her friend correct in accusing her of harboring unanticipated feelings toward Robert Bannerman? Was this affecting her plans or the way she had spoken to Sarah when she voiced the accusation?

He was a magnificent specimen of a man, she thought, picturing his handsome face and powerful features. His manners were polite but firm, as he had shown when ushering everybody into the carriage to return home. Louisa seemed to look up to him in much the same way Georgiana regarded William, and she could tell he took his responsibilities as the eldest brother seriously.

She liked the way his smile, when it appeared, lit up his face. The simple act of pulling his lips to the side in an expression of laughter or satisfaction changed his countenance, from that of a dour brother to one who loved his sister.

The picture of Robert in Georgiana's mind changed, from one of affection and regard for his sister, to one of love and devotion toward Georgiana. With a sigh, she considered the possibility of a life of wedded bliss, with children at her feet and Mr. Bannerman at her side.

Mrs. Georgiana Bannerman, what a delightful sounding name. It rolls off the tongue most appealingly.

Abruptly the dream ended, as the horse snorted and she needed to, unwillingly, face reality. Was Sarah correct? Was she allowing herself to become attached to a boy so inappropriate that William would never allow him to court, much less extend an offer of marriage?

Robert Bannerman was beneath her, and poor, a bigger sin in her opinion. The family was not of the first, or even third, circles; only Mr. Bannerman's ownership of the Kingsdown estate afforded them recognition by Derbyshire society. Her failure to acknowledge these facts would change nothing and could instead cause her grief if she continued to think otherwise.

How far Sarah would go to win this contest was also a worrisome consideration. Georgiana knew, from past competitions, that Sarah had no scruples about what she would do to win a wager. The girl would not have any compunction about leading him on with the promise of herself as the prize, bewildering the poor boy until she had him fooled into the mistaken belief that she was as besotted as him. The broken heart she left him with would not bother her, but Sarah would boast of her conquest to one and all, regardless of the hurt she caused.

She could not allow Sarah to triumph, subjecting Robert to undeserved ridicule and derision. No, she would have to win out over her friend, a goal not easily accomplished. Sarah was a wily competitor, and one Georgiana did not take lightly.

Her decision surprised her, as did the direction her thoughts had taken. Though the possibility of physical or emotional harm to people because of their contests bothered her in the past, she had not allowed it to interfere with her plans.

To recognize feelings, either of attachment to Mr. Bannerman, or guilt at the chance of harming a newly found friendship with Louisa, was an unfamiliar experience for her.

Did this herald the beginning of Georgiana's conscience, and constitute a consideration she would need to be aware of in the future? Should that be the case, it might change her outlook on life. If she now needed to consider every possible untoward consequence of her actions, she might never again find enjoyment in anything!

Georgiana was not sure she liked the changes taking place in her world, but knew it would not avail her to put up futile resistance. With a sigh she left her reverie for another time and, looking up, saw she was closer to home than she realized. She stopped the horse and adjusted herself, throwing her leg over the horn of the saddle before prodding the animal onward, through the gate and into the Pemberley stable.

"Tend to the animal please, Jacob," said she to the stable hand and, handing him the reins, made her way to the manor.

Supper was a lonely affair, with William away in London and Mrs. Annesley her only company. After the completion of her meal, she retired to her room. She enjoyed a restless sleep that night, one filled with dreams of life, both wedded and otherwise. Central to each of her dreams was Mr. Robert Bannerman, to her delight and her dread.

She woke the next morning, out of sorts and exhausted, as if she had slept not a wink the entire night.

Elizabeth placed the pen on the desk and waited for the ink to dry before picking up her reply to Jane's letter. With a feeling of satisfaction for having responded with such alacrity, and amusement at the many additions she had made before finally completing her response, she read:

Kingsdown, June 21

"Dear Jane,"

"Thank you for the latest news from Longbourn. It would appear that even without the presence of Kitty and me, things are not boring. I can sympathize about your trip home from London, but be thankful you did not have Kitty in the carriage with you.

"Our sister is a dear, but she can be a bit too much to handle. Her curiosity about our destination was unrelenting and she asked every question possible, and some more than once!

"It is good to hear that Netherfield has a tenant at last, and that he is a friendly fellow. What could Papa mean about doing something for you? Have you asked him? I agree he can be a frustrating man to talk to, but he does not answer my questions with riddles, because I think he knows I will not accept a non answer from him.

"I love it here, as does Kitty. Our cousin Amelia is almost the same age, and they have become fast friends. Louisa is a charming young woman, and as personable as anyone I have ever met.

"She is not out yet, Lizzy! I know that sounds odd, because Lydia, though younger, has been out for almost two years now, but Uncle George says she is too young and, without a dowry, unlikely to attract the attention of a potential suitor, anyway. I convinced him to let her attend a ball at his neighbor's estate if I accepted responsibility for her preparation.

"The ball arrived and Louisa enjoyed herself immensely. In fact, the host even asked her to join him for a set on the dance floor. He is a charming man and very handsome.

"Kitty mentioned it looked to her like Louisa was smitten with the man, as he showed her consideration and treated her with polite deference. He even complimented her on her skill, which pleased the girl to no end.

"I also danced a set with him and, despite his declarations to the contrary, he is among the most talented of dancers. His steps were sure and his guiding hand, when he had occasion to place it on my arm, was considerate. I had to take him to task for telling me he had no ability when he so obviously told an untruth.

"He is easy to talk with about anything, at least that is what I suspect. This was our second meeting, as we had met while Louisa and I were walking close to the Kingsdown borders and he hailed us. We shared only a few sentences, but he was polite then as well.

"Louisa has decided she loved the ball so much that she wants to go to every one Uncle George will allow, which might not be many, as he is not much on attending such events himself.

"In closing, please remember to assist Papa with minding Lydia. It is good to know she has settled down somewhat, but be careful, as I would not put it past the girl to play the part of dutiful daughter only long enough for the restrictions to be eased. In fact, Kitty tells me Lydia said in her letter that this was her plan. Do not let her return to the same wild girl we left.

"As always, give my love to our parents and siblings,

"Love, Elizabeth."

With a smile, she folded the letter for mailing and sealed the edges with wax. If she knew her sister, Jane would read it and completely ignore everything except the description of her dance with Mr. Darcy.

Jane saw romance behind every tree and under every rock, and seemed to think it her duty to see Elizabeth married. Each potential bachelor, suitable or not, was marriage material, in Jane's mind. Elizabeth had lost count of how many men, in Hertfordshire or London, Jane suggested she should someday marry.

The description of Mr. Darcy, though vague, would be enough for her to envision Elizabeth wedded and with lots of healthy offspring. She would even take it upon herself to inform Elizabeth how many children she would bear her future husband and if they would be boys or girls!

Elizabeth did not mind hearing Jane's predictions, as her sister loved her dreams of romance, whether or not they revolved around herself. She found as much joy planning her sister's future as in dreaming about her own, and Elizabeth loved her even more because of it.

She extinguished the light, climbed into bed, and pulled the covers up around her until they almost covered her head. While it was summer, the cool nights had woken her, shivering, more than once. Turning on her side, she closed her eyes and drifted off to a sleep filled with dreams of Mr. Darcy.

CHAPTER XVII

Elizabeth left the house early the next morning, having awoken to a day resplendent with a brilliant blue sky, and scarcely a cloud above to block the sunshine. Her path this morning led her outside the boundaries of the property, winding through dense thickets and stands of nearby trees growing close enough to dampen the sunlight.

The land was awash with color, from the reddish pink of the honeysuckle growing unfettered amongst the trees to the bright yellow kingcups waving in the wind which crossed the fields. The scent of flowers, growing in profusion wherever she glanced, filled the air, and added to the joy she found in her morning exercise.

Elizabeth was loving her increasingly frequent walks past the grounds of the estate, along unfamiliar paths and woods. The unexplored parts of the countryside drew her on, encouraging her to forget all about the passage of time, and she participated in the activity willingly.

This was a more rugged landscape than that surrounding Longbourn, where the only elevation of any note was Oakham

Mount. On a whim, she started up an imposing rise, hoping to get a view of the countryside.

It was not as easy to climb these hills as it was at home, and by the time she got half of the way up the incline she had chosen, she was looking for a place to stop and recuperate. Just a few feet further up, she spied a large boulder buried in the side of the hill. Its level top offered someplace to sit and directly behind it stood a tree large and sturdy enough to rest her tired back against. Scrambling up onto it, she relaxed, enjoying the support of the tree trunk, with its branches that seemed like an embrace holding her safe from the cares of the world.

The view from her perch extended across Kingsdown and Pemberley to its north. Mr. Darcy's estate was larger than she had first thought, for try as she might, she could not find any of the fences marking its border. His land appeared to go on forever, bordered only by the Bannerman lands on its southern side, the breadth of which seemed a mere pittance compared to Pemberley.

Their properties when viewed together were similar, the patchwork of fields, both fallow and seeded, giving the land a checkerboard pattern interspersed with green squares of untended forest.

One of the biggest differences between the estates was the amount of woodland on each. Kingsdown boasted few trees, apart from the wooded area she had already explored and thick stands which grew along each side of the river marking the border with Pemberley.

Trees on the neighboring estate, in contrast, grew thickly in many areas, so much so that Elizabeth thought it would be a simple matter to lose her way in one of the larger stands. Those areas, viewed from her elevated position, were beautifully verdant, and she felt an almost irresistible urge to lose herself in them.

The trees bordered the road she and Kitty had travelled when they arrived for their visit, and continued toward Lambton, some five miles east. It would be so easy to slip undetected from the roadway into the forest, and who would ever know? It was not as if they were in the middle of London, with its throngs of people and cacophony of noise, where nothing one did escaped the notice of hundreds of witnesses. She could spend an afternoon alone, with only the forest and its woodland creatures for company. What an enjoyable way to pass the day!

Elizabeth's thoughts went to Pemberley's master, and the dance she *wished* she had shared with him. Closing her eyes, she pictured herself clasped in his embrace, the two of them gliding about the dance floor. The idea of participating in a dance of such decadence was as much thrilling as scandalous, and she gave herself over to the daydream.

I would love to waltz with Mr. Darcy, thought she as her imagination caught on the dance Charlotte had described seeing at a ball in Sussex last autumn. The tale she related, of couples entwined so close there was no space between them, took her breath away for a moment before a bird's trill interrupted her thoughts.

What is wrong with me? she wondered as the dream slipped away on the breeze and sanity came in to rebuke imagination's delicate hold on her.

I will never attract a man of Mr. Darcy's consequence; I am nothing but a poor country gentleman's daughter! He must have scores of young, beautiful women vying for his affection, and I am neither young enough, nor possessed of an overabundance of beauty. Enough of these ridiculous delusions that will never come to pass.

Elizabeth rose, shaking her head at the silly notions she had entertained. How she could have entertained such thoughts she did not know, but they would not be allowed to return. Resolutely, she resumed her course, determined to make her way to the summit before the morning was too far gone.

The path ahead of her was faint, as if most of those who followed it went no further than the boulder Elizabeth had rested upon. The incline became steeper, the effort required in moving forward driving all additional thoughts from her consciousness. Her steps slowed as the trail faded, until the only clue she had that the path still existed were the absence of flowers and the stunted weeds struggling fitfully to survive.

The top of the hill, or mountain as she considered the mound, was near, she hoped. With a determination born of an innate stubbornness to accept defeat, she pressed on, unwilling to surrender to the fatigue which threatened to render her exhausted legs useless.

What animals followed this path, she wondered. Surely it was not badgers, as they were not climbers by nature, preferring to hunt along the forest floor or to dig into rabbit warrens in search of their prey.

She might be following a fox trail, although she did not think so, as they were increasingly rare in England, having been hunted almost to extinction. Maybe she simply followed the same path as everyone else who wished to conquer this elevation.

With a last push, and the help of a conveniently placed stunted tree, Elizabeth pulled herself to the peak. Proud of her accomplishment, she looked out over the surrounding terrain, amazed anew at the vast expanse of the Pemberley property. This brought her thoughts once again to the estate's owner.

Mr. Darcy impressed her as a humble individual who, despite the extent of his estate, and the wealth it must earn him, did not seem to esteem himself above those of lesser standing. On each encounter he had been polite and soft spoken, complimenting her subtly while playing down his own importance or significance.

He gave no sign that he looked down on her, or the Bannerman family. In fact, he seemed to value her uncle's friendship, as she had noticed with his presence on the estate more than once. His comments to her uncle were not derogatory, at least not those which Elizabeth had overheard. As far as she could tell, to her uncle, Mr. Darcy was that rare combination of a good neighbor and valued friend, and his actions toward them spoke louder than any words he might utter, if that were possible.

She recalled their first meeting on the road beside his estate. As she remembered, he had been a perfect gentleman, friendly and inquisitive. He had maneuvered an introduction to her, but she did not fault the man for that; they were alone, and with nobody available to properly introduce her, Mr. Darcy had taken the initiative. He had departed immediately after, in the process removing any worry that he might be the type to press a perceived advantage, and for that she was grateful.

Elizabeth realized, with mild surprise, that her thoughts toward him were changing. Where she had at first been unable or unwilling to put much trust in Louisa's or Amelia's opinions of a man she did not know, she now regarded him favorably, based upon her own experiences.

Was it possible Mr. Sadler's betrayal had not hardened her heart completely, as she thought it might? Although his desertion still caused her heart to ache with the disappointment of what might have been, she thought she might, at last, let go of the harsh feelings she harbored for the man.

With her mind pleasantly engaged in thoughts of Pemberley's master, she began her climb down from the peak she stood atop.

The descent was no easier than her climb up, and Elizabeth went slowly, choosing her footing carefully. She had almost made it back to the boulder, where she planned to stop again, when a moment of inattention threatened to bring the day to a tragic end.

Elizabeth, busy expecting the glorious rest she would achieve when she gained the resting spot, forgot to pay attention to placing her foot, and her preoccupation almost cost her dearly. Her shoe slipped when a rock she had not noticed rolled under her foot as her weight came down on it.

Before she could shift her other foot to compensate, she pitched forward onto the path with enough force to dislodge additional pebbles from the trail. These loosened stones moved under the forward motion of Elizabeth's body, propelling her down the hillside at what seemed, to her, a breakneck speed.

With no time to plan, she reacted as her body rolled, hoping to escape significant injury, or her demise. Instinctively she thrust out her arm to grasp low-hanging branches, or anything she might use to halt her mad tumble to the bottom.

Just as she completed the first of what she knew would be many full rolls of her body, her hand met something sturdy and unyielding. With an effort, she thrust her other hand out and grasped what she hoped was a branch, though it was full of thorns.

Ignoring the pain, she gripped the woody appendage tightly, the sharp points piercing the skin on her hands as she fought her natural impulse to recoil. With her grip secured, her tumble down the hill halted, and she took stock of her situation.

Releasing her death grip, she saw what turned out to be a wild rosebush, growing in an unlikely, but thankfully lifesaving, position on the hillside. It was stunted, without a doubt due to where it had germinated, on the side of this incline with abundant rainfall, but lacking adequate sunshine.

She was grateful for this plant, the only one of its kind close enough for her to grab hold of. Without it, she thought she would not have stopped before reaching the bottom, where she might have lain for days before somebody found her.

As it was, her clothing was dirty, the soil ground into her skirt, and her shoes scuffed and stained. Her hands were sore, with small drops of blood evident where the thorns had pierced her skin. Other than the minor damage to her hands, though, she found no serious injuries.

When her racing heart had slowed she picked herself up, straightened her clothing, and resumed her descent, paying careful attention this time to where she placed her feet. Upon reaching the trail at the bottom, she set off for Kingsdown, although at a slower pace than her outbound walk.

The path led around the back of the stables and through the estate's orchard, where she noted, with some dismay, that Mr. Darcy and her uncle were engaged in a discussion.

Stopping before they noticed her presence, she waited for them to conclude their conversation and leave without seeing her disheveled condition.

"Your orchard looks to be in excellent condition," Mr. Darcy was saying to her uncle. "You should have a fine harvest in a few weeks."

"I have my son to thank for that," confessed Mr. Bannerman. "He takes pride in the apples that grow on these trees. Your harvest is probably as good as mine, if not better, as your orchard is larger."

"Unfortunately, I have very few apples to pick this year, and the ones I have are not worth eating. Apparently coddling moths infested my trees, and I could not stop them from destroying this year's crop completely."

"I hope you took your gardener to task; he should have noticed the larva's first hatching and taken steps to prevent them from burrowing into the apples and laying their eggs."

"I would castigate him, but he owns the estate, so it would have done nothing to help me."

Mr. Darcy laughed at Mr. Bannerman's look of confusion before continuing: "Thomas informed me of his plans to retire at the end of the season last year. I did not take the time to hire a replacement gardener, supposing that I could get along without him."

"Probably not the best decision you ever made," said Mr. Bannerman with a laugh of commiseration. "If you had come to me, I would have sent Robert over to tend to your infestation. He might have been able to kill enough of the pests to give you a harvest, in spite of the damage."

"How were you able to save the fruit? Nothing I tried had any effect on the pests."

"My brother-in-law, Miss Bennet's father, had the problem a few years ago. His solution was to mix ammonia, vinegar, and molasses, and hang it in containers from the trees.

"The larvae went for it, rather than the fruit, and could not escape the containers. All we had to do was to empty them when they filled with larvae, and replace the container in the trees. Pests like this are lazy; the easiest food source attracts them and makes them easy to kill."

"I regret not coming to you when the problem began. I might have been able to salvage some of my fruit crop."

Mr. Bannerman gave a derisive laugh: "You will get the chance in the spring. That is when the larvae will hatch again, and the cycle will resume. They might have finished for the year, but by this time they have laid their eggs, waiting for spring."

"My regret is there will be no fruit for the cook to preserve this year, and I know our supply is getting low, as she mentioned the fact to me yesterday."

"Well then, you can have some of mine. While my harvest will be smaller this year, it appears there will be enough to satisfy the needs of both estates. I will be happy to share what I have when the apples are ready for picking."

Elizabeth watched as Mr. Darcy did not respond, seeming to be at a loss for words. His apparent reticence to speak took her by surprise, for she had assumed that he would be accustomed to offers of this sort from those who wanted to ingratiate themselves with the county's wealthiest citizen.

"I am not sure what to say," responded he at last. "Georgiana and I appreciate your kindness, but we do not want to deprive you or your family of something you had planned on helping feed everyone this winter, and after the harvest is complete."

"Think nothing of it. We have enough, and plenty to spare. While I would, in a normal year, sell the extra fruit, it is not the difference between feast and famine. Please do not assume that your acceptance will put you in my debt. Think of it as one neighbor helping another."

Mr. Darcy smiled and extended his hand to Mr. Bannerman., saying: "I will gratefully accept your kind offer." Elizabeth watched the two gentlemen shake hands in agreement.

"If there is ever anything you need, ask. If it is in my power, I will do my best to return the favor."

Elizabeth grew uncomfortable listening to the private conversation, which they had not invited her to join. She decided, in the hope of escaping notice, to make her way behind the stable and into the house through the garden. Lifting her skirts to make movement easier, she took her first step, only to be spotted when her uncle lifted his head at the same moment and saw her crossing the path.

"Elizabeth, I did not see you there. Are you at the beginning or end of your walk this morning?"

"I am returning to the house," said she, "but had hoped to escape notice until I had the chance to clean myself and change my clothes."

Mr. Darcy looked her over, his expression one of mild humor until she saw his gaze fasten on her hands, whereupon he spoke with some concern: "You injured yourself. Did you run into a problem, and are you in need of medical attention? I will have my physician, Mr. Tate, sent for to make sure you are not badly hurt. You should not be walking around in your condition. Let me help you find a comfortable seat."

"I am fine," laughed Elizabeth, raising her hands to stop Mr. Darcy, who was hurrying toward her. "My only injury is to my pride. I took a fall when coming down the hill and rolled in every bit of dirt on the incline."

"But your hands are bloody." Mr. Darcy pointed to the red spots visible on both palms. "You should have them looked at; in case a more serious injury exists. Mr. Tate is a fine doctor, one of the best I have met. Let me summon him so you can put your worries to rest."

"Thank you, but no. I am fine, Mr. Darcy, other than the extreme embarrassment I am suffering at present. The blood you see is from the rose bush I grabbed to stop my fall. When I clean myself, the blood will wash away. There is no further injury, I assure you. If there were, I doubt I could have made it back."

"Which hill did you climb, if I may be so bold as to ask?" said he, to which Elizabeth turned and pointed along the path to the tallest peak in the district.

"I decided I wanted to view the countryside from the highest place around. I made it to the top without a problem, but I became distracted on the way back down. My foot slipped, and I fell part of the way to the bottom."

Mr. Darcy regarded Elizabeth with an expression that seemed to say he did not believe her explanation. He studied the hill, then looked at her, then turned back to the hill before shaking his head and facing her again.

"Are you sure you climbed *that* hill? Could you be mistaken, and you climbed the one on either side?"

"I know which hill I climbed, Mr. Darcy, as well as which one I slid back down on. Is there some reason you doubt me?"

"Forgive me, Miss Bennet, but not even I have climbed that hill, and if I decided to, I would never try doing it alone. As you said, it is the tallest in the neighborhood. It is also the steepest. For you to climb it alone was dangerous, and your appearance proves it.

"If you wish to do so again, please take someone with you. I would hate to see you hurt anew. That hill is part of the Pemberley estate, so I would bear responsibility if you were seriously injured. I am not demanding that you stay off my property, but you need to be more careful. All I ask is that you take proper precautions, such as bringing a friend along for assistance."

"I am sorry, Mr. Darcy. I did not realize I had trespassed. I assumed your estate did not extend to the other side of the path."

"Mr. Darcy's holdings are extensive," answered her uncle. "They surround Kingsdown almost completely."

"I have not seen you since the ball." Mr. Darcy's attempt to change the subject was obvious, at least to Elizabeth. "Did you and Miss Bannerman enjoy the evening?"

"We did, although Louisa enjoyed it more than me."

"What was there about it that disappointed you?"

"Nothing at all," laughed Elizabeth. "I only meant that because I did not know any of your guests, I did not visit with as many people as I would have if the ball had been in Hertfordshire. The evening lacked nothing, and everyone I saw seemed to enjoy themselves immensely.

"Thank you for dancing with my cousin. Louisa and I appreciate your kindness in asking her to join you for a set; it helped her feel less awkward. When you brought her back at the end, she was almost giddy with excitement. Because of you, she experienced a night she will never forget."

"It was the least I could do for her. I still remember the first time I attended an event like this. I was so nervous and out of place that I wanted to find somewhere to hide. If my father had not been there to help me, I might never have attended a second one."

Turning to Mr. Bannerman, Mr. Darcy gave a quick bow and said: "I must go, but thank you for your kind offer. My kitchen staff will praise your name to the stars. Goodbye, Mr. Bannerman, Miss Bennet."

Turning on his heel, Mr. Darcy walked to the front of the house, where Elizabeth saw a horse standing and patiently waiting for its master. Mr. Darcy mounted the animal and, with a wave of his hand, gently touched his heels to the horse's flanks. The animal started for the road, where it turned toward the Pemberley estate, as if by prearranged agreement.

"You made a good impression on him," chuckled Mr. Bannerman when the man left. "He has not been this talkative in all the years I have known him, and he was certainly not as free with his speech before you arrived."

"Your imagination is getting the best of you," said Elizabeth. "Mr. Darcy is a friendly, personable man. He is easy to talk to and seems genuinely interested in the well being of his neighbors.

"I think his reason for visiting was to talk about the problems with his orchard. From what I could see, he was surprised and grateful when you offered to share your harvest with him. If you are looking for a reason for his sudden eloquence, your charity is more likely the cause."

"You have not known the man awfully long. This is not the first occasion we spoke about various problems we share as estate owners. I have visited Mr. Darcy at Pemberley more than once to discuss issues I faced. In every instance, Mr. Darcy said what he needed to, but nothing more. He was not unfriendly, nor overly gregarious.

"Not until you arrived did he share what for him must be personal viewpoints and experiences. He is paying more attention to you than to any other woman in the county."

"I did not notice Mr. Darcy showing any more interest in me than anyone else, Uncle. You are seeing things that do not exist."

Mr. Bannerman looked at Elizabeth as if studying her for the first time. Finally, he smiled and with a shake of his head, stated: "We shall see, Elizabeth. Only time will tell."

CHAPTER XVIII

When Elizabeth woke, she was sore everywhere. It seemed every muscle in her body ached, and bruises covered her arms and legs. They curtailed her morning walk, as she had no desire to suffer the agony each movement called forth, so she spent the day in the sitting-room, involving herself in some needlework to pass the time.

To add further insult to her injuries, the perfect weather mocked her misstep of the day before. She was sure she heard Mother Nature chiding her for carelessness and telling her not to be so foolish again. She then imagined she could hear a derisive taunt, daring her to attack the hill just to prove she could, in fact, make her way to the top and down again without incident.

By the end of the day Elizabeth had decided her walks would resume on the morrow, aches and pains be damned.

She rose the following morning with a groan, as her discomfort seemed to increase overnight instead of easing. Determined to abide by her choice, she dressed and made her way slowly down the stairs and into the cloakroom. There she chose a light wrap, and a worn but sturdy walking stick to lean on as she followed the path.

"May we come with you?" asked Louisa who, along with Kitty, had descended the stairs while Elizabeth was making her preparations. "It has been a while, and I miss the conversations we have as we walk; you always teach me something new, whether or not you plan to."

"Please do. Your company is always welcome. I will wait for you outside."

Elizabeth stepped out of the door and let the sun warm her face. It was another beautiful morning, although clouds in the distance suggested rain might arrive before the day ended.

"We are ready," said Louisa, coming out of the house with Kitty behind. "Where were you planning to go today?"

"I wanted to follow the same path I did previously. It is a lovely trail, and I want to explore it further, although I will probably stop frequently to rest; I am still sore from my fall two days ago."

"We should stay closer to the estate," suggested Kitty, "so you do not tire yourself. If you do too much, you might be in more pain tomorrow than you are today."

"Let me worry about that," laughed Elizabeth as they set off, passing through the gate to the path. "You just worry about keeping up."

The walk proved excellent medicine for her. As they began, Elizabeth's pace was brisk, despite protests from her aggrieved muscles, begging her to slow her steps while they went back to sleep. She ignored the stabs of pain and maintained her speed, settling into a rhythm which lulled her muscles into what she considered an agreement to cooperate, so long as she asked no more of them.

"How far did you get before you fell?" asked Louisa when they passed the fence, showing the border between Pemberley and Kingsdown.

"It is a little ahead of us. Why did you not tell me that all our walks outside your father's estate were on Mr. Darcy's property? If I had known, I might not have been so impertinent that morning we met him on the road."

"Forgive me, Elizabeth, but I assumed you knew. Everyone in Derbyshire knows the Pemberley estate goes on forever. I forgot that you, as a visitor, would be unaware we were trespassing."

"Trespassing?" said Kitty, a worried look upon her face. "Maybe we should go back; I do not want Mr. Darcy angry because we walked somewhere we had no business going."

"You worry too much," laughed Louisa. "Mr. Darcy does not care if we use these paths; they are for the enjoyment and use of anybody, as long as we show the proper respect for his land. It would upset him if he found us hunting without permission, or cutting trees or doing anything that might damage his property, but we can walk as far and as often as we like."

"He told me much the same thing after my accident," added Elizabeth, turning to address her cousin. "The man almost seems too good to be true. He is the perfect neighbor, ready and willing to lend a hand when necessary, but content to keep his nose out of other's business, unless that is all for show."

"That might be the best description of him," agreed Louisa. "Father likes it that he does not interfere in something not of his concern, but if an issue affects him or Georgiana, he will not quit until the matter is resolved."

"That is definitely something to keep in mind," said Elizabeth with a laugh. "I will be careful not to cross the man, or get on his bad side; the consequences might be serious."

Conversation lagged as Elizabeth focused her attention on their surroundings. The realization that all her walks outside the Kingsdown fences were on the Pemberley estate was a sobering thought, and one which caused her to examine Mr. Darcy in a new light.

He was not at all what she would have expected of a man with such enormous land holdings and apparent wealth. Her experience with any of the wealthier families in Hertfordshire had made her wary of anyone in like circumstances. In her experience they did not associate with those of lesser means or standing, and when they did out of necessity, their self-importance condescending manner was off-putting.

Mr. Darcy was the exact opposite, polite and unassuming, almost to a fault. His demeanor was friendly, and he seemed to take an honest interest in her uncle and the problems he might struggle with.

From her observations, he did not hesitate to offer aid, or ask for advice if he encountered a problem he could not solve on his own. To have a neighbor who offered help without expecting something in return was a rarity to Elizabeth, and something that elevated him in her opinion.

"That is the hill I climbed, and came back down quicker," said Elizabeth, pointing to her left. "I am still sore, and I can hear it laughing at me."

"And well it should," chuckled Louisa. "That is Pemberley Mount, the tallest in Derbyshire."

"Mr. Darcy told me as much, although he did not mention they named it for his estate."

"Father says they named the estate for the hill, not the other way around, although I am not familiar with the history of either."

"I wonder if Mr. Darcy knows," said Elizabeth. "It might be an interesting story."

"He might tell you about it, if you catch him in the right mood," suggested Louisa. "He is sometimes reticent in talking about his family history, or his estate. His wealth might be part of the reason. Father says he does not like to discuss that sort of thing, especially with strangers."

"I will keep that in mind," decided Elizabeth as the group entered the Kingsdown yard once again, "and we are back none too soon, if those clouds are any sign."

A peal of thunder startled everyone, its crack echoing off the stable and surrounding buildings. With a shriek, Louisa and Kitty ran for the house, with Elizabeth following at a more sedate pace.

No sooner had she entered the house than the first fat drops splattered against the dusty drive. Elizabeth watched from the sitting-room window as they grew in number, from the first few tentative droplets to a wall of water that looked, for all intents and purposes, as if the heavens had opened.

The boom of thunderclaps shook the house as the force of the downpour seemed to increase. Each was louder than the last, while the rain continued to fall with a ferocity unlike anything Elizabeth had ever seen.

A series of short, sharp, raps came at the height of the storm, which was repeated after a half minute. Again the sound came, almost blending with the noise of the thunder, and the slap of the rain hitting the roof, and pounding against the windows. When it sounded a third time, they dispatched the butler to the front door to investigate, as the noise seemed to come from that part of the house.

The door was opened to reveal the form of a bedraggled young man, drenched from the rain, and huddled in the entrance alcove against the storm, although his attempts to find shelter were futile.

"Let him in, before he drowns," directed Mr. Bannerman of the butler, who hesitated at the unexpected sight.

.or heaven's sake let him in!" said he again, grasping ᐟering young man to pull him inside and slamming the ɔn as the threshold was clear.

.t in the world are you doing out in such a storm?" asked he o. .t turned out to be a boy who, on closer inspection, looked as though he was barely Amelia's age. "Have you no respect for Mother Nature, that you would think it wise to venture out of doors in weather like this? And how did you arrive? I saw no horse, unless it was smart enough to shelter in the stable."

"Mr. Darcy sent me with an invitation," said the dripping visitor, reaching into a pouch, saturated with oil to make it watertight, and coming back out with an envelope which he thrust at Mr. Bannerman. "I am to wait for a response before returning."

"You are going nowhere until this storm ends," stated Mr. Bannerman.

Turning to the butler, he gave instructions to clean the lad up and give him some dry clothes, with his own wrung out and set over the fire to dry.

When the messenger was led away, Mr. Bannerman opened the envelope the boy had been so eager to give him. Inside, folded to fit, was a piece of paper which, when opened fully, revealed itself to be an invitation, as the young lad had claimed.

Mr. Bannerman read it through and looking up, saw their expectant faces, all of which, Elizabeth knew, were curious about the contents. Surely it was important, or Mr. Darcy would not have sent his servant out into such a deluge.

"Hmm," she heard Mr. Bannerman mumble before returning to the missive to read it through a second time.

"What does it say, George?" asked Mrs. Bannerman from the sitting-room. "And who sent it?"

"Mr. Darcy is inviting us to dine with him at Pemberley tomorrow evening," said Mr. Bannerman. "He wants to express appreciation for the kindness I showed in offering him some of Kingsdown's apples the other day."

"Do you think we should accept? With Elizabeth and Kitty visiting, it might be better to thank him for the offer and regretfully decline."

"The invitation is for the entire family, not just you and I, Rebecca. He wants all of us to join him. He tells me his sister will be there, and he thinks she would like Amelia and Louisa there as well."

"What a gracious gesture," said Mrs. Bannerman. "To thank us for something as simple as the offer of an apple or two is the mark of a true gentleman. Are you going to accept?"

"I think so unless you would rather I did not. I am honored and surprised by the gesture. This is unusual for Mr. Darcy, so unusual in fact that I cannot remember ever receiving anything like this in all the time we have been neighbors.

"It is possible he is grateful for your offer. You were under no obligation, and I cannot imagine he thought you were. Your gift was from one neighbor to another in need, and this is his way of telling you he recognizes your charity and acknowledges your kindness. It cannot hurt to have someone like him on your side."

"As I told him then, he is under no obligation to me for something as simple as a few apples. If I need his assistance, I know he will not hesitate to help."

"I agree, but Mr. Darcy is a powerful ally and a friend other people will note."

"If you insist," said he, starting toward the study. "I am going to prepare my response to Mr. Darcy's letter. If his messenger reappears before I finish, tell him to wait."

Soon enough, the messenger, dried and warm, received the response and was sent back to Pemberley, the rain having subsided.

The next day was busy. Elizabeth's aunt asked her to instruct Louisa and Amelia, as well as Christopher, in the manners they needed to learn before sharing a meal with someone like Mr. Darcy. She sent Mr. Bannerman to do the same with Robert, which he did, although begrudgingly.

At last the time arrived to depart, and the family boarded the carriage for the journey to Pemberley, although Robert had to ride beside the driver, as there was not room in the cabin for everyone.

Georgiana was not looking forward to this evening's meal; were it not for the attendance of Robert Bannerman, she might have tried to beg off, using the excuse of an upset stomach. When informed, though, that he was to be among the party, she smiled and summoned her maid, instructing the girl to prepare her in as flattering a manner as possible.

She was at the entrance with William when the carriage arrived, and waited for the family to quit the conveyance and enter the house, which they did, everyone that is except Robert. She looked around almost frantically for the missing guest and was relieved to see him climbing down from a seat beside the driver. Brushing the road dust from his clothing, he made his way into the entrance and stopped before William, who extended a hand in greeting.

"Welcome to Pemberley, Mr. Bannerman. It is so good to see you."

The younger Mr. Bannerman, it appeared, was unsure of how to respond to William's gesture, as he stood there without moving, looking at his father as if to ask what he should do. To her surprise, Georgiana felt discomfort akin to what she thought he might be suffering.

"Mr. Bannerman," was her greeting as she stepped forward quickly to welcome the young man. "How good of you to come to dinner tonight."

With a look of mild reproach for her brother, Georgiana guided Miss Bennet and Louisa to the sitting-room. Mr. Bannerman, she saw, followed at a respectable distance.

"It surprised me to hear your messenger knocking on my door in the middle of the storm last night," remarked Mr. Bannerman to William when all had chosen comfortable seats. "He appeared to have fallen into the ocean; even though the coast is nowhere near Derbyshire."

"I was embarrassed when he returned told me what had happened," said William with a laugh. "I had seen the clouds gathering and suggested he might want to wait, but the lad assured me he could make it before the storm hit. Please accept both my thanks and his for tending to him like you did."

"Think nothing of it. I could not let him leave while it was still raining, so I let him dry before releasing him again."

"He had nothing but praise for you when he got back," laughed William, "so much in fact that I had to retire to my library to get free of him."

The call to supper interrupted their conversation, which did not resume until they sat, and the meal was well underway.

"Thank you again for sharing your apples," said William. "The cook will put the fruit to good use making jams and jellies, and the occasional pie, I hope."

"I was happy to be of assistance, Mr. Darcy, but I would caution you to wait for the harvest before you thank me too profusely. While the crop looks good, an early frost or any number of other misfortunes can lessen the yield, or ruin the fruit completely."

"I agree, but wanted to at least voice my gratitude for your kindness. You were under no obligation to make it, but you did anyway, and I am in your debt."

"What are neighbors for if we cannot come to each other's assistance in times of need?"

The conversation carried on in that vein for what seemed, to Georgiana, an interminable amount of time, with neither of the men apparently willing to let the other voice the last measure of gratitude.

Although William's discussion was with Mr. Bannerman, Georgiana could see his attention focused on Miss Bennet. It looked to her as though he was noting each forkful of food she placed in her mouth, and paying attention, it seemed, to every drop of wine that passed her lips.

Was her brother losing his heart to Miss Bennet, someone who, according to Louisa, was merely the daughter of a poor country gentleman, a man who had no standing of any note outside of his home county?

She was not sure what she thought about this latest development. William had, until Miss Bennet arrived, been able to fend off the wiles and schemes of many designing women, who wanted nothing more than the fame and fortune they would achieve in marrying a Darcy. None had caught his attention, and certainly not any amount of interest, but here was a woman who, in doing absolutely nothing, was able to capture all of William's consideration, to the exclusion of everything else.

"How are you feeling today?" he was asking her. "I hope you are giving up mountain climbing, at least until you return home."

"I confess I was sore," responded she with a bit of a laugh, "but all it took was a couple of days of moderately strenuous walking to heal my aches. By this morning I was almost as good as new. My pride, however, is still recovering."

"To look at you tonight, it is not apparent that you suffered any mishap at all. Your powers of recovery are admirable."

"I ascribe it to clean living and healthy pursuits. It is easy to return to full health when you start from that position, no matter what might befall you."

"I will try to remember your words of wisdom, Miss Bennet. It sounds like advice that more of us should heed."

Was she as blithely ignorant of William's attention as she appeared to be? How was it possible she did not see the look of rapture that fastened itself to his face with every syllable she uttered? Well, two could play that game.

Georgiana cast her gaze along the table to where Robert Bannerman sat, the look on his face suggesting a level of boredom that threatened to put him to sleep. With a slight movement, accompanied by a sigh of moderate volume, she got him to look at her before looking quickly away, as if caught in some immoral or untoward act.

"Do you take walks, Mr. Bannerman?" asked she of the lad while batting her eyelids in what she considered her most seductive manner.

From the rapidity with which his eyes opened, she could tell she had caught his interest. As he stumbled to supply an appropriate comment, she knew he was disturbed and unsure of himself or even where he was at that point in time.

"I walk the cows, I mean I visit the horses. No, I mean that I have too much work to do and cannot spare the time for morning walks," said he, his face turning red with embarrassment.

"It must be a daunting task, managing an estate like Kingsdown," responded she, choosing not to call attention to his discomfort. "Every time I visit Louisa and Miss Bennet, you are hard at work. You must get so tired, having to work from sunup to sundown every day of the week."

"With adequate planning and efficient habits I can rest a few minutes in the middle of the day," said Robert, responding to her praise, she was glad to see.

Mr. Bannerman cleared his throat, prompting the boy to hastily add: "And my father works the estate also. He directs the work, and I make sure it gets done."

"I am impressed with your willingness to work so hard, day after day," offered she, aiming her brightest smile at the hapless young man. "It is a habit to be admired."

Looking back toward William, Georgiana could see that he was watching her, a bemused expression on his countenance.

"Do you not agree, William? Mr. Bannerman and his father are not afraid of work, no matter the difficulty. I think that is to be commended, don't you?"

"Yes it is, Georgiana, although most men of my acquaintance would prefer to have no fuss made over their efforts to survive."

"It is not a fuss, William, to acknowledge Mr. Bannerman's love for what he does."

"I see," said William, placing his fork onto the plate, which was empty of food.

The meal complete, the men retired to the library for some after dinner glasses of port. To his surprise, if his countenance was a reliable indicator, they invited Robert to join them, which he did without hesitation.

"I think he appreciated your compliment," said Louisa when the men disappeared. "He rarely says much, but the fact you noticed him is important."

"He is worthy of the praise," insisted Georgiana. "We should recognize any man who is not afraid to work."

She spent the rest of the evening engaged in small talk, while wondering how Robert Bannerman was enjoying the evening in the company of his father and William. After an hour, the men reappeared and Mr. Bannerman, making his apologies for ending the evening so early, gathered his family and prepared to board the carriage for their return to Kingsdown.

"I had a wonderful time," averred Louisa before entering the coach with her sister and cousins. "Would you like to visit? We usually have nothing planned and it would be nice to spend a day together."

Georgiana paused as if pondering the invitation before responding: "I agree. Would early next week be soon enough, say, Tuesday?"

"It would be perfect," was Louisa's enthusiastic answer.

"I will see you then," said Georgiana, to a smile from the girl.

And hopefully Robert as well, thought she as the carriage left the property.

"You seemed to be enjoying yourself," remarked Darcy on the walk back into the house. "It looked to me as if Mr. Bannerman had caught your attention."

"Oh William," sighed Georgiana, alarmed that he might discover the motive behind her actions, and trying to divert any suspicions he might have. "I was trying to be a gracious host. Did I do something wrong?"

"No, you were fine, although maybe a little too attentive to the young man. I would not want him to get the wrong idea. He is, if the rumors are correct, somewhat inexperienced with members of the fairer sex, and might take your friendship as something more than what you intended."

"I will make sure that does not happen," said she, thankful that her brother was not privy to her innermost thoughts and desires.

Chapter XIX

Georgiana grasped the driver's extended hand and allowed him to help her into the carriage. Seating herself as comfortably as she was able, she signalled him, upon which he put the conveyance into motion. The ride to Kingsdown was a short one, and better accomplished, in her opinion, astride one of the Pemberley horses. She did not, however, want to give the wrong impression to the Bannerman family, Robert especially, so it limited her choice of transportation to this carriage.

He had presented himself well at the dinner party, she thought as the coach jostled and swayed along the lane. Despite moments of confusion and embarrassment, some of them because of remarks she made, his comportment remained that of a gentleman.

His father raised him well. He was respectful throughout the evening, disproving the gossip Sarah and I used to spread about his lack of intelligence or sophistication. Maybe we were too quick to judge him because of his unwillingness to engage in small talk or silly attempts to demean someone. I might have misjudged the boy. Unfortunately, I encouraged others to do the same.

By the time the carriage made the turn into Kingsdown, she was almost ready to beg forgiveness for sins she did not even know she had committed.

When the coach stopped, she waited for the driver to open the door and hand her down. To her surprise, it opened almost immediately to reveal Louisa, her face beaming, and the excitement clear in her voice.

"Welcome, Georgiana. I thought you might change your mind and decide not to visit today, but here you are."

"Why would you think such a thing?" asked she, climbing from the carriage without waiting for the driver's help. "We made an appointment for today, and I always honor them. What kind of person would I be if I agreed to visit and then canceled for no good reason? It would not please William to learn I had done something like that."

"Forgive me," said Louisa, her face coloring in embarrassment. "I did not mean to impugn your character. It is just that your friendship surprised me. I know I am not well regarded in Lambton by many of my age, and have only a few acquaintances."

"I refuse to let other's opinions affect my choice of friends, so do not worry. And if, in the future, I hear of anyone making disparaging remarks, I will not let them stand. We are friends, and that is what friends do for each other."

"I know few that I can call friends, and none I would regard as close enough to invite to Kingsdown. In my experience, it is easy to break appointments without notice beforehand, or apology afterward. If you had not come, I would have understood and accepted your decision."

"As I said, we are friends, Louisa. Never forget that. Since I am here, what have you planned for the afternoon?"

"I hoped we might spend some time in the sitting-room. I can ask the cook to prepare some tea. There is no fruit, as the apples are not ripe enough to harvest, but she made scones this morning and I can ask her to set some out for us."

"The day is so beautiful," pleaded Georgiana. "Why not spend it outside in the sun? It will not be too long before summer passes, and the weather turns cool again."

"A wonderful idea. Let me tell Mother, so she does not wonder where we are."

Georgiana watched as Louisa almost skipped into the house, joy evident in her movements. She had, in the history of her friendship with Sarah, never seen the girl as happy to visit as Louisa appeared to be each time Georgiana called.

Sarah seemed almost resigned to the inevitability of Georgiana's company, although she supposedly thought of themselves as the best of friends. It was common for her to complain about Georgiana's choice of clothing, her plans, or her interests, whether Sarah shared them or not. That Georgiana showed enthusiasm for a subject or activity seemed enough sometimes for Sarah to decide that she cared not a bit for it.

Was it time to reconsider her relationship with her and pursue a closer friendship with Louisa? Georgiana suspected the girl would welcome the companionship, as she seemed starved for attention, even as superficial as that which Georgiana offered.

Her eagerness to please was something Georgiana might have considered pathetic as recent as a month ago, before she had taken time to get to know the girl better. Now she regarded her as a nice, refined girl who did not deserve the scorn and ridicule she and Sarah, along with the rest of her usual group of companions, had heaped upon her.

Louisa might be a valuable friend, or maybe even a trusted confidante, although it would take time for their relationship to progress to that extent. In the meantime, freedom from the constant competitions she and Sarah engaged in would be a welcome relief.

"Would it be acceptable if Lizzy joined us?" asked Louisa, pulling Georgiana's thoughts away from her contemplations. Beside her stood Miss Bennet, apparently smiling at Georgiana's confusion.

"Lizzy?"

"Sorry, Elizabeth," giggled Louisa. "Kitty calls her Lizzy more than Elizabeth, and I let it slip without thinking first."

"What a delightful alternative. I think it suits you, Miss Bennet."

"Please, Miss Darcy, call me Elizabeth, or Lizzy, as Louisa has adopted the name Kitty uses. We are friends, so we can forget the formalities, if you agree."

"I do, Lizzy," laughed Georgiana, "although I confess it will take some time before I am comfortable calling you by that name."

"Either is acceptable, so you may use whatever version you choose."

"Thank you, I will. Now, where should we spend our time? Is there a favorite area that you prefer, or a certain path you follow when you walk? I understand, Elizabeth, that you do it almost every day."

"I do, although most of my hiking has been on the Pemberley estate. You have some of the prettiest scenery; it almost puts my neighborhood around Longbourn to shame."

"Do you have a favorite trail," wondered Georgiana, "or do you wander, without a destination in mind?"

"I like to explore the paths around Pemberley Mount, but that is too far for us to follow today."

"What is to stop us from walking that way until we decide to turn back?" suggested Georgiana. "That way we can enjoy the weather and get some exercise at the same time. I confess I am not familiar with any of these paths because I do not spend a lot of my time walking. I prefer to ride when I can, on a horse or in a carriage does not matter."

"But riding does not let you fully admire the scenery, or experience the joys of nature," opined Elizabeth, leading her companions onto the trail. "I cannot imagine life without my daily walks. It would be too boring if it were not for these regular excursions to cheer me up."

Louisa laughed: "I bet Mr. Darcy could alleviate your boredom, and I suspect he would be more than willing."

"Mr. Darcy is a friend to Uncle, nothing more."

"From the way he was watching you at supper the other night, his interest extends to more than a simple friendship with my father."

"Nonsense, Louisa. You are letting your imagination get away on you. Georgiana did not come to Kingsdown to hear you carry on about an interest he does not share for a person he barely knows."

"Sorry, Elizabeth, but this conversation is the most interesting one I have heard in days. Go on, Louisa, what were you saying about William's interest?"

Louisa was embarrassed, if the color rising in her face was any indication: "I did not mean to spread rumors. I noticed Mr. Darcy seemed to pay attention to Lizzy that night, more so than he paid to anyone else."

Georgiana paused as if trying to recall the night in question before saying: "I believe she is correct. Although I did not notice at the time, I seem to recall that William appeared to be interested in anything you said that night.

"In fact, I can remember having to repeat myself more than once to get his attention. At the time I assumed that, as the host, he was concentrating on more important things, and that may be true. Of course, it would also be true if the most important object of his attention is you."

"Enough, both of you," laughed Elizabeth. "Mr. Darcy has no reason for this supposed interest in me, and I claim no interest in him. He is your neighbor, Louisa, and that is the end. There must be something else we can find to talk about, and besides, we should go back to Kingsdown before it gets too late."

Elizabeth turned around before the others could object, and the trio retraced their path. Georgiana was glad to follow, having wondered if she would have the chance to see or talk to Robert before she had to leave for home again.

As luck would have it, she saw him coming out of the orchard as they entered the property.

"Good afternoon, Mr. Bannerman," called she, causing him to slow and wait for them. "It is nice to see you again. Are you enjoying the day so far? The weather is certainly in our favor, not like last week."

"It is fine, I guess," said he without looking at her. To Georgiana, it appeared he was looking for an excuse to escape to the safety of the stable, where he would not need to carry on a conversation.

She, however, determined to press the advantage gained at the previous week's gathering. By the time the family departed that night, his self-confidence had arrived, and he was responding to her comments and questions with more than a word or two in reply. Georgiana was resolved that their hard won rapport would not surrender to the return of any innate shyness.

"William asked me to express his gratitude for your offer to share this year's harvest from your orchard. It was an unexpected gift that he appreciates more than he can say. Few neighbors would have been so generous, and he wants you to know that he is in your debt."

Her compliment provoked a reaction as he lifted his chin and, for the first time, looked her in the eyes while gracing her with a smile. The act, so simple and genuine, caused her breath to catch momentarily in her throat. Quickly she looked away, hoping he had not noticed her response, but when her eyes returned to him, she saw an expression of comprehension in what she had revealed.

After a moment, which seemed to her to last an eternity, he said: "The harvest looks good this year, even with the amount we lost at the start of the season. If the weather holds, we may be picking apples by the end of next week."

Georgiana heard his words, but they sounded to her as though he was reciting something already written and practiced. While he spoke she could feel his eyes studying her, as though his mere presence enabled him to peer into the deepest portions of her soul, and to see things she kept hidden from all.

"It cannot be easy to see the results of your arduous work gone so quickly. Your charity has impressed William, and he is not likely to forget what you have done for him, and for me."

"The decision was not mine to make, but if he had consulted me, I would have agreed with my father. It is not a hard choice; we often get an abundance of fruit from the orchard, so why not give some to Mr. Darcy? Father is confident that, if our roles were reversed, your brother would not hesitate to make us an offer just as generous, and it is not as though he demanded most of the crop."

"But to sacrifice your efforts, only to see a good portion of what you have nurtured through the season given away, must be troubling. It is because of your tireless work in caring for those trees that there is anything to harvest. I know from discussions with Pemberley's previous gardener, keeping a large orchard healthy is not an effortless task. There are branches to prune on every tree, and vines that would, without proper attention, rob the tree of water and stunt its growth.

"The parasites you battle are relentless and require continuous vigilance to keep at bay.

"Then when the fruit, that you labored so hard to protect and grow, is given away without notice, must be difficult to accept."

"What you are describing is a part of life, something I assume Mr. Darcy, as master of Pemberley, contends with every day. There are fields to sow in the spring and harvest in the fall, animals to feed and water, and orchards to watch over. The hardships you talk about are not onerous, rather the solving of problems is satisfying, and gives me, at least, a sense of accomplishment, not of defeat.

"If you were to ask your brother, I would wager that his response would be the same as mine. There is no shame in an honest day's work; the shame is in giving less than your best. If trouble or failure discourages you enough to quit, you should find something else to occupy your time."

Georgiana replied, in what she hoped was an alluring manner: "You are a unique individual, Mr. Bannerman. To hold such a logical point of view, and then to defend it so capably, is refreshing, and encountered too rarely."

"There is nothing to defend. The facts are undeniable. My refusal to accept them does not change anything, so why would I attempt such a foolish diversion?"

Though his statement was simple, Georgiana could see her praise affected him. As before, his posture was erect, displaying none of the fatigue he was probably feeling when their conversation began. His voice was firm, with a more pleasing resonance whenever he spoke. Each time they met, he seemed to adopt that tone of voice sooner, and she liked it.

"As much as I enjoyed my visit," said Georgiana, "I should be on my way home before William sends a search party out to find me."

"Would he really do that?" asked Louisa incredulously as they walked toward the Darcy carriage. "He must love you a lot, if he will go to such extremes to ensure your safety."

"I was joking, at his expense," she laughed. "William is not that protective, although sometimes he reminds me of a mother hen. It is just that he is at home so seldom I try to return before he worries. I am lucky to have a brother like him and try not to take his concerns too lightly."

"I stand by my judgement," stated Louisa. "Mr. Darcy sounds to me like a perfect brother."

"He is as close to perfect as he can be," agreed Georgiana, giving her hand to the driver, who helped her into the cabin and closed the door behind her.

Leaning out the cabin window, she called out to them: "You and Elizabeth should come to Pemberley next time. I will send an invitation in a day or so if you like."

"Please do," said Louisa. "We would love to visit you at home again."

With a wave, Georgiana settled into the seat as the driver put the horses in motion. She had enjoyed her visit, which did not surprise her. She considered every visit to Kingsdown well spent, and today was no exception. Louisa and all her family, including her cousins, were friendly people. She could see no artifice in any, a trait so unusual it surprised her.

To her knowledge, not one of the Bannermans had spoken an untruth, unlike her usual companions, most notably Sarah, whose every word was suspect. With Louisa, though, she could detect no hesitancy, even when answering a question that Georgiana would have shied away from. To her, honesty really seemed to count.

Robert Bannerman was, however, something of a conundrum. While Georgiana originally befriended Louisa to meet her brother, things had changed. The young man she considered uneducated was proving her wrong, and it confused her.

What she had taken as discomfort seemed, as she got to know him, a disinclination toward becoming too familiar, or friendly, with someone he did not know. To be honest, Georgiana had shown no desire for friendship with Louisa or Amelia, so why would he suppose she had suddenly developed an interest in him?

The first time they spoke, Georgiana thought him tongue-tied and afraid of the possibility that she would take offense at anything he might say.

On this occasion, though, something about him was different. He sounded surer of himself and less timid, as though he had decided he was her equal. Whether or not that was true they could settle another time, but for now Georgiana liked this improved version of Robert Bannerman. The time had come, she decided, to let him know how much she appreciated his attention. With the proper approach, he would be so enamored of her he would do almost anything she wanted. That might be the best way to win the wager and put Sarah in her place forever.

Elizabeth Bennet was another story. Georgiana had seen William show an inordinate amount of attention to her, but she had not realized others had seen it as well. Elizabeth's acceptance of his interest complicated things, something she had not counted on.

What would happen if William were to get the idea that she returned his interest? He might throw caution to the wind and pursue her! The realization she inadvertently encouraged the woman with her ill-advised answer to Louisa's statement was regrettable, but she could not retract her remarks.

Georgiana harbored no ill feelings toward Elizabeth, but she did not understand what her brother found attractive about the woman. She was a gentleman's daughter, but that, in Georgiana's opinion, stretched the facts beyond reason.

Mr. Bennet, according to Louisa, was a country gentleman, with an estate only marginally bigger than Kingsdown. Georgiana could see from her visits that Mr. Bannerman was not a wealthy man. He employed few servants and had only two tenants, which meant he did much of the farming himself.

Mr. Bennet, with a comparable sized estate, was probably in the same situation. His daughter, although friendly, was in Georgiana's opinion too carefree and easy with her manners to fit in at Pemberley. Should William become enamored of the woman, the loss of face would result in a lower class of suitor vying for her hand, and that was something she would not accept.

Elizabeth's sister Kitty might, all by herself, cause William's friends to disassociate themselves with him. She was flighty and impulsive, according to Louisa, and from what Georgiana had witnessed, it was true. If the rest of their sisters were alike, the disgrace might ruin the Darcy name.

All together, from what Georgiana had seen of the Bennet family, she would not accept the possibility of their inclusion in the society that William inhabited. But what might she do about this impending calamity?

She could not allow them to become familiar with each other. At all costs, any potential romance would have to be discouraged. Georgiana would try to dissuade her brother, but, failing that, she would do anything it took to keep them apart. No sacrifice was too great to protect the Darcy name.

"I like her," was Louisa's statement when Georgiana's carriage entered the road leading back to Pemberley. "She is a pleasant person, and I am ashamed of myself for misjudging her."

"She seems to like Robert," teased Elizabeth, laughing at the scowl her remarks brought forth from her cousin before he made his way to the stable. Louisa turned and entered the manor, leaving Elizabeth alone to contemplate Georgiana's visit.

She seems to be less charitable toward me, thought she in reviewing the visit just concluded. It had begun as a meeting of friends, and Georgiana looked to Elizabeth as though she was enjoying herself. Their banter had been amiable and lighthearted until the subject of her brother arose, after which Elizabeth had noticed a definite change in the girl, from that of a friend to someone wary about saying too much.

Was she displeased with the prospect of Mr. Darcy's interest in Elizabeth? She did not appear to appreciate Louisa raising the subject. As there was nothing she could do about the matter, Elizabeth forgot about the rumor her cousin seemed determined to raise.

"I overheard some of your conversation," said Kitty, coming up beside her. "And I also noticed Mr. Darcy paying more than a casual amount of attention to you at supper that night. It is good Lydia was not here to witness it. She would have had something to say immediately, I am sure. Poor Mr. Darcy would have been so embarrassed that we caught him!"

"Lydia is not a good example of how to behave at a dinner party. She has a knack for saying the wrong thing at the wrong time and causing an uproar. Do not let her become an influence on you again; your demeanor has transformed, and for the better."

"Do not worry, Lizzy. I forgot Lydia when we arrived and see no reason to change."

"If you are exchanging letters, she cannot help but influence you in some manner. Please be careful, Kitty. It would be a shame to see you go back to the insensitive and submissive girl you were at Longbourn."

"Lydia has sent no letters since her first. I chose not to respond to it because, as you said, she was encouraging me to flout the Kingsdown rules and make a fool of myself. I hoped if I ignored her she would not bother me with any additional letters. It turns out I was correct. She only sent the one letter."

"Good for you, Kitty. You are growing up and maturing into the young woman Papa encouraged you to become. I am proud of you, and I will let our father know the next time I write home."

"I guess my absence has led to some positive changes. Thank you, Lizzy, for having the faith to invite me along. I like all of our cousins, and Uncle and Aunt are not too bad themselves."

"I will pass your praise along," laughed Elizabeth. "They will appreciate the vote of confidence, I am sure."

CHAPTER XX

"Good morning, Miss Bennet," was Mr. Darcy's greeting to Elizabeth as she arrived back at Kingsdown the morning after Georgiana's visit. "Returning from your morning constitutional, I presume? Did you enjoy the walk today?"

"Good morning, Mr. Darcy," responded Elizabeth. "It was delightful, but of course I take pleasure in every morning I spend out of doors. My walks inspire me, but they also remind me how insignificant I am in this world."

The look Mr. Darcy fastened upon her was hard to decipher. Was he in agreement with her opinion, or was he going to mock her statement as trite and meaningless? His countenance was calm and without expression which to her was disturbing.

"You, Miss Bennet, are not insignificant." His statement, coming as it did without warning, surprised her: "Since the beginning of your visit, I have noticed a lot of changes, all of them for the better."

"I have no opinion on any changes or my role in them, although what you are referring to are probably nothing more than coincidences, and my presence had little bearing on them."

"You are too modest. Life in Derbyshire and at Pemberley shifted with your arrival, and I am not the only one with this opinion. Even your uncle has commented on the fact."

"I cannot agree or disagree with your claim, as I do not know anything of life in the county before these so-called changes happened. To me, everything is the same as it was when Kitty and I first arrived."

"I beg to differ, Miss Bennet. Your friendly nature has gained the admiration of many in Lambton and beyond. I hear you are the most popular subject of the town gossips, most of it favorable, I might add. That alone is unusual, for they rarely have anything good to report, and when they do, it is always in addition to the denigrating tales they like to traffic in.

"Even Georgiana has changed. To me, she is quieter and not so apt to waste her time in frivolous pursuits with Miss Haversham. She has befriended your cousin and spends her days either planning her next visit here or deciding to have Miss Bannerman visit Pemberley. Her interest in the welfare of this estate and its residents is new, and something I had not expected to see."

"I will have to take you at your word. I am not aware of these changes you say I am responsible for, but I doubt you can lay the credit at my feet."

"You are as entitled to your opinion," smiled Mr. Darcy, "as I am to mine, but it seems to me you are a bit too intent on avoiding an honest compliment. As someone told me recently, false modesty is a sin of the same magnitude as vanity. I cannot recall exactly who said it, but as I remember, it made an impression on me."

"You have made your point, Mr. Darcy," laughed Elizabeth, "and I accept your censure. In the future, I will allow your compliments, but only when they are honest, and I feel I am deserving."

"I ask for nothing more," Mr. Darcy agreed before saying his farewells and departing.

Elizabeth saw him again the next day and frequently over the following week. When she stopped to ponder his visits, she thought he might be spending more time at Kingsdown than at his own estate. On returning from her morning walks, she often saw talking with her uncle, usually positioned in such a way that he could see her as soon as she entered the yard.

Mr. Darcy would nod and exchange pleasantries regarding the weather, the route she took on her walk, or other meaningless subjects. She did not mind; he was always polite, taking time to compliment her on her appearance, her astute point of view, and anything else that came to mind.

Elizabeth looked forward to these conversations, and hoped he would continue to call, for whatever reason he might profess. Her uncle was also enjoying himself immensely, and was not hesitant about saying so.

"He likes you," stated the man one day as Mr. Darcy said his goodbyes and left to deal with a recent issue he claimed had arisen at Pemberley.

"And I like Mr. Darcy," rejoined Elizabeth. "He is a friendly neighbor, always polite and easy to talk to. That is a quality that is sometimes in short supply, usually more so with someone of his wealth and importance. And he seems to like your company, Uncle. I hope you enjoy his visits as much as he seems to relish coming here."

"He is not calling to bask in the joy of conversing with me. It is you he is coming to see. The man is interested in you, and his attraction is growing as I mentioned before, if you recall. Of course he needs an excuse to visit, so he fabricates a problem that requires my invaluable advice to solve as it is a delicate issue or some such blather."

"Why do you call it blather? Has he given you reason to suspect his motives? I would assume there are many problems on an estate the size of Pemberley. Kingsdown might be a smaller property, but you probably face the same issues, on a lesser scale of course. Why would he not avail himself of your greater experience and knowledge? It seems only logical."

"It is the size of Mr. Darcy's estate that convinces me he is looking for excuses to come to Kingsdown every day."

"Why should that make any difference? You face similar problems, and your knowledge is a valuable resource, is it not? You should be proud that he recognizes your wisdom and appreciates your insight."

Mr. Bannerman's head shook in disagreement with Elizabeth's opinion. When she finished, he gave a short laugh which sounded to her almost like a snort of derision.

"Let me explain," said he before she could object to his reaction. "Your father is in much the same position as Mr. Darcy, is he not? What I mean is, he is the master of Longbourn, and has several tenants working his fields. They plant and tend the crops, and at the end of the season, they harvest those crops and pay your father the rent they owe for their use of the land, correct?"

At her nod of agreement, he continued: "Your father does not work Longbourn land himself; his tenants do that."

"What does this have to do with Mr. Darcy?" asked Elizabeth, unsure of the point her uncle was trying to make. "He has tenants, I agree, but Mr. Darcy probably has four tenants to every one of Longbourn's."

"Mr. Darcy also has servants that see to the maintenance and upkeep of the estate, much like your father has. Again, he has many more, but their duties are comparable, are they not?"

Elizabeth nodded her head and sighed, wondering if her uncle would ever arrive at the point he was approaching, to which he held up his hands in a placating gesture.

"When a problem arises in the fields or with the crops, one that he has not yet faced, what does he do? Does he immediately go to his neighbor to ask for direction, or does he consult his steward, the man hired to manage the property? If the problem is with the animals, he consults his head groomsman, assuming the problem is bad enough that the groom or stable boys are worried.

"Have you ever known a problem so serious that your father's servants were unable to solve it themselves?"

"Not that I can recall," acknowledged Elizabeth, the explanation beginning now to make sense. "To the best of my knowledge, one of them has always taken care of any problems that have arisen."

"Exactly. So, knowing that, how likely do you suppose it is that Mr. Darcy's servants cannot solve any issue that comes up at Pemberley? Remember, he employs a lot more servants than your father, and they probably have experience resolving myriad different dilemmas.

"Mr. Darcy is not coming to consult with me, he is using it as a pretext to visit you. You have attracted the man's attention, whether or not you want to acknowledge the fact. I am not a seer, but even I can see that he might ask permission to court you soon. He might or might not approach me about this, but I would most likely allow his request, with the understanding that your father could rescind the permission."

Elizabeth had nothing to say in response, but she was pleased and flattered that someone of Mr. Darcy's importance would deign to take notice of her. She liked the man, and appreciated their daily conversations, which he also enjoyed, if she was any judge of character.

As the day passed, she again imagined being wedded to him and mistress of Pemberley. It would be a wonderful life, with nothing but love and happiness between them. They would be blessed with children, six in total. Their first, a boy, would grow up hale and hearty to be a champion of the downtrodden and ill-treated.

A daughter would come next, and Elizabeth saw herself nurturing the girl and raising her as a proper gentlewoman. A thought, unbidden, of Lydia sprang to Elizabeth's mind, bringing forth a shudder and a vow that no child of hers, son or daughter, would behave in such an impertinent manner. Why, the loss of stature from such a child would horrify Mr. Darcy.

She would encourage all their children to explore their world and delight in the discovery of knowledge. Mr. Darcy might not agree, but if she had her way, they would all receive the best education money could buy, and this was something she vowed to accomplish. No daughter of hers would be denied proper and competent instruction.

These thoughts occupied Elizabeth for the rest of the day and into the evening. By the time she retired, her decision was made. If her uncle were correct and Mr. Darcy was, in fact, interested in her, she would make sure that her daily walks continued, and would time them to coincide with his visits to the estate.

Life went on in that vein for the next few days and it seemed, from Mr. Darcy's demeanor and good humor, he had no intention to quit calling at Kingsdown. Elizabeth's walks began early each morning and followed an identical path, finishing the same time every day at the estate. Mr. Darcy, ostensibly in conversation with her uncle, would greet her and comment with one platitude or another, most often concerning the weather or state of her health.

Her uncle had nothing further to say on the matter, but his expression of self-confidence informed Elizabeth of his conceit in predicting Mr. Darcy's continued interest.

"I am looking forward to our visit to Pemberley tomorrow," confessed Louisa to Elizabeth and Kitty as they walked together on the third morning after Georgiana's visit. "I confess, it surprised me when her invitation arrived yesterday."

"Why is that?" asked Kitty. "She said she was going to send one, and she did."

"Her friendship was so unexpected," explained Louisa, "and I am still wondering what prompted her first visit. We had been neighbors our entire lives and had not spoken so much as one sentence to each other since the death of her father. For her to arrive at our door unannounced like she did was strange."

"It seems to be a Darcy trait," giggled Kitty. "From what I have seen, Mr. Darcy likes to spend his mornings visiting Uncle."

"He is not visiting Father," stated Louisa. "That is just an excuse to see Lizzy when she finishes her walk. It lets him speak to her with no one thinking he has designs on her, or so he thinks."

"Are the banns ready for reading?" said Kitty, to which Louisa laughed, but which caused Elizabeth to frown.

"He is not *that* interested in me, Kitty. Kindly control your imagination and watch what you say. If a rumor like that got started because somebody overheard your remarks, it would upset Mr. Darcy, with good reason."

"I meant nothing by it," smiled Kitty nonchalantly. Elizabeth knew that, despite her protestations of innocence, she was not willing to let the subject go, and this was a concern.

Kitty, while not as impetuous as Lydia, was prone to ill-advised outbursts. If the wrong person overheard something she said, the resulting rumors would cover all of Derbyshire before the sun set. Elizabeth had no wish to anger Mr. Darcy and wanted to impress the seriousness of the matter upon her sister.

Upon their return, Mr. Bannerman met them and, as was usual these days, Mr. Darcy was there to greet them with a smile and a comment about the weather. Louisa and Kitty left the group almost at once, and Elizabeth heard them laughing uproariously until they entered the manor.

They were finding the situation hugely entertaining, as girls their age were wont to do. It flattered her that Mr. Darcy's interest continued, and she wondered if he could see that she felt the same.

"Welcome to Pemberley," greeted Georgiana as Elizabeth and Louisa exited the carriage early on the afternoon of the following day. "I hope your ride was comfortable."

"As much as it can be over a rough road," remarked Elizabeth. "Unfortunately, the Derbyshire lanes, like those anywhere except for the paved highways in and around London, are not of stone. Sometimes I think the drivers of these vehicles take aim at every pothole they can find. I know how petty that sounds, but it does not stop me from complaining. That is my right, and I refuse to give it up."

"And I would not expect you to," said Georgiana with a laugh. "If we cannot raise valid concerns, what else is there?

"How is life at Kingsdown? I trust everyone is in fine fettle."

"We are all as healthy as we were three days ago," offered Louisa, "although Robert seems somewhat distracted. He has been this way since Mr. Darcy's ball, and it is more noticeable since we came for supper."

An unanticipated thrill ran through Georgiana in response to Louisa's news. Could she be the cause of his preoccupation? If so, what was the best way to exploit the advantage it gave her? She needed to take some time, she thought, and carefully plan her next steps. With luck, the victory would be hers and would in turn humiliate Sarah, once and for all.

"Maybe he has a problem that is not easily solved," said she, plans already running through her head. "William sometimes gets that way when he worries about a solution for a problem he is considering. He appears distracted but is just working the cure over in his mind.

"At any rate, thank you for coming. To confess, I experienced a little worry that you might decide to reject *my* invitation. In that respect we are not so different, are we Louisa?"

"Thankfully, I am not the only one who worries about such things," was the answer, "although I had not realized you also suffered from those kinds of insecurities."

"Is this a common occurrence?" asked Elizabeth, "and if so, why? In Hertfordshire, when we arrange a visit, and agree upon a date, it does not change on a whim or because one party has a change of mind.

"From what I am hearing, people in Derbyshire change their plans without taking the simple courtesy of informing the other party. It is a wonder any of you are on speaking terms with each other."

"No, Elizabeth, it is not that way at all," laughed Louisa. "Derbyshire residents are among the most considerate of any, according to Father. We honor commitments without fail, and have called on our neighbors without prior notice, like Mr. Darcy has been doing every morning at Kingsdown.

"Of course, it may be nothing more than his desire to see more of you, I suppose. He seems to be happier when you get back from your walks."

"Mr. Darcy is visiting Uncle, not me," said Elizabeth, although Georgiana saw her cheeks becoming flushed as she refuted her cousin's insinuation.

The visit continued in this fashion for the rest of the afternoon, although the subject of Mr. Darcy and Elizabeth was soon dropped in favor of more interesting topics of conversation, at least to Louisa and Elizabeth.

Georgiana had much to ponder when her guests left for home. The possibility of the Bannerman son's interest was too delicious to forget and occupied her imagination until they served supper. By the time she sat for the meal, she knew what to do. All she needed to carry it out was Sarah.

William was another matter. If he pursued Elizabeth, the consequences might be disastrous. She would not let that happen.

"A post arrived for you," announced Mr. Bannerman that evening at supper. "I had the upstairs maid put it on the desk in your room."

"Thank you, Uncle. It is probably a letter from Jane containing the latest news from home. I plan to read it before I go to bed. It will be full of good cheerful news, as she tends not to dwell on the negative."

Alone in her room after supper, Elizabeth broke the envelope seal and pulled out several neatly written pages. Making herself comfortable at the desk, she unfolded them and read:

Longbourn, July 10

"Dear Lizzy,"

"I should have written sooner, but until recently there was little of interest worth reporting, and Papa and I have been busy minding Lydia.

"Thank you for informing us of her plans. When we confronted her with what you wrote, she denied it, but confessed when Papa showed her your letter.

"Lydia claims the letter she sent Kitty was written in a fit of pique, but she has since repented of her wanton ways and is no longer that same person. Papa was unconvinced until an event at Netherfield changed his mind.

"Mr. Bingley decided, shortly after his arrival, that he would host a ball. When the invitation arrived, it was for everyone, including Lydia. Papa was going to keep her at Longbourn that night, but Lydia, with our mother's help, convinced him to give his permission, and she behaved the entire night. It would appear the girl is changing for the better.

"Mr. Bingley's event was a wonderful affair, and he was the consummate gentleman. He asked for the first dance when he delivered the invitation, and we shared one more before the evening ended.

"As a dance companion, he was wonderful. He seemed to go out of his way to compliment my dancing ability and would not accept it when I insisted he take credit for guiding me so ably through the steps.

"Of course, our mother was there to express her gratitude to him for inviting me to dance, as if without Mr. Bingley's invitation I would have had to spend the night with Mama, ignored and forgotten by everyone.

"Mr. Bingley's response was to tell her he considered himself lucky to dance with me at all, and there were many who, through no fault of their own, did not have the chance.

"He is such a gentleman, Lizzy. Even Mama likes him, and invited him to dine with us next week, which he accepted. She is beside herself with joy and claims she accomplished what Papa could not, although she refused to explain herself.

"Mr. Bingley's sister, Caroline, was there and enjoyed herself, as much as she was able to, although she confessed to me, she wants to return to London for winter, if Mr. Bingley agrees.

"She is afraid her suitor has paid his attention to someone else because she has been away so long. My suggestion was to stay the winter, and if the man were serious he would wait, but she is desperate to return and wants permission to stay with her aunt in Scarborough. I hope she is not going back just to find disappointment.

"There is nothing more to say, so I will express again my love for you and Kitty, and hope to see you soon, although Papa says you will stay another few months. Be well and give my best to everyone at Kingsdown.

"Love, Jane."

Elizabeth finished the letter, which had taken up only two of the pages included in the envelope. Curious, she put the completed pages to the side and looked at the next in the bundle, which was another letter addressed to her.

This letter was as unlike the previous one as it was possible to be. The first few sentences, difficult though they were to decipher, gave her a reason to smile, and by the time she finished, tears of joy creased her face.

Longbourn, August 4

"My Dearest Lizzy,"

"Please forgive my penmanship, but I can hardly hold the instrument to write. I have the most wonderful news; Mr. Bingley has asked for my hand in marriage, and I told him yes!

"I know this comes as a surprise, so I will attempt to detail the events of the past month. Before I do, I really meant to send the other letter when I wrote it, but life got in the way, and I completely forgot.

"As I mentioned before, we attended a ball at Netherfield, where Mama took it upon herself to invite him and his sister to dinner. He accepted, and the evening was almost a dream for me. Mama placed him across from me at the table, and he paid almost exclusive attention to me throughout supper.

"When the time came for him to depart, Papa invited him to return whenever he wanted, and they have hunted together frequently, as I explained in an earlier letter.

"Every time he called, he was sure to exchange pleasantries with me. He took to sitting with me while waiting for our father to get ready, which seemed to take him longer on each occasion. The same thing would happen when Mr. Bingley needed to consult him about problems he was encountering at Netherfield.

"Papa would invite him into the sitting-room to wait while he finished one important thing or another. I did not mind his company, and I thought at the time Mr. Bingley shared the feeling.

"Mr. Bingley asked Papa for permission to court me and received it immediately. He said Papa's only comment was to ask why it took him so long to get around to raising the question.

"The poor man was so nervous and unsure of my response that it took him a full two weeks after receiving permission to offer his proposal. Of course, I accepted without hesitation, as I already knew that he was the only one I would ever love.

"Oh Lizzy, I am so deliriously happy I might burst. We are planning the wedding for spring, in part because the courtship was so quick that people might wonder if we rushed into the arrangement too soon. This will give us the rest of this year and the beginning of the next to get to know each other better than we do now.

"Mama is beside herself with happiness. All she can do is repeat: 'five thousand a year. What pin money you will have!'

"I guess to her, the money is as important as my happiness. Yes, he is moderately well off, but to me that is of secondary importance.

"I hope you are as happy for me as I am, Lizzy. Just wait until you meet him; I have no doubt you will think almost as highly of him as I do.

"It is time for bed, although I doubt sleep will come easily on this or any night until we marry.

"I love you, Lizzy, and hope to see you soon.

"Your sister, Jane."

Elizabeth was overjoyed. Jane betrothed, and Elizabeth so far away that she could not celebrate with her. With a smile stretching from one ear to the other, she put out the light and went to bed.

CHAPTER XXI

Georgiana was having a good day. Sarah had called unexpectedly, and the surprise visit furthered two necessary components of her plan. First, it gave her the opportunity to introduce some unwelcome doubt to her friend's self-confidence, and second, allowed her the additional convenience of provoking Sarah into rash actions to impede the influence she feared Georgiana had gained. Overall things were progressing nicely, although if asked, her friend might disagree.

"He is a nice young man, and so polite," gloated Georgiana, further aggravating her friend, a result she found most satisfying. "When I visit, he makes a point of greeting me and enquiring as to my health, along with sundry other concerns.

"Our little wager will be over soon, and you will be the loser again. Of course, that should not come as a surprise; I win more of these contests than I lose."

"That is because you always cheat," said Sarah, the fire in her eyes a continual source of amusement, and a confirmation that her friend worried about the possibility of losing again to Georgiana.

"Please explain, if you can, how I have been cheating."

"You have been calling on him almost daily and using the fact that Kingsdown and Pemberley are neighboring estates to unfair advantage!"

Georgiana's laughter at this declaration did nothing to calm her friend, which was evident from the crimson shade of Sarah's face. A voice in the back of her head, though, urged her to placate the girl before the growing tumult attracted William's attention.

"Lower your voice," said she, "and come with me." Turning from the girl, she led the way to a forested area far enough from the house to be out of earshot. When she found a little-used trail, she drew Sarah into the secluded stand of trees before stopping to address her.

"In the future, try to behave when you visit, or William might hear. Do you want him to discover what we are doing? I know my brother, and he would put an immediate stop to our competition. He would also inform your father, and probably Mr. Bannerman, something I warned you about in the past.

"I have no desire to explain the circumstances of our wager, and neither should you. William would punish me, and I assume your father would do likewise."

"If you followed the rules, I would have no reason to raise my voice," spat Sarah, pacing back and forth, her apparent agitation increasing as she spoke. "I should know better than to let you talk me into these ridiculous games. The only reason you win so often is because you never let something as silly as the notion of fair play interfere with your plans."

"For you to accuse me of cheating is the funniest thing I have heard in weeks," laughed Georgiana, further raising Sarah's ire. "Your attitude is a little too high and mighty, when compared with any sins you accuse me of committing. You are also not above seizing any advantage you can, if you suspect it might give you the slightest edge.

"I have Robert Bannerman just where I want him. When I call on Louisa, and *she* is the person I go to visit, *not* her brother, he finds an excuse to speak to her. He frames his comments so that I am pulled into the conversation. He might think I am unaware of his intentions, but I am not so naïve I cannot see his transparent attempt to make it seem like he is responding to a remark Louisa made."

"That is so like you," said Sarah, her voice loud enough that Georgiana was glad they had moved away from the house. "Rather than taking the time to attract the boy without ambiguity or pretension, you have him fooled into thinking your friendship was unplanned and came about by fortunate coincidence. Your innocence is false, just like your modesty. You hope to keep him so confused that the mere mention of your name will have him swooning, unable to form a coherent thought."

"And your anger is unjustified," laughed Georgiana. "I see through your protestations of dishonesty on my part. It upsets you because I pressed the advantage I created, and you cannot accept the fact that I was the one to devise such a plan.

"Your objections are pathetic, more so because they result from your failure to compensate for steps I have taken. You must have been aware of what I had planned; I did not try to hide what I was doing. Grow up and face the reality of your situation. You have lost once again, although I cannot understand why you are surprised."

"I am of half a mind to inform young Mr. Bannerman of our game," said Sarah. "What would he do if I told him this is nothing but a wager, and he is the prize in a game devised because of your conceited opinion of your own beauty and appeal?

"All I would need to do after that is convince the poor boy that my affection is unfeigned and true. He would be mine by the end of the day, and you? I doubt he would give you any more consideration, other than to advise his sister and father of your treachery."

"You are correct," laughed Georgiana, "you do possess half a mind, if you think he would believe any of that gibberish. I have made no announcements of affection or interest. The attraction he feels is his own, not because of any untruths I have expressed. I have no hidden agenda because, unlike you, I do not need to use trickery or deception. Anything I have told Mr. Bannerman is true; there has been no dishonesty, and you owe me an apology for suggesting I would resort to such things.

"Mr. Bannerman is not someone I would even contemplate deceiving. To be honest, I admire and respect him, and would regret losing his friendship. If I were you, I would think about any consequences that you might suffer for telling Mr. Bannerman lies like that."

"When did he become *Mr.* Bannerman instead of Robert?" jeered Sarah, her contempt easy to perceive.

"I do not have permission to use his given name, nor have I asked. Louisa is my friend; Mr. Bannerman is just her brother. When he expresses his desire to court, I will ask permission to use his given name."

"Am I to assume that you like the boy?" laughed Sarah. "I never suspected the day would come with the great Georgiana Darcy smitten, and by a poor gentleman's son, no less."

"Think what you want, but the game is over, and you have lost. Mr. Robert Bannerman is mine, to do with as I please," said Georgiana, turning back toward Pemberley.

"No! You will never have him!" she heard before a flash of light burst behind her eyes, followed by darkness.

Red is the best flavor, she thought, reaching for an orb that hung suspended beyond her outstretched fingers. *I must give it to him.*

This is not real, she guessed as the object danced away, its rhythmic pulse changing to a steady throb at the back of her head.

She opened her eyes to learn that she lay on the ground amongst a stand of trees; the twigs, branches, and pebbles pressing into her shoulders and back. A gurgle of water tumbling over rocks was easy to hear, but the attempt to turn her head toward the sound caused a stab of pain, forcing her to reconsider the effort and close her eyes.

If I am still this might go away, she decided as pain rolled over her in waves, each one stronger than the previous.

For minutes she lay unmoving until at last the agony eased and she felt she should rise. She opened her eyes again to take stock of her position but waited a few minutes to gather her strength. Then, with an effort, she rolled onto her stomach while bringing her arms under her shoulders. With her hands flat upon the ground, she drew her knees to her chest and pushed against the dirt, at the same time straightening her legs to rise to a standing position.

When upright, she stood still, fighting to keep her balance as the world spun in uneven circles and her vision refused to fasten itself on any single point. She wanted to close the lids again but feared if she did, she would fall. To compensate, she shut them as much as she dared and waited for the dizziness to pass.

When it eased, she peered through slits opened enough to inspect her surroundings again. Hopeful that her world would remain settled, she allowed her lids to part until objects came into focus.

She was in a tiny clearing, not much more than a widening of the woods, with a brook along one side and a path on the other. The trees grew close, branches intertwining in a dense canopy that reduced the sunlight within, rendering it impossible to approximate the time of day. The path was faint, overtaken by weeds growing in clumps on the surface. It entered the clearing at one end and disappeared from view at the other, with no sign of its source or destination.

Uncertainty taunted her as if deriding the options and her capacity to choose. With no idea where she was or how far it might be to the nearest road, she briefly considered climbing a tree so she might view the surrounding landscape, but knew she was too weak.

With an effort she shook her head, fighting a tendril of panic. Instead, she looked up and down the path again for any sign to suggest which way she should proceed, but found none, which angered her, the emotion surprising her with its appearance.

The danger of a night alone in the woods at last overrode her hesitation, and she moved along the trail, hopeful the direction she chose would lead to a road or a more substantial path. She stumbled as the dizziness returned, threatening her paltry progress.

In desperation she clutched a low-hanging branch and stood while the trees whirled in ever increasing orbits, her grip the only thing keeping her upright. She fought the discomfort, her will battling for control of her body until at last her balance recovered.

Again, she set off, this time less confident in her ability to demand the obedience of her protesting muscles and doubting her body's reserves of strength.

She could not tell how long she trudged on, whether it was minutes or hours, because the branches obscuring the sky also masked the passage of time. She refused to heed growing protests from tired flesh and her aching head and struggled to keep going, despite a desire to find shelter beneath a tree and give herself over into the blessed arms of sleep.

No, she thought, annoyance at her weakness pushing her fears aside, *I will not give in.*

The image of an estate sprang to her mind, its clarity and detail shocking. An impressive house, well-kept and massive, its grounds maintained and beautiful in their simplicity, tugged at her memory, but the knowledge of its relevance remained out of reach. The familiarity of the property was both tantalizing and disheartening. She knew that house and had been there, she was sure. In her mind she saw the estate master, though not his visage; she had met him, but was unable to unmask his face.

If she could only see him her confusion might retreat, and with it her unease.

So preoccupied was she with the mystery that she stepped onto the lane before she saw it, the sensation of her feet kicking the edge pulling her thoughts back to the present.

Tears welled and coursed down her cheeks as she stood upon her goal. With a sigh, her muscles released their control, and she allowed herself to collapse against the nearest tree, this one welcome company.

She surveyed the road, first one way and then the other, but spied no traffic. Content with the achievement of her immediate aim, she closed her eyes for just a minute to regain her strength and was soon fast asleep.

"Should we wake her?" pulled her from a dream of soft beds and warm blankets.

"We cannot just leave her," came a second voice, that of a woman, "She is alone, and might need our assistance."

Her eyes opened to the sight of a carriage stopped on the road and a woman bending over her, while a man stood nearby.

"Are you hurt?" asked the woman, an expression of worry upon her face.

"My head aches," was her response, lifting her hand to touch the part of her head that still throbbed. With a gasp, she pulled it away, noting as she did that her hair was matted and wet. She would have the maid brush it out tonight, she decided, as it would not do to be seen in this condition.

I have a maid? she wondered, trying in vain to hold on to the fleeting thought which had leapt to her mind.

"You are injured," gasped the woman, trying to inspect the wound without touching it, for which she was grateful.

"I wanted to sit for a minute," said she, trying without success to remember anything of the day prior to waking in the woods. "I am sorry if I trespassed, but the temptation to rest against this tree was so inviting, and I was so tired, I could not resist."

"You are probably not trespassing," suggested the woman with a smile, "as this is a public road. But why, pray tell, are you sleeping against a tree, instead of somewhere more comfortable, like your home?"

"I have no idea where that is," whispered she, fear at last gaining the upper hand as the tears resumed their cascade down her cheeks.

"Then what is your name?" asked the woman, to a snort from the man.

"If she cannot recall where she lives, what makes you think she can remember what her name is?"

"Hush, dear. I am trying to assist this poor girl, and your interruptions are not helping," said the woman, resuming her ministrations by leaning forward, as though her proximity would aid in restoring the missing memory.

"He means well but is not the best at expressing his intentions."

"I do not remember my name," was the response she offered through the sobs she was trying, without success, to control.

"Shh, my dear, everything will be fine," said the woman, her soft compassionate voice helping to staunch the flow of tears.

"I am sorry, but your question reminded me of what I had not realized until now. I cannot remember my name, or how I hurt myself."

The woman stood and offered her hand, saying: "We cannot leave you here now, can we?" Georgiana gratefully accepted the outstretched hand. Once upon her feet, she was led to the carriage and helped inside, followed by the rescuers.

"Do you have any idea what direction we should take?" asked the woman after making her comfortable. "While we are familiar with the county, we do not know any of its residents. It was pure coincidence that we chose this road, instead of the one we usually follow.

"Forgive me, I have completely forgotten my manners. I am Lady Ridlington, and the gentleman wearing the scowl is my husband, Lawrence, the Earl of Sheffield.

"It was our driver who noticed you and brought it to our attention. Lawrence had him stop in case you needed help. It was a good thing that we did; our arrival was a blessing, I think."

"By all that is holy, let the poor girl answer your question," demanded her husband, "or we will never get her home!"

"I am sorry," said Lady Ridlington. "When I am nervous or upset, I prattle on without thinking, and finding you here has made me both. Which direction should we tell the driver to go?"

"I do not know. I am unsure where we are, or where I live."

"Then we will continue in the direction we were travelling," stated Lady Ridlington. "There must be another estate along this road, as it is well traveled."

The carriage started up with a jerk, and she laid her head back to concentrate on the hazy memories that lay just out of reach. Her attempts to force them to the surface were fruitless, as they remained tantalizingly hidden, covered by the thinnest of veils.

"Is this your home?" asked Lady Ridlington, pointing to a house they were approaching.

The residence stirred something in her mind, but she could not identify the source of the feeling. As the building came into sharper focus though, her heart raced and panic pushed its way forward, blotting out all other thoughts.

"No." Her throat closed around the words, as if attempting to rob her of the power to speak. "Please, I cannot return there. They will never understand."

The words pushed themselves out from between her lips before she knew what she was saying.

Please do not let them see me, thought she as the distance to the house narrowed. In a panic, she pushed as far back from the opening as possible, her fear an insurmountable barrier between herself and the world beyond the carriage door.

The earl rapped on the cabin's roof, causing the driver to bring it to a stop.

"Wait," was his command to the driver when the conveyance was still. "It seems there might be a problem."

"I do not belong here," said she, to their consternation. "Can we go to another estate? I do no belong here."

"What about the property we passed before we found her?" asked Lady Ridlington. "The owner might be able to tell us who she is."

"We cannot leave her there," was the earl's opinion, pointing to the house framed in the carriage window. "The place terrifies her."

After a brief discussion with the driver, the coach turned in the opposite direction and the journey recommenced.

What is there about that house that terrifies me? Was that where I hurt myself?

She leaned back and closed her eyes to view the house again in her memory. It was familiar, which was one piece of the puzzle, but the source of her panic refused to reveal itself, to her growing frustration.

The carriage was silent as the horses retraced their path to the property in question. She opened her eyes a small amount to see that Lady Ridlington was watching her. Twice she opened her mouth as if to speak but shut it again without offering a word. Beside her, the earl seemed to contemplate something important although, like his wife, he did not speak.

"We are nearing the property." Lady Ridlington words as the carriage turned, encouraged her to open her eyes fully. "I hope someone here knows you, or I do not know what we will do."

"We will do whatever we must," said the earl in a voice of authority. "She is under our care, and I intend to treat her well."

"Of course, Lawrence," agreed his wife. "I was not suggesting that we abandon her. On the contrary, I too want to make sure she is where she belongs."

The drive they followed gently turned, revealing a stately manor. With a start, she realized this was the house she had seen in her mind's eye. Like a dam failing under the onslaught of excessive water, memories flooded her mind.

At last, she was home. The knowledge left her unable to give voice to the feelings washing over her. Lady Ridlington, watching the emotions as they played across her face, reached over to grasp her hands.

"You have been here before, I assume," was her comment, spoken with surety rather than as a question.

"I live here," was her reply as movement from the corner of her eye brought her head around to see a man approaching the carriage. His gait was familiar, as was his appearance. With a shock, she knew this was the man she had seen in her vision, and from his relieved expression she could tell he knew her.

"Georgiana?" asked the man as his eyes came to rest on her pale face, peering from the window.

"William," cried she, throwing the carriage door open and stumbling from the conveyance into her brother's arms as the last impediment to her memory crumbled.

"It appears we have found her home," observed Lady Ridlington as brother and sister embraced joyously.

"We should let them be," suggested the earl, "it looks like they have something to celebrate."

"Wait," called Darcy before the horses were put in motion. "Thank you for returning my sister to me. We had been searching the property without success, and I was unsure where to look next."

"Thanks are unnecessary," said the earl. "We discovered her at the side of the road and stopped to lend a hand. It seemed she did not know where, or even who, she was, so we took her first to your neighbor, because that was the closest property.

"She became agitated and insisted that we bring her here, so I agreed. I apologize for the delay in getting her back to you; if we had come here in the first place, she would have been home an hour or more ago."

"All that matters is that she is here, and I have you to thank for that. I am Fitzwilliam Darcy, and the young woman you so kindly rescued is my sister, Georgiana. Let me say that it is an honor to meet you and express my gratitude, however lacking it may be."

"Your thanks are enough," the earl assured him. "And since we appear to have dispensed with formalities, the woman who comforted Miss Darcy is my wife, Lady Ridlington. I am Lawrence Ridlington, the Earl of Sheffield."

"It is good to make your acquaintance," said Darcy. "My aunt, Lady Catherine de Bourgh, who I assume you are familiar with, speaks highly of you, and her regard does not come easily."

"She can be a formidable woman," laughed the earl, "but also the best of friends, once you gain her respect."

"A perfect description," agreed Darcy before becoming serious again. "Please, let me offer a proper thank you over dinner tonight. I will have the cook prepare something special. That is the least I can do for the charity you showed Georgiana."

"Thank you," said the earl, "I appreciate your kind offer but must decline, with regret. Your sister needs your attention more than Lady Ridlington or I. Please see to her, and do not worry about us. We had planned to stop in Lambton for supper and to tend to our horses anyway. If we remain, it will interfere with the care Miss Darcy requires from you right now. That is something I cannot agree to, in good conscience."

"I understand, and will let you go, on the understanding that you call the next time you pass through Derbyshire."

"Agreed," said the earl as he assisted his wife into the carriage, which was put in motion almost as soon as the cabin door closed.

"You had me worried." Darcy turned to Georgiana when they were alone: "What happened, and how did you meet the Earl and his wife?"

Georgiana, wincing as a breeze lifted her hair, reminding her of the wound, said: "They found me on the side of the road, and brought me home. Please, William, may we talk about this later? My head hurts and I am dirty. I would like to clean myself up before I face your questions. The truth is I remember little of what happened, other than waking up in unfamiliar woodland and making my way to the road, which is where they found me."

"You are going to bed," was his declaration, "and I will summon Dr. Tate to examine your wound. Your maid can give you a light washing, but anything else will have to wait until he gives his approval."

"I am fine," Georgiana smiled, "but I need a bath. I am filthy, as you can probably see. Please have my maid draw some water so I can clean myself before Mr. Tate examines me."

Turning on her heel, she took two steps and stopped. Grabbing Darcy's arm, she stood still while the room turned in rapid circles around her.

"I can see how fine you are," was Darcy's sardonic comment. Summoning Georgiana's maid, who had come at the news of her return, he said: "Take her upstairs and put her to bed. If she insists, you can wash her lightly, but be gentle, and do not let her talk you into doing more. Anything else can wait until the physician has examined her and treated her injury."

Georgiana allowed the maid to take her upstairs, knowing protests would not change her brother's mind. Despite wanting a thorough washing, by the time the maid finished cleaning the worst of the dirt from her, the physician had arrived, and commenced treating her injury.

When the examination was complete and her wound cleaned and bandaged, Mr. Tate summoned Darcy.

"She suffers from a concussion caused by a blow to her head. She is recovering, but I would keep her in bed for three or four days. I will leave some laudanum for the pain, but be careful not to give her too much."

The rest of the conversation carried on without Georgiana, as she was by this time falling asleep.

CHAPTER XXII

Georgiana slept in fits and starts through the night. It was not hard to fall sleep but staying there was. The wound began to throb, and the pain woke her. Turning on her side, she dozed off again, whereupon her mind replayed the incident, the dream causing her to thrash about as she tried to ward off the attack.

The movement of her head irritated the injury, and the resulting stab of pain woke her again. The servant Darcy had stationed in the bedchamber did what she could to ease the discomfort, but it was not until he was summoned and administered a measure of laudanum, mixed with some lemonade, that she gained some much-needed rest.

She heard quiet voices upon waking. "How well did she sleep?" an unfamiliar male voice was asking as she opened her eyes and tried to sit up.

"Be still," the voice demanded, while hands on her shoulders prevented her from rising. "You must stay in bed today and rest."

"No, I need to go home, or William will worry. Let me go!"

"Georgiana, you are home. Stop thrashing about, or you will hurt yourself further."

"William?" asked she, opening her eyes to see him standing over her, his brows knitted with worry as his hands kept her from moving.

"Oh William, I was so scared because I did not remember where I was. Then I heard your voice, but it sounded strange and unfamiliar. I cannot stay here. Please take me home; I want to sleep in my bed."

"You are home, Georgiana, and in your bedroom. You have been since last night, when I had the maid put you to bed while I sent for Mr. Tate."

What does he mean, and why would he send me to bed? I do not know where I am, but it is not at home, so this cannot be my room.

Georgiana struggled to free herself from Darcy's grip while she cast her eyes around the room, desperately trying to make sense of the situation. She fought with all her strength until at last, unable to break free of his hold, she collapsed onto the pillow, exhausted.

"Bring me the laudanum and a glass of lemonade," were Darcy's instructions to the servant, who hurried from the room.

"You *are* at home, Georgiana. There is nothing to fear; calm yourself."

"But this is not my room, or my bed. Why do you insist it is? What has happened, and why are we not at Pemberley?"

"We are at Pemberley," sighed Darcy as the maid re-entered the room carrying a tray, which she set on the bedside table. On it were the glass of lemonade, as requested, and a vial.

"Stay where you are." Turning to his side, he opened the vial and added some of its contents to the lemonade, which he handed to Georgiana.

"Drink this," his voice allowed for no argument. "It will help you go back to sleep. We will talk when you wake. Hopefully by that time you will have regained your senses enough so you can accept my answers."

Obediently, she accepted the glass and, lifting it to her lips, took a sip. The lemonade, although cloyingly sweet, left an aftertaste in her mouth, and she handed it back to him.

"I cannot," said she when Darcy refused to take it from her. "It tastes terrible."

"I know it is bitter. Holding your nose will help, and the medicine will be taking effect by the time you finish the glass."

Reluctantly she raised the glass to her lips and, pinching her nose as Darcy suggested, emptied it while trying not to retch. Finished, she handed it back and laid her head onto the pillow, offering a smile to calm any fears he still entertained.

"Now go to sleep." Bending over, he placed a light kiss on her forehead. She tried to smile, but the effort was too hard, as her eyes were closing.

"Call me if anything changes," she heard him say before she fell asleep, her fears forgotten as the narcotic took effect.

When next she woke, her thoughts were less confused as the events preceding her injury came into focus. Despite gaps which she could not seem to fill, she remembered Sarah's visit, the argument she feared William would overhear, and their walk into the woods to ensure that did not happen. Try as she might, however, she remembered nothing beyond that; the span between entering the forest and waking was a blank.

Did Sarah hit me? Why would she do such a thing? Surely, she knew I was only teasing her; she does the same to me. Maybe someone attacked us both. If so, I hope she escaped without injury. But if that happened, why did she not send anyone to help me? She might be lying injured in the woods. If nobody looked for her, she might be unable to move, or worse.

"You look better than you did yesterday," offered Darcy, entering the room and seating himself on a chair beside her bed. "Would you like to talk? I can spend the day with you, at least until you tire of me and want more than my stimulating conversation."

"I was thinking about what happened yesterday. Did you send someone to look for Sarah? We were in the woods together."

"You have been in bed for three days, and Sarah was not with you. She was in Bath with her father, according to what she told me two days ago when she called to see you. I asked her to come back next week."

"I was sure she was with me," said Georgiana, "but maybe I was mistaken."

"That has been a common occurrence this last while." He gave her a commiserating smile, showing the depth of his concern. "Yesterday and the day before, you wanted to return home. I tried to tell you that you were in your own bed, but you refused to believe me, and seemed determined to prove me a liar.

"You were so upset I had to sedate you for your own good. It would not do to have you wandering the estate in such a condition, so you have been unconscious for most of the last two days. Believe me, I hated drugging you, but I was more afraid of you hurting yourself, so I ignored my misgivings and mixed it into some lemonade I had you drink."

"I remember drinking something, but everything else is unclear," said Georgiana. "I seemed to be dreaming, but could not seem to wake, and it worried me. And you made me drink the same thing over and over, no matter how much I protested."

"That was the laudanum Mr. Tate prescribed. I hope we can put it away now that the worst has passed, thankfully. Forcing you to take it was not my first choice, but you were so agitated and determined to find your way home that it became necessary."

As she listened to him, Georgiana could imagine how uneasy he had been giving her the medicine, and his relief that she would not need another dose.

For as long as she could remember, William had refused to use laudanum, something he called a dangerous and immoral drug. He had never, to her knowledge, taken the narcotic himself for an injury, and derided those who did so. In his opinion, they took it for no other reason than the stupefying feelings the drug induced.

For him to allow any physician, even Mr. Tate, whom he held in high regard, to prescribe something so potent showed how much he feared for her health.

"I remember someone asking me questions but cannot remember what they were about. I just wanted to sleep."

"You were lucky, as Mr. Tate was in the neighborhood examining someone else, so he arrived quickly. You struck your head and were showing signs of concussion, so he prescribed laudanum, which I had to give you more than once."

"You dislike that drug, so why did you make me take it? My memory is not the best, but I know it tasted vile, and you would not let me give it back to you."

"You were so upset when you woke that I decided the drug would do more good than harm. If not for its calming effects, you would have run from the house in search of Pemberley. I could not convince you the bed was your own and was not about to allow you to leave in your delirium.

"The only treatment that seemed to work was the narcotic. I did not want to force it on you, but I was left with no choice."

Georgiana tried not to laugh as Darcy described his quandary, but the picture his story painted in her mind was too much, and she could not stop. The movement, though, allowed the pain to return, causing her to wince.

"You need to rest," a cadence of worry colored his voice. "I can give you one more measure of the drug, if it will help."

"No, I will be fine. When I remembered how much you detest the mere mention of that narcotic, only to be told it was necessary for my recovery, I could not help but laugh. And to realize you have it in the house is more amusing. I do not want anymore of it; the confusion it caused was almost as bad as the pain."

Rising and crossing the room to the door, he turned back to her: "Go to sleep. I will come back when you are rested.

"Goodnight William." Closing her eyes, she thought briefly that the room was certainly bright this evening. She would have to ask William about it when she woke.

Darcy shut the door behind him and waited for a minute while he considered the events of the last few days.

To see Georgiana in such a state of distress, her clothing tattered and her face and hands filthy, shocked him in a way he had not felt since the passing of his father. The injury to her head frightened him; if she had not stumbled, he might have stood there, immobile, for the rest of the evening.

The nature of her trauma was distressing because it was not the result of a fall, as she seemed to think. Since inheriting Pemberley, he had seen many head injuries to his tenants and servants, and Georgiana's wound was not the result of something as simple as a stumble while walking.

Someone attacked his sister, of that he was sure, and the fact enraged him. What had she done that her assailant decided she deserved to be beaten? Had it not occurred to them that a blow of such force might kill her?

With the vow of an eye for an eye in retribution, he descended the stairs and left the house to attend to tasks neglected much too long.

He worked without stopping until Snell came to inform him that Georgiana was awake. His pocket watch, when he looked at it, told him the workday was finished, and the cook would serve supper in the next hour.

With regret at failing to complete all the tasks he had set for himself; he bid goodbye to the tenant he had been speaking with and returned to the house.

"Enter, William," called Georgiana at his knock.

"I knew it was you," she stated when he sat beside her bed. "There is no mistaking your hand against the door."

"I liked you better unconscious," was his comment, to which she laughed, the sound a welcome change from her moans and cries of the previous days.

"So that is why you took the laudanum from Mr. Tate; you prefer me in a stupor! I will remember that the next time you want help with an issue you cannot solve on your own."

"You were less demanding, and easier to live with when you slept all day, and I cannot remember a circumstance where I have needed your help. As I recall, you are always more of a hindrance."

"That is not what you say when I save you from those embarrassing situations you seem so capable of getting into."

"I am glad you are feeling better," said he, the banter gone from his voice. "What do you remember about the day of your injury? Why were you in those woods, rather than on the paths closer to the house? Who was with you, and why did they attack you and leave you alone, injured and unconscious?"

"I am sorry, William, I do not recall any attack. I thought Sarah was with me but you told me she was in Bath with Mr. Haversham. I must have gone there by myself, although I cannot recall doing that, either."

"You could not have been alone, Georgiana. A fall did not cause your injury; somebody, most probably a man from the extent of the wound, hit you with something. When I find out who it was, I will make them pay."

"I do not remember seeing a man, William. In fact, I cannot remember much of the day at all," mumbled she, fighting and failing to keep from yawning.

"You are tired." Darcy stood as her eyes closed: "Go to sleep, and I will see you again in the morning."

Thoughts of revenge occupied him the rest of the night and were the first thing on his mind when he rose. They continued through the day, interrupted only by visitors from Kingsdown early in the afternoon.

"We came as soon as we could," stated Miss Bennet upon exiting the carriage, followed by her sister and cousin. "How is Georgiana? Is she strong enough to receive visitors?"

"She is recovering nicely," was his assurance upon showing them into the sitting-room, "and your presence will cheer her up. Make yourself comfortable and I will bring her downstairs."

"Elizabeth, how nice of you to call," said Georgiana when Darcy led her into the room. "And you brought Louisa and Kitty with you. Thank you for thinking of me."

"We wanted to come before this," was Louisa's comment, "but Elizabeth thought we needed to leave you alone for a few days to recover without interference."

"Thank you again, Elizabeth." Georgiana's smile, and the reply which followed, looked forced to Darcy: "I would not have been good company the last few days, and I appreciate your thoughtfulness."

"Think nothing of it." Miss Bennet also seemed affected in some manner. Whether this was in response to Georgiana's reticence or some other reason, she had changed from the amiable woman who had last called.

The visit went on in this fashion until Georgiana began to yawn. At this, Darcy promptly declared, over her protests, that it was time for them to leave so his sister could return to her bed.

Gathering her companions, Miss Bennet offered farewells on their behalf and, after wishing Georgiana a speedy recovery, the party climbed into their carriage and departed.

When the visitors left, Darcy took his sister by the hand and escorted her back to bed, ignoring her protests that she was fine and should be able to join him for supper. She continued to insist that he allow her to eat at the supper table, stopping only when he observed how useful a portion of the laudanum would be in helping her get back to sleep.

With a huff of displeasure, she gave in and let him arrange the bedcovers before leaving the room. She met his goodnight with silence, which he took as a hopeful sign that the Georgiana he knew and loved was returning to him.

Supper was a solitary affair, allowing him to ponder Miss Bennet's visit, and consider whether the tension he noticed between her and Georgiana was real or merely a product of his imagination.

From what he had observed in watching the two, it appeared as though his sister was not overjoyed at Miss Bennet's decision to call. She had showed a reticence to speak, which was unlike her.

Miss Bennet's demeanor had also shifted, from a friendly, confident woman to one who seemed reluctant to engage in anything more than the most basic of conversations. Apart from Georgiana's health, they had discussed nothing of any significance, which by itself was, Darcy knew, no cause for alarm. What troubled him was that neither Georgiana nor Miss Bennet had issued an invitation for future visits at either estate, as they had on past occasions.

At length, concluding that no amount of worry would change things, he retired for the night.

The morning sun woke him as it crested the horizon, beaming into the room through his open bedroom window. Darcy, ever a light sleeper, knew returning to what had been a most pleasant dream about Miss Bennet was impossible, and cursed himself for leaving the curtains open the previous night.

With a mild imprecation, he tossed the blanket to the side and rose to face the day. Even through bleary eyes, the beauty of the morning beyond his window beckoned, waking in him an urge to walk the Pemberley paths before the day's business interfered.

Dressing hurriedly, he left the house and crossed the garden to the nearest trail, the one which coincidentally led past Kingsdown, or so he told himself.

This morning, although cool, was beautiful. The sun, still low on the horizon, cast its rays across the path, accenting the late August flowers as they seemed to strain toward its life-giving warmth.

Asters competed with Queen Anne's Lace for supremacy along the path's borders, the purples and whites of the flowers contrasting but complimenting each other. The beauty of nature's floral bouquet struck Darcy, who rarely noticed such things, and he could not help imagining Miss Bennet, her face framed by a laurel composed of these blossoms.

"They are beautiful, are they not?"

With a start, Darcy looked around to find the object of his daydream watching him, a most appealing smile upon her face.

Embarrassment at her appearance found its way to his voice, which seemed unable to form a coherent sentence, to her amusement.

"Forgive me," said he at last with an embarrassed laugh, "I was admiring the flowers and did not see you sneaking up on me."

"Excuse me," came with an answering smile, "But I did not sneak up on you. I came around the corner and saw you standing there, lost in thought. The way you were gazing at the path, I assumed the flowers had caught your imagination."

"They had, which is unusual for me. I am not normally an avid lover of nature and am more interested in the trees growing on Pemberley. I find their size and strength remarkable. Flowers, to me, are of little use unless you need some color in your garden."

"Spoken like a man," laughed Elizabeth. "You remind me of my father. When he looks at a tree, he sees something to be cut down and used for fuel in the winter or logs to construct a barn or stable, or even an assembly hall. He has no time or inclination for the more delicate and pretty parts of nature."

"A wise man, and one I should like to meet someday." The words were out of his mouth before they entered his mind and he stopped, mentally kicking himself for giving voice to his thoughts.

"How is Georgiana?" asked Elizabeth when he did not continue. "I hope she is mending."

"She is, although she still does not recall the details surrounding her injury. Many of her memories of that day are confused; I hope they straighten themselves out, but according to Mr. Tate they may never."

"That must be distressing. If there is anything I can do, please call on me."

"Thank you, I will," was his response as they parted ways.

Thoughts of her occupied the rest of his walk, replacing his appreciation of the beautiful surroundings with the realization of his growing attraction toward her.

His almost daily visits to Kingsdown had not been to consult with Mr. Bannerman, he confessed to himself, but in the hope of seeing Miss Bennet. He was aware of her penchant for morning walks, and timed his visits to coincide with her return. Her uncle was unaware of his interest, for which he was thankful, as he had no desire to answer the awkward questions such knowledge would give rise to.

Her comely appearance was appealing, but more important to Darcy was her wit and charm. When combined with her intelligence, she was as close to his idea of a perfect companion as he could imagine.

His thoughts of this woman, and the possibility of a union with her, consumed him, blocking all other considerations as he entered the house. Once inside, he climbed the stairs to the second floor and paused in from of Georgiana's room to collect himself before knocking on her door.

"What has happened?" said Georgiana when he entered her bedroom.

"What makes you think something happened?" asked he, wondering, not for the first time, how she could tell he had decided.

"I know you, William, and know when something is bothering you, or when you have reached a decision. Now out with it, what has happened to you? It came about this morning, because you did not look like this last night."

"I was thinking about you and worrying about your recovery while I am gone."

"Gone? Do you have to go to London again, William? Why now when I am still confined to bed? Can it not wait?"

"I am sorry, but the choice is not mine. This trip was postponed once, and I cannot do it again without incurring additional expenses. My absence will be less than a week, if I can settle the problems my delay caused."

"Fine, I guess," pouted she, her arms crossed and her lips pursed. "Now, what else do you have to tell me?"

"That is everything," he replied, unwilling to confess to his unformed plan.

"Nonsense," said she, the slyest of smiles crossing her lips. "I am not fooled by your attempt to hide the contented, almost rapturous look upon your face. You have decided on something that pleases you immensely. And before you try to deny it, remember that I know you better than anyone, and can tell you have decided, although not what the issue might be."

"I saw Miss Bennet this morning while I was walking. She expressed her best wishes and hopes for your speedy recovery."

"She is a good person, William, but what has this to do with anything?"

Darcy looked away from his sister, unsure if he was ready to confess his attraction. Would it be better to wait until he was able to explain himself with more clarity? Would Georgiana understand, after watching him reject so many, most of them having nothing more than designs on the status and wealth a marriage to him would gain them?

"Out with it, William. You are not leaving until you tell me, so you might as well get it over with."

"Miss Bennet has impressed me with the care she has shown since your injury. Her first question is always about the state of your recovery, and she has insisted that I call upon her if you need anything. I find her company pleasant and our conversations stimulating.

"She is an intelligent, witty woman, and I have decided I would like to know her better. I will speak with her uncle about this when I return from London."

Darcy had no idea what his sister was thinking. He thought he saw an expression of fear or alarm in her eyes, but it passed so quickly he could not be sure. Before he could ask her about it, she smiled and, with tears in her eyes, leaned forward to embrace him tightly.

"I hope you are happy," whispered his sister, "but please consider your intentions carefully. It would be unbearable to see you hurt if she rejects your approach. I want the best for you, no matter what happens."

CHAPTER XXIII

Elizabeth entered the dining-room and sat to eat her breakfast. Kitty and Louisa, busy with their own meals, paid scant attention to her until Robert stepped into the doorway.

"Are you almost ready?" asked he. "We need to leave soon, or I will be hard-pressed finish the day's work before I have to come get you again. Amelia is already waiting in the carriage."

"I just need to finish my breakfast. Give me a minute and I will be ready."

Kitty and Louisa looked at each other; their meals forgotten.

"Was there something on your mind?" wondered Elizabeth of the girls, whose expressions displayed what she assumed was concern she might not include them in her plans. "If so, tell me now because Robert needs to leave."

"Are you calling on Georgiana?" was Louisa's query, "And may we go with you?"

"I am going to leave her alone until she is feeling better. Uncle gave me permission to visit Lambton today to purchase books and some other items. He was not going to, as he could spare nobody to drive the carriage, but Robert volunteered if I got myself ready within an hour. Amelia asked to accompany me, and she was given permission, so long as she minds me and causes no problems."

"Is Mother going with you?" asked Louisa.

"No, she has too much work to complete."

"Then how is it you are taking Amelia? Mother has always said she is too young to go without supervision."

"Amelia begged her, and Aunt gave permission after I promised to pay close attention to her."

"May we come?" asked Kitty. "I want to visit the sweetshop again. And go to the milliner's as well if there is time. I love trying on the bonnets and looking in the mirror. Picturing myself wearing them to an assembly or a ball is so much fun."

"Remember what happened the last time I took you with me? More time was wasted chasing you than browsing the shops. I have no desire to go through that again."

"I will behave. Please let us come; there is little to do here, and less if there is no one here to do it with."

"There is a lot to do if you put your mind to it. The estate has paths to walk, and according to Mr. Darcy, you are free to explore the Pemberley paths as well. You can do needlework, a skill you need to practice, a lot.

"It would not hurt you to find something to read; you told Papa you wanted to learn, and reading is the best way to do that. Or you might volunteer to help your aunt with whatever she is doing. She would probably appreciate the offer."

"But you are going to Lambton with Amelia, and we want to go with you. Please, Lizzy? I will not give you any trouble, I promise. It is only fair if Amelia can go. Please, please, please?"

Elizabeth knew Kitty meant every word, as she had experienced her sister's heartfelt entreaties on more than one occasion. The problem was with Kitty's propensity to forget her promises in the excitement of discovering something new.

Should that happen, and Elizabeth was not foolish enough to assume it would not, Kitty would disappear without so much as a thought for the inconvenience her actions might cause.

She was not a disobedient girl; it was her thoughtlessness that got her into trouble more often than not, a fault Lydia used to advantage whenever it suited her. Lydia had, with the benefit of years of practice, become accustomed to the ease with which she controlled her elder sister.

Elizabeth believed Kitty's biggest shortcoming was that she lacked self-confidence and discipline. When asked for an opinion she would, no matter the circumstance, defer either to the person who posed the question or the one with the most imposing presence.

Her relationship with Lydia was one such example. Even though Lydia was younger, her character was one of questioning authority, often vehemently, while Kitty, though not a timid girl, avoided confrontation.

Lydia was by nature a headstrong girl who refused to accept Mr. Bennet's restrictions, or the reasons for them. To her, his rules were imposed to deny her any amusement, rather than to keep her safe and the family's dignity unblemished, or so she exclaimed whenever she was taken to task for untoward behavior.

Regretfully, her defiance was never a solitary affair. Without fail, she would enlist Kitty in her feats of derring-do mainly, Elizabeth guessed, because Kitty possessed the intellect to devise a plan enabling them to escape unnoticed from Longbourn.

She did not want to reject their company in Lambton; it was the difficulty of controlling Kitty's rash impulses she found so disconcerting. She did not have the patience or the energy to go chasing after a sister who, like a cat chasing a mouse, was apt to dart in many directions.

So why not keep Kitty busy by focusing her attention where Elizabeth wanted? If she successfully arranged it, the visit to Lambton might well be an enjoyable experience for everyone, including Kitty.

"It so happens," said she, the details of the idea coming together as she spoke, "there is something you can both help me with in Lambton."

A look of confusion passed between the two girls before they turned their attention back to Elizabeth, whose expression was, she hoped, cryptic.

"What kind of help are you talking about?" wondered Kitty. "Are you planning on buying so many books you will need someone to help carry them? We do not mind, but will you let us browse the shops first? It is only fair."

"I have no plans to use you as mules," laughed Elizabeth as the image of her sister and Louisa, each overburdened with armloads of books, came to mind. "I want your help with Amelia."

"Amelia is a problem?" asked Louisa. "That is a surprise. She can be persistent when she wants something but, to my knowledge, no one considers her a problem."

"I did not mean it like that. What I meant is that she will not enjoy spending most of the day with me in a bookshop, but she is too young to leave on her own. If you agree to mind her, you can come with us. You might even find something of interest, Kitty. You told Papa about wanting to explore Longbourn's library when we return. Why not start with the bookseller in Lambton? It is as good a place as any to find something of interest."

"So all we have to do is keep Amelia out of trouble? We can do that, don't you think, Louisa?"

The closing of the front door and the sound of heavy footsteps approaching the dining-room interrupted the conversation. As one, their gazes looked to the entrance to see Robert appear, a grim expression on his face.

"We need to get going," Robert's tone was one of exasperation. "I have work to do and cannot start until I take you into town. Please hurry, or I will unharness the horses and get to my tasks."

"We are ready," said Elizabeth, standing to follow her cousin to the carriage.

"Are you coming?" asked she, to which Kitty and Louisa nodded enthusiastically and hurried to catch up to her.

A flurry of activity ensued, with the two girls dashing about to find shoes and coats suitable for a day in town. Elizabeth watched the organized confusion, amused at the comments exchanged while making their preparations.

"Where did I leave my coat? Louisa, did you wear it? It is not hanging where I put it yesterday."

"I have not seen it, Kitty. And why would you assume I wore it? We are different sizes, and neither of us went out yesterday."

"Then where is it? I cannot go to town without a proper coat; today is not warm enough, and there are clouds in the sky. What if it rains? That would soak me through and ruin the rest of my day."

"Is this it? Right where you left it, on the other side of the room from where you are looking?"

"So it is. Thank you, Louisa. Now where is my bonnet? It should be right here with my coat."

Louisa emerged from the cloakroom ready for the excursion, and came to stand beside Elizabeth, whose patience with Kitty's continued muttering and panicked rushing about was waning.

"Hurry, Kitty," called she when the girl did not appear, "or we will leave you here with Christopher and your aunt. Robert is waiting."

"I cannot find a decent hat to wear. My favorite is missing, and there is nothing else suitable in here."

"What about the one on the rack directly above where you found your coat?" asked Elizabeth. "It looks like the one you usually wear."

Silence from the cloakroom was the response to her query, followed by a subdued Kitty exiting the room with the bonnet in question perched upon her head. Though Elizabeth was tempted to comment, she chose instead to usher everyone out to the carriage, and an increasingly impatient Robert.

As soon as the cabin door closed, Robert shook the reins to get the horses moving at a rapid trot, leaving the girls to seat themselves as well as they could.

"He might have waited for us to get settled," muttered Kitty as the horses' pace increased from a trot to a canter, making the cabin pitch and sway from side to side.

"There is work to do, and our delay is affecting his ability to finish before he has to come back," said Louisa. "I think we can put up with some minor discomfort."

"She is correct," agreed Elizabeth. "We should thank your cousin for giving up so much of his day just so we can go to town. He might have told Uncle he had too much work to complete today. We should all thank him when we get to Lambton, and again when he returns for us tonight, don't you think?"

"I guess," mumbled a chastened Kitty, fighting to find a comfortable position as the cabin continued to roll and pitch from the increased gait of the horses. "But I wish he would slow to a more respectable speed before we are jostled to death."

Elizabeth chose not to respond, knowing that to say anything would invite Kitty to indulge in a continual stream of complaints, each more vehement than the last. Of all the habits she appeared to have learned from Lydia, this was, in Elizabeth's opinion, the worst. The sole means of disabusing her of this sense of outrage at Robert's supposed ill treatment was to ignore her complaints until they had run their course.

The journey finished before Kitty did, which came as a relief to everyone, Elizabeth thought. Even Louisa, for once, seemed impatient for the carriage to come to a stop. When it did, she was the first out of the cabin, alighting from it as soon as it was safe.

Elizabeth, as the last to step from the coach, waved to Robert, who turned the vehicle about and set off back to Kingsdown.

"Wait for the rest of us," said she to the others, who were walking toward the nearest shop. "We need to remain together, so we do not have to waste our time looking for each other."

Louisa stopped in the center of the walkway and turned to observe the others. In doing so, she blocked the passage of others on the walk.

"Would you be so kind as to move to one side or the other, so others can use the street as well?" The request, although worded politely, came in a quite uncivil manner to the group. Elizabeth, looking up at the sound of the voice, observed a gentleman bearing an expression of distaste as he watched them mill about on the walkway.

"I am sorry we inconvenienced you," was her apology, while gesturing at Louisa and Kitty to step out of the way. "My sister and cousins let their anticipation overrule their common sense."

"I cannot speak for the county you came from," grumbled the gentleman, stepping around the girls, "but here we do not make a habit of impeding others."

Elizabeth watched him walk away from them along the street until he turned the corner at its end. Only then did she notice the attention their encounter had attracted. Of those in their vicinity, and the street today was reasonably full, most had witnessed the exchange.

Elizabeth felt surprise and concern at the reactions to their conversation. Unlike their first visit to Lambton, when everyone met them with cheerful greetings and almost universal smiles of welcome, the people she saw today regarded them with undisguised animosity. Try as she might, Elizabeth did not see a smile on a single face.

"We seem to have made a spectacle of ourselves," remarked she to Louisa, "but I am not sure what we did wrong. Did you recognize the gentleman we offended?"

"I cannot remember seeing him before, but I rarely come to Lambton."

"We must have done something," stated Elizabeth. "I hope we avoid offending anybody else. Please behave yourselves until we leave.

"Where is the bookseller? The one in Lambton must be larger than Meryton's, and I would like to meet the shop owner. The merchant in

Meryton always suggests the best books, and I expect it will be the same here. He is probably an avid reader; from my experience they usually are. Who wants to come with me?"

"He is in the next street over," answered Louisa. "I can show you. There is a milliner a few doors away that I want to visit. The shop will have new bonnets, and I want to see them. It has been a few months since I have been there, so I expect the displays are changed."

"Lead the way," Elizabeth indicated with a flourish of her hand, "and we will follow. Kitty, you are in charge of Amelia. Please make sure she is with you when we get to the bookshop."

"I will, Lizzy," promised Kitty, grabbing Amelia's hand and hurrying to catch up, as Louisa was by this time nearing the corner.

The walk, although short, was not an overly pleasant experience. Rather than the smiles and welcoming greetings they had encountered on the previous visit, a good number of those they passed met them with sullen faces and dour expressions. The change was so drastic that Elizabeth wondered if they had come to the same town.

"Here is your bookstore," pointed Louisa while gesturing to a shop that, while smaller than many of those around it, was still much larger than the one in Meryton.

"Thank you," muttered Elizabeth, peering with anticipation through the shop's small front window. From the little she saw, the interior was much like the merchants she was used to in Meryton and London. A shiver of excitement went through her at the thought of the books within, just waiting to be purchased and poured over upon their return to Kingsdown tonight.

"The milliner is just down this street," directed Louisa, pointing to a shop three doors distant. "I will be there, looking at her newest bonnets."

"I will meet you there in two hours," said Elizabeth. "Are you coming with me, Kitty?"

"May I stay with Louisa? I would rather browse the milliner's."

A tug at her sleeve drew Elizabeth's attention to Amelia, who was wearing a hopeful expression. "May I go with you, Elizabeth? I would like to see the books so I can find something interesting to read."

"Yes, you may." Elizabeth chuckled at the way her plans had been altered, "and I will help you."

Pulling the door open, she followed her young cousin into a room filled with so much reading material it took her breath away.

The shop, although small, almost overflowed with printed materials of every shape and kind. Shelves, built from floor to ceiling, covered the walls and stood in rows running the length of the room. Each shelf was tightly packed with books of all types, from novels to scientific treatises on every subject imaginable.

Along the front of the shop was a counter which held an assortment of recent newspapers, published in London and various other towns and cities.

"There is too much. How can we find anything interesting?" asked Amelia, her voice hushed as if in reverence.

"Everything will be in some sort of order, at least it has been in every bookshop I have visited. With a bit of effort, and a lot of browsing, we will make sense of the system, and find something to purchase."

"I hope so," said Amelia, "but I am not even sure where to begin."

With a laugh, Elizabeth began at the front of the store and, upon studying the contents of the first shelf, was able to explain the manner of organization the bookseller used to group his various titles. Amelia proved to be a quick study, understanding the pattern almost at once and browsing with an intensity Elizabeth found surprising.

The time passed in a haze of discovery and satisfaction, ending when the two approached the counter, Amelia carrying a book of poetry and Elizabeth with two novels and a periodical that had caught her eye.

"Did you find everything you were looking for?" asked the bookseller, totalling their purchase on a pad of paper. "I try to stock something for all interests. My customers come from as far away as Sheffield and Derby, so I must be doing something right."

"You have a far better selection than I am used to," praised Elizabeth. "Meryton's bookstore is much smaller, and does not have the room you do. It is unfortunate, because I love to read but often cannot find anything to my liking there."

"Meryton, you say? I am not familiar with that town. Is it far from here?"

"It is small, not much larger than a hamlet. We are a few hours from London, in Hertfordshire County. I am here visiting my cousins, the Bannermans. You are familiar with the family, I presume."

"I am," growled the merchant as he snatched the books from the counter and placed them out of reach behind him. "And I have nothing to sell you. Leave, at once!"

Shocked at the outburst, Elizabeth could muster no response to this sudden vitriol. The merchant, seemingly unsatisfied with her hesitation, came around the counter and, throwing open the door, hastened them outside, slamming it behind them.

Elizabeth looked at Amelia, whose confusion seemed to match her own. "What did we do to upset him?" she asked her cousin, who responded with a shrug of her shoulders.

"I hope it was not something I did," said Amelia. "Although I cannot recall doing anything but look at his books. Most of them I did not touch, as I was afraid I might drop or damage them."

"You did nothing wrong. Oh well, maybe we should locate Louisa and Kitty, so we can go back to our meeting spot. I promised Robert we would be waiting when he arrived."

"Is that Louisa?" asked Amelia, pointing down the street to where she saw the girl walking toward them, Kitty following.

To Elizabeth, they looked dejected, as though the day had been a complete disappointment. Neither girl wore the cheerful, excited expression they had when Elizabeth left them earlier, their countenances the saddest Elizabeth had seen in a long while.

"Why the glum faces?" wondered she when they stopped in front of her. "Was the milliner's display uninspiring?"

"It was fine," sighed Kitty, "but she would not let us touch them. When I tried, she told us to leave and not come back. She said I was a disgrace, and she wanted nothing to do with me. She was less friendly to Louisa. I thought the other patrons were going to object until she told them our names. Then they looked as though they wanted to punish us, but I cannot say why."

"We visited the confectioner instead, but they were no better," said Louisa. "I was told they did not want my business, so we thought it best that we come back here."

"I wonder what has happened since our first visit. Maybe Robert will know. We should get back, so he does not need to wait for us." With that, Elizabeth set off toward the street on which their visit had begun.

The return to the meeting place was an uncomfortable walk. It seemed to Elizabeth that everybody they met scowled at them or looked away in disgust. It was a relief to see Robert had arrived early, so she urged them on at a faster pace, escaping the town with its unfriendly, hostile residents, her only desire.

"I did not expect you so soon," said she when they got to Robert. "But I am grateful you are. If you are ready, we want to go home."

"Has something happened?" asked he. "You look upset."

"We can talk about it at Kingsdown. Please leave, we have been here long enough."

Robert shut the carriage door and, climbing up to the driver's seat, reached down to take the reins in his hands.

"You should be ashamed, associating with that degenerate!" yelled a woman passing the carriage. "There will be consequences."

"Excuse me?" said he, clearly confused. "To whom are you referring?"

"You know very well, or you should. If not, you are as bad as she is, and I want nothing to do with you."

She concluded her diatribe by spitting at him, the act shocking in its unladylike vehemence.

With a shake of the reins, Robert put the carriage into motion while, in the cabin, Elizabeth tried without success to understand the difference in Lambton's residents since they last visited.

"What did we do?" asked Kitty. "I did not misbehave, not intentionally, anyway."

"I cannot imagine." Elizabeth was confused at the reception they had received. "Maybe Robert or Uncle will know. Hopefully, this has nothing to do with us, but it certainly seems like it does."

The conversation continued in this manner until they reached Kingsdown, where the subject was dropped and forgotten in the preparations for the evening meal. By the time Elizabeth retired for the night she had concluded that, because she had done nothing to provoke the animosity, she would not stay awake half the night worrying about it.

She climbed into bed and fell promptly into a sleep whose dreams were again about Mr. Darcy and the wedded bliss they would enjoy.

Chapter XXIV

Georgiana signed her name and placed the pen on the desk while she waited for the ink to dry. In the meantime, she read over her composition to be sure her writing was legible, and it might prompt the intended recipient to act accordingly.

Her purpose in composing the letter, she told herself, was not to cause undue hardship, but to keep her brother from making what she considered a terrible mistake.

Georgiana loved William and felt a responsibility for his future happiness. This path he wanted to follow would not, in her opinion, allow that result. If something as simple as a letter sent to the correct person was enough to dissuade him, she would try.

When the ink was sufficiently dry, she took the page from the desk and folded it before placing the correspondence into the envelope and sealing the flap.

A knock on her bedroom door announced her maid, Annabelle, who entered at her summons.

"You have a caller, Miss Darcy. Miss Haversham is enquiring after your health and would like to visit if you are agreeable."

"Of course, Annabelle, I am always available for Sarah. Please show her up, but say nothing concerning my present state."

Taking the finished letter from the desk, she handed it to the servant: "And please have this posted immediately. I would like it delivered as soon as possible."

"Yes, Miss Darcy," said the girl, accepting the envelope and leaving the room to retrieve Georgiana's friend, a delay which allowed her to ponder the events of the past week.

To wake alone in the woods was unsettling. Georgiana remembered, in the finest of details, the smells of the various trees, vines, and other plants surrounding her, and the sound of the brook gurgling away merrily beside her.

She knew Sarah was with her that day, despite her assertions to the contrary, and recalled their conversations with little effort. The girl had been angry, and Georgiana remembered her satisfaction in the knowledge she held the upper hand in their little contest.

What was missing from her memory, no matter how hard she tried, were the events immediately preceding her injury, or of Sarah leaving.

Had she been alone, Sarah having departed for some as yet unknown reason, or had Sarah witnessed the attack and fled, hoping to avoid a similar fate?

She could recall no additional presence in the woods that day, although it was possible someone else had been there, unnoticed by either of them. But if that were the case, why would Sarah leave her to fend for herself, rather than running back to Pemberley for William? And why would she then tell William she was away from Derbyshire altogether? These and other questions bothered Georgiana, causing sleepless nights and restless days, until in frustration she had resolved to put them from her mind.

No, Sarah struck her, of that she was sure, having arrived at the conclusion when no other scenario she came up with answered the questions satisfactorily.

This visit would be a welcome respite from the otherwise unrelenting tedium of the previous few days. William, upon departing for London, had left strict instructions confining his sister to her bed until his expected return at week's end.

Georgiana discovered to her dismay that she was unable, on this occasion, to ignore his demands that she stay shut up in her room. Snell, who was left behind to ensure her recovery proceeded as it should, thwarted all her attempts to leave.

That William had gone to London unaccompanied was uncharacteristic of him, and to leave his manservant in charge of her care was something he had never done before. Snell's displeasure with the decision was clear in his demeanor which, while not sullen, was also not cheerful or overly pleasant.

To be sure, the man had never been a source of humor or glad tidings, but he had always treated her with a certain amount of deference. That was at present in short supply, as he would not allow her to leave the bedroom, not even for something as innocent as to sit on a bench in the garden for an hour.

"My instructions from Mr. Darcy were that you keep to your chambers," was his only reply when Georgiana protested. "I have no desire to face his wrath which, I am certain, would be fierce should he discover I failed to look after you as he demanded."

"But the day is so nice," she pleaded. "Is it too much to allow me to feel the sun's warmth on my face? I need to do something which does not involve watching shadows cross my bedroom walls. Please, Snell? I will not breathe a word of this to William, I promise, and it will free you from having to monitor me."

Snell considered her request, or so Georgiana thought, until he dashed her hopes. "I will not ignore my instructions," said he. "You are to stay in your room; on this Mr. Darcy was clear."

Georgiana considered going outside anyway, but when she tried, Snell appeared as if out of nowhere, almost before she had closed her bedroom door.

"You are not allowed in the hall," she heard, causing her to start at his silent approach. "Please stay in your room. If you need a book to read, tell me and I will bring it from the library. I can have the cook send something up if you are hungry. Should you need something else, I will inform your maid and she will attend to your needs."

Georgiana marched back into her room and slammed the door behind her, all the while muttering a mild oath.

William even prohibited Mrs. Annesley from entering the room to resume her instruction, which he had paused because of her injury. Initially, Georgiana found it preferable not having to concentrate on lessons that in her opinion were ridiculous anyway.

Of what use was an ability to understand French or Italian if she would never use those languages? Why did Mrs. Annesley refuse to offer instruction in mathematics which, despite William's expressions of doubt in her intelligence, fascinated her? What was there about the subject that made even the idea of its instruction so abhorrent?

She was not a stupid person, as her brother seemed to think. Just because she was not interested in the study of approved languages, or the proper method of mending a torn sleeve, it did not mean she was incapable of learning.

Her relief had, however, changed to restlessness at her forced confinement and its resulting monotony. Could William not see that a complete recovery would not happen if he restricted her to this room?

"Is Georgiana's recovery proceeding apace?"

Sarah's voice, tinged with worry, roused Georgiana from her contemplations. Moving from her writing desk, she crossed to the window and, seating herself in the settee placed before it, pulled a blanket across her legs as the door opened to admit her friend.

Sarah stood in the entrance, looking, Georgiana thought, apprehensive and a trifle unsure of herself. Georgiana said nothing, regarding Sarah in such a way as to suggest her injury was more severe than it was.

Sarah was afraid, that much was easy to see. She was trembling, so much that Georgiana almost expected her to collapse, or burst into tears at any moment. Georgiana was content to let her friend's sense of guilt raise the spectre of extreme punishment for her actions. Although she would never tell Sarah, this was simply another part of the competition they had entered.

"Thank you for coming to see me," said she in a quiet voice. "I have missed the pleasure of your company."

At the sound of Georgiana's voice, Sarah seemed to break free of the trepidation that had seized her. In a rush, she was at Georgiana's side, her apology bursting forth in a tumult of words difficult to separate one from the other.

"It is such a relief to see you here, alive and well. Oh, Georgiana, please forgive me, I cannot excuse my actions, but you made me so mad I lost all control. Can you ever forgive me? I know that what I did was inexcusable, but all I could think of was that you were going to win and I was not going to stand for it. I will never do that again; you must forgive me. Please, Georgiana, say that you will!"

Sarah's ramblings showed no sign of ending, and Georgiana had no desire to make her suffer any more, so she raised her hand and motioned her to silence. When Sarah quieted, Georgiana noticed her cheeks were wet, a sign of the anguish she had suffered since the attack she had visited upon her friend.

"What did I do that was so bad you had to beat me and leave me alone in the forest?" was her sedate response. "I thought we were friends, but one friend would not do that to another, especially not with the history we share. We have been each other's closest companions since we were children. In all that time we have never come close to blows, at least I have not."

Georgiana introduced the observation with a smile, deciding there was no better way to relieve Sarah's torment than to introduce a bit of humor to lessen her anxiety.

"I am sorry, but when you claimed Robert Bannerman was yours, and described the plan you had devised, I lost my temper. Then you gloated about my incompetence in pursuing him, and I could not stand it anymore."

"I do not recall saying you were incompetent," corrected Georgiana softly. "I remember discussing the way I had attracted the boy, and laughing at your insistence that I cheated, which I still maintain I did not need to do."

"It was the way you told me. You seemed to enjoy belittling me so much and pointing to the fact that you are always the victor in our contests. I should not have let you provoke me so easily. After all it is something you excel at, and I fall for it every time."

Sarah's words affected Georgiana in a way that would have surprised her before the incident. Sarah's statement was true, there was no other way of looking at it. Georgiana had acted selfishly, consumed by the need to triumph over her friend, no matter the cost. To do so, she had exploited her advantages, and mocked Sarah's indignation.

She was ashamed of herself, and of her actions which led Sarah to lash out in anger, almost killing her in the process.

Still, there remained unanswered questions, at least one of which had bothered her since the first night, when William forced her to take the laudanum so she could sleep. Those questions, if her memory of that night was correct, returned in her drug induced stupor, becoming a recurring nightmare she could not seem to wake from.

"What did you hit me with? You were not carrying a weapon, and I did not see one lying near me when I woke. I wondered at first if you used a rock, but there were none of any size in the vicinity, unless you threw it into the water before leaving."

"There was a dead branch lying on the path. You stepped over it, probably without even noticing it was there. In my anger, I picked it up and hit you with it. When I left you, I threw it into the trees. It is probably still there."

"Then why, after beating me senseless, did you leave? Did it not occur to you I needed help?"

"You dropped so quickly that I was sure I had killed you. The horror of what I had done overtook me, and I wanted nothing more than to escape before someone discovered me standing over your body. In a panic, I ran back to the stables and, as luck would have it, was able to take my horse and leave without being seen."

"How did you manage such a thing, and do it without William seeing you? The stable and paddock are busy places; somebody should have noticed what you were doing and come to offer help."

"For all I know, it was *because* they were busy that I left unnoticed. There was a commotion of some sort in the stable, and the saddle was still on my horse, forgotten, I suspect, in the excitement. I led him around to the back of the stable, mounted, and left for home. I thanked my good fortune in riding to Pemberley, instead of taking the carriage, as I had originally planned."

"So you left me alone to die? I thought we were better friends than that. To realize that you left without a care for my safety hurts me deeply."

"I returned! I was only half of the way home when better sense convinced me to go back. I searched the woods, but you were not where I left you. That convinced me someone had discovered you and carried you back to Pemberley, so I went home as well."

"Why did you tell William you had been in Bath with your father? Did it not occur to you that a simple conversation between the two would expose your lie?"

"I called on you because the rumors of your rescue were circulating in Lambton. When I spoke with Mr. Darcy, he told me you were sure that I was lying injured somewhere in the woods. In my panic to avoid his censure, and the certainty of severe punishment, I told him I was with my father, and had only just returned.

"I also told him I was alone at Haversham Lodge again, as my father went to London suddenly and would not return for another week. It was my hope that by the time they met again your brother might not raise the subject."

"Please forgive me, Georgiana. I am so sorry for my actions. I will do anything to make it up to you."

Sarah's earnest plea brought a smile to Georgiana, and relief at the knowledge that her friend harbored no feelings of hatred towards her, despite Georgiana's treatment. She had to mend her ways, she realized, before losing Sarah's friendship forever, and today seemed like an opportune moment to begin.

"There is nothing to forgive. My conduct was inexcusable, and I caused the anger that drove you to lash out like you did.

"We should call off this silly contest. It is harming our friendship and doing nothing for Mr. Bannerman. I cannot find a reason to justify what we have been doing. If you agree, we can drop this competition, and any others we might find to wager on in the future."

Georgiana watched as many emotions, moving from anger to distrust, and from distrust to relief, passed across her friend's visage, until acceptance at last seemed to settle in place.

"I would like that," said Sarah. "The only reason I entered any of these competitions was my fear that, should I refuse, you would find others to enjoy them with. But what about Mr. Bannerman? By now the poor fellow is probably so confused that he cannot tell up from down. It might be cruel to suddenly stop paying attention to him."

"Let me worry about that," smiled Georgiana, to a fleeting look of suspicion from Sarah. "I have no intention of misleading him any longer, but it might be best to let him down slowly. My visits to Kingsdown will continue, although not as often, and I will pay less attention to him when I am there. He will eventually lose interest in me, although it might take a while."

"I hope you know what you are doing," said a visibly relieved Sarah. "It would be a shame to disappoint him but in reality, there was never a chance that he could court either of us, anyway."

"To be honest, I am thankful you attacked me," stated Georgiana, to Sarah's confusion.

"When my rescuers found me, they took me toward Kingsdown, as they were already going in that direction. At the time I was confused, but when we neared the property, I was sure I did not belong there, so they turned around and brought me here. In my addled state I begged them not to leave me at the Bannerman estate and, from reports I have since heard, they assumed my attacker was resident there.

"I chose not to correct them, either then or since. Annabelle tells me that rumors abound in Lambton about my attack and the person responsible. Apparently, everyone blames Elizabeth Bennet, most likely because she is not from Derbyshire, so to most people she is a stranger."

"Why not correct their assumptions? An accusation like this might damage her reputation and turn everyone in Derbyshire against her."

"I know, and it helps me immensely. William is growing fond of Miss Bennet and told me he is going to ask permission to call on her."

"And?"

"She is a nice enough person, but not one he should want as a part of the Darcy family. She is too uncultured, and her personality is much too forceful. I was afraid she would dominate him, to where my brother would disappear, and in his place would be a mere shell of the man I know and love, unable to make a decision without her approval.

"A union such as that would bring shame and derision to the Darcy name, and the result would be William's loss of standing in the circles he inhabits. Of course, such a loss would reflect poorly on me, and my chances of marriage to any of the eligible members of the Ton would suffer. I cannot, in good conscience, let a circumstance of that misfortune befall him."

"Certainly Mr. Darcy would not allow himself to fall in love with a woman like you describe. He is too intelligent, and his own personality is too forceful to fall prey to such an odious person."

"You have not seen how much he has changed. He walks around in a daze, and every second sentence concerns Miss Bennet, and how smart, or attractive, or intelligent she is. No, Sarah, I am afraid the woman has landed him, and is only waiting for the opportune moment to lay her claim. He does not realize what she is doing, so enamored has he become.

"If I do not act now, I will lose the chance, so I am doing something about the problem. A letter has been posted that should arouse concern in the proper places and, if I am not mistaken, result in corrective actions being taken."

"You are making a mistake, Georgiana, one that could have unforeseen consequences. Once begun, you will have no control over its outcome. If you want my advice, change your mind before it is too late."

"I know exactly what I am doing, and am fully prepared for the consequences, whatever they may be."

Sarah was unsure, of that Georgiana was certain. If she were honest with herself, Georgiana also harbored doubts about the wisdom of her plan, but the future of the Darcy name was too important. She was not going to stand idly by while William threw his future, and the future of the family, away on an ill-advised romance that would, she knew in her heart, leave him unhappy for the rest of his life.

"I should go," said Sarah, "but please reconsider. The life most affected by a successful completion of your plan could very well be your own."

With a wave and a quick hug, Sarah let herself out, leaving Georgiana alone to ponder their conversation.

CHAPTER XXV

Elizabeth skipped along the path, her steps light and her mood buoyant. The morning was warm, a light breeze redolent with aromas from the foxglove and enchanter's nightshade growing abundantly on either side and extending, like a colorful carpet, to the woods beyond. The clouds above were few and insubstantial, existing only, in her opinion, to draw attention to the brilliant blue in which they floated, proud of their apparent indolence.

Her thoughts concerned Mr. Darcy, as they did every morning, it seemed.

These daily walks, which she had continued since arriving at Kingsdown, were fast becoming the highlight of her day. It was not because of the beauty and variety of the flora and fauna in and around the paths she trod, but because of Mr. Darcy's regular presence when she returned each morning.

She looked forward, with greater anticipation each day, to his amiable greeting as she concluded her walk, and the pleasant conversation that seemed to flow so naturally from the man. Their conversations varied, ranging from mundane topics concerning the day's weather to subjects where a woman's opinion did not matter, such as the conflict with France or the latest gossip concerning the House of Lords.

Elizabeth was not afraid to forward a viewpoint opposing Mr. Darcy's, and enjoyed the lively debate her views occasionally caused. She was confident in her ability to hold her ground in any difference of opinion and had, more than once, given the man something to consider as she explained her position.

She valued his opinion, never offered, it seemed, before careful consideration of the subject under discussion. It was invariably defensible, getting to the core of the matter with unerring accuracy.

Of all the debates she had engaged in through the years, those with Mr. Darcy were, without a doubt, the most rewarding. His ability to challenge her statements with lucid arguments of his own intrigued her in a manner she had never experienced.

She loved his way of questioning what he determined were erroneous ideas on her part. His attitude was not dismissive or condescending, an approach she appreciated, as it suggested he found her comments worthy of consideration.

His ability to carry on an intelligent conversation was but one attribute she found attractive. He also possessed a keen sense of humor that ranged widely, from poking fun at himself and illustrious members of the Ton, to instances he described, which to Elizabeth bordered on the absurd. His penchant to laugh at his own errors was an endearing quality that proved he was not apt to take himself, or any of his acquaintances, too seriously, regardless of their status.

Thoughts of Mr. Darcy became daydreams, as the world around her faded and a picture of herself, wedded and mistress of Pemberley, replaced the awareness of her surroundings.

She saw their children, first a boy brought up as heir to the estate, followed by three girls, each the picture of health and beauty. The life she envisioned was idyllic, with nary a problem to disturb them, or a disagreement between husband and wife, whose love for each other would be all-encompassing.

Their son would grow to be a just and compassionate man, taught to value truth and charity above all else. He would learn from the most eminent of instructors and attend the finest schools, where his intelligence and thirst for knowledge would drive him onward, his search for enlightenment an unrelenting passion.

Elizabeth would see to her daughters' education herself. She would never allow their gender to impede their future and would accept nothing but the best tutors. Nobody would deny her daughters an opportunity to learn.

With a sigh, Elizabeth opened her eyes to find she had wandered far from Kingsdown to within sight of Pemberley. The house was massive, a building that looked large enough to billet an entire regiment, and one even Elizabeth's imagination, fanciful though it was, did not picture living in without a multitude of children to raise.

Georgiana must feel so abandoned, all by herself so often and denied the companionship of the parents who loved her with all their hearts. She must ache for the company of her mother and father, or her brother. I wish there were something I could do to ease her loneliness.

With a last look at the Darcy home, Elizabeth turned to retrace her steps, her thoughts now drawn to Georgiana and the pain she must constantly endure, being left essentially to herself in a house of that size. She recalled their first meeting, and Georgiana's seeming reticence to expose much of her inner self.

Elizabeth at first ascribed it to conceit regarding her superior status, but their friendship dispelled that opinion. Her regard for Georgiana had changed, from that of a spoiled, somewhat disrespectful girl badly in need of correction, to a shy, insecure young woman trying desperately to establish friendships, amid fear of rejection.

She would not ignore what looked to her like pleas for acceptance, which the girl expected Elizabeth to ridicule, or worse. She was not as self-assured as she let on. What she needed, more than anything, was a friend to offer support in times of need, and Elizabeth was up to the task.

Her attempt to encourage Georgiana was initially resisted, she thought, but her persistence was paying off in friendship. At each meeting, she had grown more comfortable, or so Elizabeth supposed.

The young woman she called on after the injury was not the same one who accepted her friendship when Elizabeth arrived. She appeared uncomfortable with Elizabeth's presence, so much that Elizabeth came close to offering the obligatory wishes for a complete and rapid recovery, and shepherding Louisa and Kitty back to the carriage. What stopped her was Mr. Darcy's concern for his sister's health, and the gratitude he expressed at their compassionate visit. She was not prepared to leave in the face of his relief at the concern they had all shown in visiting.

There was nothing to be done about it, she decided, other than to support both Mr. Darcy and his sister as she mended. Perhaps, when she recovered, whatever was troubling her would resolve itself.

Elizabeth sighed and looked again at the beauty of the day. How she loved this area, with its solitary paths bordered by the abundance of flowers, continuously changing with the seasons, from spring to summer. Each new month saw different blossoms appear, vying for supremacy with the stragglers from the month previous.

The woodlands, steadfast and silent, had seemed content with spring's budding of leaves on branches and the growth of parasitic vines that in some ways benefitted both host and intruder.

As spring gave way to summer, the now leafy branches shaded the ground below. They reminded her of guardians, watching over the countryside while providing safety and shelter for the wildlife whose homes were within the forest canopy.

When autumn drew near, she knew the leaves would turn and begin to fall, and the flowers would die in preparation for the snows of winter. To her, each season was beautiful in its own way, and she could honestly say that none of them was preferable to another.

Too soon, the gate appeared, and her walk ended. She entered the property, feeling a touch of melancholy at having to leave the serenity of the path for the often chaotic world.

Kingsdown was quiet this morning, an uncommon state, in her experience. Other than two tenants tending to their fields she saw nobody, which was puzzling. Of greater importance to her was the absence of Mr. Darcy, who had been there to greet her on each of the previous eight or ten mornings.

Her disappointment was not surprising; she was accustomed to their discussions and the lively repartee that passed between them, further enhancing the conversation. Her uncle was missing as well, she noticed upon scanning the grounds.

"Everyone is inside," came Robert's voice, his form hidden in the darker stable entrance, "and Mr. Darcy is not here, if you were looking for him. I was told to send you to the house as soon as you arrived."

"Why? Has something happened? I hope Georgiana is no worse. Mr. Darcy thought she was healing when we visited last week."

Robert regarded her for almost a minute without speaking. To Elizabeth, he looked to be judging her for committing some sin, although she had no idea what it might be. He seemed to find her lacking in some way, and that made her uneasy.

"Georgiana is still recovering, and is doing well, according to the gossip in Lambton."

"That is good news. I was so worried about her. She did not look well when I saw her, despite Mr. Darcy's assurances."

"I suppose not, considering what she suffered. The rumors I heard say she almost died. Mr. Darcy is beside himself with anger and has sworn vengeance upon her attacker. I would not want to be the guilty party."

"Nor would I," agreed Elizabeth, which drew a sharp, piercing glare from her cousin, surprising in its intensity.

"You should go inside," said he, bending to retrieve a pitchfork from the stable floor. "They are waiting for you. Your delay is probably making matters worse."

Robert retreated into the structure, leaving Elizabeth to puzzle over his last remark. Why would her speed in returning make matters worse, and what matters was he referring to? There were no indications of trouble when she left this morning, so what had occurred since then?

Had Kitty done or said something she ought not to? If that were the case, Elizabeth did not know what it might be, although in the past she had, without realizing, caused trouble for herself and others. Kitty never created problems out of spite; she was the happiest of her sisters and was not in the habit of holding grudges. She was slow to anger, and usually unable to recall an argument the day after, a quality Elizabeth envied.

She quickened her steps, hoping that whatever the issue, they might resolve it rapidly and with little fuss.

The house was quiet when she entered, the only sound that of the pianoforte in the music room. Elizabeth turned in that direction and proceeded down the hall. As she approached the library, the door opened and her uncle stepped into the hall to block her passage.

"Your aunt and I need to talk with you," said he, pointing to Mrs. Bannerman, who sat by the fire, a mournful expression on her face.

Obediently, Elizabeth went into the room and sat in the chair her uncle pointed to, across from her relatives.

"You can probably guess why I sent for you," was his surprising declaration, "but I wanted first to give you the chance to explain yourself."

"Forgive me, Uncle, but I don't know what you mean."

"The time for declaring your innocence is past, Elizabeth. From reports circulating in Lambton, you are the guilty party. My only question is, did you act alone or was your sister with you?"

"I did nothing wrong, Uncle, and even if I had, I cannot give you an answer until you tell me what I am accused of."

Mr. Bannerman had risen to his feet at Elizabeth's protestations of innocence, and now he paced the room, his face set in what she presumed was anger at her declaration.

"Calm yourself, George," said Mrs. Bannerman. "Let Elizabeth give us her version."

"He is referring to rumors that you attacked Miss Darcy and left her for dead," she explained. "According to what we were told, a couple found her and took her to Pemberley. After delivering her to Mr. Darcy, they stopped in Lambton to feed and water their horses and to eat supper at the inn.

"Someone overheard them discussing the affair over their meal, and the conversation was mostly about the terror she exhibited when she saw they were bringing her here. Apparently, she pleaded and begged them to take her anywhere else but would not tell them why she was so afraid of Kingsdown.

"The rumor grew, and in each telling the account probably expanded, until everyone in Lambton became certain you were the person who assaulted poor Miss Darcy and then left without a second thought."

"I did no such thing!" exclaimed Elizabeth. "I would never commit an act so vile; please believe me."

"If that is so," objected Mr. Bannerman, "why were you accused? As much as I want to trust you, rumors are usually based on at least a bit of truth."

"But I was nowhere near Pemberley. I spent the day with Louisa and Amelia and did not leave the estate. Ask Kitty, she was with us as well."

"That is true, Father," said Louisa from the hall. "Forgive me for interrupting, but the door was open, and I heard your voices. Elizabeth was with us in the music room, helping me with a piece I was having difficulty mastering. She did not leave my side at all that day.

"When the maid called us for supper, she mentioned she had no chance to enjoy her regular walk in the morning. I had interrupted her on the way out, so my request confined her to the house all day, or so she said. Of course, she was joking, and we both laughed at the comment.

"She did not attack Georgiana; she was with me when it happened."

"I trust her, George. Louisa has never lied to us before, and I do not think she would start now."

Mr. Bannerman shook his head, looking to Elizabeth as if he believed denying the truth of Louisa's statement would put the matter to rest.

"Even if what you say is true, and I do not doubt you," said he before Louisa could add anything else, "that does not settle the issue."

"We need to make Mr. Darcy see that these rumors are false," implored Mrs. Bannerman. "We have to do whatever it takes to protect our niece from these lies and suppositions. George, we cannot let them stand."

"The problem," observed Mr. Bannerman, "is that we can take to the rooftops to proclaim her innocence and our support for her, but it will not help. At present, it is Elizabeth's word against Miss Darcy's. Lambton's residents, and all of Derbyshire, will believe Miss Darcy, not Elizabeth.

"She has lived here all her life, while Elizabeth is a visitor, unknown to any of Lambton's residents. When you combine that with the fact that she was reportedly terrified about coming here, suspicions regarding the newcomer would have changed to certainty she is the guilty party. Miss Darcy is his sister, and that means people will believe her, not Elizabeth.

"My support will not help Elizabeth, but it might affect our family, badly, I might add."

Mrs. Bannerman was getting angry, that much was clear, and it worried Elizabeth. She appreciated the support her aunt was giving her but did not want such a matter to come between them.

"Maybe we can settle this if we call on Mr. Darcy and talk to him about it," proposed she, hoping to calm the situation and restore peace. "He is a reasonable man, is he not? Surely if I am there to give him the truth, he will see that I was not her attacker."

"Ahem," interrupted Bertram from the library door. "Mr. Darcy is asking if he might confer with you in private. Shall I show him to the sitting-room?"

"No, Bertram, bring him to the library," directed Mr. Bannerman.

"It looks like Mr. Darcy also wants to put the matter to rest. We will continue our conversation later," said he, motioning everyone out of the room. "If I am not mistaken, this situation will end quickly."

"What could he want?" asked Kitty, joining Elizabeth in the garden, where she had gone to escape the stress. "I hope he apologizes for these nasty, unfounded rumors."

"That is probably not the reason for his visit," Elizabeth replied, "but we will see, I suppose. He did not come to discuss the weather; of that I am sure."

"I have a mind to give him my opinion of his sister," said Kitty, stamping her foot to emphasize her indignation. "How dare he accuse you! If I never see him again, it will be entirely too soon!"

Her point made, Kitty strode away, her back straight and wearing a look so outraged it caused Elizabeth to chuckle at her righteous indignation. If left up to Kitty, she would straighten things out in short order. The picture that sprang to mind, of Kitty browbeating poor Mr. Darcy into submission over Elizabeth's treatment at the hands of the Lambton busybodies, was delicious.

Her uncle and Mr. Darcy came out of the house as Kitty went in, the expression on her face appearing to dare either of the men to address her. To Elizabeth, Mr. Darcy looked concerned yet resolute, suggesting he had arrived at a decision which gave him no pleasure.

"Miss Bennet," said he, waving her back to the bench she had risen from at their approach. "All of Lambton is talking about the attack on Georgiana, and your part in it. I will not accuse you without reason, but I need the truth. Were you the one who assaulted her so violently and then left her to die?"

"Mr. Darcy, I am not the person everybody seems to think I am. I could no more inflict such harm on your sister than upon the vilest of criminals. I do not countenance such a thing, not even for the most deplorable acts of debauchery. Please believe me."

"I want to, but we are not so well acquainted that I can rule out any possibility. What can you tell me about that day that I do not yet know?"

"There is nothing I can offer you, as I did not see or speak with Georgiana the day of her attack. As I told Uncle, I spent the day with Louisa and Amelia, as well as Kitty. They can vouch for me, and to the truth of what I am saying.

"I had no reason to cause her harm, then or now. I consider her a friend, and thought she returned my regard."

"My sister is not a liar, Miss Bennet," declared Mr. Darcy, his visage stern as he regarded her with a look most venomous and angry.

"I did not say she was," said Elizabeth, her worry increasing as the conversation looked to be on the verge of descending into nothing more than vitriol. "My intent was to suggest that she might be confused, nothing more. An injury as serious as hers must have been disorienting, or worse. Why she would lay the cause of her wound at my feet I cannot guess, but I had nothing to do with it. I spent my day at Kingsdown."

Mr. Darcy listened, thankfully without interruption, but whether he accepted her assertions of innocence, she could not tell. To her his anger seemed unappeased, the fire in his eyes unchanged.

Elizabeth's emotions were turbulent, ranging from the fear of losing his respect and friendship to anger at the false accusation leveled upon her, and even toward the Bannerman family for their invitation to visit this year.

If he were unwilling to accept her insistence that she was telling the truth, he could leave. She would not stand here and accept his censure when she had done nothing to earn it.

"What about the sympathetic words you expressed the last time we walked together," asked he, still upset and apparently unwilling to acknowledge her declaration of innocence. "Were they just that, words, designed to throw suspicion elsewhere? You impressed me as one of the few truly decent and honorable people I had ever met, but maybe I was wrong."

"I meant what I said then, and my feelings have not changed. The attack was horrible, and the extent of Georgiana's injuries more so. I would tell you again that I did not do this, but it seems there is nothing I can do to change your mind. If that is so, I see no reason to waste time with useless vows of innocence."

"I had grown fond of you, Miss Bennet, to the degree that I considered asking Mr. Bannerman's permission to court you. That is now impossible. I want to believe you, but Georgiana is more important to me than you or any possible marriage companion. Until I can resolve this matter you are not welcome at Pemberley. Do not call on Georgiana, as I will leave instructions to send you away."

Mr. Darcy turned from Elizabeth, showing his unwillingness to speak further with her, or to so much as acknowledge her presence any longer.

Setting his back to her, he addressed Kingsdown's master: "Forgive me, Mr. Bannerman, but I will not visit while your niece is here. I have no quarrel with you or your family, but I made my decision and it will not change. Please inform your daughters that their company is not welcome at Pemberley while Miss Bennet is welcome here. Their presence will only remind Georgiana of what she has suffered, and Miss Bennet's continued presence in your house is a constant reminder that I will not allow her to experience."

With that, he walked away, going around rather than through the house, which Elizabeth knew was a sign of his displeasure.

CHAPTER XXVI

Elizabeth watched Mr. Darcy walk away, her inner turmoil changing her mood rapidly, from anger at his surprising attack on her character to sorrow at the loss of his friendship.

He had some nerve accusing her! And then refusing to accept her insistence of innocence, or even listen to what she had to say about the matter. It was contemptible, and she would not stand for it.

Still, she would miss his company, and the daily conversations they had shared. She enjoyed the back and forth of their discussions and his tendency to laugh at himself when she bested him in debate. The absence of his cheery greeting would lessen her day's enjoyment upon returning from her walk each morning.

Had his order to stay away extended to walking those paths on Pemberley property? She might as well assume as much, having no desire to further inflame the hatred he now appeared to hold for her.

She would find other areas to explore. Mr. Darcy did not own every piece of land in Derbyshire, did he?

Unfortunately, he did, or at least it seemed that way based upon what she had viewed from the top of the hills she occasionally climbed. And Kingsdown sat surrounded by Darcy property, which limited the available paths to explore.

She could always retrace her steps each day and circle the property two or three times. In this way, she thought with a chuckle, she would become familiar with every stone and piece of grass on the estate. She would find Kingsdown's hidden meadows or any undiscovered areas.

"I cannot decide if I am disappointed in you or not," said her uncle from his position beside the garden door, where he had been since their irate caller departed.

"On the one hand, the attack on Miss Darcy was uncalled for and unconscionable. There is no acceptable excuse for such an act, no matter the justification. On the other, you say that you were not involved, and I want to believe you.

"But there is also the consideration of Mr. Darcy's position on this matter, and the consequences of ignoring his demand. He is a respected resident of Derbyshire, and once people are told of his censure, I might find it difficult to conduct business with any of the Lambton merchants.

"What are you to do, Uncle? Maybe things will not be as bad as you fear. In my admittedly limited experience, most merchants will not pass up the opportunity to sell their wares. What they say in public and what they do in private are often two different things."

"I am undecided. If I agree to this demand, I fear it will embolden him the next time we disagree on something. Should I act as he wishes again, he might increase his demands until I am ruined. Cowardice like that leaves only one victor, and in this case, it would not be me.

"It is unacceptable to debase myself like that, and I resent Mr. Darcy for demanding it, the injury to his sister notwithstanding."

"I am sorry, Uncle. If I suspected that something like this might occur, I would have avoided them both. I am sorry for Georgiana and what she has endured but refuse to take the blame for an attack I had no part of and would have done my best to prevent if I had been present."

"I understand, Elizabeth, but my duty is to my family. This is a situation I need to think about, and one for which I can see no straightforward solution. If you will excuse me, I will be in my study."

Elizabeth watched him go, hopeful he might arrive at a fair solution to the dilemma, but doubtful there was one to be had. If Mr.

Darcy would not move from his position, the blame would, in the eyes of friends and foes alike, rest upon her, regardless of any proof she might offer.

Elizabeth rose from the bench and made her way into the house, where her aunt was waiting for her.

"Please tell me you believe me," pleaded Elizabeth, not interested in reviewing her account a third, or fourth, time, "because there is nothing I can add to what I already told you."

"I want to, I really do," sighed Mrs. Bannerman, "but I cannot dismiss Miss Darcy's accusation out of hand. To do so is to invite terrible consequences, as I am sure George has told you."

"I believe her," Louisa's voice, the tone more than her words, left no doubt that personally, she brooked no dispute. Elizabeth would have laughed in reaction to her cousin's somewhat comical expression had the situation been less serious.

"That is to be commended," said Mrs. Bannerman, "but it gains us nothing. If Mr. Darcy believes his sister, we would be wise to accept whatever form his censure takes. Remember, he is a gentleman and she is his sister, and a Darcy."

"You would never know it from the rumors in Lambton," mentioned Louisa. "This is not the first time she has caused problems for someone. Just ask her friends, if you can find any willing to tell the truth."

"What are you saying? Has she levelled accusations like this in the past?"

"No, this is the first time she has done something like *this*, but that does not mean she is as innocent as she claims. She has little use for the rules they expect her to obey. I heard, from more than one acquaintance, that she ignores them, assuming none of her friends will expose her disobedience.

"I was told of one occasion where she stretched the truth so much it bore little relation to the event in question. If it were me, I would want to find out what actually happened that day. There is probably more to the story than she has shared.

"She wants our friendship, and I would like to believe she is sincere, but I cannot let something like this go unchallenged."

"But what could she hope to gain by lying? She is ruining a reputation and harming Mr. Darcy's friendship with his neighbors. Can she be so hard-hearted that this does not bother her? What type of person is she?"

"I cannot say, Aunt, because I am not well acquainted with her. What I know is that I had no contact with Georgiana the day she was attacked. I spent the day indoors with Louisa, Amelia, and Kitty. I passed most of the time in the music room, practicing on the pianoforte.

"While I first said that Louisa needed help with a difficult composition, I was incorrect. We both used the instrument to master the number. I apologize, until now I had not remembered my own struggle to control my uncooperative fingers.

"The only time any of us, or at least Louisa and I, left the room was for the noon meal. Other than that, we remained there.

"I had not seen Georgiana for a day or two before the incident, and I did not speak to her until all three of us called at Pemberley. The reason for that visit was to offer our support in her recovery."

Mrs. Bannerman's regard was essential to Elizabeth, who worried what her aunt was thinking while she proclaimed, once again, her complete and utter innocence in the attack.

She liked the woman and respected her opinion. In the weeks she and Kitty had been at Kingsdown, Aunt Bannerman had welcomed them and treated her as one of the family. She had supported Elizabeth's desire to ready Louisa for her first ball and assisted them both in the preparations for the event.

Elizabeth had yet to hear her aunt utter a disparaging remark about her husband or children, a habit her own mother seemed to exult in practicing. Her countenance was often cheerful despite the cares and worries that beset her, and Elizabeth intended to adopt a like manner.

As much as she hoped her aunt would accept the truth of her claims, she would not take responsibility simply to appease the woman, or anybody else. Elizabeth had not attacked Georgiana Darcy, and she would never confess to the crime to preserve her uncle's friendship with Georgiana's brother.

"I believe you, Elizabeth, and will support you in this as much as I can. That might be little more than a moral victory, however, as I cannot defy my husband's decision in the matter, though I might disagree.

"George is not an unreasonable man, and he will do his best to see you treated fairly, by everyone. He is not one to meekly accept an injustice, especially one involving a member of his family, and that includes you and Kitty. All we can do is wait. He is in the library thinking it over, and I cannot push him into a rash decision."

The walk back to Pemberley was not pleasant for Darcy, whose thoughts kept returning to Miss Bennet, and the disappointment he had seen in her eyes when he delivered his ultimatum.

What a fool he had been, to become involved with such a woman. Why had he let himself become fond of her and, more important, consider her a potential wife? How had he missed the evil lurking behind those beautiful amber eyes?

He had not planned to bar her from the estate, but the more he discussed the situation, the more vehement her declarations of innocence became. Her refusal to accept responsibility was the last straw, causing him to lash out in anger.

The inability to control his temper was shameful, but the damage was done, and his decision was final. As much as he liked the woman, a mere affection was not sufficient to overrule the responsibility to his sister. So why did his attraction to the woman remain unchanged? Had her womanly charms so clouded his judgement that his every thought was suspect?

No! He would put her from his mind and move on. Miss Bennet was not the only beautiful, intelligent woman in the world. He could easily find another to take her place.

Of course, any replacement needed to possess those same qualities, but that was not an impossible task, was it?

Darcy cursed his decision to walk instead of taking his horse to Kingsdown. This method of travel allowed him too much time for introspection, and the process was uncomfortable.

The day was warm, and the path was far from quiet. From birds calling out, to squirrels chattering to one another, the air was alive with the sounds of woodland creatures.

As he listened, the voices became a cacophony of discontent, each a condemnation of his actions at Kingsdown.

Miss Bennet is not a criminal, they seemed to say. *You should have held your temper and listened to her. It might not be too late yet to change your mind. Go and beg her forgiveness. Do you want to live with regret for the rest of your life?*

"Enough!" cried he as the voices crowded in on him, each more insistent than the last. "I cannot. Her callous disdain for Georgiana will not go unchallenged."

As the sound of his voice died away, he looked around, embarrassed at the outburst. To his relief, the path was empty and quiet, the animal noises gone as though, having accomplished their purpose, they were free to return to the business of survival.

Darcy did not intend to let a guilty conscience rule him. He had acted in the best interests of his sister. If he were to turn around and deny the woman's perfidy by courting her, he might as well climb to the rooftops and announce his disregard for the calamity she had visited upon Georgiana.

What of his reputation and standing in Derbyshire and London? People would treat him as an outcast, with good reason. No, forget the heartache. Fitzwilliam Darcy's course was set. If his fate was the life of a bachelor, so be it.

Darcy spent the rest of the walk concentrating on the path before him and the flowers gracing him with their presence on either side. Slowly, the tension diminished, departing almost completely by the time he entered the house.

The relative peace of mind he had with difficulty achieved lasted almost three days, only to be interrupted by a most unwelcome visitor.

The new week had just begun when it descended into confusion. A knock on the door interrupted Darcy, who was in his library reviewing the accounts. At his invitation, the butler opened it and, with a look of consternation and a glance over his shoulder at something that seemed to almost terrify the man, spoke.

"Y-y-you have a visitor, Mr. Darcy," stammered he. "When I requested her name, she demanded I quit wasting time and summon you at once. I showed her to the sitting room before coming to get you. I am sorry, but it was all I could do to accomplish even that much, as she would not wait."

"Do not worry, Finch, I can guess our visitor's identity," said Darcy, rising from his chair at the beleaguered servant's tale of woe, all the while wondering what prompted this visit. Had someone informed her of Georgiana's mishap? If so, who took it upon themselves to tell the woman? He had purposely left off sending word for fear she would react in this exact manner.

The only person Darcy had notified was Fitzwilliam, out of respect for the man's shared responsibility as Georgiana's guardian. If he had forwarded the information in defiance of Darcy's request not to, there would be hell to pay when next they met.

"You may go," said he to Finch, rising and crossing to the library door, which gave rise to a look of great relief on the man's face. "I will look after her."

"Is this how you manage the affairs of this house? I cannot imagine Darcy is so lenient as to allow it. If you were in my employ, you would correct your incompetency, or you would look for another situation."

Darcy heard the woman's voice clearly as he approached the sitting-room, where it sounded like she was berating the housekeeper. The nature of the poor servant's sin, while unknown, was likely minor, although the level of any perceived infraction mattered not a whit to her.

Inhaling deeply to armor himself against the coming invective, he entered the room and stopped, forcing a smile he did not feel.

"Lady Catherine, how good of you to call. How was your journey from Rosings Park? I trust it was comfortable."

"It was abominable if you must know. And the accommodations I was forced to accept along the way were just as bad, if not worse. How the innkeepers outside of London stay in business is a mystery to me, what with the paucity of decent rooms and edible food. It is a wonder I survived long enough to make it this far."

"To what do we owe the pleasure of this visit? I had expected to call on you the next time I was in London on business, but that will not be for a month or more."

"I came to see my niece, who from what I was told, somebody beat and abandoned. Why was I not informed? Am I not her favorite relation, and her closest?"

Darcy knew he should have written Lady Catherine. It was because of his desire to avoid a situation such as this that he had not.

She was a formidable woman, with a demanding, unapologetic mien. She entertained no misgivings about interfering in matters of no concern to her, stating that it was her duty to correct any shortcomings she found. To object was to invite a scathing rebuke, along with questions regarding the offender's upbringing, lineage, and any other subject she might decide to raise.

Darcy found the best response was quiet acceptance of her opinion, followed by apologies to the offended party, or parties, once she departed. All too often, her inflammatory remarks had reduced the maids in her own household to tears, en masse!

In some ways Darcy envied the woman her forceful way with people, but that was on rare occasions only, when he had to deal with a difficult problem involving intractable persons.

Contrary to Lady Catherine's assertion, she was not Georgiana's favorite relative. While she was Georgiana's favorite aunt, the only reason for that was because she was also Georgiana's *only* aunt, and even then, the question was moot.

"Well, what happened to her, and what steps are you taking to exact justice?"

"She suffered a significant injury, one that left her concussed. Mr. Tate tended her wound, and confined her to bed until she was sufficiently healed."

"And what about her attacker? Was the guilty person punished? I hope you addressed this issue promptly."

"I said nothing about an attacker, Lady Catherine, but to answer your question, yes, I took steps to correct the situation."

"Why was I not informed of this immediately? Why did I hear about it so long after the fact? If it were up to you, I would have never been told about what amounts to a shameless, incomprehensible attempt on her life."

"I would not describe it as an attempt to murder her," protested Darcy, worried that the conversation was slipping out of his control, not that he had ever been in control to begin with.

"Then what would you call it? She attacked the poor girl and left her to fend for herself. It was only through the grace of God and the luck of providence that the Earl and his wife happened upon her. If not for their timely intervention she might be dead."

So that was how she found out. Darcy had forgotten all about Georgiana's rescuers. That explained his aunt's arrival. They probably wrote when they stopped for the night and dispatched the letter with some urgency. He could not fault them, no matter how much it inconvenienced him. They had done what they thought at the time was necessary.

"And what of this trollop you are involved with? Where is the respect for your sainted mother's feelings? She must turn in her grave at the insult. And the Darcy name. How can you countenance dragging it through the mud like this?"

"To whom are you referring? To my knowledge, there are no women of that type in Derbyshire."

"You know who I am talking about. I have it on good authority you are involved with the very person who assaulted your sister!

How could you? Did you lose your mind? The woman has neither morals nor scruples, if she will make love with you one day and viciously attack Georgiana the next.

"You need to stop this inappropriate affair at once and focus attention on your sister, instead of women with questionable motives and character."

Lady Catherine's attack on Miss Bennet's character wounded Darcy despite his vow to be done with her. She was not the licentious harridan Lady Catherine painted her to be, and the idea she was a schemer did not describe the woman he knew.

Darcy felt his self-control slipping, as it did whenever he endured one of Lady Catherine's harangues. He had to end this before he said something she found unforgiveable. As much as he disliked visiting with her, she was his aunt and, other than Fitzwilliam, his only other relative. Still, it was essential that he get the situation under control, for the sake of his sanity, and the well-being of the Pemberley servants.

"I am not having an 'affair' with Miss Bennet. She is an acquaintance, because she has been visiting Kingsdown, the neighboring estate. When I learned of her involvement, I spoke with Mr. Bannerman, the estate's master, and then with Miss Bennet. As a result of that conversation, I informed her she is not welcome here, nor are any of the Bannerman family."

"If you married Anne, in obedience to your dear mother's wishes, you would not be in this position, with Georgiana fighting for her life."

"She is not fighting for her life, and Anne passed over three years ago," he reminded her, wondering how much longer this insanity would continue before he could escape, to the comfort of his library and a glass of his strongest malt whiskey. "Even if I had married your daughter, I would have been without a wife, and susceptible to the same inconvenient situation."

"At least you took steps to distance yourselves from her," said Lady Catherine, mollified but still determined to carry her point. "Now see that you protect your sister from further calamities."

"How long were you planning to visit?" asked Darcy, hoping she would decide to leave after a good night's sleep.

"I will remain until week's end so I can see to Georgiana's recovery. Your untoward interest in the woman who attacked her has deprived my niece of the care she needs to properly mend, so I will make sure she is tended to properly."

"Georgiana is receiving the best treatment possible. She is under constant supervision, and I sent for Mr. Tate immediately. He examined and treated her the night of her injury and I put a maid in her room with orders to wake me at once if she requires anything.

"She is not in any danger and is, in fact, free to roam the house, although I do not allow her out of doors. That will come in time, but not before Mr. Tate approves. There is really no need for you to stay if your company is needed somewhere else."

"I will be judge whether my niece is receiving adequate attention. I am an excellent judge of the medical profession, and you would do well to remember that. Until I am satisfied, I will not be leaving, not until I can be confident Georgiana will survive the care she is getting."

"The houseman will take your things upstairs," said Darcy resignedly, knowing that arguing would not avail him. If he wanted to make it through the week, it would be vital that he find tasks to occupy himself. Engaging his aunt in as little conversation as possible might salvage his sanity, but even that was no foregone conclusion.

Chapter XXVII

Elizabeth slept little that night, and the nights following. She tried, but closing her eyes brought Mr. Darcy's face to mind, and with that mental picture came a replay of the whole sordid mess again.

What might she have done to lessen his anger? The question hounded her day and night until she thought she might go mad, but there was no answer.

He had been in no mood to listen to anything she said, if it did not conclude with a confession and a tearful plea for mercy. But how much was she to abase herself before he would grant absolution for a crime she had not committed?

If she were to call, clothed in sackcloth and ashes, would that mollify him? Or would he expect a lifetime of penance and abject, humiliating supplication to him and his sister? Would that be enough for Mr. Darcy to resume his courting, or would he demand another, more onerous punishment?

That was no way to start, or to nurture, a relationship. The choice of whether or not to believe her, was his alone. Elizabeth Bennet would never grovel or shame herself to attract a suitor, even one as handsome as Mr. Darcy, who affected her in ways she could not ignore.

The man wanted to court her! That revelation had come as a complete surprise for, despite her growing attraction towards him, she had been blissfully unaware that he felt the same.

To Elizabeth, Mr. Darcy was an enigma. She looked forward to his greetings upon the conclusion of her morning walks and considered it the best portion of her day.

The topics he raised were thought-provoking and stimulating. She knew, without a doubt, that Mr. Darcy expected his comments, offered casually in the course of his greeting, would set her to pondering his remark, and her responses would set the tone for the ensuing conversation.

He challenged her to justify her opinions, usually without exposing his own position on the subject. Elizabeth enjoyed these discussions with him for many reasons.

Mr. Darcy, unlike every one of the men she seemed to meet, listened without interruption. He never belittled her or acted as though she knew nothing of what she was saying. When he voiced an opposing point of view, it was with respect. On over one occasion, he had complimented Elizabeth on her ability to offer an intelligent discourse. He had once even compared her, favorably, to other women in his circle of acquaintances, telling her what a pleasure it was to carry on a conversation without reverting to platitudes and empty compliments.

Still, until he stated his intentions regarding courting, she had assumed his interest was in the conversation, rather than the person he was speaking with.

Thoughts of this nature kept her awake, unable to fall asleep until almost morning. She took to rising later each day, exhausted from the repeated bouts of insomnia. As a result, she changed, from a cheerful, friendly young lady to one who was short-tempered and prone to snap at others for the smallest things.

In desperation she resumed her morning walks, although later than she was used to, which did precious little to calm her. The attraction of the morning constitutional had always been the beauty of the early hours. Elizabeth loved the solitude walking afforded her, as it gave her the opportunity to ponder problems and practical solutions, and to admire God's creations and the harmonious way each complimented the other.

By starting two or three hours later, she lost the feeling of serenity and quiet peace, now swallowed up in the day's activity. As a result, the practice, while retaining value in the exercise it afforded her, did nothing to settle her acrimonious attitude.

The parson directed his Sunday sermon, on the deadly sins of pride and vanity, at her, she just knew. From his opening sentence, she could feel his eyes upon her, as if calling on her to mend her ways and submit to Mr. Darcy's censure and its accompanying punishment.

Her uncle intended to remain at home that day, wanting to avoid the unpleasantness he was sure to encounter. Elizabeth, however, was adamant that they should attend, if for no other reason than to show their defiance in the face of the unwarranted accusations leveled at her.

Mr. Bannerman relented and, in spite of his misgivings, told them to prepare for the journey to the chapel in Kympton.

They arrived forty-five minutes early, which was their practice, as it let them find unoccupied pews in the normally crowded chapel before they filled. Unfortunately, this Sunday it allowed for an uncomfortable wait before the service began.

Most of the worshippers studiously ignored the family. Those who deigned to offer greetings paid no attention to Elizabeth, giving her the impression they held her in contempt for her supposed sin. One of the so-called Christians even threatened to pull her from the pew and take her outside for a severe lashing.

Her uncle, bless his heart, defended her vigorously, going so far as to berate the fellow, in a quiet voice and respectful manner, to which her would-be attacker slunk away, his displeasure unabated but silenced, albeit temporarily.

When the service concluded, the family was treated with scorn and shunned by everyone, including the parson. Mr. Bannerman's attempts to engage in conversation, with just one exception, were met with silence or open hostility, until he gathered everyone and set off for home.

"The parson would have done better to offer a sermon on charity and love," opined he as they left the church grounds. "There was little of either in evidence today, from those I counted as friends, to the parson himself. Though it pains me to confess, I am not in the least surprised that Mr. Darcy's decision on your guilt has infected Kympton. Hopefully, Lambton is unaffected, although that is doubtful."

"Mr. Hoskins spoke with you at least," observed Mrs. Bannerman, "so there is one person, anyway, who is not afraid to be seen in your company."

"My conversation with Mr. Hoskins was not as innocuous as you assume. He gave me something else to think about, besides repeating the same message I heard from everybody who bothered to acknowledge my existence."

"What can we do to prove Elizabeth is innocent?" asked Mrs. Bannerman.

"I have thought about this for three days," said her uncle, "and fear there may be only one answer. Let me consider it another day before I give you my decision."

It was a somber group that arrived back at Kingsdown. The Sabbath, Elizabeth's favorite day of the week, was anything but peaceful today, and she felt responsible. Had she listened to her uncle, they would have remained at home, avoiding the uncomfortable glares and impolite comments of those at church. Because of her insistence they attend, the family was rejected by everyone, a humiliation she had brought upon them.

She went directly to her room and stayed there until morning. When informed the evening meal was ready, she sent her regrets with the maid, asking her uncle to excuse her. She spent the evening studying the bible, trying with moderate success to find solace in Matthew's account of the Sermon on the Mount, which she read four times over.

When she could no longer keep her eyes open, she retired to her bed, where exhaustion at last took her. She slept without interruption and woke refreshed, resolved that the cares of the previous week would not interfere with her enjoyment of this new day.

Dressing quickly, she opened the door to her bedroom to find Kitty there waiting for her.

"Were you going to walk today?" asked she timidly, as though the mere question might offend her sister. "If so, may I come along?"

"I was, and your company is welcome," invited Elizabeth, leading the way downstairs to the cloakroom. "Dress warmly, it is cool this morning."

Kitty jumped to it with alacrity, as though she feared Elizabeth might rescind her permission if she took too long.

"Which way do you want to go?" asked she when they reached the gate. "Are we still allowed to walk the paths on Pemberley property?"

"I do not know, and have no wish to find out, so we will go the other way. The path is not as long, but it keeps to Uncle's land, so we can use it without fear of further offending Mr. Darcy."

Kitty looked like she wanted to object to Elizabeth's comment, but after a moment she shrugged her shoulders and nodded her acceptance of the decision.

"Was there something you wanted to say?" asked Elizabeth as they proceeded along the path, away from Pemberley.

"No, I just want to enjoy a walk with my favorite sister," was her explanation, although to Elizabeth it looked as though something was weighing on her.

"Thank you, Kitty," replied Elizabeth in return. "And in case you were unaware, you are my favorite sister at Kingsdown as well."

Kitty's radiant smile was brief, as what Elizabeth actually said had just occurred to her.

"That is not what I meant," insisted she to Elizabeth's laugh, the amusement lifting Elizabeth's spirits with the love she felt for her sister.

"I could not resist a bit of fun at your expense. I love you, Kitty, and appreciate your company. You have a way of cheering me when I am down, and I needed that this morning."

Kitty smiled at the compliment, which lit up her face most becomingly, prompting Elizabeth to ponder what, to her, had started as an unplanned confession of regard for her younger sister.

Kitty was often a handful but there was no mistaking her love of life, which included everyone she met. She owned an infectious laugh and a way of looking at the world that Elizabeth almost envied.

She was not one to judge, but in Elizabeth's experience, her good opinion, once lost, was nigh impossible to restore. That she held such high regard for Lydia, who seemed to consider her nothing more than a convenient scapegoat, was puzzling, for she would not allow that type of conduct from anyone else.

"Mr. Darcy's treatment of you has been abominable," stated Kitty, pulling Elizabeth's attention back from where it had wandered. "He should be ashamed of himself."

"Mr. Darcy defended Georgiana, and his actions are beyond reproach. If I had a brother, I would want him to be as zealous in protecting me."

"I suppose, but it makes me so mad when I see how they misused you. You did not attack Georgiana, why does he not believe you?

Does it not matter that Louisa, Amelia, and I all said you are telling the truth? I hate him, I truly do!"

"You are being a little rash, Kitty. He does not deserve your hatred. I think the truth will come out; it usually does. In the meantime, Georgiana needs our love and support while she heals."

"That might be awkward, considering they banned us from the estate."

"Then our moral support will have to suffice."

Their conversation continued, Kitty moving without warning from one subject to another, until the walk reached its end, returning to Kingsdown before Kitty ran out of things to say.

Elizabeth left the cloakroom to find her uncle waiting in the hallway.

"I see you walked this morning," commented he. "That is good, I have been worried about you."

"There is only so long I can go without my morning exercise. The sun was shining when I woke, and I could not resist. I even had company today, which was a welcome change."

"It is good to see your mood is improving. If you can spare a moment though, there is something we need to discuss. I will wait in the library."

Elizabeth watched him walk toward the room in question, dread rising in her at the morose sound of his voice. Obediently she followed, taking the seat he indicated.

"I tried to find a solution to this problem," said he upon closing the door to ensure their privacy. "From what I can see, my only recourse is to send you back to Longbourn, so I have written to your father and sent it by express. We will leave for Northampton in three days time. That should give him time to meet us.

"I am sorry, Elizabeth, but I must do what is best for my family. While I do not believe you are the guilty party, the rest of Derbyshire seems convinced that you are, something Mr. Hoskins took pains to tell me on Sunday."

"I understand," said Elizabeth, who had been expecting something of this nature. "Kitty and I will be ready to leave. It is unfortunate that it has come to this point, but I cannot fault your decision. I hope that once we leave, your relationship with Mr. Darcy, and Derbyshire as a whole, will go back to what it was."

"I hope you are correct, but we shall see," replied her uncle, rising to show their conversation was complete.

Elizabeth did not relish having to return to Longbourn under a cloud of suspicion but found no fault in the idea. Kitty, however, was not as accepting of the decision.

"It is not fair," said she upon hearing of their impending return. "Just because Mr. Darcy has seen fit to accuse you does not mean that we should turn tail and run."

"That is not what we are doing. This is the best solution, and the only one that makes any sense, given the prevailing sentiment in Lambton, and the entire county, from what I hear.

"With you and me gone, people will forget about this affair. It might take most of the winter, but by spring there will be something else to engage their attention."

"But they accused you of something you did not do! And our leaving, without so much as stating our case, tells everyone their suspicions were correct. How are we to show our face again, if they consider you the vilest of people, having attacked an innocent girl? I do not for a minute believe she does not know her attacker.

"Mark my words, the truth will come out, but by then it will be too late, as everyone will remember you as the most despicable person ever to set foot in Derbyshire."

"That is out of my control. I cannot dictate another's thoughts, nor would I try. If that is how I am to be remembered, so be it."

"They treated us poorly, and nobody cares! And what about Louisa or Amelia? I thought they would support you, but I guess they are as worried about the appearance of friendship as everyone else. I for one will be glad to say goodbye to Derbyshire."

"Need I remind you, Kitty, that Louisa came to my defense as soon as the accusation was made? She has been a steadfast ally, telling anyone who would listen that the charges are without merit, and that I could no more have accosted Georgiana than the Prince Regent. Of course, she tends toward hyperbole when she gets excited, but if anyone has treated us fairly, it is Louisa.

"And Amelia, while she has not offered an opinion to anyone outside of the family, has told me, in no uncertain terms, she is on my side. This censure of your cousins is unwarranted. I would advise you to rethink your attitude; they both deserve better."

"Forgive me," said Kitty, hanging her head at Elizabeth's correction. "I was angry because of this indignity and let my emotions control me. They trust you and I should not have said such a thing."

"Thank heaven they did not hear you accusing them. Take care, and in the future, think before you speak. I find it is easier to hold my tongue than it is to make amends for a poorly expressed opinion."

"I will, but that does not change the fact that I am still mad at the way you were treated."

"Fine," laughed Elizabeth, the tension of the moment broken, "you may be as mad as you like, but keep your thoughts private."

The next morning saw Elizabeth rising early for her walk, having decided that to deprive herself of the habit was contributing to her poor mood. Her walk was a solitary exercise, as Kitty, having assured Elizabeth of her support, remained in her warm bed.

The morning was cool, and Elizabeth was grateful for the autumn coat she wore. She could see her breath, a warning that winter was fast approaching. The flowers of summer were almost gone, with only an occasional witch's thimble still visible, its bright blue blossoms easily spotted bordering the fields. It would be only a week, she thought, before the last blossom died, killed by the dropping temperatures.

As the walk progressed, she sang, something she had not wanted to do since the troubles began. The song lifted her spirits, and she sang with abandon, her voice ringing out in harmony with the winged chorus surrounding her, or so it seemed.

Her steps grew lighter as her mood improved, until she felt her cares depart at last, a welcome respite from the darkness she had labored under for a week or more. When she reached the path's end, she joyfully turned around to return to the house, her mood immeasurably improved.

Movement from the corner of her eye caught her attention as she stepped through the gate into the garden. Turning her head in that direction informed her it was Robert, working diligently in the orchard. To her dismay, she realized that, in the fuss and bother of what had been happening, she had completely forgotten about him.

Mentally chastising herself for her lack of manners, she decided to correct the slight, unintentional though it was.

"It looks like the harvest will be good," said she to the lad, whose back was to her as he worked away.

"Father agrees," responded he without pausing his task.

"A little late this year, it appears," said she when he volunteered nothing more.

"Spring was late arriving, and moths appeared at the beginning of the season," explained he, continuing his work, to her consternation.

"Is something bothering you, Robert?" asked she when he began moving away from her, as though the trees at the opposite corner of the orchard required more of his attention than the one he had been working on.

"It is nothing," was his comment, although his tone of voice suggested otherwise.

"Please, Robert, talk to me," she pleaded. "Don't ignore me or walk away hoping I will leave you alone. If I offended you, let me apologize and do my best to make amends."

"I am not offended," said he, standing still, his back toward her. "There is nothing you need to apologize for."

"Then what has come between us? Please, tell me. I do not want to leave, knowing I had done something to lower your opinion, which I value."

"Georgiana," was his response.

"What about her?" asked Elizabeth, a sour feeling growing in her stomach. Did Robert believe the rumors?

"Everybody I talk to says you assaulted her. Some even say you wanted her dead so Mr. Darcy would be free to marry you."

"What about you? Do you think I am so callous that I could do such a thing? In all the time since I arrived at Kingsdown, did I ever do anything that might lead you to suspect I was capable of such an act?"

"I cannot say. I want to accept what you claim as the truth, but if I do, then I must defend your honor."

"Why should that matter? Are you uncomfortable with the idea that I might need your protection, even though I am leaving in two days?"

"That does not bother me," said Robert, although the unsettled aura he gave off did nothing to convince Elizabeth he was telling the truth.

"Then what is the problem? Tell me, so we can put it behind us."

"If I defend you, what will become of my friendship with Miss Darcy, Miss Haversham, and their friends? Will they decide they want nothing to do with me because I will not join them in denouncing you?"

Elizabeth saw the anguish in her cousin's eyes as he spoke. It could be difficult, she knew, to stand alone against the common opinion. For Robert, who had never enjoyed the attention of a single young woman, let alone two, the fear of losing their regard must be doubly concerning.

"Do you have feelings for Georgiana or Sarah?" she asked as the cause of his anguish became clear to her.

"I value my friendship with both." His statement, which Elizabeth accepted as true, did not answer the question she posed.

"That is commendable, but I would advise you to take care. Do what is best for you, but do not let a winsome smile and demure countenance deceive you. I cannot pretend to know why Georgiana accused me of hitting her, but there is a reason, one that may never come to light. Please, be careful."

Elizabeth left him standing in the orchard, his look of pained confusion in no way lessened.

She pitied him, and wished she had some way of easing his misery, but this was a problem he would need to solve by himself.

CHAPTER XXVIII

It was with some sadness that Elizabeth settled herself in the for the journey back to Longbourn. Her farewell to her aunt had been melancholy, despite her efforts to show a cheerful face.

"Goodbye, Elizabeth," Mrs. Bannerman has said somberly. "Thank you for coming to visit. We enjoyed your company, Louisa most of all. Your willingness to help her prepare for her first ball eased her nerves and let her enjoy herself without obsessing over so many of the things girls of that age fear, unnecessarily, I might add."

"She was easy to teach," stated Elizabeth with conviction, "mostly because she listened to me and remembered what I taught. I knew within five minutes of beginning that she would make her parents proud. I consider myself lucky to have spent my summer with you."

Louisa fought to control her emotions, and Elizabeth watched as a solitary tear made its way along her cheek, dropping to the ground upon reaching her chin.

Her voice quavering, she struggled to express herself: "I will miss you, Elizabeth. Please write when you can and tell me about your journey. Include all the details; I want to know everything."

"As soon as I get home, I promise to write, and send it on the next post. And I will miss you as much, if not more…"

She stopped as Louisa sprang forward, wrapping her arms about Elizabeth in a tight embrace, which she returned fourfold.

Amelia said nothing, an unusual occurrence for the normally cheerful girl. Her mumbled goodbye was difficult to hear, and if Elizabeth had not been watching, she would have missed it. She impulsively grabbed her cousin and pulled her close to give her as warm an embrace as Louisa's, which Amelia returned fervently before stepping back to regard her with a teary smile.

"Goodbye, Elizabeth." A wan smile accompanied her words. "I wish you a safe journey."

"Thank you," responded Elizabeth, "and keep practicing your dance steps. Your own coming out is not too far away."

Amelia nodded once before turning to run back into the house as the tears finally overcame her ability to hold them back.

"She will be fine," promised her aunt. "All she needs is a bit of time. I will see to her once you leave."

"She is a wonderful cousin," said Elizabeth, watching Amelia until she entered the house.

Christopher stood beside his mother, watching the proceedings with an impassive expression. His silence tugged at her heart strings, prompting her to include him in her farewells: "I will miss you also. Promise not to forget me, and I will do the same, although to be honest, you are unforgettable anyway."

Elizabeth leaned forward and gave him a light kiss before he hid behind his mother's skirt. When she stood again, his hand flew to his cheek to rub the spot she had graced with her lips, amusing both Elizabeth and his mother.

"It is a shame Robert was too busy to say goodbye," Elizabet observed regretfully. "Please express our love for him and tell him Kitty and I will remember him in our prayers. We will remember all of you, won't we, Kitty?"

"Yes, Lizzy," said Kitty glumly. "May we go now? If we stay very much longer, I will burst into tears like Amelia."

"It is only proper to express our gratitude for the time we spent at Kingsdown. I am surprised you need reminding. Where are your manners?"

"I am sorry. It is just that I am still upset with Mr. Darcy and his sister. I may never forgive them."

"You must and you will forgive them," scolded Elizabeth. "This is nothing more than a misunderstanding, even if it is serious. The truth will come out, and holding a grudge will not change things, not in the tiniest bit."

"Sorry," mumbled Kitty, "I am trying to find the good in this, but it is difficult."

"As long as you are trying, Papa would say that is good enough," reminded Elizabeth, before turning her attention back to her aunt. "It is time, I guess. Now that we are leaving, everything might return to normal. I wish you all the best, and please tell Robert goodbye."

"I will," said Mrs. Bannerman as her husband handed Elizabeth into the carriage and followed her, settling on the seat across the cabin.

Upon his signal, the driver put the horses into motion and the coach pulled away, to waves and calls of best wishes between those in the coach and on the drive.

Elizabeth was of two minds regarding her departure. On the one hand, she would not have traded her time at Kingsdown for anything. She would cherish her friendships with Louisa and Amelia forever.

From the moment she met her cousins, she loved them both. They had changed over the summer, Louisa much more than her sister.

Elizabeth had some pride in the mature, confident young woman Louisa would grow into, which she had encouraged. She still possessed a hesitant nature in new situations, but she accepted the fact she was a comely young woman, and that gave her enough confidence to move forward instead of back.

Elizabeth had watched her debate some of her views with Georgiana, whose self-confidence never faltered. Louisa was now unafraid to voice a contrary opinion and defend it, a welcome improvement in her opinion.

Amelia remained a bit more reserved, it seemed to Elizabeth. She was not so eager to monopolize a conversation, and Elizabeth had even observed her accepting a differing opinion, although on a minor disagreement.

On the other hand, the stain of leaving under a cloud was difficult to accept, no matter how much she tried to justify her uncle's decision.

Elizabeth, watching the passing scenery, could see that autumn had arrived. The leaves on the trees, so brilliantly green when they arrived, were slowly changing colors as the warmth of the summer gave way to early morning frost and cooler daytime temperatures. Soon they would fall as the trees made their preparations for a long winter's sleep.

If only I could sleep through the winter. Maybe this situation would resolve itself by the time I awoke.

With a vigorous shake of her head, Elizabeth determined to put thoughts like that from her mind. She would not let Mr. Darcy or his unfounded accusations ruin her return home!

"I enjoyed myself this summer," said she to Kitty, wanting to change the direction of her thoughts. "You did as well, if I am not mistaken."

"Everything was fine until Mr. Darcy slandered you so carelessly." Kitty spoke in a voice devoid of malice, sounding as if she were discussing something as commonplace as the weather. "He ruined the rest of my visit."

"Mr. Darcy's actions were justified," stated Mr. Bannerman. "His response to the attack on Georgiana was less severe than mine might have been, had someone attacked Louisa or Amelia like that. She is the only remaining member of his family, so his reaction is commendable, although misplaced."

"I am not complaining," was Kitty's response, her voice displaying no emotion. "I am only stating the fact of the matter. His accusation may have been reasonable had he reached his conclusion after listening to Elizabeth's explanation.

"We all know he refused to accept what she said and dismissed the proof she offered. That, to me, is not the way a gentleman should act."

"It is all in the past now. We gain nothing by discussing the issue ad infinitum, and my suggestion is that we let it rest, so the injustice, real or supposed, does not color our relations with friends and acquaintances."

Kitty was silent until they stopped for the night. She did not seem to be upset or pouting because of her uncle's mild rebuke. To Elizabeth, she appeared to have nothing further to say on that or any other subject, a welcome difference from the chatty, excited girl of a few months previous. She would not complain about this change for fear of awakening the ghost of the former Kitty Bennet.

The journey continued through the rest of the day, stopping only when necessary, until the daylight faded and the horses needed to rest. At Mr. Bannerman's instructions, the driver pulled the carriage into a reasonably presentable inn, where he arranged for two rooms and supper.

The journey recommenced early the next morning, and by late afternoon they arrived at the Northampton inn, where Mr. Bennet waited.

The girls went to the room their father had rented for them, where they freshened themselves for the evening meal. Mr. Bannerman found the innkeeper to arrange for his own.

When Elizabeth and her sister joined the men, they had become engaged in an intense discussion.

"She seemed sure that Elizabeth had been her attacker, and I could not refute her argument."

"But did you believe her? It is my understanding that Elizabeth offered irrefutable proof that she had not been the girl's attacker."

"I saw no reason to disbelieve Miss Darcy."

"George, you are a fool. To take the word of a stranger over that of a family member is beyond the pale."

"Mr. Darcy is my neighbor, and my friend. He is also the largest landowner in the county. To defy him is to invite the ruin of my name and the loss of Kingsdown when the merchants everywhere in Derbyshire refuse to do business with me. I saw no other way to calm an unpleasant situation, so I did what I thought best, under the circumstances. If the situation were reversed, you would probably do the same."

"That is possible, I suppose, but highly unlikely. I have never shied away from problems, no matter how distasteful they might be, while you appear to be running away from yours as fast as you can.

"It is time for bed. We both have long journeys ahead of us, and our discussion is not proving fruitful, to either of us."

Mr. Bennet rose to his feet and led his daughters from the dining-room, leaving Mr. Bannerman alone.

"Maybe you were too hard on him, Papa," commented Elizabeth at the door to her room. "He did what he could, but Mr. Darcy would be a formidable foe. Uncle made the best choice available in sending us home. He has to live beside the man, we do not."

"I know," sighed he. "But as a father, I reserve the right to my righteous indignation. I will speak with him in the morning and straighten things between us."

"Thank you, Papa." Elizabeth reached up to give him a peck on the cheek. With a quick goodnight, she entered her room, closing the door on her smiling father.

She rose early the next morning and roused her sister, wanting to be on the way as soon as possible. Mr. Bennet, it seemed, was of like mind, and waiting in the dining-room when they came down the stairs.

"Your uncle has already gone," said he to Elizabeth's reminder of their last conversation. "He left at daylight, according to the innkeeper, so I will write him when we get to Longbourn."

"Thank you, Papa. It is important to mend your relationship as soon as you can. It would be a shame to see you become distant from each other again."

"You have nothing to worry about, Lizzy. I will be the bigger man and apologize."

They ate quickly, and the party repaired to the carriage for the second half of the journey. Although Elizabeth wanted to enjoy the increasingly familiar landscape, the only thing she thought about was the level of her father's disappointment. Guilt ate at her until, in her mind, she could see his accusing glare and hear his condemnation for her heinous action.

As the day wore on, her feelings of shame grew, until she feared she might never again enjoy her father's love and trust. Reviewing the circumstances did nothing to relieve her and bring peace to her soul until she had convinced herself that her father's anger consumed him. She wanted to beg his forgiveness but feared his censure would be unbearable.

With the beginning of the second day of their journey with their father, Elizabeth concluded that to remain quiet was no longer possible. She needed her father's absolution for the trouble that forced him to rescue her: "Forgive me, Papa, for the harm I have done to the Bennet name.

"I never intended to shame you or Mama, but I would not accept responsibility for an attack that I had no part of. I did not attack Georgiana Darcy, and do not know who might have."

"You have not shamed us, Lizzy, and there is nothing for which you need to beg my forgiveness. I have never doubted your innocence, and your uncle should not have, either. Remember, I am your father, and know what you are capable of. No matter what George Bannerman, or Mr. Darcy say, you did not attack that girl, so we do not need to review the matter again."

"Thank you, Papa." The happiness arising from his support was almost enough to bring tears to her eyes. "It is good to have your trust. I cannot wait to get home, and to see Jane, especially. It has been so long since we spent any time together. And the changes to Lydia she described! I will believe that when I see it with my own eyes."

"Lydia has changed," laughed Mr. Bennet, "probably because she had no choice, what with Kitty gone and Mary unwilling to chase after the regiment, who have decamped, by the way."

"That must be a relief," was Elizabeth's response, "not having to tie her to a chair so she will stay away from them."

"Poor Lydia must be at her wit's end," laughed Kitty. "What will she do, without handsome men in uniform to pursue?"

"Fear not, they are due back before the snow falls," said Mr. Bennet. "But I suspect her priorities have changed. She is not the girl she was when you left. The new Lydia is a quieter, more reserved, version, and Mary is the one responsible for that."

"Mary?" asked the girls, almost in unison.

"Yes, Mary," replied he. "I caught them in conversation one day, about two weeks after you left. Lydia was listening to her sister explain some of the finer points of proper behavior as taught by Fordyce. Although tempted, I did not offer an opinion as to the absence of any kind of finer point in his so-called sermons."

"A laudable decision," laughed Elizabeth. "You have told me, on many occasions, how much you disagree with his opinions, and how it irks you when the parson references the man in his Sunday sermons."

"Yes, I suppose I have. To continue, a few days later Lydia came to ask me about the books in my library and showed some interest in looking through them. I gave her the same instructions and restrictions as you and Kitty.

"Your youngest sister has taken to spending her days reading. Her tastes seem to encompass almost everything in the library. Most surprising are the questions she asks, which are a lot like the ones you used to pose when you first showed an interest in my books. Not once in the last month has she tried to sneak off to Meryton."

"Forgive me, Papa, but that is not the same Lydia we left you with, and I am not convinced you are telling the truth. I will reserve judgement until I see this change myself."

"The more things change, the more they stay the same. Before you discovered the charm of the printed word, you were another Lydia, as I recall. You might have been younger, but thank God you found an interest in reading, because if you had not, I would have sold you to the gypsies."

"Really, Papa?" asked Kitty, her interest captured by the revelation. "Lizzy was as bad as Lydia?"

"Yes, although to be honest, she started to read at the age of ten. The mischief she got herself involved in before that vexed her mother and me to no end but did no harm."

"Lizzy, a holy terror!" laughed Kitty. "I can hardly wait to tell Lydia."

"Thank you, Father," remarked Elizabeth. "Because of your tales, I will never be able to live it down."

"You are welcome. I hope my little voyage into the past lifted your spirits. You seemed down, and I could not allow that."

"My spirits are fine," said she with a smile she did not truly feel, although she would never tell her father. The pain she carried was hers alone. She might decide to share it with Jane, but only if Jane promised to keep her secret. Elizabeth was happy to see her father, and looking forward to getting home, but what she saw as another betrayal, this time at Mr. Darcy's hands, would be a long while fading from memory.

"What about Jane?" she asked, to divert her father's thoughts. "Is her intended as perfect as she seems to think?"

"More, it you can believe half of what she says. He is a nice enough fellow, and very attentive to Jane and her various moods. If her spirits are low, his are in sympathy. It is almost as if he views it as a requirement."

"You must be exaggerating, no one can be that solicitous."

"He is always asking after my health, and the state of my mood. It is the same for your mother. If Jane had refused his offer, your mother would have wed him herself."

"You must be stretching the truth. Jane did not extoll his virtues to that extent, and she would be the first to do so."

"Judge for yourself. If you find I have lied, you can inflict your own punishment on me, and your sister can join you.

"As for Mr. Bingley, the man loves to hunt, or at least he likes to join me when I go out. If he is trying to gain my good opinion, he had that before he asked permission to call on Jane. I have yet to find anyone, in Meryton or anywhere in Hertfordshire, who has an unkind word to say about him.

"His attitude is, without fail, cheerful, and I have yet to hear anything close to a cross word or imprecation, no matter how mild, cross the man's lips. Though I hesitate to say so, he might be as perfect as Jane claims."

"How did he come to let Netherfield? There must have been others he looked at. And what did you mean, that Jane would one day thank you?"

"When we learned someone had leased Netherfield—a wealthy, single, tenant, no less— your mother prevailed on me to introduce myself and, while there, invite the man and his party to supper. When I made his acquaintance, his good humor and friendly manner convinced me he would make Jane a perfect husband. I thereafter made every reasonable attempt to encourage his interest in Jane, and hers in him.

"As to the decision to lease, that was a matter of luck, nothing more. Apparently, he toured this estate first, and decided he liked it. Part of the attraction, I am told, is its proximity to London, which has been his home for several years now."

"In case Jane forgets, I will thank you for her. You are the best father. Now, what of his family? According to Jane's letter, he arrived with his sister, and of course, Jane thinks the world of her, as she is wont to do with everyone she meets."

"Miss Bingley did not stay long. Apparently she returned to London to stay with an aunt in Scarborough. Something about a potential suitor who expressed interest before Mr. Bingley leased Netherfield. She worried he would find another if she stayed away too long."

Elizabeth sympathized with the woman, having twice experienced the loss of a suitor in the previous twelvemonth. To lose the interest of a man because of a prolonged absence, though, suggested to her that Miss Bingley was better off without him. If the man genuinely loved her, he would wait for her to return, however long it took.

"Is she a good person, or does her family's money affect her attitude?" said she, considering the sense of entitlement she had, upon reflection, felt from Georgiana.

"She has always been polite and friendly toward me and your mother. I suspect she is not foolish enough to let something like that color her view of the world and her place in it."

"What do you mean? Is there a problem with her brother's wealth?"

"That would depend on your definition of a problem. Miss Bingley returned to Netherfield about a month later, this time with her sister and her sister's husband. They seem to be decent people, although the sister and brother-in-law are a bit full of themselves.

"They apparently consider themselves above the Hertfordshire residents, which is the joke of the county at the present time."

"What do you mean, and why would people laugh at them, especially if they are that wealthy? That does not sound like our neighbors, or anyone in Hertfordshire, to be honest."

"The family made their wealth in the trades. For them to take the attitude that we are beneath them is presumptuous from my point of view. They are not evil, and, in fact, I quite enjoy visiting with Mr. Hurst. It is Mrs. Hurst who, from what I can gather, is full of herself."

"I am looking forward to meeting Mr. Bingley," stated she as the coach turned into Longbourn's drive. "It will be nice to see Jane's perfect man."

"Good," said her father, "because your mother has issued a standing invitation for his presence at supper, and he avails himself of the opportunity almost every night. He will not be here tonight, though. As I told Mrs. Bennet before we left, the journey would tire us too much to be acceptable company, so we would not want a full and active dinner table."

"Thank you, Papa," responded Elizabeth. "You truly are a good man. If I find someone a quarter as good, I will consider myself the luckiest girl in the world."

"Never fear, Lizzy," offered Mr. Bennet, "you will, but first you must separate the wheat from the tares. When you accomplish that, it will leave you with your perfect husband. Or you might decide to become a spinster and live a life of seclusion, visited only by your nieces and nephews, and occasionally by one or more of your sisters, themselves all happily married."

"Do not even joke about something like that, Papa, it depresses me. There is someone for me, I just need to find him, or he needs to find me, whichever the case may be."

"I know, my dear. Forgive your old father for his ill-timed levity. You will, in time, find someone to marry. All it requires is patience while you wait, and faith that your future husband will move heaven and earth to be with you."

CHAPTER XXIX

The sun had reached its zenith when Elizabeth woke the following day. With a languid stretch, she surveyed the room, noting her unopened trunk and the clothes thrown haphazardly as she undressed to prepare for bed the previous evening.

Her bedchamber's state of disarray reminded her of the exhaustion that had overtaken her upon entering the room. The sight of her bed, unused in the months she had been away, had lured her when she came through the door, filling her mind with thoughts of blessed, uninterrupted sleep for at least a week, or so she hoped.

In her haste to climb beneath the covers and close her eyes, she had undressed without concern for where her garments landed. The result was a mess, her dress sitting only half on the trunk and her stockings draped, one across the chair back and the other on the desk beside.

It surprised her, when looking at the state of the room, that she had even bothered to don bedclothes, but a quick peek under the covers confirmed she was, in fact, wearing her nightdress.

The amount of light in the room brought on a momentary pang of guilt at sleeping past the time of her morning walk, but she swept it aside. Had she not just returned from Kingsdown, after suffering an arduous journey in two uncomfortable coaches? Surely she could take one day to recover.

Reluctantly she pulled the blankets to one side and, pushing her feet into slippers, rose from the bed and made her way to the window where she parted the curtains, Sunlight flooded the room, banishing the semi-darkness to the closets and crannies.

The world beyond her window was bright, the sun directly overhead. She noted with pleasure that the leaves on the bushes and trees alongside her walking paths were mostly green. Winter did not seem so close as it had in Derbyshire. Hopefully, autumn was still a week or three distant.

Not that Elizabeth disliked the changing of the seasons, but this year had been difficult. A few more warm days might lift her sagging spirits before the dreariness of autumn became the norm.

It was too late today to walk, she decided, so she would stay in and spend some time with her mother.

I hope she has forgotten that unfortunate mess with Mr. Collins. The last thing I need is for Mama to start up again with complaints about his marrying Charlotte instead of me.

Elizabeth turned from the window to dress for the day. As she fussed with the buttons and clasps, her thoughts went to Georgiana and the friendship she had thought they shared.

What sin did she commit to turn the girl against her? They had met less than a dozen times, and had, in those meetings, engaged in no serious discussions that Elizabeth remembered.

Did she fail to do something, and in the process upset Georgiana? That made no sense, as she had turned down no requests, nor had she made promises that were later broken. She had not even mentioned the attraction she had seen growing between Georgiana and Robert, which, because of the obvious mismatch in terms of wealth and social standing, might have given Mr. Darcy cause for concern.

She had two reasons to keep the matter to herself. To her, the interest resembled simple infatuation, at least on Robert's part. If Georgiana's attraction was of a more romantic nature, she had been careful about displaying her feelings too openly.

But even if she had, that was a matter for her brother and Mr. Bannerman to deal with, and Elizabeth would not have dared to interfere in so private a matter.

No, there was something else, but Elizabeth did not know what it might be. The worst part of the whole affair, besides the injury to Georgiana, was Elizabeth's banishment from Kingsdown, and indeed, all of Derbyshire.

She missed the Bannermans, especially Louisa. From their first meeting, Elizabeth had a kindred spirit in her cousin, whose joy of life and thirst for knowledge were not unlike her own.

She considered her time in Derbyshire to be among the best of her life. From the first day, she and Kitty were treated like daughters by their aunt and uncle, and sisters by their cousins.

Even Robert, whose diffidence was at first off-putting, had, by the time she left for home, warmed to her. Though he projected an air of unconcern, she was by this time well enough acquainted with him to know he had some doubt about the charges laid at her feet, but whether he would voice his thoughts was improbable.

His fear that he might lose the friendship with Georgiana and her friend was not surprising. Elizabeth knew he felt a certain amount of affection for one of the two girls, probably Georgiana, if she was to hazard a guess. She thought, from observing the young man, that this attraction was something he had never dealt with, and the confusion it caused him was uncomfortable.

And what about Louisa? The idea of her cousin being denied some sort of coming-out ball distressed her, almost as much as the accusation which forced Elizabeth to leave Kingsdown.

Louisa's happiness at the conclusion of the Pemberley ball had her heaping praise upon Elizabeth and her father. To witness her cousin's joy, a happiness that seemed to permeate the girl's attitude for a week or more, gave her the idea to suggest arranging Louisa's coming-out.

Regrettably, she considered the idea too long, it seemed, because before she had the opportunity to raise it with her aunt, Georgiana's injury occurred, forcing Elizabeth to suspend her plan until the excitement subsided.

Faced with Georgiana's accusation and her inability to defend herself to Mr. Darcy's satisfaction, she abandoned the idea, forgetting it in the uproar that followed. Upon considering her uncle's reticence to the original idea of Louisa attending the ball at Pemberley, Elizabeth wondered if she would ever have the opportunity.

A coming-out ball was a formality not much practiced outside of London, but in Louisa's case, the advantages of attending any such event as an eligible young woman would be enormous.

Until Mr. Darcy's ball, with its invitation that included Louisa, she had not been to such an exciting evening, nor had she dared ask her father for permission. To Elizabeth this was unacceptable, but not a subject she had any business raising. The occasion presented by his invitation gave her the excuse she needed to bring it up, anyway.

It shocked Elizabeth to learn the man had no plans to present his daughter, or encourage suitors at all, having apparently decided that his lack of wealth was an impediment large enough to prevent any possibility of a favorable match.

In Elizabeth's opinion, Louisa's paltry dowry would not make it impossible for her to attract an honorable man. He would have to look past the disadvantage, but if he were attracted to her, and given leave to court, genuine love could easily blossom.

She believed fervently in the concept of love, and its ability to vanquish seemingly insurmountable barriers, even though the circumstances of her own life seemed determined to prove her foolish to entertain such a preposterous idea.

This was her second betrayal this year, at the hands of a man she thought returned her regard and might even want to court, and eventually offer for her.

The sudden lack of interest depressed her, but Elizabeth was grateful he left off pursuing her before beginning the game of courtship, rather than waiting until she became hopelessly lost. The humiliation would have destroyed her, coming as it did upon the heels of Mr. Sadler's similar betrayal.

As changing the past was impossible, she could do nothing but go on with her life. She would not forget her summer in Kingsdown, or the cousins she now held in such high esteem. Letters would have to suffice, until she could convince Louisa, and maybe Amelia as well, to come to Longbourn for an extended visit.

It might not be such a bad idea to raise the subject, in a roundabout way, in her letter to Louisa tonight. Subtle hints, written in such a way as to influence hers and Amelia's thoughts, would go further than the issuing of a direct invitation, as their father might decide to deny them permission.

Elizabeth had left under a cloud, and to send his daughters on an extended visit to Georgiana's accused attacker might strain relations with Mr. Darcy more than they already were. The man's reaction upon learning of plans to do so might be severe, although it truly was none of his business.

She would worry about that when she composed her letter tonight after supper. Until then she had things to do at Longbourn, important things like sharing the latest gossip with Jane, and pressing her for all the details about Mr. Bingley. As Jane was, without a doubt, bursting with the anticipation of doing just that, she had no worries about boredom, at least for today.

Elizabeth closed the last button and stood to go downstairs and greet her mother, but looking at the untidy mess that was in her room stopped her. She was not about to leave the room in this condition and expect the maid to clean up after her.

She had no compunction about employing servants to maintain the house, but the clutter she saw was an embarrassment. Clothes were strewn everywhere, from the floor in front of the closet to the top of the wardrobe.

What state had she been in last night, that she thought nothing of throwing her garments on the floor, or dropping them where she stood, instead of placing them neatly on the chair?

This would never do, she decided as she picked up the offending articles to place them in an orderly pile on top of her trunk. Her mother had not raised a slovenly daughter, unconcerned with unreasonable demands she might make of the household servants, and Elizabeth would not become one now. She would leave the room tidy before she left, and escape the guilt she would suffer otherwise.

Her reception was nothing like she anticipated. When she entered the sitting-room, Mrs. Bennet sat, concentrating on the intricate cross-stitch on her lap. It was a pattern that, when complete, would become a richly detailed rose, so she crossed the room silently to avoid interrupting her mother's progress.

"Hello, Lizzy," her mother greeted her with a smile as she put the needlework aside, "or should I say good afternoon? I hoped you would not sleep the day away and forget to come downstairs to see me."

"I would never do that, Mama. I slept longer than I planned, but the journey home was more difficult than the one to Derbyshire, and tired me more than I expected."

"I suspected as much, which is why I told Lydia not to wake you. She was disappointed, but to her credit, she listened. The girl has changed so much in your absence that I doubt you would recognize her if she were not your own sister. Now, come and give me a proper greeting. It seems forever since I last saw you, and I have missed you ever so much."

Elizabeth did not know how to respond to her mother's invitation, for it came as a complete surprise. In all her years, from childhood to this very moment, the woman had never been profuse in welcoming her home after an extended absence. On previous occasions she had, at most, voiced a one or two word welcome before turning back to whatever she was doing.

The warmth of her mother's greeting confused her, as Elizabeth clearly remembered the strain in their relationship when she left in the spring.

She recovered quickly and hurried across the room to give her mother an enthusiastic hug and a warm kiss. The opportunity to enjoy her mother's approbation was something she did not want to waste, it being a rare occurrence and one to be cherished.

"How was your visit? I hope Mr. and Mrs. Bannerman treated you and Kitty with the respect you deserved. And what about Kitty? Did she behave, or did she embarrass you, and the entire family?"

"The Bannermans treated us well. They welcomed us warmly and made us feel like members of their family. We could not have asked for better treatment, from our aunt and uncle, or from our cousins, even Robert, who was more reserved than Louisa and Amelia. And Kitty was the perfect gentlewoman. She gave me no trouble and got along extremely well with Louisa and Amelia."

"Did you hear about Jane's intended? Such a nice man, and rich! He is so good to her, and so polite to everyone. And five thousand a year! She will want for nothing."

This was the mother she knew and loved; her initial diffidence swiftly replaced by her need to impart the latest news.

"Come, sit next to me so we can talk quietly. This way we can share our feelings with each other, instead of letting everyone in the house, including the servants, know the intimate details of our business."

Another momentary bit of confusion struck her. Was this the same mother who complained continually about Elizabeth's stubborn impertinence and refusal to accept her demands, unreasonable though they often were? A woman who retired to her room many evenings with an affliction of nerves? What had encouraged so dramatic a change? And was this improved, more sensible version a permanent part of her mother, or would the other, familiar woman reappear?

Elizabeth did not know, but she would accept the transformation and enjoy it while it lasted.

The hour that ensued became one of the best Elizabeth had ever spent with her mother. The woman was chatty but not frivolous, her comments and observations astute but not supercilious, and the opinions she ventured were reasonable and seemingly well thought out.

Elizabeth found it difficult to reconcile the mother beside her, engaged in stimulating conversation with the parent she had known all her life, and expected to find upon her return.

She was almost sad when the conversation came to its end, which happened when Jane rushed into the room and stopped in front of the chair she occupied.

"Lizzy," cried she, reaching out to grasp her sister's hands and pull her from the chair into the tightest of embraces. "It is so good to see you! Summer was such a bore with you gone."

"Oh? Was Mr. Bingley's company not enough of a diversion? From what Papa said, you and he have been close to inseparable, and he eats here more than he does at Netherfield."

"Mr. Bingley has been wonderful, and a welcome diversion from the boredom, but nobody can replace you, Lizzy."

"Is your fiancé aware that he is nothing more than a 'diversion from boredom,' as you so eloquently put it? I will have to ask him when you introduce us."

"You know perfectly well what I meant," said Jane with a laugh that contained what Elizabeth suspected was a little nervousness at her teasing.

"The day is so beautiful," continued she, "it would be a shame to waste it inside. Let us continue in the garden, where I can tell you all about my summer."

Though Elizabeth wanted to be outside, she could not simply abandon the conversation with her mother, given the absence of rancor and the genial nature of their discussion.

"Go with Jane," directed Mrs. Bennet, surprising Elizabeth for the second time by understanding the need for her eldest daughters to bring each other up to date. "My needlework will keep me busy. Maybe we can talk after supper tonight."

"Thank you, Mama." Elizabeth gave her mother an affectionate kiss before following Jane, who waited for her in the garden.

"So much has changed," exclaimed Jane before Elizabeth had seated herself. "Lydia is a different person altogether, and Mary is to blame.

"She is better behaved, and not so prone to impulsive outbursts. She is more likely to be found in the library than outside. Can you believe it?"

"I will have to, not having seen her yet. Why are you blaming Mary for changing Lydia? Papa seems to think the difference is commendable."

"It is, and I am not implying what Mary accomplished was wrong. She is to be commended. Mary's influence has been the example that Lydia needed, and I am grateful for what she did, and Papa is as well.

"As for Mary, she is unchanged. She still prefers Fordyce to anything in the library, and you can count on hearing her sermons on the evils and shortcomings of any visitor to Longbourn, as well as me and Lydia. It is too bad that she did not adopt some of Lydia's cheery attitude in exchange for the soberness and propriety she gave her sister."

"It would have surprised me if she had changed, in even the smallest amount."

"There is more." Jane's excitement was almost enough to infect Elizabeth. "Lydia has not been to Meryton in weeks, and has not once asked permission to go. Without Kitty to blame for her indiscretions, she had no desire to leave the estate.

"I am sorry, but that does not sound like Lydia at all. I hope now that Kitty is back, they are not tempted to return to old habits."

"Lydia tells me she has no interest in chasing men in uniform. When I asked her why she felt that way now, when she used to sneak away every day or so, she laughed and said she had no desire to live a life of poverty. Then she declared she would not settle for anyone who did not have many, if not all, of the qualities Mr. Bingley is so blessed with!"

"Careful Jane, it sounds like Lydia has fallen in love with your fiancé," laughed Elizabeth, although Jane did not seem to find amusement in her jest.

"Lydia has finally realized that better manners and a demure countenance are the best way to attract a proper gentleman. She has been asking me how she can develop such traits, or if it is too late for her.

"I promised to do everything possible to teach her, and that it is never too late to adopt the behaviors of a gentlewoman."

"That is the thing I love most about you, Jane. You are never too busy to help. I hope Lydia realizes she has the best teacher in Hertfordshire."

"She has been both grateful and receptive. She really is a wonderful student, eager to learn, and to practice what she is learning. The sister you left is not the sister you are coming home to."

"It would seem that taking Kitty away was good for both of them," suggested Elizabeth, to Jane's nod of agreement. "She has improved in many of the same ways. Together they were holy terrors, but apart they have matured."

"Miss Bennet," came from Hill, interrupting their conversation, "Mr. Bingley is here to see you."

"Please tell him we are in the garden," instructed Jane, to which Hill nodded and went to fetch the young man.

"Finally, I will meet this perfect man," laughed Elizabeth, "and judge for myself if he is as good as you and Papa claim."

"He is, and better," declared Jane as the visitor appeared on the garden path, his countenance nothing but a smile from one ear to the other and beyond.

"Mr. Bingley," said she as he approached at a pace just short of running, his anticipation of being with his love seeming to overcome his manners, "Elizabeth has returned at last."

At Jane's words, he stopped so fast that Elizabeth expected to see his body continue despite his feet having planted themselves. The sight was so comical that she looked away, not wanting to embarrass the man by breaking into laughter.

"Mr. Bingley," continued Jane, evidently missing the humor Elizabeth tried to contain, "I would like you to meet Elizabeth, my next younger sister and best friend in the world. Elizabeth, this is Mr. Bingley, my future husband and, I hope, your future friend."

"I am so pleased to meet you, Miss Elizabeth." Mr. Bingley bowed and gave a flourish with his hand, so overly eloquent she was tempted again to break into laughter.

"The pleasure is mine, Mr. Bingley," giggled she, curtseying in response. "Jane is the happiest I have ever seen her, and I am told you are to blame."

"While I cannot claim responsibility for that, I will say that your sister made me the happiest man in England when she accepted my proposal."

"I can see that she feels much the same, if not more so."

"Miss Bennet tells me you spent the summer in Derbyshire?"

"Yes, with relations I had not seen since our childhood. I enjoyed meeting them and spent a wonderful summer there."

"My closest friend lives in that county. He is the best friend a man could want, and a gentleman among gentlemen. His judgement is above reproach, and his charity toward his fellow man surpasses anyone else I have ever met.

"His friendship, while not given lightly, is absolute and steadfast and once earned, never rescinded."

"He sounds like a great man. You should count yourself lucky to have made his acquaintance. As for his judgement, I would have to agree, since he extended his hand to you, Mr. Bingley. I should like to meet him some day."

"I am surprised you did not have the opportunity while you were visiting your cousins. His estate is the largest in the county, and everyone knows his name.

"You will have the chance, I hope, at our wedding. I have sent an invitation but have not yet received a reply. If Mr. Darcy can attend, I will introduce him to you. You will come to regard him as favorably as I do, without a doubt."

For a moment that seemed to stretch into an eternity, Elizabeth was unable to speak. Surely, he did not mean the same man who had treated her so poorly, forcing her expulsion from Kingsdown and her shameful return home?

But how many Darcys lived in Derbyshire? Only the one family to her knowledge. So this man, who had broken her heart, had to be the same whose virtues Mr. Bingley so heartily extolled.

Tears threatened to fill her eyes as memories came flooding back in defiance of her efforts to keep them at bay. She could not let Jane see them. Her sister seemed so happy, as did Mr. Bingley, and Elizabeth had no desire to disturb their felicity.

"I think it is time I returned to my room," was all she could say, wanting to escape before the accursed tears exposed her misery. "I am more tired from my journey than I realized, and I need to lie down again. It was nice meeting you, Mr. Bingley, and I look forward to seeing you again the next time you call."

With a wan smile she hoped did not show her distress, Elizabeth hurried from the garden and to her room where she could let her tears flow freely at this reminder of the future she had lost with a man who would never love her.

Barely five minutes passed before she heard the door open and felt the bed shift as Jane sat beside her.

"What is it, Lizzy?" asked Jane tentatively, as though she feared she had done something to cause Elizabeth's sorrow. "Please tell me, so I can help."

"There is nothing you can do," said Elizabeth. "Please apologize to Mr. Bingley; I did not mean to ruin his evening."

"You ruined nothing, and Mr. Bingley wants to help as much as I do. What is the matter, Lizzy? What has affected you so?"

Elizabeth fought to control her emotions while Jane sat patiently, waiting for her sister to speak. Finally, the disappointment holding her heart in a vice-like grip abated enough for her to inhale deeply, and with the intake of air, a feeling of calm descended upon her.

"Can you talk about it yet?" asked Jane softly, to which Elizabeth shook her head, unsure of her ability to speak without succumbing once again to the sorrow.

"No," responded she, grateful for a sister willing to wait as long as it took for her to recover enough to give voice to her feelings of hopelessness and loss.

The sisters spent an hour in silence, neither wanting to speak, until Elizabeth decided she would never be free of the heartache if she chose not to explain, to her sister at least, her loss of control.

"Mr. Bingley's friend is the man who accused me of assaulting his sister and refused to accept any proof of my innocence."

"Mr. Darcy? Are you sure?"

"He is the only Darcy in the county, and in England, from what I have been told, so they have to be the same."

At the news, Jane threw her arms around Elizabeth, as much to comfort her sister as herself, she knew.

"I am so sorry, Lizzy." Janes tears were now flowing in sympathy for her sister. "Please forgive me; I did not know."

"How could you?" asked Elizabeth, "when I said nothing about it? The fault is mine, not yours."

"Supper is being served," announced Mrs. Hill with a knock on the door.

"Come, Lizzy," said Jane, rising to her feet. "You need to eat."

"Could you have something sent up? I would like to stay in my room until morning."

"Of course, but you will have to come out sometime. If you hide in your bedroom, it will only make matters worse."

"And I will, but not tonight. Please, Jane, let me have one night to myself, with no more questions, or recriminations regarding our sudden return to Longbourn."

Jane nodded and left the room, promising to return with a plate from the cook. With a sigh, Elizabeth lay back on the bed to wait for her plate, but soon fell asleep. When Jane returned, she took the time to pull the covers over her sister before taking the plate back to the kitchen.

CHAPTER XXX

By the end of the week, Darcy's patience had worn thin. He loved his aunt but her imperious, condescending attitude toward the Pemberley servants was creating problems.

It seemed not a day went by that he did not come upon at least one of them, reduced to tears because of Lady Catherine's scathing rebuke over some minor error. Mrs. Reynolds, the Pemberley housekeeper, seemed to spend more of her time comforting these devastated servants than tending to her own duties, and he was grateful to have a woman like her in his employ.

After the third such occasion, Darcy decided enough was enough and thought he would either change his aunt's attitude or show her the door. Mrs. Reynolds, however, guessed his thoughts and cautioned him against creating a scene.

"This is not your fault," was her firm direction, "and all the servants agree. You are a fair man, not easily provoked and considerate to all. If I may offer an opinion, your aunt will leave soon, and life will return to normal. Until she does, we will tend to her needs with as much grace and forbearance as we can give."

To Darcy's surprise, the servant receiving Mrs. Reynolds' comfort, a normally timid girl who had been in his employ less than a year, smiled and nodded her agreement. Life at Pemberley did not improve before Lady Catherine finally departed, but the servants accepted the incessant insults and daily diatribes stoically, or so it seemed.

Even Snell, who displayed a lot of the same haughtiness as Lady Catherine, appeared to find the woman somewhat off-putting.

"Incompetent? If madam had been paying proper attention, she would not have put me in such a position," Darcy heard him muttering on the Thursday of that interminable week.

"I beg your pardon, Snell?" asked he, amused at the indignant expression on the man's face. "Is there a problem you wish to discuss with me?"

"It is nothing," grumbled Snell, although Darcy saw clearly that something had upset him.

In all the years he had been in Darcy's employ, the man had never displayed an emotion other than disdain for those he considered beneath him. Of course, as the master's personal manservant, he considered every other Pemberley servant beneath him, and had no hesitation when it came to informing them of this. Darcy found it amusing to find Snell flustered, although he had Darcy's sympathies.

He took to spending as much time out of doors, tending to the business of the estate, as he could. When Lady Catherine mentioned this, Darcy justified his absence with a recitation of the problems a property the size of Pemberley encountered daily. Although she chose not to argue the point, he could tell that she did not accept his excuses.

By the time Lady Catherine departed at week's end, his goodbye was perfunctory and brief, as he found himself unable to even pretend to have regrets over her leaving.

An unintended consequence of avoiding Lady Catherine was that he had a lot of time to ponder the subject of Miss Bennet, and the circumstances leading to her departure. His attraction toward her remained, and that bothered him. How was it possible to entertain feelings for someone who stood accused of such a heartless act?

But she was a woman unlike any other he had met, and it was doubtful he would again have the good fortune to meet another possessing her qualities. No matter how he tried, his thoughts remained focused on her, to the exclusion of almost everything else.

The woman was witty and intelligent, apparently unafraid of exposing herself to the possibility of ridicule for holding an opinion different from the accepted norm. Debating her proved to be an exhilarating experience; he found her points of view considered and rational, but never bombastic.

If not for the matter of Georgiana's injury, he might have been well on his way to asking for her hand in marriage. Even then, his decision to cut all ties and ban her from the estate did not come easily.

Autumn progressed, as had the autumn before it, and the one before that, into the snows and colder temperatures of winter, but Darcy took no notice. His thoughts centered on Miss Elizabeth Bennet, and what might occupy her interests, or the amusements she might be engaged in at present.

Did she attend the balls and assemblies that occurred in celebration of the changing seasons? Was she enjoying the traditional goose in honor of Michaelmas? Darcy saw, in his mind's eye, the table, laden with food and full of guests partaking in the fun and frolic such a party would invite, and the picture bothered him.

His thoughts did not confine themselves to the daylight hours. When he closed his eyes at night she appeared, surrounded by suitors, each of them doing their utmost to attract her interest.

Night after night these dreams returned to torment his sleep, leaving him increasingly exhausted and out of sorts upon waking each morning.

In desperation, he took a trip to London, hopeful that in the conducting of business, with its intricate moves and counter-moves, he might find respite from the moroseness which had overtaken him at Pemberley.

He returned a week before Christmas, invigorated with his success at putting former thoughts and obsessions from his mind. His spirits restored; he gave permission for placing evergreen boughs to decorate the sitting-room on Christmas Eve.

Christmas Day, and Boxing Day following it, were neither festive nor uplifting. The absence of Mr. Bannerman and his family at any of the season's balls muted the celebrations and commemorations of the Savior's birth. He really should talk to his neighbor, he thought, and do his best to mend the breach in their friendship.

Darcy liked the man and valued his insights regarding issues of mutual concern. Since the unfortunate incident, with its resulting strained feelings, he had missed their frequent conversations and camaraderie. He would, he decided, make an effort to restore their previous accord. He lost the choice the third week of March, in a most surprising way.

Darcy was in his library on the Tuesday morning of that week, pouring over his accounts in preparation for the planting to be done in the coming months.

As was his custom, he had given the butler instructions not to disturb him, so he answered the knock with a less than enthusiastic invitation to open the door.

"Mr. Bannerman is here," the butler announced before Darcy could demand an explanation for the interruption. "I told him you did not wish to be disturbed, but he was insistent that I inform you of his need to see you."

"Show him in," instructed Darcy, rising to greet this unexpected visitor while a thousand guesses ran unhindered through his mind.

What does he want? Is there news of Miss Bennet? If so, why would he suppose I should want to be informed? But if not, what other reason can there be? We have not spoken in months, notwithstanding my decision to attempt re-establishing our friendship.

The appearance of Miss Bennet at the top of his questions was no surprise, as the woman had not been far from his thoughts throughout the autumn and into the winter just past. What concerned him, though, was the quickening of his heartbeat, and the hope that she was the reason for this visit. This led to the fear that Mr. Bannerman's news might not be felicitous.

"Mr. Bannerman," Darcy greeted him as the man entered the room, "how good to see you. I meant to call on you myself but, to my shame, I let other issues take precedence."

"I understand and sympathize with you. There is always too much to do, and not enough time to get everything done."

"Well said, my friend." The declaration was out before he could stop himself. While he had always considered his neighbor a friend, the circumstances of the previous year might have caused Mr. Bannerman to reconsider the matter.

"Thank you, Mr. Darcy, for your regard. I feared our friendship had ended, and that assumption almost prevented my calling on you today."

"I did not hold you responsible for what happened to Georgiana. I regret my reaction to it but wanted only to protect my sister."

"Understood." Mr. Bannerman, although appearing relieved at Darcy's confirmation of their friendship still looked uncomfortable, as though what he had to say was not likely to please Pemberley's master.

"Please, have a seat," Darcy directed his visitor to a chair drawn up by the fire. "We can talk over here, where it is warm. May I offer you some brandy? Or would a cup of tea be more to your liking?"

"Brandy would be nice," said Mr. Bannerman, sitting in the indicated chair. "The weather is a touch cool today."

"To what do I owe the pleasure of your company?" asked Darcy, handing the glass to his guest and seating himself in the chair opposite.

Mr. Bannerman sipped from his glass, his eyes fixed on the dancing flames as they gamboled over the logs and danced against the grate.

What troubled him so much that he was uncomfortable raising the issue? Was it something Darcy would find cause for anger at hearing, or did the man require help and did not want to confess the fact?

"I need to speak with you about young Miss Darcy," stated Mr. Bannerman. "Believe me, I would rather not raise the issue, but I cannot keep it from you."

"Continue," Darcy felt unease settling in the pit of his stomach like a tainted meal.

"She has been calling at Kingsdown since Elizabeth left in the autumn, and to my knowledge, your instruction that she stay away is unchanged. We see her whenever you are away from home, whether you are in Lambton for a day, or London for a week.

"I have said nothing to her because I can tell that she takes care to escape my notice. This cannot, however, continue without some assurance that she has your permission."

"Thank you for bringing this to my attention," Darcy stated as Mr. Bannerman rose to his feet and made his way to the door. "I have not given permission for Georgiana to visit with your daughter, and she has not asked me."

For an instant it looked like Mr. Bannerman had something to add to the conversation, but the moment passed. Instead, he said goodbye and departed, leaving Darcy to ponder their conversation.

Why had Georgiana deliberately disobeyed the instructions he had given to protect her from further injury? While Miss Bennet was no longer in Derbyshire, that did not mean she had permission to do whatever she pleased. He needed to address this situation now, instead of waiting for the problems that would surely arise from ignoring the rules he had instituted last autumn.

With his decision made, Darcy left the library, intending to find Georgiana to ask her for an explanation. He was halfway up the stairs when Mrs. Reynolds called to him.

"She is not in her room, Mr. Darcy," the housekeeper informed him. "She went out an hour ago, for a bit of fresh air, she claimed."

"Thank you, Mrs. Reynolds," was his response in turning to retrace his steps. "Kindly send her to the library when she returns."

"I will," said she as he shut the door and turned his attention once again to his books.

While he made progress in his planning for spring, it was slow and tedious work when he would rather concentrate on Georgiana and her disobedience, which was troublesome.

What would lead her to ignore his counsel and directions? Did she believe herself immune to further attacks, or retaliation over Miss Bennet's banishment from Derbyshire? While he did not worry about Mr. Bannerman or his wife, their children were another matter. What if Miss Bannerman, or Miss Amelia, chose to retaliate for what they viewed as his mistreatment of their cousin?

Darcy could not be with her every moment of every day, so she needed to remain at home until he resolved the matter properly. At present, though Miss Bennet was gone, Georgiana had still not identified her, or anybody, as the assailant, which worried him further.

"You wanted to see me, William?" asked Georgiana, breaking his concentration as she stepped into the library.

"Close the door behind you," said he, "and have a seat. This is a matter best kept private."

Darcy waited until she settled in a chair across the desk from him before speaking. As she made herself comfortable, he studied her, noticing anew how much she had matured over the past year.

Gone was the thin, awkward little sister he had raised essentially alone over the previous ten years. In her place he beheld a beautiful young woman, graceful and sure of herself, and one who would, in the next few years, have the suitors beating down his door for the chance to court. Her smile alone would melt many hearts, he was sure, and he felt acutely the responsibility of keeping the worst of them far away from her. Nobody would break her heart if Darcy had anything to say about it.

"What did you want to see me about?" asked Georgiana, disturbing his reveries, and displaying the impish smile he found so disarming. "Or did you simply want to spend an hour in my presence? The idea is flattering, but not overly exciting for me."

"You are visiting Kingsdown, despite my instructions to stay away."

"Who told you such a thing?" demanded she, a response that did not deny the accusation, he noticed.

"That is not important. What is important is the fact that you called on Miss Bannerman, even though I told you to stay away from the property. Why would you do such a thing, and what did you hope your disobedience might accomplish? Nothing has changed; you are to stay away from Kingsdown. I want you to have nothing to do with them."

Darcy knew his sister was ready with a sharp retort; he saw it in the skin's tightening around her eyes and the outthrust jaw that happened whenever she was angry. He braced himself for the coming argument, as Georgiana was determined to voice her opinion whenever she disagreed with his rules or opinions.

To his surprise, he saw her countenance soften in acceptance of his censure. It happened so rapidly that it caught him off guard.

"You are correct, William," her apology came softly. "I will stay at home until you give permission for me to leave."

"Thank you." Darcy rose from his chair and came around the desk to enwrap her in his arms. "I want to protect you but cannot if you do not listen. The rules are there to keep you safe, not because I want to restrict your movements."

"I understand. Now please, let me go. You are suffocating me."

With a laugh, Darcy released her and stepped back to watch her walk out of the room. Pausing at the door, she waved and blew him a kiss before laughing and capering away into the house.

Darcy returned to his books, relieved that he would not have to punish her for a simple act of girlish foolishness.

His relief was short-lived as Georgiana, it seemed, chose not to abide by her restrictions.

Two days after their discussion, he saw her leaving Kingsdown as he passed by on one of his infrequent walks. So intent did she seem to be on slipping away from the estate without being noticed that she failed to see him standing at the Pemberley border.

"A lovely day today, is it not?" asked he as she neared, causing Georgiana to shriek and turn so fast she almost lost her balance.

"William! I came to find you," said she with a nervous laugh. "I hoped you were here, but I must have been mistaken."

"It would seem so," he agreed. "Need I say again, you may not call at Kingsdown, not even to find me?"

"I am sorry, William. It will not happen again."

"Why is it I doubt your promise? No, I think it best that you remain at Pemberley, inside the house, to be exact. That way you will not have to come find me, and I will know where you are at all times."

"But that is not fair," cried Georgiana. "I will obey, you can trust me. This was nothing more than an error and it will not reoccur."

"On that point you are correct. You will remain in the house until I am convinced you are abiding by the rules."

It incensed Georgiana, Darcy knew, but that did not change the fact that she had willfully disobeyed, and he would not let that go unpunished.

For the rest of the week, she would not talk to him. Her anger was such that she took her meals in her room until he forbade the cook from taking the food up to her. When she returned to the dining-room to eat with him, she refused to do anything but consume her food and return upstairs. Her manner hurt him, but he could not in good conscience rescind his punishment. To do so would invite further disobedience, or outright rebellion.

The matter came to a head on Monday when Darcy, partaking of a portion of brandy in the library after the evening meal, heard a knock on the door. Opening the portal revealed a repentant Georgiana, her manner hesitant, as if afraid to interrupt her brother.

"May I speak with you?" asked she softly.

"Of course," stepping aside, he allowed her entry.

When she sat, uncomfortably if he was any judge of her demeanor, he spoke: "What is the matter?"

"Please don't hate me," began she so softly that he strained to understand what she was saying.

"I could never hate you. You are my sister, and the only remaining member of our family. That alone guarantees my love."

His vow seemed to give her a measure of comfort, as she relaxed into the chair. For a minute she did not speak, and he could see that she struggled, as if looking for the proper words to convey her feelings.

"I lied," at last came forth before she dropped her head to stare at the floor, where her focus remained.

"Lied? What did you lie about?" asked he, unsure if he heard her correctly.

"Elizabeth Bennet did not attack me. I should have said something when the rumors started, but I chose to remain silent. Sarah Haversham hit me because I taunted and belittled her."

"What do you mean, Miss Bennet did not attack you? And why not correct the rumors, which had spread all over Derbyshire? What reason could you possibly have for letting me think she attacked, and almost killed, you? I accused her and barred her from Pemberley. She left Derbyshire because of my censure, and the condemnation I delivered because of your injury! You owe me an explanation."

"I know, and I am sorry, but I could not let you marry a woman so far beneath you. It would have made us the laughingstock of England."

"What gave you the right to decide who I should fall in love with, or marry? Miss Bennet is a gentleman's daughter, and perfectly acceptable as a bride, even for London society."

"I worried that if you married her, I would be sent to live with Lady Catherine so you and your wife could live here alone. I know she is my aunt, but the thought of living with her was something I could not accept."

Darcy was angry and more upset with Georgiana than he had ever been, but something about her confession rang false. She had spent more than one summer with her aunt and, while Lady Catherine was a strict and unforgiving woman, Georgiana always returned with tales of the fun they had shared. No, there was another reason, and he suspected he knew what it was.

"You are not telling me the complete truth are you, Georgiana? While I realize that life with Lady Catherine would not be appealing, that is not the only reason for this confession, is it?"

"No, William. I want you to ease your restrictions on visiting Kingsdown. I have missed Louisa and want permission to visit her again. That is why I have been sneaking away. She is a friend, and I want to see her."

"Is it really Miss Bannerman, or is there someone else at the estate that you are visiting? Mr. Bannerman tells me that Louisa is uncomfortable with your visits, and has told you, in no uncertain terms, to remain at Pemberley, but you keep calling, so she has refused to meet with you. Tell me the truth or the rules will remain, unchanged."

Georgiana was caught, and Darcy saw the recognition of that fact dawn in her eyes. Would she confess, or would the charade continue? He wanted to discuss the matter with her, but not if she insisted on hiding the truth.

"Yes, there is someone else!" she exclaimed, drawing herself up and impaling him with a fierce glare before again dropping her head. "I want to see Robert Bannerman. And I care not that you disapprove. He is the kindest man I have ever met, and he treats me as his equal, despite our difference in status. I love watching him, especially when he is unaware of my presence. Please allow him to pay attention to me. He will not defy you, or his father, and has told me that until you remove these restrictions, I can no longer visit Kingsdown."

"You should not be calling on any man, restrictions or not. Where is your sense of decorum? You have received proper instruction, so you are not ignorant of the rules you flaunt by calling on him.

"The Bannerman family is not wealthy, so if you and he *were* to marry, your situation would not be as comfortable as it is at Pemberley. Are you prepared for such a change in your life?"

"I think so, but unless you give him permission to court me, I cannot make such a decision. Please allow it, William, and let us find out if we suit."

Darcy was unsure how to react to her confession, even though it did not surprise him. Unfortunately, the injury to his neighbors reputation and shunning by most of Lambton's merchants would be difficult to repair. Still, Georgiana had owned up to her misdeed. The only question that remained was whether she wanted to face the consequences.

"Get your wrap," instructed he, reaching a decision he hoped was correct. "We are going to Kingsdown, where you will apologize to the family and hope they forgive you."

"Now?" asked Georgiana incredulously. "Should this not wait until morning? I can offer a more sincere apology, and Mr. Bannerman will have the entire day to think about what I say."

"There is no time like the present." Darcy took her hand, pulling her after him as he left the library.

"Finch," called he upon entering the front hall. "Have the carriage readied. Georgiana and I are going to call upon a friend."

"I expect a full confession from you when we arrive," was all he could say while they waited for the conveyance. "Do not attempt to lessen your role in this affair, or I *might* send you to live with your aunt anyway. She would have little trouble changing your behavior for the better."

"Yes William," said she as the coach arrived at the door. "I will tell the truth."

"That would be best," stated Darcy as he handed her into the vehicle and got in himself.

CHAPTER XXXI

Georgiana had nothing to say on their way to Kingsdown, and Darcy decided it was best not to engage her in conversation.

He was angry, more so than at anything she had done in the past. What was she thinking to assume such a plan was an advisable course of action? And what had Miss Bennet done to deserve this kind of treatment? Try as he might, Darcy did not recall any action on her part that might have given Georgiana the idea to attempt something so reprehensible.

He considered sending her to Rosings Park to stay with Lady Catherine. Georgiana needed correction, and her aunt might instill the respect and proper reverence for her elders she seemed to lack.

But Georgiana might also pick up what Darcy considered Lady Catherine's haughty, unforgiving, sense of superiority and condescending manner, and that was a chance he was not about to take. No, Georgiana was his responsibility, and it was up to him to mold her into a respectable woman, one who cared for those less fortunate and looked down upon no one.

"We have arrived," was Georgiana's comment as the carriage turned into Kingsdown's drive.

"We have," observed he while they waited for the cabin door to be opened. Georgiana nervously fidgeted and shifted on her seat as comfort clearly eluded her. Darcy knew somewhat how she felt, having been in similar situations with their father in years previous.

His sister, without a doubt, wanted to be somewhere else, and avoid the embarrassing confession she had to make. She probably wanted the whole affair finished and put behind her.

He had been in the identical position when he was younger than Georgiana, punished for having broken a window in one of the tenant's houses at Pemberley. It had been an accident, but instead of telling his father immediately, he had tried to put the blame on the shoulders of someone else. When Mr. Darcy finally pried the truth out of him, he took Darcy to the tenant's home to confess. Darcy remembered the shame and humiliation of that day. Although he sympathized with his sister, this was a lesson she needed to learn.

Upon exiting the carriage, she hesitated briefly before following Darcy to the manor's entrance, where Bertram stood waiting with the door open. With a slight bow, he waved them into the hall, closing the door behind them.

"Please tell Mr. Bannerman I wish to speak with him, and his family," asked he, whereupon the butler nodded and left to pass along the request.

"I am scared, William," pleaded Georgiana. "Is there not another way to do this?"

"No. You need to confess and beg their forgiveness. This is a good family, who will accept your remorse, but only if it is genuine. You will need to earn it, but that is for Mr. and Mrs. Bannerman to decide. I cannot demand such a thing and would not consider making the attempt."

"Mr. Bannerman is in the sitting-room," said Bertram upon entering the hall again. "Please follow me."

It did not surprise Darcy to see Georgiana hesitate; she had to be worried about how Mr. Bannerman would react to the disclosure of her guilt in this affair. Would he listen and accept her apology, or would he choose to banish her from Kingsdown forever?

With a gentle push and a nod toward Bertram, Darcy got Georgiana moving, although her steps were slow at first.

"The faster you follow him," said Darcy with a nod toward the butler, "the faster this will be over, and we can return home."

When Georgiana's pace did not increase, Darcy took her by the hand and led her into the sitting-room, where the Bannermans were waiting for them.

Mr. Bannerman appeared to be curious, which in Darcy's mind was better than the animosity he expected to be greeted with. Stopping in front of the man's chair, Darcy bent down to speak without being overheard.

"Georgiana has something to tell you. I thought it best that she do it in front of your family as it involves all of you."

Darcy stepped back and motioned to his sister to come forward and stand beside him. When she was in place, he turned to her.

"Tell Mr. and Mrs. Bannerman what you told me."

Georgiana's eyes went to Darcy, a look of fear fastened upon her face. With a shake of her head, she stepped back as if to flee, but Darcy, anticipating such a move, kept his hand on her back so she could not escape.

"Go ahead. Waiting will not make this any easier, so it is best to get it over with."

Georgiana was still, her eyes looking everywhere but at the people she was there to address. Darcy watched a moment of panic cross her countenance before she closed her eyes and spoke. As she did, a solitary tear leaked from each eye and sat on her cheeks.

"The accusations against Elizabeth Bennet are not true," began she, her voice quivering with emotion. "She did not attack me. I should have told you earlier, but I was afraid that William was going to ask permission to court her, and I did not want him to do that. Please forgive me; what I did was wrong. I am so deeply sorry."

Darcy had prepared himself for their reaction to her confession, but the silence which followed was a surprise. Mr. Bannerman was angry, that much Darcy could tell, but he did not speak. For a minute, then two, the room was still.

"Everybody in Lambton shuns us," said Miss Bannerman. "Many of the merchants refuse to sell to us. I cannot go to town, for fear of being attacked in retribution for what happened to you."

"I will go to Lambton tomorrow," stated Darcy, "and let everyone know what happened. I will restore your good name; I promise."

"That will do little to restore our good opinion and regard for Miss Darcy," came from Robert, who until now had been silent as the confession unfolded. "Nor will it be enough to remove the hatred and suspicion we have been subjected to in Lambton, at least not immediately, and maybe never."

"You have my word the damage will be repaired," said Darcy. "As for the other, I suspect Georgiana is anxious to reclaim her good standing with you, no matter what it takes."

"What will happen to her?" asked Mrs. Bannerman. "Does it worry you this will damage the Darcy name and reputation? The town gossips can be vicious in spreading rumors and half truths."

"I am prepared for that. As far as Georgiana is concerned, she needs to earn your trust and respect again. That is not something I can, or should, demand."

"I can forgive you," sighed Miss Bannerman, "but if I may, what prompted you to confess your error? If you had remained quiet, the truth would not have come out, and you would not be subject to the punishment you are facing."

At the question, Darcy looked to Mr. Bannerman, who appeared to be pondering the same thing.

"Can I speak to you in private? The answer is not something that everyone needs to hear."

With a nod, Mr. Bannerman took Darcy to the study and bade him sit. When both settled in chairs, Darcy spoke.

"Georgiana came to me because of her restrictions on calling at Kingsdown. She claimed it was to visit your eldest daughter, but the truth of the matter is that she has developed feelings for your son. She seems to think he feels the same."

Mr. Bannerman sighed and nodded in agreement: "Your sister is correct. Robert also has been despondent and short tempered since the attack on Miss Darcy and the resulting discord between us. It would seem he is attracted to her as well."

"Would you oppose letting them visit, with Miss Bannerman in attendance as well? This might be no more than a simple infatuation. Georgiana is only seventeen and has not yet been the object of a young man's attention."

"While Robert is nineteen, and just as inexperienced in matters of the heart. I have no objections; if you are comfortable letting Miss Darcy visit, I am as well.

"She will not, however, find it as easy with Robert as she assumes. Although he never told me, this affected him, and I doubt he will trust her immediately.

"She is welcome at Kingsdown, but only with your permission."

"I will allow it, but only in the company of you or Mrs. Bannerman. Georgiana's chaperone, Mrs. Annesley, will always accompany her, so there should be no worries in that regard.

"This will not happen until Georgiana satisfies me she is truly repentant. She does not know yet, but I am confining her to the estate for the next month. If she misbehaves, the restriction will double, and double again each time it happens. She will have to decide just how badly she wants to entertain the company of your son."

"A fitting punishment," laughed Mr. Bannerman. "You are a wise disciplinarian."

"A craft I learned at my father's knee," said Darcy, rising to his feet. "Thank you for your willingness to forgive. It might have been easier to withhold your charity, and I would not censure you for doing so."

"But that would not profit either of our families, would it?" asked Mr. Bannerman.

The men returned to the sitting-room to find Georgiana sitting beside Miss Bannerman, the two young women talking as if the problems of the previous months had never occurred. Her elder brother sat a little way off, watching the two with interest, as if he wished to be included in the conversation. Darcy glanced to Mr. Bannerman to see that he, too, had noticed and seemed to find a little humor in the situation.

"We should leave," suggested Darcy, "so Mr. Bannerman and his family can finish their evening peacefully."

"May I return tomorrow?" asked Georgiana as she stood. "There is so much that we need to discuss."

"That is a conversation we will have at home. Now bid Miss Bannerman, and the rest of the family, good evening."

The families exchanged farewells, after which Darcy ushered his sister back to the carriage for the journey home. In response to Georgiana's impatient questioning, Darcy informed her of the punishment she would need to serve before regaining any freedom.

It was an angry but subdued Georgiana who arrived back at Pemberley. Her pleas for mercy fell on deaf ears; nothing she said changed his mind. Only when he spelled out the consequences of disobedience did her displeasure soften and change to grudging acceptance.

Georgiana seemed resigned to her punishment, to Darcy's relief. For the first few days she was pensive and unusually quiet, but by week's end her usual good spirits were appearing again. By unspoken agreement, they did not discuss her misdeed, which was agreeable to Darcy, who had no desire to revisit the subject.

With Georgiana's confession and its accompanying revelation of what she had put in motion, his melancholy returned. He knew common decency demanded that he put things right with Miss Bennet and apologize, but the fear she might reject his attempts weighed on him until, in near desperation, he put the matter aside. If he forgot about Miss Elizabeth Bennet, his world would hopefully return to its normal state.

On a fine spring morning early in April, Fitzwilliam came to visit, and his arrival put into motion a series of events leading to a momentous change in Darcy's life.

Darcy was in the orchard talking with someone when his cousin entered the drive, riding a beautiful chestnut colored stallion, whose high-stepping gait and spirited walk showed it was an animal with energy to spare.

Fitzwilliam dismounted and, giving the reins to a stable hand, waited while Darcy finished his business and came to greet him.

"Is that a new gardener I saw you with?" asked he when Darcy neared. "Don't tell me you finally broke down and hired someone to rescue Pemberley's orchard from your mismanagement."

"He comes highly recommended," responded Darcy, choosing to ignore the gibe. "Because of last year's moth infestation, I approached Thomas for help in finding a replacement. His nephew was at loose ends, and Thomas claimed the lad was as competent a gardener as he had been, so I took him at his word. The young man has not disappointed me; he has in fact done a lot to help the orchard recover from last year's damage. I am impressed with his knowledge and work ethic and think the harvest this year will be acceptable."

"May I assume that your help mostly comprises staying out of the fellow's way?"

"You may assume whatever you wish. I would correct your misconception, but you ignore everything I tell you anyway, so why try now?"

"Have I touched on a sore spot, cousin? If so, let me know so I can keep raising the offending subject."

"Was there a reason you came all this way to see me, other than to insult my intelligence and deride my management of Pemberley?"

"If you must know, I came to see both of you," stated Fitzwilliam.

"Although I am reconsidering my decision to visit you," laughed he at Darcy's scowl. "Is this an inconvenient time? You seem less than pleased I am here."

Darcy appreciated Fitzwilliam's attempt to lift his spirits and his ability to sense something was bothering him. The man had always cheered him, but his depression this time was completely out of the norm, and more profound than ever before.

"There is a problem, and it involves Georgiana," said Darcy, deciding that, as his sister's other guardian, Fitzwilliam had the right to know what had transpired over the winter. "We can discuss the matter inside, over a glass of whiskey."

"Ahh, the magic word," laughed Fitzwilliam at Darcy's sudden look of confusion. "Whiskey, my friend, is the magic word. I would follow you to the ends of the earth for a sample of that nectar of the gods you keep in such abundant supply."

Darcy laughed despite himself. Fitzwilliam was not the great connoisseur of alcohol his claim suggested. He sipped only occasionally, and even then, allowed himself only one serving. Darcy had never seen his cousin drunk, and probably never would. The man valued self-control and would not consider surrendering it to an over-indulgence in anything, especially not a liquid that would leave him ill the following day.

Darcy led the way into the house and, when they were in the library, glasses in hand, gave his cousin a look of gratitude.

"Thank you for lightening my mood. The respite is unfortunately temporary, but I will take whatever I am given."

"And this involves Georgiana?"

Darcy took a moment to organize his thoughts. The memory of her involvement in the events of the past few months aroused the anger that he had fought so hard to overcome. It would not do to surrender to the emotion now.

"Do you recall the circumstances of Georgiana's attack and the resulting departure of the person I accused of causing her injury?" said he when he regained possession of his mental state.

"I do, but only vaguely, as you never gave me the full story. Your last letter informed me that you knew the identity of the guilty party, and they would not attack her again. As I recall, she is a cousin to your neighbors, and they sent her home because of her involvement in the incident. I would have demanded a more severe punishment, but you seemed to think being driven from the neighborhood would suffice."

Darcy's neck grew warm as Fitzwilliam recounted the steps he had taken. Embarrassment, and the temptation to conceal the indignity forced upon Miss Bennet, urged him to remain quiet, but his conscience would not allow him to take the easy, cowardly way out of his predicament.

"Miss Bennet was innocent, as she claimed, but at the time I was in no mood to listen to what I thought were blatant lies and pathetic attempts to shift the blame."

"A reasonable assumption, I would guess, but of course I was not here when it happened."

"I have been kicking myself for not accepting her denials. I refused to listen, and it bothers me."

"Was there any reason to think Miss Bennet was telling the truth? It is easy to claim innocence; the guilty do it all the time."

"She claimed she was with her cousins and her aunt the entire day, and they supported her. I refused to listen and became angry when she would not retract her claim. In retaliation I barred the entire family from visiting Georgiana at Pemberley and swore I would not set foot on Kingsdown property if Miss Bennet remained."

"And, of course, you have been miserable ever since."

"It was only recently that Georgiana came to me and confessed to wanting the blame placed on Miss Bennet, who was telling the truth. Georgiana's attacker was her friend, Miss Haversham, and Georgiana concealed that, knowing I would retaliate against the person I thought had harmed my sister."

"A reasonable assumption, but what was her motive? Was she angry for some perceived slight? Did Miss Bennet publicly cut her, and she wanted to even the score? I am sorry, but that does not sound like the Georgiana I know."

Darcy had risen from his chair and was restlessly pacing the library floor while his anger again fought for supremacy. As he considered the matter, he realized that, while Georgiana's deceitful actions were upsetting in the extreme, it was his hesitancy to set the matter right that was more bothersome. He would not let it go unresolved, but how best to confess his shame and guilt? Would a letter suffice, after the manner he treated her? It would have to, because he had no desire to go to Hertfordshire, hat in hand, to beg forgiveness.

"Georgiana took it upon herself to judge the worth of Miss Bennet to be seen in my company."

"What would that matter? It was not as though you were chasing her with your tongue hanging out and your self-regard abandoned, was it?"

"I told Georgiana my thoughts that Miss Bennet and I might suit each other, and that I was going to ask permission to pay my attention. Georgiana took it upon herself to decide that Miss Bennet was unworthy of such an honor and took steps to ensure things progressed no further."

"That does not sound like your sister. We raised her to look past surface imperfections, to the person within. There must have been a reason for her behavior."

"She claimed to fear being sent to live with Lady Catherine if we married. When I pressed her for the truth, she confessed she was growing fond of Mr. Bannerman's eldest son Robert, and wanted my restrictions lifted so she could call on him."

"Not very ladylike or appropriate, but she can be willful when she sets her mind to something. I would hope she realizes that to call on a man is unacceptable, but that is a matter for another time, I suppose. Meanwhile, what are you doing to make amends to Miss Bennet?"

"I am not sure what I can do. The woman does not live in Derbyshire, and would probably refuse to see me, or accept an apology. We treated her shamefully, and I am responsible."

"Go see her," urged Fitzwilliam. "Apologize, on your hands and knees if you must, and repair your relationship."

"Why would I want to do that? Our parting words were not the most amicable. If I were in Miss Bennet's place, I would not accept any attempts to reconcile."

"Get over yourself, Darcy. Either swallow your pride and confess that you still love her, or be miserable, but for your own sake, do something."

Fitzwilliam was correct, and Darcy knew it. But was he brave enough to face the wrath of a woman he had treated so poorly? She might throw him off the property, and he could not blame her if she did. Still, if he was going to find any peace and serenity, he had to take the chance.

"I will, and I know when to do it," said he to Fitzwilliam's look of satisfaction. "Bingley is to be wed next week, and he invited me to be his best man. I sent my apologies, as he is marrying Miss Bennet's elder sister, but what better time to beg forgiveness, when the marriage has already softened her heart?"

"Careful, Darcy, or your schemes might have the opposite affect. Be honest with the woman, and trust in her ability to see that you love her and are ashamed of your actions. Subterfuge can only further damage your relationship."

"You are correct, as always. That must be why I allow you to bother me here," said Darcy with a smile. "It is not your wisdom, or the support you rarely give, but the fact you occasionally stumble on the truth, by accident of course."

"That is the Darcy I know and love, obtuse and insulting in the same breath," laughed Fitzwilliam.

"Are you able to stay with Georgiana while I am gone?" asked he, plans already forming in his head. "I know she would appreciate the company."

"Sorry, but I cannot. I have a commitment of my own, something I have been looking forward to all winter."

"Heaven forbid the thought of you allowing anything to interfere with your plans," laughed Darcy.

He stepped into the hall, summoned Snell, and instructed the man to pack enough clothing for an extended journey. Snell, upon being told he was to remain behind, set off to do as he was told, grumbling all the way about being abandoned again while his master left on a merry adventure. Darcy, his good humor restored, let the man think his complaints went unnoticed.

Darcy had Snell call the servants together before leaving the following morning. With a curricle loaded, his trunk lashed to the back, and the horses harnessed and waiting it seemed, as they pranced and whinnied, they were urging him to climb aboard and start the journey.

He entered the house and approached the servants, lined up and awaiting his instructions. With a nod of thanks to Snell, he said: "I will attend Bingley's wedding after all, and expect to be gone for a month, or six weeks at the most. While I am away, Georgiana is not to leave the house for any reason.

"She is to have no visitors for the next two weeks, after which Miss Bannerman may visit, if she decides to call. Under no circumstances is Miss Haversham allowed on the property, even with her father.

"If I return to discover you failed to enforce these instructions, I will end the employment of the servant responsible. Are there any questions?"

Darcy paused to let those assembled ponder his words. He trusted his people, but he was aware of the sympathy many of the upstairs maids held for his sister and wanted to be sure Georgiana would not tempt them to bend the rules in her favor. When he was sure he had made the point, he continued.

"Remember, I confined Georgiana to the house. I have tasked some of you with watching her and will expect a report upon my return. If she has behaved herself, and given you no trouble, I will consider restoring her freedoms, but that is my decision alone.

"Most of you have been in my employ for many years, and I trust you will follow my instructions. Please, be mindful of my sister, and each other, while I am gone."

Darcy turned to join Fitzwilliam, who was standing by the entrance, listening. With a nod to Finch, and one to Snell, he left the house and walked to his conveyance. Taking the reins from the stable hand, he climbed into the vehicle.

"Why not use the carriage, or the chaise and four?" asked his cousin.

"Because the wedding is in four days, and I want to get there with time to spare."

"Be careful. These things might be fast, but they are dangerous, and easily upset. It would be a shame to kill yourself because you were in too much of a hurry."

"I am skilled enough to drive two horses and a light carriage," laughed Darcy as he shook the reins to get the horses moving. "And if not, you can finish raising Georgiana, if she will let you."

With a wave of Darcy's hand, the curricle entered the road and picked up speed. Fitzwilliam watched until he was out of sight before mounting his horse and setting off toward his own destination.

CHAPTER XXXII

Darcy set a fast pace, pushing the horses almost to a gallop in his haste to arrive at his destination. The breakneck speed was dangerous, he knew, but he was willing to risk everything in his desperation to complete the journey. When the horses tired, he slowed them to a walk to let them regain their strength before shaking the reins to speed them up again.

The approach to Derby was a sharp turn, and well known to Darcy, who had ridden this road many times on his way to London, by coach and perched on a horse. For reasons he could not explain, the treacherous characteristics of the curve fell by the wayside as he urged the horses to greater speed. The animals, strong and seeming to enjoy the exercise, responded with enthusiasm, entering the curve much too fast to allow safe transit around the corner.

Designed for speed, the curricle sat well above the axles, which gave it a high center of gravity and a predilection for sudden, and unforeseen, upsets. As the horses started into the curve, it tilted, rising on the inside wheel. Darcy threw himself to the top of the rapidly rising side, hoping his weight would be enough to return the errant wheel to the ground.

Slowly, or so it seemed, the side of the vehicle rose, until Darcy feared an upset was inevitable. In desperation, he braced his foot against the lower part of the curricle and, using the placement of his foot, pushed himself hard against the rising side, trying to shift enough of his weight to force the wheel back onto the surface of the road. As he did, the reins slipped from his hands and dropped to the ground, where they dragged behind the fast-charging horses.

I hope I survive this, he thought as the vehicle seemed intent on upending and strewing its contents across the hard surface of the road. To his grateful surprise, the horses, feeling the reins loosen, slowed their gait and lessened their path through the curve, both of which allowed the free-floating wheel to regain contact with the road.

Instead of continuing to run, they came to a stop in the middle of the lane, for unknown reasons. It had been his experience in the past that a horse, once given its head, would run until exhausted, especially when spurred on by a carriage trailing behind.

Here, however, the opposite had happened, and Darcy, leaving the vehicle to settle his nerves, was tempted to throw his arms around the neck of each animal to show his gratitude.

"An extra measure of oats for you tonight," said he instead, gathering the reins and climbing back into the curricle. With a shake, he got the horses underway, this time at a pace more suitable, both for the road and the vehicle he was driving. He had no desire to risk himself further; the journey would finish in good time, and he wanted to arrive in one healthy piece.

Lethargy arrived suddenly, in consequence, he surmised, from the harrowing experience he had been through. Fatigue stole over him, threatening to close his eyes if he did not find an inn at once.

It was a relief to see the Pig and Whistle at the end of the street, before sleep claimed him. Pulling up to the inn, he gave instructions to treat his horses, including the extra ration he had promised. It would not do, he thought, to make a promise to his animals and neglect to follow through. Though they did not understand his vow, they deserved the treat, and the reward for getting him here safely.

The innkeeper was no stranger to Darcy, who rented a room almost every time he journeyed to London. His inspection, conducted as Darcy approached the counter, was quick and accurate.

"Had a rough day?" was his guess as Darcy leaned on the wooden counter, a piece of oak burnished until one saw himself reflected in the surface. Darcy had been in the habit of remarking on the quality of the finish, but the day had exhausted him, to where he thought he might fall asleep before paying for his room.

Reaching behind him, the man took a key from its place on the wall and handed it to Darcy. "Room seven, just at the top of the stairs. You go ahead, and I will have your trunk brought up."

"I need to pay for my accommodation," mumbled Darcy, fumbling for his wallet as he reached for the key.

"You can pay me tomorrow. I know you are good for it."

"Thank you, Edward. You are the reason I stay here and recommend you to my friends and acquaintances."

"And I appreciate your praise, but now is not the time for small talk. Take yourself upstairs before you collapse. I would offer to bring you a plate of supper, but I doubt you will be awake much longer."

With a nod of gratitude, Darcy took the key and climbed the stairs, thankful that the room was at the top and directly in front of the staircase. Exhausted, he put the key into the lock, turning it to retract the bolt and open the door.

It was only a minute or two later the servant delivered his trunk to the room. "The master told me to get this up here without delay, as you were in a hurry," said the servant, placing the item under the window. Backing from the room, he pulled the door closed.

Darcy wanted to undress, but the bed was so inviting he could not resist its allure. He sat, intending to rest for a minute before completing his preparations, but his eyes closed and he slumped to the side, fast asleep.

When he woke, the room was dark, and the building was quiet. Darcy, knowing it was too late for a meal, got himself undressed and settled into bed, pulling the covers up to ward off the spring chill. His attempt to plan the next day's travel was unsuccessful, as his eyes closed again almost as soon as he relaxed.

When Darcy woke, the sun was well on its way across the sky, the morning dew having evaporated long before. Throwing the covers off, he left the bed and made his way to the nightstand, with its pitcher of water standing beside the bowl. He washed himself quickly, then dressed and left the room in less than fifteen minutes.

He enjoyed a hearty breakfast, despite the innkeeper's teasing about rising long after most of the inn's guests had departed for the day. Darcy was used to Edward's manner, and counted him a friend, so he knew the man's taunts were light-hearted and well meant.

Upon finishing his meal, he settled his bill and climbed into the curricle, which was ready and waiting for him, his trunk lashed securely in place.

"Keep an eye on the horizon," remarked Edward, pointing in the direction of Darcy's travel. "It is clouding over, and the sky looks pretty dark to me. You might be better off laying over for another day, so this weather can pass. Your curricle will provide no shelter should the storm catch you before arriving at your destination."

"I cannot, Edward, but thank you for the warning. I have someplace to be, and a day's delay will make me late."

"Then I wish you a safe journey, and pray you escape the worst of it," said he as Darcy shook the reins to get the horses moving.

The speed today was slower than yesterday's, but Darcy had no desire to risk himself, or the horses, on another dangerous upset. The pace they set was a trot, which devoured the miles while giving him time to consider the welcome he might expect upon arriving at Bingley's leased estate.

Would Miss Bennet let him apologize and, if she did, what were the chances she might accept what he said? He had hurt her by unjustly accusing her of a crime she had not committed. Her denials had fallen on deaf ears, and he was ashamed of himself for refusing to extend her the courtesy of listening to any of the proof she offered.

Were it not for the feelings he held onto through the long, cold winter, he would have rejected Fitzwilliam's suggestion to call on her and beg forgiveness for his treatment. If she rejected his supplications, he would leave, knowing he had done everything possible to repair the relationship and regain her former regard.

Darcy's thoughts turned to Miss Bennet as her image appeared in his mind. She was a comely woman with a pleasing figure, but it was her impertinent nature that had ensnared him. Before he knew what was happening, he was smitten. Not that he minded in the least. He could not imagine himself courting another should she turn him away, as he doubted there was someone else with her qualities in all of England.

The rain Edward had warned him about began in the late afternoon as big, lazy droplets, but within fifteen minutes the sky had opened up and looked to be intent on drowning him. It came in sheets, driven by a strong, gusting wind that cut straight through him. Forced to the side of the road by the rain, he unlashed his trunk and opened it, looking for the greatcoat he had packed in case the weather turned.

He pulled it on but found only brief respite from the deluge, as his coat was not watertight, and the rain soon soaked it through. Darcy kept on, knowing that to stop and shelter for any amount of time would put him in danger of arriving too late to accomplish his goal, and there was nowhere he might stop that would shelter him, anyway.

Luton's appearance was a relief and stopping at the entrance to the first inn he came upon, Darcy bounded from the curricle and hurried inside, where it was dry and warm.

"Not the best day to be traveling," offered the innkeeper as Darcy shook some of the water from his clothing. "Were you needing a room? There is only one left, as it seems everybody is waiting for the storm to pass. The room charge includes supper; if you eat is up to you."

"Thank you," said Darcy. "Is there somebody who can unlash my trunk and place it in my room? I fear the rain soaked everything inside, and I would like to hang some of it out to dry, if possible."

"I can arrange that, but it will cost you," said the innkeeper, a greedy look in his eye.

"That is fine," Darcy wanted nothing more than the key to his room so he could light a fire and dry himself. "If it is not too much trouble, will you send the meal to my room? I will pay an extra farthing if necessary."

Darcy was familiar with this type of man, having met his like more than once. He would grasp at any amount, and swindle his guests for more, so Darcy decided he might just as well make the offer first. He hoped to save a bit of his money by suggesting an amount for the requested service.

The trunk was wet through and through; a full half inch of water remained at the bottom when he removed the clothes. He took it downstairs to empty before returning to his room and placing it in front of the roaring fire he had built to dry his apparel.

After a meal that was particularly good, Darcy went to bed and slept as well as expected, what with dreams of Miss Bennet running through his imagination all night long.

With morning came a return of the sun, and a milder temperature, which was a welcome relief. He rose early and, eschewing breakfast in favor of a quick departure, set off on the last leg of his journey. The beauty of the day lifted his spirits but heightened his anxiety regarding the reception he might receive when he showed up, unannounced, at Netherfield. He knew Bingley would welcome him with open arms, but he rather doubted Bingley's betrothed would. And certainly not her sister, Miss Elizabeth.

As he neared Hertfordshire, Darcy realized he had neglected to bring Bingley's carefully written directions with him. He stopped to ask for the best way to Netherfield, which was given, along with the gentleman's profuse praise for Bingley's pleasant nature and friendly attitude.

Darcy thanked the man and left, promising that he would pass the compliments along to his friend. An hour later he turned into Netherfield and brought the curricle to a halt in front of the entrance.

Before he alighted from his vehicle, the door opened, and Bingley was upon him, shaking his hand and welcoming him warmly to Hertfordshire, his leased estate, and his wedding, to be held the next day.

"I thought you could not attend?" Bingley tried, but failed, to sound upset. "If I had known you were going to be here, I would have prepared a room for you to sleep in."

"I will sleep in the stable, if that is all you have available," said Darcy, intending the statement as a joke, but realizing as he spoke, he meant every word. "Just clean out a stall and I will be happy."

"Nonsense," laughed Bingley. "I will have a room prepared, and a bed made up. But tell me, what made you change your mind? In your letter, you thought it best if you were not present."

"I came to beg Miss Elizabeth's forgiveness. I was foolish to treat her the way I did, and I need to tell her. My fear is that she will turn me away like I did her, and she would be justified in doing so."

"Why did you wait so long? She has been miserable since coming back from Derbyshire. It is only in the past month that her spirits returned, according to her sister. You might have avoided this if you had reached out to her last winter, instead of waiting until now."

"Georgiana had me convinced Miss Elizabeth was the person who attacked her so viciously, and that was something I could not forgive. It was only recently I learned the truth, and I was unsure what to do about it. I was going to write, but thought a letter was too impersonal to do an apology justice.

"When I finally decided to come and ask her to forgive me, and possibly overlook my faults, I loaded my clothing and personal affects on the curricle and came as fast as I could. That reminds me, I drove through a fearful storm yesterday, and it soaked everything I brought. Could a maid dry and press my clothing for tomorrow?"

"I will have it done." Bingley, motioned to his housekeeper, giving instructions to have the items tended to.

"About Miss Elizabeth," said Bingley, turning his attention back to his friend, "she might not want to have anything to do with you. Your rejection crushed her, and according to Jane, it was her second betrayal last year.

"She might not want to take another chance, because if you were to decide, after winning her heart again, that the two of you do not suit after all, she might never recover."

"All I can do is make the attempt. If she has turned against me and decided she wants nothing to do with me, I will leave with regrets, but without putting up an argument. I hope that, however this turns out, you can forgive me for hurting your future sister-in-law the way I did."

Bingley's response was to sweep Darcy into an embrace. He was not surprised, as his friend normally wore his heart on his sleeve and was quick to show his emotions. To his credit, there was not so much as a single ounce of insincerity in the man. With Bingley, the face he presented to the world was a mirror of the man inside. It was his open and trusting nature that endeared him to Darcy, in spite of the unflattering opinions his friends at first held regarding the man.

"Of course I forgive you," was his statement as the embrace tightened, pulling Darcy closer than he desired. "I am your best friend, and even they make mistakes. What matters is that you have recognized your error and decided to atone for it, or at least as much as she will let you."

"Could you not have expressed that emotion from a distance?" asked Darcy as Bingley's hug showed no signs of loosening. "You are going to smother me, and then what use will I be in speaking to Miss Elizabeth?"

With a laugh, Bingley dropped his arms and, taking a step back, took hold of Darcy's hand, which he shook with the same amount of enthusiasm he had shown in capturing Darcy in his embrace.

"Is this more appropriate?" said he, to which Darcy laughed.

"It is, but be careful, as I might need that hand to feed myself tonight, unless you are fasting until your wedding breakfast tomorrow. If that is the case, I will find the nearest town and check myself into the inn. Surely they will offer me some sustenance."

"Heaven forbid! I would be too weak to make it through the ceremony, and Jane might never forgive me, although she is of a mind to forgive everyone their faults, as far as I can tell.

"No, I will ask the cook to prepare us a little something to tide us over until supper. I am sure she will not mind, the preparations for the wedding breakfast are almost complete."

"Thank you Bingley, I appreciate your kindness, as always."

"Think nothing of it, Darcy. The butler will show you to your room while the cook prepares something for us to eat."

Darcy's room faced the front of the house, and the morning sun, which would help to rouse him in plenty of time to prepare for Bingley's wedding. It was tidy, possessing a comfortable bed and spacious closet to hang his clothes once the servant finished cleaning them. He unpacked his shaving brush, razor, and perfume, for his stubble would need to be removed before venturing out in the morning.

After putting his personal items away, Darcy went downstairs to the dining-room where Bingley was waiting, an assortment of sandwiches on plates in front of him. At the sight of the food, Darcy's stomach growled, reminding him he had not eaten yet today. The sound was so loud in his ears that he looked to Bingley, positive his friend was laughing, but Bingley did not seem to notice.

"Help yourself," mumbled the man, his mouth full. "They are delicious. I think the cook might deserve a bonus in her pay envelope if she is going to keep feeding me like this."

"Careful, or your generosity will impoverish you before your first child is born."

"Not to worry, the servants have heard statements like this before. They know I am not serious, and I pay them well enough that they rarely need to ask for a raise, or an advance on their pay."

"I am not sure I would get away with such an easy tongue at Pemberley. They would probably band together to insist that I honor my promises."

"That might be the biggest lie you ever told. I have spoken to your servants, and they all, without exception, consider themselves lucky to be in your employ, especially Mrs. Reynolds who has been there since before you were even born."

"You caught me," laughed Darcy, "but in my defense, I was only trying to compete with you.

"Not to change the subject, but are Miss Elizabeth or Miss Bennet aware of my arrival? If so, I hope they do not feel annoyed with you or me for surprising them like this."

"Your arrival is still a secret. I thought it best to wait until tomorrow before the wedding to let them know, although that might well put a strain on the ceremony. It will surprise Elizabeth, I am certain, but I cannot guess what affect the shock will have on her."

"Thank you for keeping this quiet. I agree, it is best to wait until tomorrow, otherwise they both might be too upset to get any sleep. I would prefer to wait until after the wedding, but one or the other will surely see me and the shock might ruin your special day."

"We can leave early for the church. I sent word to Jane, asking her to meet me an hour earlier than we planned. That should give you enough time to plead your case. Whether Miss Elizabeth is prepared to decide is another question, one whose answer will not come before tomorrow morning, unfortunately."

They ate the rest of the meal in silence, Darcy concentrating on sating his appetite at first, and then wondering about Miss Elizabeth. Bingley, he presumed, was busy envisioning his beloved voicing her vows before the parson.

At meal's end, Darcy returned to his room while Bingley busied himself with preparations for the next day's momentous occurrence. At supper that evening he was quiet, which for Bingley was a rare event. Darcy assumed the stress of the day, and the preceding week, had finally worn the man down.

At the conclusion of supper, Bingley begged off Darcy's invitation to join him in a celebratory glass of fine port, which he had brought as a gift. With an apology, he retired to his bedroom in hopes of getting enough rest to carry him through the excitement of the coming day.

Darcy was happy to go to bed himself, and enjoyed his most refreshing sleep in months.

CHAPTER XXXIII

"The note did not explain why he wanted us there," stated Jane, settling into her seat so the carriage could depart Longbourn. "All it said was that something had occurred, and it was important for us to be at the church early."

Elizabeth studied her sister as the coach entered the road and turned in the direction of the church. She looked happier this morning than on any occasion Elizabeth had ever seen, which surprised her, considering the girl had slept little the night before. She was too excited over the upcoming wedding ceremony, and the bliss she was sure could only naturally follow her marriage to a man as perfect, in Jane's opinion, as Mr. Bingley. Elizabeth, ever the supportive sister, sat up with her as late as she was able, but excused herself sometime well after midnight when she was unable to keep her eyes open any longer.

Elizabeth knew she looked tired this morning, despite the copious amount of icy water she splashed on her face upon rising, scarcely five hours after turning in last night. The water, though, was unfortunately not the cure for what ailed her, nor was it likely to improve her appearance very much.

The previous winter had been difficult to bear. She had tried to appreciate the enchanting and intricate patterns of hoarfrost coating everything. This winter, however, found her unable to set her imagination to work as it usually did, picturing tiny fairies painting the world in shades of icy white, so much of her joy in the season was absent.

Instead of winter's beauty, she saw only trees devoid of leaves and dirty brown woodlands, lifeless and depressed by the absence of the sun's warmth. Not even the arrival of Michaelmas before winter's onset brought her any happiness; the obligatory balls and assemblies celebrating a successful harvest and the beginning of autumn were too depressing to attend.

Unlike previous years, where she had looked forward to the season, with its almost weekly gatherings of celebration and evenings spent dancing, just the thought of donning a gown and attending those types of events saddened her.

Christmas was no better. The sight of the yule log blazing merrily in the fireplace, along with Jane and her beau capering about in the garden, sent Elizabeth to her room with claims of sudden headaches. It would never do, she thought, to ruin Jane's enjoyment of the season by confessing to heartache she could not escape, no matter how hard she tried.

Watching Jane and Mr. Bingley, so much in love the rest of the family were forgotten, had her remembering Mr. Darcy's public rejection. Their display conjured up her shame upon being told she was no longer welcome, either at her aunt and uncle's home or at Mr. Darcy's estate.

Jane was positively glowing this morning, and Elizabeth was happy for her. She was a little disturbed, however, over the cryptic note that was delivered late in the afternoon of the previous day. Though seemingly innocuous, its delivery raised her suspicions, despite her inability to identify a reason for concern. Maybe she was suffering from wedding day nerves, a malady she expected would have afflicted Jane, but which did not appear to be the case.

"But why send such a note, without even a hint regarding the reason for his strange request?" asked Elizabeth again, for the third, or possibly the fourth time. "Why could it not wait until after the service or the wedding breakfast? Surely this was not more important than allowing you a proper night's sleep and an adequate amount of time to ready yourself this morning."

"We will know soon enough." Jane was not about to let something so insignificant as an unexpected missive from the man she loved ruin a perfectly delightful day. Yesterday's messenger might have come with word of an unforeseen calamity, but if the news did not affect her directly, it was not to be allowed to interfere with her wedding.

Elizabeth envied her sister's ability to set aside the unpleasantness of life to find pleasure in the simple things, like the appearance of spring's first daisy or the surprise of a friend's unannounced visit. She was not the type of person prone to losing herself in depression over disappointment but would instead pick herself up and go on with her life.

While Elizabeth strove to display a sunny disposition, the vicissitudes of the daily existence often managed to steal any enjoyment she might otherwise experience. More and more over the past few months, she found herself out of sorts and cross over the simplest of unexpected occurrences.

The change in her personality did not go unnoticed. Jane, who almost never found fault with anyone, Elizabeth in particular, took to hinting at the difference. Elizabeth's response was to tell her sister, in a less than kind manner, to mind her own business.

The hurt she saw in Jane's eyes had her begging for forgiveness as soon as she spoke the offending words, but the damage was done, and Jane never mentioned the matter again. Even now, over two months since the verbal altercation, Jane was still reserved and not as open as before, as if unwilling to provoke her again.

"We are here." Jane interrupted Elizabeth's thoughts as the carriage passed through the entrance to the church yard. "I see Charles has arrived, and it would appear he has company."

Jane pointed to the Bingley carriage waiting alongside the church, its driver napping in his seat. Beside it stood a horse, eating the grass that grew along the side of the building.

"I do not see him," said Jane when they had exited the coach, "which is odd. I thought he would be waiting for us."

"He is probably inside," stated Elizabeth with a smile, pointing to the church door moving slightly in the morning breeze. "He wanted to find a private part within the chancel from which to declare his everlasting love again before the service begins."

Jane's progress toward the church paused at Elizabeth's jest. When she looked back, Elizabeth was pleased to see the emotions that ran across her face, from excitement to adoration for the man she was about to wed. Stepping forward, she took hold of her sister's arm and led her into the nave, where Mr. Bingley stood waiting nervously, or so it appeared.

"Jane, Miss Elizabeth," said he, an uncommon quaver in his voice, "thank you for arriving early. I feared you might not."

"Why would you entertain such a preposterous idea?" asked Jane, sounding insulted he would have thoughts of that nature. "Your request puzzled me, but it was something I could not ignore."

"Thank you," muttered he, although to Elizabeth his unease seemed to grow.

Mr. Bingley cleared his throat as if he had more to say but remained mute. As the silence lengthened, she saw a bead of sweat appear on his forehead, which he quickly wiped away.

He cleared his throat a second time while looking to his side, as though whatever was waiting there, out of sight, was something to fear. Finally, he motioned with his hand, a quick summoning wave, which resulted in the appearance of the last man in the world Elizabeth expected to see and, in spite of herself, the man she wanted to see more than any other.

"Hello, Miss Elizabeth." Mr. Darcy's eyes searched hers, as though wondering if she would acknowledge his presence or turn away in disgust.

"Charles?" Jane's confusion gave way to concern as she watched Elizabeth struggle to keep her emotions under control. "Who is this, and why has his appearance upset Lizzy so much?"

"This is Mr. Darcy, my closest friend. He arrived yesterday and wanted to speak with Miss Elizabeth before our wedding. I think he should be given the opportunity to say his piece."

"No." Elizabeth's astonishment gave way to anger at his appearance, and his unmitigated conceit if he supposed that the mere act of showing himself would erase the indignity and hurt she had suffered at his hand. "I do not need to be insulted again. Once was enough for a lifetime."

"He wants to apologize for the harm he caused," said Mr. Bingley before she could turn away. "When I told him how his actions hurt you, and the changes his decision had caused in your demeanor, he begged me to let him try and atone for his sin. Please allow him to express his remorse. If you decide you cannot accept his confession, I will escort him from the property, and he will return to Pemberley."

"Listen to him, Lizzy," pleaded Jane softly. "Let him make the attempt before turning him away. I have watched you wither, becoming a shell of the loving, spirited woman you used to be. I think you owe it to yourself to at least listen. If you decide not to forgive him, you will not have the added burden of wondering what he might have said."

Elizabeth was torn between her desire for the return of his good opinion and the restoration of his affection, or the urge to deliver a stinging rebuke for breaking her heart and destroying her reputation. How could she listen to such a man, who had not even bothered to acknowledge her claims of innocence?

She opened her mouth, intending to refuse, but stopped at the sight of him standing forlornly beside Mr. Bingley, head down while he awaited her decision. She looked to Jane, whose moist eyes declared her support for whatever Elizabeth might decide, and the hope she would allow this penitent intruder to speak. Mr. Bingley wore an expression that she could not mistake for anything but trust in the inevitability of her decision in favor of his friend. It seemed she was the only person in the church who was hesitant to hear what Mr. Darcy had to say, and the realization tore at her heartstrings as it conquered her resistance.

"You may try," she stated at last, "but Jane and Mr. Bingley must stay. If they are not a welcome part of the conversation, we have nothing to discuss."

"Agreed," Mr. Darcy responded quickly, as though he feared she might change her mind.

Some of the anxiety left Darcy's body at Miss Elizabeth's willingness to hear him, replaced with apprehension that she might find his excuses unacceptable and turn him away forever. He would not let that happen. If there was any way to convince this woman of his sorrow, and his unceasing love, he needed to find it now, before it was too late. To think of better, more convincing words tonight or tomorrow would be of no use after she reached her decision.

He could do this! He had not spent last night and this morning rehearsing his confession for nothing. There would be only one chance to win her over, and he was not going to waste it on platitudes or meaningless protestations of innocence; what she needed was to hear an honest expression of sorrow and regret for his actions.

"Forgive me," said he, watching her face for any sign that his words were softening her heart. "What I did was inexcusable. If I could do anything to change the past, believe me, I would.

"You were telling me the truth, but I chose not to listen, an error I will always carry with shame. She is my sister, and my need to protect her drove me to accept her story and refuse your claims of innocence. If I had listened, I could have avoided the unpleasant, hurtful result. Please forgive me or tell me what I must do if you are not ready to entertain the idea. I promise to do everything possible to regain your good opinion."

Darcy waited for her response, doubts assailing him. Had she believed him, or was the hurt too deep to forgive? Was she willing to trust his sincerity and vow to repair the damage he caused, or was her heart now hardened to where nothing he said would change her mind?

He wanted to restate his sorrow, but worried that any sound from his lips might cause her to reject him, and his apology, forever.

Her prolonged silence was unnerving, as his imagination dreamed up countless ways she might plan to humiliate him. If she made that choice he would accept it, knowing that he deserved any punishment she decided upon, or scorn she expressed.

"You tell me how sorry you are, but not what you will do in the future if the situation should reoccur. How can I trust you if I must constantly worry that you will turn on me again?"

"I wish I could promise that it will not happen, but I would be lying. If something like this was to reoccur, my reaction would probably be the same, and whether I was defending Georgiana or my wife would not matter. My family is the most important thing in the world. My father and mother raised me to protect those I love, and I cannot go against what I have been taught."

"Your honesty is admirable, but your complete disregard hurt me more than you will ever know."

"All I can do is ask for the chance to earn your forgiveness," pleaded Darcy, desperate to convince her of his sincerity. "If you can find it in your heart to let me try, I will repair the damage I caused, no matter how long it might take."

"Forgive my doubt, but what changed your mind? The last we spoke, you were convinced I was the one who attacked Georgiana and refused to listen to anything I had to say."

This was the moment Darcy most feared. If Miss Elizabeth were the type of person to nurse a grudge, the knowledge of Georgiana's duplicity would undo everything he was trying to accomplish. If she was of a forgiving nature, she might put her wounded feelings aside.

"Georgiana could not bear to remain confined to Pemberley. She wanted the freedom to visit Kingsdown, not because she missed Miss Bannerman's company, but because she had become enamored of Robert Bannerman, and he apparently felt the same.

"When she would not stay on the property, I confined her to the house, which convinced her to come to me and confess her deception. When she finished, I took her directly to the Bannerman estate and had her repeat herself in front of the family. Upon returning to Pemberley, I said I was coming to visit Bingley, and confined her to the house, with a promise that any disobedience would end with sending her to live with our aunt, Lady Catherine.

"She is a formidable lady, and one who would not treat Georgiana's behavior with any amount of pity. There is no doubt that when I return, reports from the servants will praise Georgiana's newly discovered piety and respect for others."

Darcy saw tears in Miss Elizabeth's eyes, and it added to his worry. If they were tears of anger, his reason for coming to Hertfordshire did not matter, as she would probably reject him outright. If, however, they were tears of sympathy, he would do his utmost to comfort her. He could only wait for her to speak and hope she did not decide Georgiana was contemptible and he, as her brother, equally so.

"I would be less than charitable if I refused to accept any attempts to repair the damage to our friendship. I am not ready to forgive you, but maybe that will come in time."

"May I call on you then?" asked Darcy with relief. "If not, I will understand. I want you to know that my feelings are undiminished from last year; if anything, they are stronger."

"You may if my father is in favor, but he will not give his permission easily. He has expressed some anger toward you and might not allow you on the property."

"If you provide me with an introduction, I will do my best to win his approval."

"It will have to be your very best," responded Miss Elizabeth with a smile.

"That is true," giggled Miss Bennet. "Lizzy is his favorite daughter, and he might not welcome the attentions of the man who wounded her so terribly."

"Wonderful," said Darcy cheerfully, hoping Miss Elizabeth did not detect the trepidation that suddenly beset him.

"What a wonderful resolution to a fearful problem," cried Bingley. "And just in time, as our guests are arriving."

"I will find a quiet bench from which to view the service." Darcy, thinking it might be better to go unnoticed until after the wedding ceremony finished, looked around for an advantageous seat from where he would watch events unfold.

"You will do no such thing," exclaimed Bingley, taking hold of his friend's shoulder to keep him from moving. "I invited you to stand up as my best man, and no one else can take your place. There is no need to worry about those attending; they are here to support Jane and celebrate with her family. Nobody knows who you are, so you may remain anonymous if you wish."

Darcy looked toward the narthex, which was filling with people. Bingley was correct in his claim of Darcy's anonymity, though one gentleman seemed to show an extra measure of interest in them. His gaze, when fastened upon Miss Bennet and Miss Elizabeth, was tender and loving. When it shifted to Darcy, the genial expression hardened and became the sternest of glares, prompting Darcy to drop his eyes to the floor before the gentleman took exception to his unplanned presence.

"I see Papa has noticed you," mentioned Miss Elizabeth from behind him. "He seems less than pleased to see you here, which is unusual since he does not know for sure who you are."

"It would seem he has guessed my identity and is not pleased about my showing up for the wedding. I should leave, so we can avoid an unpleasant scene."

"Let me talk to him," Miss Elizabeth offered, stepping into the aisle. "I will explain what has happened and promise to introduce you before the wedding breakfast. Do not worry; my father is a reasonable man who only wants the best for his daughters."

"Hurry, Lizzy," called Miss Bennet as her sister moved away, "the guests are sitting, and the parson is ready to begin."

Darcy watched Miss Elizabeth walk toward her father, whose acrimony seemed to be increasing. How was it possible that this man, who looked as if he wanted to tear Darcy limb from limb, might allow him to call on his favorite daughter? From the look of him, Darcy wondered if he would survive making the request.

"Papa wants to meet you before the wedding breakfast," Elizabeth, who had approached while Darcy stood thinking, told him. "He wants you to know he is looking forward to meeting you and judging if you are worthy of calling on me. He would take the time now, but the wedding is about to begin, and his attention is too much on giving Jane away to 'concentrate on other foolery', as he puts it."

"I can hardly wait," sighed Darcy dejectedly. "It will be the best part of my day, I am sure."

"He is not an ogre," giggled Miss Elizabeth. "Just be honest, and everything will be fine. Now come, Jane and Mr. Bingley are waiting for us."

Darcy let her lead him to his assigned place, after which she joined her sister, and the ceremony began.

Throughout the service, Darcy kept his eyes on Miss Elizabeth. The woman was radiant, eclipsed only slightly by the bride. Her poise and grace were perfect, and her eyes shone with nothing but love for her sister and soon to be brother-in-law.

So captivated was he by her beauty and elegance that he almost missed the exchange of vows between Bingley and his bride. His attempt to pay closer attention to the ceremony, however, failed when he glanced to his side and discovered Miss Elizabeth watching him, her eyes damp with tears that he hoped showed happiness rather than disappointment.

The ceremony's conclusion brought a surprise, as Darcy heard a familiar voice calling his name, and his cousin appeared in the company of a most comely young woman.

"So this is the engagement you dared not miss?" asked he as Fitzwilliam drew near. "I might have known that it involved a member of the fairer sex. How are you, Miss Bingley?"

"And I was not aware that this was the wedding you planned to attend," countered Fitzwilliam with a laugh. "Or that you knew Miss Bingley."

"She is the sister to my closest friend," explained Darcy, "and I have known her almost as long as her brother."

"That is convenient for me," said Fitzwilliam, which elicited a look of confusion from Darcy. "I am not well suited to the niceties of introductions, as I usually say or do something wrong. If you will excuse me, Miss Bingley, there is a matter I wish to discuss with your brother."

Fitzwilliam left on his quest to locate the newly married groom, leaving Miss Bingley and Darcy standing together amongst the well-wishers, all of them determined to congratulate the lucky couple and express their fondest hopes for a life of married bliss.

"Mr. Darcy, I presume," said the gentleman Darcy had observed prior to the wedding ceremony. His approach had not been unexpected, and Darcy prepared for an unpleasant discussion.

"Mr. Bennet," replied he, hoping they might share an amicable introduction, and possible further conversation. "Miss Elizabeth informed me you wanted to talk."

"Lizzy was correct," said Mr. Bennet. "While I wanted to meet you, my reason for approaching without first getting a proper introduction was to satisfy myself that your appearance today would not cause Elizabeth further injury."

"There are no words to explain my actions, nor excuse for my treatment of her." Darcy, suddenly nervous despite his preparations, was unsure of the response he was expected to give. "All I can say is that I was misinformed, and I based my response on the information I had at the time. Someone deliberately misled me but even then, I was too quick to judge.

"I came to beg Miss Elizabeth's forgiveness, but to do that, I was told I must first confess my sins to her father. She informed me that until I got your approval she would not entertain, or even acknowledge, my attentions."

Mr. Bennet regarded him with a critical eye, and Darcy attempted to prepare himself for the rejection he feared was coming.

"Lizzy has always been the most intelligent of my daughters, and the child I am closest to," was his comment after a moment of silence. "If it were not for Bingley, who I regard as a son, I would not let you anywhere near her. Bingley, though, has nothing but praise for you, and has defended you on every occasion."

"Bingley is a good man and a better friend. I would trust him with my life; while he is alive, no harm will come to Miss Bennet, or Mrs. Bingley, I guess I should say now."

Darcy thought he detected a hint of amusement in Mr. Bennet's manner, which was concerning. Did the man view him as a clown, someone not to be taken seriously? What was there about this conversation that was funny? Maybe he had been mistaken in his hope that Miss Elizabeth might accept his feeble attempts to reconcile, although she had not appeared insincere this morning.

"We all make mistakes of varying importance," responded Mr. Bennet, a smile appearing so suddenly on his face that Darcy found himself taken aback. "What matters is our fortitude in correcting our errors. You, Mr. Darcy, impressed me with the courage you showed in entering the lion's den, so to speak, to face an angry father. I think you might be just what Lizzy needs.

"Let me warn you though," the smile disappeared and a stern countenance again took its place. "If you treat her poorly again, though, I will hunt you down and demand satisfaction."

"You have my promise, sir," said Darcy. "Miss Elizabeth will never know pain or disappointment at my hand; her every wish will be my duty to fulfill."

"I would not go that far," laughed Mr. Bennet. "It would never do to spoil the girl. Do your best, and she will return your efforts. Now, if we wait much longer, the food will not last, and I am feeling somewhat peckish. There will be time enough later to discuss your atonement."

CHAPTER XXXIV

Life at Longbourn did not return to anything resembling normal after Jane's wedding, and Elizabeth was uncertain whether she was in favor of the change, or regretful it had occurred.

Darcy's cousin left at the conclusion of his conversation with Bingley, telling Miss Bingley that he would call upon her in London.

The newlyweds departed on their honeymoon after partaking of the wedding breakfast, leaving to well wishes from the guests and tears from Mrs. Bennet over the loss of her first daughter to marriage. Elizabeth's attempts to calm her were ineffectual, serving instead to encourage the woman to cry harder. It was not until Mr. Bennet reminded his wife of Bingley's intent to purchase Netherfield that the hysterics she had worked herself into ceased, after which peace returned to the estate.

Miss Bingley accepted the couple's offer to ride with them as far as her aunt's home in Scarborough, where they were spending some time together as husband and wife. She would remain until her brother and newly gained sister-in-law returned from their honeymoon, leaving Mr. Darcy alone at Netherfield.

When Elizabeth remarked on the solitude he would suffer, his response was to deny he would experience anything of the sort.

"I will be much too busy working my way back into your good graces to worry about loneliness," affirmed he, to which she laughingly wished him good luck in his endeavors. Although his declaration pleased her, she was not yet ready to give him too much encouragement. If he proved his assertion of renewed love was true, she would welcome and encourage his attention. Something might come of this, or it might all come to naught.

He began his attempts without delay, as he called upon her two days after the wedding.

"Lizzy," said her father, his words interrupting the needlework she was concentrating on, "you have a visitor."

He stepped to the side, allowing Mr. Darcy to enter the sitting-room. His manner, she saw, was that of a man in doubt of a warm welcome or the reception he might expect from her.

Elizabeth finished her stitch and, putting the piece aside, regarded the man standing just inside the doorway. To her, he looked ready to flee at the slightest hint his calling upon her was at an inopportune time. His smile was uncertain, and his eyes fixed on the floor instead of the person he had come to visit.

"Mr. Darcy, how good to see you." Elizabeth was trying to ease the man's discomfort, an attempt he seemed to resist. "Please, come in and take a seat."

"If it is all the same to you, I would rather walk the grounds of the property." With a slight smile, he seemed to regain some of his composure. "It would be a shame to waste such a beautiful day indoors."

"What a delightful idea," interjected Mrs. Bennet, looking from Mr. Darcy to Elizabeth as if trying to make a point, although Elizabeth was unsure what it might be. "Show him around the garden and along the paths you like to walk. The estate, and Mr. Bennet's management of it, might impress him. Although our property is probably nothing compared to Mr. Darcy's, we are content."

"I suppose we could," agreed Elizabeth, "as it is within sight of the house, so we would not require a chaperone."

"Take Kitty with you," invited her mother, as if the idea were so self-evident it should have occurred to her without prompting. "She knows Mr. Darcy, so introductions are unnecessary."

"Where is she?" continued Mrs. Bennet as if noticing only now that the girl was elsewhere. "She was here not twenty minutes ago, but now that I want her, she is nowhere to be found."

"Kitty is in the library, Mama," stated Elizabeth, "where she is every afternoon, remember? She has discovered the joy of reading, something Papa and I have encouraged. I will find her and ask if she wants to come for a walk."

Kitty was swiftly located and agreed to accompany them. In short order, the trio left the house.

"Did you have a destination in mind?" asked Elizabeth to break the silence before it became oppressive. "If you like I can suggest the path I like to follow."

"Might we go by Lucas Lodge?" asked Kitty. "I would like to visit my friend Maria."

"But that would leave me without company for the rest of my walk," Elizabeth informed her.

"I am willing to continue if you are," was Mr. Darcy's surprising suggestion. "Your reputation will not suffer if we confine ourselves to the less travelled paths. If nobody sees us, there will be no danger of rumors starting.

"I promise, you will have no reason for regret if you decide we can press on without Miss Kitty."

Elizabeth bit her tongue to hold back the laughter threatening to burst from her lips. To her, Mr. Darcy looked so hopeful she would accept his offer that she feared he might cry if she declined.

"We can continue without Kitty, but it will have to be toward Longbourn," stated she, to what she interpreted as a look of joy that she would decide to walk on, followed by disappointment upon hearing she would not entertain the idea of continuing in their original direction.

"I understand." His disappointment, strangely comforting to Elizabeth, encouraged her in ways she had not anticipated.

Mr. Darcy did not speak again until Kitty bid them goodbye at her friend's home. When she did, he turned back in the direction they had come, but stopped when Elizabeth touched his arm.

"There is another, more secluded way," said she with a smile, "if you are interested in seeing more of the property."

"Lead on," his jubilant voice proclaimed, "I would love to see any of the property you want to show me."

Elizabeth led him toward the side of the road, and a spot which looked identical to the rest of the tree lined lane they were walking along. Upon arriving, she reached out to pull two of the leafier branches aside, revealing what appeared to be a well-used path.

"Shall we?" said she and, slipping inside the branches, waited for him to join her. Mr. Darcy, after looking to each side, followed her onto the path, whereupon Elizabeth let the branches close, effectively concealing them from the view of any who might pass by on the road.

The trail, although clearly well-trodden, was narrow and secluded, one of its endearing features, in Elizabeth's view. It led them into the woods separating Longbourn from Lucas Lodge, which had the effect of further concealing them from anyone's notice. To someone unfamiliar with the countryside, it would be easy to perceive this small stand of forest encompassed a vast area, when it was only a dividing line between Lucas Lodge and Longbourn, standing barely thirty yards wide. The solitude made it Elizabeth's favorite path for her morning walks.

"A beautiful area," remarked Mr. Darcy, walking close behind Elizabeth as she moved along the path, "and a familiar one, it would seem."

"This is the route I follow more than any other," offered she by way of explanation. "I love the peace; it gives me the chance to think without interruption and savor the beauty of my surroundings."

"And what about when you walk? Do matters of the heart take precedence, or are you more concerned with the latest absurdity coming out of the House of Commons?"

"Why would you suppose I care a fig about anything in London, when there is plenty of foolishness to keep me busy in Hertfordshire?"

"You are a woman with varied interests, and I assumed they would include such things," replied Mr. Darcy, wearing the hint of a smile that reminded Elizabeth of a cat toying with a mouse. "And your father intimated as much in our conversation when I arrived this afternoon. He let it slip that you possess a keen interest in expanding your knowledge and told me politics was a special passion."

"If I know my father, he let nothing 'slip'," said Elizabeth with a shake of her head. "This was most likely his way of warning you not to take me for granted. I am grateful for his gesture, but capable of looking out for myself."

"Your father loves you and is, in his own way, trying to protect you from me. Though he is a fine example of good humor and friendship, he has not yet decided if I am to be trusted."

"Are you surprised? If you recall, I left Derbyshire under a cloud, accused of a vicious attack on your sister. I suffered shame all last winter from your dismissing my claims of innocence.

"To have you now appear, without warning I might add, to beg my forgiveness and declare your love is disconcerting, to be blunt. Papa probably wanted to satisfy himself that you would not decide to abandon me again should you hear someone share an unflattering opinion. To be honest, I have had the same thoughts."

"And I intend to do whatever it takes to convince you of my affection and sincerity," stated Mr. Darcy in a manner that almost suggested he would get down on his knees to plead his case if that was what she wanted. "It would help to know what you expect of me, but I am willing to proceed cautiously. The last thing I want is to drive you away with unwanted approaches or gestures."

"I would appreciate honesty and patience," said Elizabeth, her answer spoken without having to consider it first. "Honesty about your feelings toward me and patience, so I can decide for myself if I want to take another chance and welcome your attention. If you cannot give me those considerations, there is no need for us to continue.

"Or, if you are more inclined to fun and frivolity, we could chase each other around the rose bushes in the garden, like Jane and I used to do when we were young girls. That might amuse us, although Papa would probably not see the humor."

The shock on Mr. Darcy's face was just what Elizabeth hoped to provoke with her indelicate remark. He had stopped walking, and now stood still, studying her. She was certain he had a response ready, but he appeared uncertain about voicing it aloud, so she waited, showing what she hoped was an inviting smile to assist his decision.

"I would never engage in something so juvenile," she heard him say, his face now serious as if even the mention of such an idea was an affront to his dignity. "Sooner or later one of us would end up amid the thorns, and it would not be me. Your father would have to come to your rescue, and probably banish me from the property forever.

"How am I supposed to call on you if I may not set foot on Longbourn?" His countenance softened as he spoke, to display a twinkle of merriment in his eye.

"And you would never forgive me for such an injustice. I can see it now, the roses destroyed by your attack on the bush, and your rage at being bested by a superior gentleman such as myself. The embarrassment would follow you for the rest of your life; a tale to be related whenever your sisters come for a visit.

"Our children would tease you mercilessly, although it would not surprise them that I could easily catch you and prove my superiority, for they would see it every day of their life. No, out of pity for your weakness and lack of skill, I cannot allow you to engage in such a one-sided contest."

Their arrival at Longbourn put an end to their conversation, and the mirth which had risen between them. Elizabeth almost regretted her decision to walk with Mr. Darcy, as the return of his sober mien reminded her of the reason for his visit and his goal of winning her hand in marriage.

She had enjoyed their time together, more than she wanted to acknowledge, but the fear of another rejection by this man was almost too much to consider.

"May I call on you again tomorrow?" asked Mr. Darcy, just as her fears threatened to overwhelm her.

"You may," said she, her former feelings toward him rekindling despite her efforts to avoid such an entanglement.

"I will be here at the same time, then. And please, tell Mr. Bennet that I look forward to seeing him again. With any luck, he will give me further insights regarding his favorite daughter, something to help me win her heart."

With a farewell nod, Mr. Darcy went in search of the stable boy and the horse he had ridden to Longbourn. Scant minutes later, Elizabeth saw him ride from the yard, waving to her as the mount turned onto the roadway.

He visited the next day as promised, and every day that week and the next. His manner was always respectful, especially toward Mr. and Mrs. Bennet, who voiced their approval of him to Elizabeth.

To her he was the perfect gentleman, solicitous of her mood and desires in every respect, and attentive to her every whim. He was trying, almost desperately it seemed, to work his way back into her heart, but though she welcomed his attention, it was not easy to forget the way things had ended between them the previous year.

His frustration with her hesitance came between them, erecting a symbolic wall that she was unable to dismantle. She saw his patience was wearing thin, and the consequences worried her.

If only Jane were back from her honeymoon, they could discuss the problem. Her elder sister had a unique way of examining a situation, and Elizabeth felt the loss of her advice acutely.

Friday of the second week brought the very situation she had feared when, instead of his usual visit, a messenger delivered a letter addressed to her. On the rear of the envelope, the Darcy crest showed in the wax used to seal the letter.

Elizabeth took it and almost ran to her room, hoping against hope that it was not a rebuke from him, and a statement of his decision to end all contact with her.

Upon seating herself at her dressing table, she tore open the envelope, unfolding the page to reveal the contents, which were straightforward yet confusing, hopeful yet depressing.

"Miss Bennet,"

"Please forgive me, but I have made the decision to return to Pemberley, so I can decide whether to reconsider what is beginning to resemble an ill-fated courtship for your hand in marriage.

"I have enjoyed my time at Netherfield, and the days I have spent in your company have been among the best of my life, but it does not seem to me as though you are of like mind in this matter.

"When I saw you, the morning of Bingley's wedding, I vowed to win your heart again, if you would let me try. Your permission was both uplifting and sobering, as I knew I faced what might be an insurmountable task to regain your love and trust, which I so foolishly wasted.

"I have done my best to rebuild our relationship and want to believe your desires are akin to mine. Unfortunately, my attempts seem doomed to fail, because you cannot, or will not, allow yourself to surrender to your own feelings.

"This situation has convinced me it is best to return home, where I can think about any future efforts without your proximity, which is both a blessing and a curse. Please believe I love you and am willing to do whatever I must to win your hand.

"I cannot remain away from Georgiana or my responsibilities at Pemberley forever, so it is with heavy heart that I bid you farewell, at least for the present time. I cannot say when, or even if, I will return."

"Fitzwilliam Darcy"

Elizabeth's heart caught in her throat. Was this the finish to Mr. Darcy's courtship, which again had ended before it began? Had her hesitation driven him away, never to return? What was she to do without his attentions and his regular visits to Longbourn?

Recriminations ran through her mind, each more demeaning than the last. She lamented the loss of a wonderful man and the respect he had expressed for her. His absence would haunt her, she was sure, turning this year into another one of dashed hopes and wasted love, too much like the one preceding it.

Elizabeth refolded the letter and placed it into a drawer, unwilling to destroy this reminder of her failure to find happiness. She was going to keep it close to read his words of love again. She did not share its contents with her father, who accepted her refusal to discuss it with him. For all his imperfections as a parent, he was considerate with Elizabeth, and the problems she faced.

She was pensive the following day, not inclined to talk unless directly addressed. Although she kept to her habit of morning walks, she did not take notice of her surroundings, as the day seemed dreary and uninteresting.

Until Jane's arrival almost two weeks later, the world around Elizabeth remained depressing and without cheer. Mr. Darcy's departure had wounded her again, but this time she could find nothing to lift her spirits. She continued to tread the paths, but that was more out of habit and a sense of duty to her health than because of any joy she found in her daily constitutionals.

Life passed, but Elizabeth found it less than enjoyable. She woke each day and kept to her established rituals of an early walk, followed by breakfast. The rest of her day she spent in the sitting-room with her mother, or in her room, pouring over Mr. Darcy's letter.

The page was unfolded and refolded so many times that it began to tear along the creases. Still, she acted on her compulsion. Although there was nothing in the letter to possibly misunderstand, that did not stop her from studying it intently.

A commotion downstairs interrupted her on the Friday of the second week of her loneliness. The noise was such that she rose from her desk and peered out the window to see a carriage pulling up to the house, one that she knew, and had been anxiously awaiting. Hurriedly, she placed the letter back in its place and almost ran down the stairs to greet the new arrivals.

"Lizzy!" called Jane, rushing forward to greet her sister upon exiting the cabin. "I missed you terribly all the time Charles and I were away."

"Really?" wondered Elizabeth, smiling in response to Jane's exaggeration. "Is Mr. Bingley aware of his inability to keep his bride occupied on their honeymoon? If I were you, I would hide that information from him or it might damage his self-esteem."

"Charles knows he is the love of my life, and he also knows how close we are as sisters. He is not so fragile that it would crush him to learn I missed your company."

"How was your honeymoon? Did you visit most of England, or did you spend all your time gazing into each other's eyes whilst professing undying love? You appear to be wasting away; were you unable to tear your eyes from one another long enough to share a meal, or two?"

Jane's face took on a far away look at Elizabeth's jest, and Elizabeth could guess what her sister was contemplating. She had seen it before, most notably when the subject of her then future, and now current, husband arose in conversation.

"We brought a guest, or rather, two guests, back with us," said Jane, with a shake of her head and a smile. "They came specifically to see you, Lizzy, so please, hear what they have to say before you turn them away."

"Hello, Miss Bennet." The appearance of Mr. Darcy stepping from the carriage sent Elizabeth's heart racing. "It is good to see you again. I hope you don't mind that I brought Georgiana with me."

Turning back to the carriage, he beckoned to his sister, who sat with her head down. When his summons brought no reaction, he reached in to grasp her hand, pulling her from the coach to stand beside him.

"Hello, Miss Bennet," offered she when prodded by her brother. "It is gratifying to see you in good health."

"She has more to tell you," explained Mr. Darcy, "but it would be better to speak in private. Might we continue our conversation in the garden? I seem to remember some benches toward the rear of the space; one of them would serve our purpose nicely."

Elizabeth nodded and turned to lead her guests to the back of the house, afraid to speak lest her self-control fail, exposing her to unwanted pity from Mr. Darcy and scorn from his sister.

Upon reaching the garden, she took them to the bench sitting farthest from the house. She, like Mr. Darcy, had no desire to have their conversation overheard.

"Was this the one you had in mind?" asked Elizabeth, cringing inwardly at her statement of the obvious. This was the only one near, but for once, she had nothing else to say. His appearance had unsettled her, and she was not so sure she even wanted to have this discussion.

While its conclusion might be the answer to her desires and nightly dreams, it might also be one more heartache to add to her growing list. She thought, for an instant, that she would be better off not knowing than to endure the shattering of her world again.

"This is perfect," said he, and gesturing toward Georgiana, he sat and beckoned for Elizabeth to join him on the bench. She did, placing herself as far from him as the bench allowed without sitting on the path itself.

"You may begin," he told his sister, who stood silent as tears slowly made their way down her cheeks.

CHAPTER XXXV

"Please begin," repeated he when Georgiana remained silent. "Miss Bennet needs to hear this, and you need to confess your role in this affair. I hope she can find it in her heart to forgive you, but I will leave that up to her.

"From what I have seen of her character, she will accept your confession and apology, but I cannot guarantee that outcome. I can say with confidence, though, unless you are sincere she will turn you away, and I will not blame her if she does. Now speak, or you might find yourself unwelcome, here or in Derbyshire."

"Please, William, I am sorry," mumbled Georgiana, her cheeks now glistening from the tears running down her face.

"So you have told me, many times but you need to show Miss Bennet the courtesy of acknowledging your guilt."

Georgiana reminded Elizabeth of a trapped animal, desperate to escape its imprisonment but unwilling to take the obvious path in front of it. Her gaze flitted everywhere but toward Elizabeth, who would not have been surprised to see the girl bolt from the garden to avoid the task Darcy demanded she complete.

Elizabeth felt sorry for Georgiana and understood the fear ruling her. A confession of this gravity was difficult to make, especially when the outcome was unknown. Although she did not possess Jane's ability to extend comfort so easily in times such as this, she had to offer something, even if it did not solve the dilemma.

"I am satisfied that she feels remorse for her error. You will gain nothing by forcing her to do something she is not prepared for and watching her discomfort will not make me feel any better."

"I disagree," was his firm response. "Georgiana, you will speak to Miss Bennet, or you will find yourself with new, undesirable accommodations by this time tomorrow. Do you understand what I am saying, or do I need to explain in front of Miss Bennet?"

Fear, mixed with what looked like mild disgust, crossed the girl's face as Darcy explained the consequences of continued disobedience. Shaking her head in denial did not seem to change his mind as he gestured once more for her to speak.

Finally, with a small shudder and look of resignation, she raised her eyes and addressed Elizabeth directly.

"Miss Bennet," she began, "I am sorry. You did not attack me, and I knew that from the start. While I never accused you, I chose not to correct those who did, and for that I apologize. I hope that you can forgive me, and I realize that might not happen quickly. This should never have progressed as far as it did, and I accept responsibility for letting the situation degenerate so terribly."

Elizabeth listened to the words pour out of Georgiana, starting slowly but with increasing speed and fervor as she spoke. She knew the girl was telling the truth; what bothered her now were the reasons for Georgiana's betrayal. What had she done to deserve such treatment? Try as she might, Elizabeth was unable to recall any action she had committed to justify her removal from Derbyshire in such a manner.

"I am not opposed to forgiving you, but I need to know what prompted you to act in such a way. Did I hurt you, did I embarrass you to Mr. Darcy, or your friend Miss Haversham? If so, I cannot remember the instance."

"You did nothing wrong," said Georgiana, although she did not continue, choosing instead to drop her eyes back to the ground, as if in shame.

"Then why did you not step up and correct the misconceptions that were being thrown about by everyone in Lambton, and probably all of Derbyshire?"

"I was at home in bed, and unable to leave Pemberley for any reason. William had called Mr. Tate, who left orders I was not to be moved under any circumstances. By the time I learned the attack was attributed to you, the damage was done, and I saw no benefit in correcting the error."

"Forgive me, Georgiana, but I do not believe you. The damage extended to my aunt and uncle, as well as my cousins at Kingsdown. The Lambton citizens shunned them, and most of the merchants refused to conduct business of any kind with Mr. Bannerman.

"If you had spoken up, attitudes would have changed, maybe not overnight, but in time the Bannerman's reputation, and good name, would have been restored. Your silence guaranteed that everyone treated them with more animosity and disdain as time passed."

"I know," said Georgiana plaintively, "and I have apologized. What more do you want from me?"

"The truth," insisted Elizabeth. "All I want is the truth."

Georgiana did not respond, regarding Elizabeth with a look almost of enmity, which surprised her. What was there about her that antagonized this girl so much? And why did she resist giving the explanation that could very well resolve the issue?

As much as Elizabeth wanted to get on with her life, and hoped it would include Mr. Darcy, she was not going to become entangled in something which looked increasingly as though it was a family affair. If they did not bring the problem to a satisfactory conclusion, she would not accept further approaches from him.

"Out with it, Georgiana," demanded he, seeming to realize what Elizabeth was on the verge of declaring. "Tell Miss Bennet the rest of the story, and do it now. She has every right to your explanation, and if you are unwilling to offer it, I will."

A look of panic flashed across Georgiana's countenance before she could hide her reactions, after which her lips tightened, as if she was biting her tongue to defy her brother.

She was a willful girl, that much was apparent, but what she might fear in giving in to her brother's demands Elizabeth could not guess.

Was the story so deplorable she feared Elizabeth would hate her forever? If that were the case, she did not know Elizabeth as well as she supposed. While she might harbor an unfriendly opinion or two, Elizabeth always forgave, in spite of what people subjected her to. Why, she had even forgiven Mr. Sadler for the indignity he had caused in deserting her to sail the seven seas! That had not happened overnight, but she thought she might be able to encounter the man at a ball or assembly, and not surrender to the temptation to expose him to ridicule and censure.

If she had forgiven him, she would forgive Miss Georgiana Darcy, no matter what she had done.

"I did not want William to get involved in courting you," said Georgiana finally. "I feared that, should he be successful in his pursuit, you would have me removed from Pemberley, and sent to live with my aunt. The thought of losing my home convinced me to hold my tongue when the rumors began."

"What made you think I would ever consider such a demand? You are his sister, and have as much right to Pemberley as anybody, including whatever woman Mr. Darcy takes as his wife. I would never try to come between you, and I hope you would extend the same consideration."

"I realize that now, but the possibility consumed me when William confessed his interest in you. Fear influenced my actions, to the detriment of your continued presence on the Bannerman estate."

Elizabeth knew Georgiana was trying to keep a portion of her confession hidden, but also knew that she could never accept the girl's claims if she continued to withhold vital information. "I want to believe you, but your answer sounds too contrived, as though you are telling me what you suppose I want to hear. What you are offering are excuses, which I might expect from someone afraid, or unwilling, to tell the truth. That is something I cannot accept, no matter how much you dress it up in platitudes and expressions that you hope will pull at my heart and call up my sympathies."

Turning to Mr. Darcy, she continued: "I am sorry, but if that is all she has to offer, you might as well take her back to Pemberley. As much as I want to accept your affection, and encourage your attentions, I will not do so under the pretext of hurt feelings and apologies based on lies and half truths.

"If you expect me to welcome your attempts to secure my hand in marriage, you are mistaken. While it hurts me to say this, more than you will ever know, I will not subject myself to any more of this debasement."

Elizabeth turned to go, her hopes for a secure and happy future defeated. She wished, with every fiber of her being, that she could change the past, but the die was cast, and she would never accept Mr. Darcy under those circumstances.

With her head held high, she set off toward the house and her bedroom, where she could begin to put her life together again.

"Wait!," called he before she had gone two steps. "Please, Miss Bennet, come back."

Elizabeth stopped, uncertain if returning would accomplish anything, or if it would lead to more heartbreak for her, and further triumph for Georgiana. There was something about the girl that she was not seeing, and it bothered her.

She had a reason for interfering in her brother's plans, that was certain. What was more certain, Elizabeth knew, was that it had nothing to do with sending Georgiana to live with her aunt.

"Please, Miss Bennet, do not walk away. All I ask is one last chance to regain your trust and the interest you once held in my affections. They are unchanged, as I stated. Let us all attempt to put this in the past, I beg you."

Something in his voice overcame Elizabeth's intentions to have done with the whole affair. Mr. Darcy sounded, for the first time, as though her refusal to listen would absolutely destroy him. He sounded lost, it seemed to her, and she had the power to change his fortunes; all it would take was her agreement to listen just one more time.

And what would it cost her, other than a few minutes that she would have spent weeping and feeling sorry for herself, anyway? Surely she might postpone her self-pity for an hour, or two at the most.

"I will listen," said she, turning to face him again, "but only if she is ready to tell me the truth. If she wants to continue with her deceit, I will leave, and you can see yourselves out. As you told me in much the same situation last year, I will not receive you, and I am sure Papa will not allow you on the property again once you leave."

Mr. Darcy nodded as Elizabeth spoke, his countenance set in determination. He hoped that he might yet prevail, she was sure, but she could also tell he had reached a decision, one that did not bode well for his sister.

"Thank you." Facing Georgiana, he fixed her with a look that told Elizabeth he had reached the end of his patience with the obstinate girl.

Elizabeth felt his anger and watched the worry grow on Georgiana's face. If she refused again, there was no telling what he might do, and Elizabeth had no desire to witness the consequence of such a refusal.

"The time for games has passed," said he firmly, the set of his countenance looking as though cast in stone. "Either you tell Miss Bennet what she needs to hear, or I will remove you from Pemberley.

"Remember, Georgiana, what that means for the future you are dreaming about. This is the last opportunity you will have to repair the injustice Miss Bennet suffered. I suggest you make the most of it."

It was obvious to Elizabeth that Georgiana did not want to speak, but something in her brother's demand affected her, accomplishing more than any previous pleading or threats had managed. She looked to be considering his words, and seriously weighing the consequences if she continued to defy his demands to answer Elizabeth's question. What had she missed that had caused such a reaction in Georgiana?

"I feared the loss of status if William was to marry you," was her simple statement, the defiance suddenly absent. "To me, you were the daughter of someone who was only a country gentleman, and that just barely. If the people in William's circle of acquaintances were to find out that he was intent on pursuing someone so utterly inappropriate, they might decide to sever all ties with him.

"If that were to happen I feared that the quality of suitors I could attract would suffer tremendously. It would reduce me to marrying someone whose only interest was my dowry, and William's fortune.

"I was not willing to let that happen, and my injury came at a fortuitous moment, one which I put to good use. When the rumors began, I decided it was best to remain quiet about what had happened, and to claim a loss of memory regarding the perpetrator."

"But you must have been aware that Mr. Darcy would suffer no loss of respect in marrying someone like me. Like you said, I am a gentleman's daughter, and my family enjoys a level in society that is almost the same as yours and your brother's."

Georgiana did not agree with Elizabeth, if the vigorous shaking of her head was any sign.

"The way society regarded you was unimportant to me," responded she to Elizabeth's explanation. "What I saw was a country woman, with little or no sophistication, and nothing to recommend her to my brother. Your friendly demeanor was suspect, and your tendency to extend an offer of companionship to almost everyone you met was, to put it mildly, troubling.

"I could see no way for William to find happiness with you as his wife, and it was up to me to change his mind. I was wrong, and I truly am sorry.

"It took me some time to accept the harm I caused, but I do, and I ask your forgiveness. I now believe you and William would be perfect for each other."

Georgiana was finally telling the truth, of this Elizabeth was sure. There was still something she was not saying, but Elizabeth was content to let her hold on to one secret. Georgiana might decide to tell her someday, but she would not force the issue.

"Georgiana has decided she likes your cousin, Robert," added Mr. Darcy, to his sister's obvious horror. "And it would appear the attraction is mutual. The condition that I attached to any potential courting, and Mr. Bannerman agreed, was that Georgiana confess to you, to Miss Bannerman, to the residents and merchants in Lambton, and to everyone else her deception affected.

"When we return to Pemberley, I will confine her to the house for a time. Not until she has proven to me that she is a changed woman will I allow her to visit Kingsdown. When that happens, the Bannerman lad may call on her, but only under the strictest of conditions. She is only just turned seventeen this past winter, after all.

"Her chaperone, Mrs. Annesley, will have her hands full with those two lovers, I would guess, but I believe she is more than capable of supervising them."

Georgiana was not pleased with her brother's decision to share the most intimate details of the affair, of that Elizabeth was certain.

"If you ever wish to discuss my cousin, or any problems you might encounter with him or his courting, come to me," offered Elizabeth. "I would be happy to offer any advice I can, without judging or making fun of your confidences.

"Thank you," said Georgiana, her countenance brightening for the first time, "but for the time being I would prefer to keep things to myself."

"I understand and would not feel any different. Just remember that I will help you in whatever way I can. All you need to do is ask."

Georgiana's response suggested to Elizabeth that the girl would give thoughtful consideration to her offer. This could go a long way toward re-establishing their previous friendship, something Elizabeth would welcome. There was only one thing remaining, a question that had puzzled her since leaving Derbyshire.

Georgiana might not want to answer Elizabeth's query, but she needed to make the attempt to settle it in her own mind. If the girl refused to provide the information, Elizabeth would not take offense, and let the issue fade into memory.

"I confess to some curiosity about the incident that caused the problem. If I may be so bold, was your friend, Miss Haversham, your attacker?" asked Elizabeth, to looks of surprise from Georgiana and satisfaction from Mr. Darcy.

"Why do you ask?" wondered Georgiana, her demeanor once again wary, as though Elizabeth's question might harbor another sinister motive.

Elizabeth almost laughed at the reaction, which confirmed her suspicions without hearing an answer. "I had months to think about everything, from the beginning of my Derbyshire visit to my premature departure.

"In pondering the question that, to me, was the center of the problem, I remembered only one time I witnessed you involved in anything even resembling an altercation.

"It happened, if you recall, during the ball Mr. Darcy hosted at Pemberley. You and Miss Haversham became embroiled in an argument which became heated, forcing Mr. Darcy's cousin to step in and settle the matter.

"It looked like she was ready to attack you, right there in the ballroom. Something from your conversation inflamed her, and your raised voices attracted the attention of most of the guests.

"When I remembered her anger at the ball, I started to wonder if you might have provoked her that day, to where she lost her temper. With no one to step in and calm her this time, she might have picked something up and hit you with it."

Georgiana's surprise was plain to see, but she did not try to deny Elizabeth's supposition. She did not try to confirm it either, but it satisfied Elizabeth that she finally knew the truth. She would sleep well tonight, with the matter at last put to rest.

Mr. Darcy laughed, a short bark that surprised Elizabeth, but not Georgiana, who, it seemed, had expected a response like this from her brother. "You are an intelligent woman, Miss Bennet, of that I am convinced.

"The fact you recalled seemingly unrelated occurrences and used them to arrive at the truth amazes me. If I had not been a party to the entire episode, and its conclusion, I would not have been able to work out such a solution. Remind me to never attempt to lie to you; I would not get away with it."

"So, my assumption is correct," said Elizabeth with a smile toward Georgiana, who still seemed nonplussed at Elizabeth's ability to arrive at the crux of the matter so quickly. "I thought so; no other answer made sense.

"What about Miss Haversham? Has anyone taken her to task for her actions that day?"

"I reviewed the matter with her father. His solution was to send her to a private school, for instruction in the proper manners and attitudes a genteel young woman should have. I believe she will return a changed person.

"Mr. Haversham and I agreed they are to have no further contact. We hope that, if they are not together, they will learn to behave as they should."

"A wise decision, Mr. Darcy. I wish you, and Georgiana, success in the future. Hopefully, we can be friends again. I am willing if you are, Miss Darcy."

"Does this mean that you will also accept my attentions?" asked Mr. Darcy, a little too confidently, in her opinion.

"We will see. Let me consider the matter overnight and I will give you my answer when you call tomorrow."

Mr. Darcy looked crestfallen as he listened to her response. It was not until he reconsidered her words that his face took on a hopeful expression, as the full meaning of her statement occurred to him.

"I will call on you tomorrow," was his statement as he tried, but failed, to maintain a placid expression, "to hear your decision whether I can call on you."

"Until then," Elizabeth rose to her feet as Mr. Darcy and his sister began their walk back to the front of the house. "And please be considerate of Jane and Mr. Bingley's feelings and plans while you are their guests. They are probably still getting to know each other, and do not need interference from you or Georgiana."

"They will get none from us," declared Georgiana, sounding more like the girl Elizabeth had met in Derbyshire. "I will keep William away from them, at least for tonight."

"I suspect Jane will thank you if you do," remarked Elizabeth as they reached Bingley's carriage, which had taken the couple to Netherfield and returned for Mr. Darcy and his sister.

When they were settled in the coach, Mr. Darcy leaned out of the window to fix Elizabeth with an affectionate look.

"I will be back tomorrow," said he with a wave as the carriage departed, leaving Elizabeth alone on the drive to watch them disappear, before returning to the house.

CHAPTER XXXVI

True to his word, Darcy returned early the next afternoon, accompanied by Jane and Mr. Bingley. Upon arriving, he first went to pay his respects to Mr. Bennet, and to inform the gentleman that he would resume his visits to Longbourn, intending to court Elizabeth.

"You know," mentioned her father at supper that evening, "Mr. Darcy's persistence and determination impresses me."

"He is persistent?" wondered Elizabeth, innocently. "I had not noticed."

Mr. Bennet studied her for a moment before turning his attention back to his meal.

"He came into my library today to announce his intention to resume calling upon you. He stated, firmly I might add, that he intended to have you as his wife, eventually. I encouraged him, though I doubt he needed it."

"The man is wasting no time," agreed Elizabeth with a smile as she recalled the day's visit. "He promised to call every day this week, to prepare for his journey home on Saturday. When I asked what he meant, he referred to it as 'planting the seed' for his triumphant return once he has taken his sister back to Pemberley."

"Take care you do not drive him away this time," said Mrs. Bennet. "The man will not chase you forever. Give him some encouragement."

"Lizzy has given him all the encouragement he needs. If he requires more, he is not as intelligent as I thought."

The week flew past, and all too soon Elizabeth was standing in front of the house, waving goodbye to Mr. Darcy's carriage as it left Longbourn. The time until his return would go slowly, but it would pass, and she intended to keep herself as busy as possible while he was gone.

"Mr. Darcy is waiting for you in the garden," said Mr. Bennet, late on a morning some two weeks after his departure. "He looks anxious to enjoy your company once again. Please, put the man out of his misery and get him to make an offer of marriage. You want him to, and he wants to, so what is the problem?"

"There is no problem, Papa," insisted Elizabeth. "Mr. Darcy does not want to rush things, and I will wait until he decides he is ready."

"If you do not encourage him, I will," was her father's reply. "Enough with the delays. Get the thing done, so you can plan your life together. I am eager to have you gone, so I can expand the library. It is getting crowded, and I need more room for my books."

"It would interest me to see how you plan to accomplish that, when my bedroom is a floor above, and at the opposite end of the house from the library."

"I never said it would be easy, only that I wanted to do it."

Elizabeth laughed at her father as she left to welcome her caller. He had no intention of expanding his library; he wanted to visit Pemberley and explore Mr. Darcy's, which Elizabeth had teased might be more than twice the size of Longbourn's.

She considered her father's advice on the way to greet her suitor. His assessment regarding the state of hers and Mr. Darcy's relationship was correct. She wanted him, and he returned her feelings, so why had he not made any attempt to secure her hand?

Since Georgiana's confession, hard won though it was, the man had made clear his intention to make her his wife, and Elizabeth had encouraged him willingly. Their time together was all she hoped it could be, now that his sister's actions were addressed.

Georgiana accompanied her brother the day before their departure for Pemberley, and Elizabeth warmly welcomed the girl, whose demeanor had completely changed since their uncomfortable confrontation.

This was a young woman who was gracious and friendly. Her greeting was warm, having transformed from the sullen and defensive sister forced to confess her sin, into the happy and vivacious young girl Elizabeth first met in Derbyshire. The change was remarkable and appreciated.

Mr. Darcy was not in sight when she entered the garden, which was no surprise. They had lately taken to meeting in the grove to speak in private, at the farthest point in the garden from the house. Her steps went in that direction almost of their own accord, her anticipation building as she neared the place where her lover waited.

He sat on the bench, lost in thought. His eyes were closed, but his lips were moving as he spoke to himself, his voice quiet enough to make the words indistinguishable.

Twice he shook his head violently, as if in disagreement with himself, but his lips continued to move as he appeared to be working on a vexing problem, the solution difficult to find.

Elizabeth cleared her throat softly, prompting his eyes to open. Upon seeing her, Mr. Darcy sprang to his feet and gestured for her to come closer.

"Please, sit down," urged he when she neared. "I have something to ask you."

When she was comfortable, Mr. Darcy lowered himself. After placing one knee on the grass in front of her, he grasped her hands in his. Raising his eyes to look at her directly, he began:

"Miss Bennet, I have decided that life without you would be boring. Your joy of facing the unknown, and your insatiable quest for knowledge and understanding inspire me in ways you cannot imagine. I love our time together, and when we are apart, I count the minutes until I can see you again. Please, never change."

Elizabeth listened to his heartfelt plea with some amusement and a tender heart. She understood what he was trying to say, but his manner was indirect, giving her the impression that he was afraid of her response.

"Are you, Mr. Darcy, making an offer of marriage? If so, my answer is yes, with all my heart. If not, what exactly are you proposing?"

The embarrassment she saw on his face was endearing and heartwarming. This was a first for Elizabeth, to whom he had always been the most proper, self-assured person she had ever met. It was gratifying to see this softer, gentler side of the man she was going to spend the rest of her life with.

"Come," demanded she, jumping to her feet and hurrying toward the house, her hand still intertwined with his.

"Where are we going?" asked Mr. Darcy, scrambling to keep up with his intended.

"Why, to tell Papa and Mama, of course," said she, wondering how he could have assumed anything else. "They will be so pleased, especially Papa, who has been lusting after your library since I described it to him. Be prepared, he will be a regular visitor once we marry."

"And a welcome guest," was his answer as Elizabeth pulled him into the house for the big announcement.

The news of Elizabeth's engagement was the biggest story of the year in Meryton, eclipsing the gossip that usually abounded in English country towns. By the time the wedding took place, rumors of Mr. Darcy's wealth and status had grown, aided by Mrs. Bennet's prideful boasts concerning her future son-in-law.

Mr. Darcy took no notice, preferring instead to divide his attentions between his fiancé and his sister, who, although accepting of the restrictions he had placed upon her, tested them continually.

Their wedding took place at the end of August, a period of only three months, which gave rise to rumors concerning the probable reasons for such a rapid ceremony. Neither of the couple paid any attention, the desire to conclude their unattached lives pushing them forward. Mr. Bennet, however, took matters into his own hands, threatening to challenge any repeating the unflattering stories to a duel, the illegality of such a contest conveniently ignored.

When the banns were read, the rumors ceased. Anyone familiar with the Longbourn parson knew he would never agree to take part in a marriage ceremony for a couple forced to marry in sin.

The wedding and subsequent breakfast were almost too much for Mrs. Bennet, who was beside herself with pride at having arranged advantageous marriages for two of her daughters. Her boasts that she would do the same for her remaining children were embarrassing and stopped only when Mr. Bennet told her directly that he would take her back to Longbourn if she did not quit immediately.

The happy couple spent their honeymoon visiting various places in England and Scotland, returning to Pemberley after spending a month getting acquainted as husband and wife.

Shortly thereafter, Elizabeth informed Darcy there would be an addition to their family, which news excited him beyond rational reason.

She bore him, in quick order, two sons and four daughters, of which both boys, and three of the girls, grew up healthy, raised to be perfect gentlemen and caring gentlewomen. Their second daughter, a sickly child from birth, succumbed before her first birthday to the sorrow of both parents, Elizabeth more so than Darcy.

EPILOGUE

Elizabeth and Darcy's marriage was fulfilling, bringing joy to both. As their children matured, Elizabeth advised them all to marry for love, not money, as that was the only way, in her opinion, to guarantee a happy life.

Lady Catherine, once she was over the shock of Georgiana's revelation of guilt in causing the misconceptions and unfounded accusations, came to respect and admire the stability Elizabeth brought with her to Pemberley.

While she remained aloof, and somewhat cold and reserved toward Darcy's bride, her love for their children and affection for Darcy endeared her to Elizabeth. Her eventual passing left a hole in Elizabeth's heart, which came as a surprise for which she was not prepared.

Bingley purchased Netherfield, calming Mrs. Bennet's fears that Jane and her husband would become strangers if he should purchase a distant estate. Jane, she was sure, would inevitably choose to ignore her mother in favor of other pursuits. They lived at Netherfield for many years but visited Pemberley whenever Mrs. Bennet's company proved too much for Bingley to bear, which was often.

Jane blessed him with four wonderful children, each growing into an exceptional, caring individual who went out of their way to help the less fortunate, without exception.

Mrs. Bennet passed away twenty years after the wedding. To the end of her life she was the same person, flighty and given to wild imaginings. Her grandchildren were her life, and she never tired of spoiling them terribly, ignoring the pleas of their parents to enforce rules regarding behavior and expectations that Mrs. Bennet considered nonsensical for a grandmother to follow.

Mr. Bennet survived his wife by fifteen years. Though he never said so, Elizabeth and Jane knew that he missed his wife in his own way. He spent most of his life as a widower in Longbourn's library, although he was a frequent visitor to Pemberley, which Elizabeth always enjoyed. He was a doting grandfather to all his grandchildren and was never too busy to spend time with them, either keeping them amused or teaching them when they would listen.

When Elizabeth complimented him for the attention he paid to his grandchildren he brushed it aside, responding that it was his duty to pass along whatever knowledge he had while they still valued his company.

A new parson at Longbourn led to Mary's eventual marriage, something which surprised both parents and all her siblings. Mary never gave him children, which seemed to suit her, although not him.

She was never a favorite aunt, and always seemed uncomfortable when her sisters visited. As the years progressed, contact between them diminished until it became practically nonexistent, although she had no reservations toward writing long, detailed letters which frequently descended into rants concerning the sinful behaviors of Longbourn's parishioners.

Kitty Bennet married and followed her husband to a new life in America, to Mrs. Bennet's horror at losing her 'favorite' daughter forever. She bore her husband two children, a boy, and a girl, who were the principal subjects of her monthly letters to her parents, which were shared with all of Kitty's sisters. They anticipated her missives eagerly and read each one avidly before passing it along to the next, and so on until it finally returned to Longbourn. Mrs. Bennet cherished every one of them and took to lamenting them as her only remaining contact with Kitty.

Lydia attracted the attention of a solicitor in Luton through the machinations of her uncle Philips in Meryton. He was a virile and handsome man, according to her, which she claimed was the deciding factor in her decision to accept his marriage offer. Their union lasted many years and was blessed with numerous children and a life of happiness and love.

Georgiana's release from Darcy's restrictions was not the start of an extended courtship by Mr. Robert Bannerman, as she had hoped. He seemed to avoid her as much as he could, but she was just as determined to rekindle the interest he once seemed to have.

When the subject arose in conversation with Mr. Bannerman, Robert talked about his fear of trusting the woman after the pain and tribulation she had caused the family. His interest in her was unchanged, but he was decided that, until she could convince him she had well and truly repented of her sins, he would have as little to do with her as possible.

To her credit, Georgiana refused to give up, and pursued Robert as much as propriety and good manners would allow. It was not an easy conquest, but with the passage of a year, wherein she did her utmost to prove herself to Robert and Louisa, along with the rest of the family, his worries were assuaged.

With Darcy's permission he began to court Georgiana, under the restrictions originally pronounced. Her protests regarding the onerous nature of his rules fell on deaf ears, and subsisted only when he threatened to withdraw his approval.

As Darcy promised, they were never alone, as they were not allowed to spend their time only with each other.

Despite the problems this presented for the two, their friendship and mutual affection evolved into love and respect. In Georgiana's twenty-first year, Robert approached Darcy for permission to propose marriage, declaring his complete devotion to the young woman.

Darcy, while inclined to allow the request, spoke to him first about his lack of property or finances that would allow him to support Georgiana in any kind of comfort.

Robert proved his ability to plan for the future, stating he had first discussed the matter with his father, who offered the couple a small but serviceable home situated on the property. It needed repair, but Robert would see it completed before the marriage took place.

He further stated that because he was the heir to his father's estate, he would inherit the land upon Mr. Bannerman's passing. He was content to wait and continue his work at Kingsdown until that inevitable event.

The lad made such an impression upon Darcy that he informed them his wedding present would be the gift of a fully renovated house situated along the border of the two estates, along with one hundred acres. The couple lived there seventeen years and, when Mr. Bannerman passed away, combined the property with Kingsdown, enlarging the estate into one that provided the family a good living.

Darcy, ever the good neighbor but better brother, offered advice as to the managing of Kingsdown, which improved the estate and increased their yearly income.

Louisa and Amelia surprised their father by attracting the interest of a sizable number of Darcy's friends. Louisa's charming, good nature was highly regarded, and she suffered no lack of suitors, at last marrying a man who loved her without reserve. Their union was blessed with many children, to the joy of the couple and both bride's and groom's parents.

Amelia, on the other hand, waited for the right man to come along, one who would love her, but who would not fear her love of knowledge or ability to debate intelligently any number of subjects.

Her marriage, to Sarah Haversham's cousin no less, was a union of equals, blessed with children who seemed to inherit their mother's love of the unknown and persistence in solving any mystery they encountered.

Mr. Bannerman, upon seeing Elizabeth's happy satisfying marriage, secured without the advantage of a sizable dowry, accepted the foolishness of his assumptions, and begged his daughter's forgiveness, which they readily extended.

Christopher shocked his parents in choosing a life in service to the Lord. With Darcy's assistance, he attended Cambridge and received the finest in religious instruction. Upon graduation he was offered the Kympton parsonage, which he accepted readily. It was there he met his future wife.

Fitzwilliam married Miss Bingley after an appropriate courtship. Their home was Thornhill, his estate a good distance from London. Although they were far away from his bride's friends in the city, she grew to love the estate and its neighbors, who became good and valued friends. They were always on the best of terms with Elizabeth and Jane, and their families, of course.

Mrs. Fitzwilliam could never provide him with offspring, but their love was strong and satisfying to both.

Nieces and nephews compensated for their lack of children, and visits were frequent. The sole source of contention between the sisters was their tendency to spoil their visitors, despite requests not to, which were routinely ignored.

Elizabeth aged gracefully, becoming a favorite of many Derbyshire residents, and sought after for her views and opinions on matters of importance, or local gossip. Darcy never gave her cause to regret the long and tortuous path she trod to find the one man, in all of England, who loved her unconditionally and satisfied her every whim or desire. To the end of her days, she was grateful for the heartache that precipitated her visit to Kingsdown, where she met the man of her dreams.

"We are truly blessed," declared Elizabeth to her husband one night after the light was extinguished.

"Why is that?" asked he, pulling her close enough to wrap his arms around her waist. "Other than the obvious reason of your marriage to the county's most handsome, virile man?"

"You, Mr. Darcy, are a little too full of yourself," laughed she, knowing that he was only teasing her, as he was wont to do occasionally. "When you finish extolling your dubious virtues, I will continue."

"Dubious? There is nothing dubious about the truth. I was, and still am, the handsomest man in Derbyshire, if not all of England. Everyone speaks of my virtues, and I know that many, if not all, of the young women compare their prospective suitors to me. Of course, the poor men always fall short, but that is to be expected."

Elizabeth chose not to respond, having listened to this identical discourse many times through their twenty-five years of marriage. He would eventually finish, and she would answer his question.

When the room had been silent for half a minute, Elizabeth continued: "What I meant was that I am blessed with a man who loves me, and five healthy children who have grown into outstanding men and women.

"Georgiana is happy in her marriage, and Robert has done wonders with Kingsdown. With your help and advice, they have improved the estate, from a somewhat rundown property that barely supported the family, to a well run and prosperous one.

"Robert is respected, and so is Georgiana, in her own way. The Lambton gossips rarely bother starting rumors about her anymore, because her sincere, loving manner is easy to see."

"Was there a reason you brought this up now, instead of tomorrow at breakfast?" asked Darcy, snuggling close enough to place a kiss on her neck, which sent shivers down her back, as it always did.

"No," was her reply in turning to face her husband. "I was just thinking about the first time we met, and how close we came to going our separate ways. If it had not been for my persistence and unwillingness to let you go, our marriage would never have happened."

"Now who is a little full of themselves?" said he, his hands going to her sensitive spots, where his tickling soon had her reduced to tears as she convulsed in laughter.

"Stop!" she was finally able to utter when the merriment had run its course and her husband, ever solicitous, obeyed. Her final thought that evening before she drifted off to sleep was of Darcy, sleeping peacefully with his arms wrapped around her as if his protection were required even in the privacy of their bedchambers.

The End

More Great Titles from One Good Sonnet Publishing!

PRIDE AND PREJUDICE VARIATIONS

By Colin Rowland

The Parson's Rescue
Hidden Desires
Disgraceful Conduct

By Jann Rowland

Acting on Faith
A Life from the Ashes (Sequel to *Acting on Faith*)
Open Your Eyes
Implacable Resentment
An Unlikely Friendship
Bound by Love
Cassandra
Obsession
Shadows Over Longbourn
The Mistress of Longbourn
My Brother's Keeper
Coincidence
The Angel of Longbourn
Chaos Comes to Kent
In the Wilds of Derbyshire
The Companion
Out of Obscurity
What Comes Between Cousins
A Tale of Two Courtships
Murder at Netherfield
Whispers of the Heart
A Gift for Elizabeth
Mr. Bennet Takes Charge
The Impulse of the Moment
The Challenge of Entail
A Matchmaking Mother
Another Proposal
With Love's Light Wings
Flight to Gretna Green
Mrs. Bennet's Favorite Daughter

By Lelia Eye

Netherfield's Secret

Also from One Good Sonnet Publishing
A Collection of Collaborations

PRIDE AND PREJUDICE VARIATIONS

By Jann Rowland & Lelia Eye

WAITING FOR AN ECHO

Waiting for an Echo Volume One: Words in the Darkness
Waiting for an Echo Volume Two: Echoes at Dawn

A Summer in Brighton
A Bevy of Suitors
Love and Laughter: A Pride and Prejudice Short Stories Anthology

By Jann Rowland, Lelia Eye, & Colin Rowland

Mistletoe and Mischief: A Pride and Prejudice Christmas Anthology

PRIDE AND PREJUDICE SERIES

By Jann Rowland

COURAGE ALWAYS RISES: THE BENNET SAGA

The Heir's Disgrace
*Volume II Untitled**
*Volume III Untitled**

Other Genres by One Good Sonnet Publishing

FANTASY

By Jann Rowland & Lelia Eye

EARTH AND SKY SERIES

On Wings of Air
On Lonely Paths
*On Tides of Fate**

FAIRYTALE

By Lelia Eye

The Princes and the Peas: A Tale of Robin Hood

SMOTHERED ROSE TRILOGY

Thorny
Unsoiled
Roseblood

About the Author

Colin Rowland

Colin Rowland is the brother of Jann Rowland, a well-known author in the realm of transformative works centered around Pride and Prejudice. Colin's interest in the works of Jane Austen began with advice from Jann to read Pride and Prejudice. After having done so, Colin felt inspired by Austen's work, and he now spends his free time penning manuscripts centered around the Regency England period. Such a genre has been a natural choice for him, for while he has always loved to read and enjoys almost every genre there is, his favorites delve into historical periods, from Ancient Rome to World War Two and everything in between.

Though Colin has lived most of his life in Canada, he dislikes cold weather with a passion. This dislike led him to sell his house and move with his wife to the big island of Hawaii, where he loved every minute of the eighteen months they were there. After returning to Canada, he has settled down in Calgary with his wife of forty-plus years. Together, they are the proud parents of two sons and two daughters. They also act as servants to three dogs, a Border Collie and a Shih Tzu, who have been with them since they were puppies, and a Sheltie they took in as a rescue.

Website: **http://onegoodsonnet.com/**
Facebook: **https://facebook.com/OneGoodSonnetPublishing/**
Twitter: **@OneGoodSonnet**
Mailing List: **http://eepurl.com/bol2p9**

Made in the USA
Middletown, DE
31 July 2021

45033581R00215